John Connolly

The Instruments of Darkness

HODDER &
STOUGHTON

First published in Great Britain in 2024 by Hodder & Stoughton Limited
An Hachette UK company

1

A CIP catalogue record for this title is available from the British Library

Hardback ISBN 978 1 529 39186 2
Trade Paperback ISBN 978 1 529 39187 9
ebook ISBN 978 1 529 39188 6

Typeset in Sabon LT Std by
Palimpsest Book Production Limited, Falkirk, Stirlingshire

Printed and bound in Great Britain by Clays Ltd, Elcograf S.p.A.

Hodder & Stoughton policy is to use papers that are natural,
renewable and recyclable products and made from wood grown in
sustainable forests. The logging and manufacturing processes are expected
to conform to the environmental regulations of the country of origin.

Hodder & Stoughton Limited
Carmelite House
50 Victoria Embankment
London EC4Y 0DZ

www.hodder.co.uk

The Instruments
of Darkness

Also by John Connolly

For Jo Dickinson. Welcome to the fold . . .

Acknowledgements

Lines from the poem 'You Are Afraid of the Dark' by Kathryn Nuernberger, from her collection *Rag & Bone* (2011), are used by kind permission of the author www.kathrynnuernberger.com and Elixir Press www.elixirpress.com.

Extract from *Rosencrantz & Guildenstern Are Dead* by Tom Stoppard, reprinted by permission of Faber & Faber, 3 Queen Square, London WC1N 3AK.

I

And oftentimes, to win us to our harm,
The instruments of darkness tell us truths . . .

William Shakespeare, *Macbeth*

Chapter I

Moxie Castin was easy to underestimate, but only on first impression. He was overweight by the equivalent of a small child, didn't use one word in public when five others were loitering nearby with nothing better to do, and had a taste for ties with patterns reminiscent of the markings of poisonous insects or the nightmares of LSD survivors. He subsisted largely on fried food, coffee, and the Maine soda that had given him his nickname now long since passed into common usage: since he had been christened Oleg, Moxie sounded better to him. He lost cases, but not many, and his friends far outnumbered his enemies.

Currently, Moxie was sitting in a booth at Becky's on Commercial, performing a vanishing act on his patented version of the Hobson's Wharf Special, which basically meant changing 'or' to 'and' when it came to the options: hence, bacon *and* sausage, two pancakes *and* French toast, along with the requisite two eggs over easy, home fries, and regular toast. Any cardiologist who had yet to slip Moxie a business card was missing a trick.

He looked doubtfully at my dry toast and coffee as he squirted ketchup on his bacon.

'Are you trying to make me feel bad?' he said.

'That depends on how bad you already feel,' I said. 'I wouldn't want to be responsible for tipping you over the edge.'

'I get my heart checked regularly.'

'You get your heart restarted regularly. It's not the same thing.'

'Ha-ha. I ought to have met you after breakfast. You're raining on my food parade.'

One sausage link, a slice of bacon, and half an egg met their

1

fate while I was still lifting my coffee mug to my mouth. If I was ruining Moxie's appetite, it probably just meant he wouldn't be able to eat the plate.

'I have a new client,' he said.

'Congratulations.'

'It's Colleen Clark.'

'I take it back.'

A week earlier, Colleen Clark had been questioned by the Portland PD in connection with the disappearance and suspected death of her two-year-old son, Henry. The actual evidence amounted to a bloodstained blanket discovered beneath the spare tire of her car ten days after the boy went missing, and the testimony of her husband, Stephen, who told police that Colleen had been struggling with anger issues and depression. He had also, he claimed, discovered bruises on the child's arms, which his wife had attributed to Henry's undeniably rambunctious nature; the boy was a little ball of energy, and when he wasn't running, he was falling. Regardless, Stephen Clark had been on the verge of reporting his suspicions to the family physician when Henry disappeared.

As in every parent's nightmare, Henry Clark had seemingly been abducted from his toddler bed while his mother was asleep in the next room and his father was away on a business trip to New York. An exhausted Colleen told investigators that she'd slept comparatively late on the morning in question. A night of undisturbed rest was a rarity for her, and on those occasions when Henry didn't look for attention during the night, her body went into shutdown. She woke shortly after seven and went to check on her son, only to find the bed empty and the window standing open. She immediately searched the garden, in case he had some-how managed to climb out before calling her husband, quickly followed by the police.

Both parents made appeals for Henry's safe return, but it was noted by some observers that the husband was more tearful than his wife, who appeared oddly detached and unemotional. It didn't matter that there was more than one way to respond to trauma, and shock and guilt could make mannequins of the best of us.

The mob wanted a show, but only one of the actors was prepared to provide it. Within days, rumors were beginning to circulate. They were unfounded, but that was no obstacle, unfounded rumors being the best kind.

It was only after Stephen Clark persisted in raising his concerns about his wife with the police that her car was searched more thoroughly, and the blanket found concealed in the well. Tests subsequently revealed it to be soaked with Henry's blood. Colleen was interviewed by police without a lawyer present. She was convinced she didn't need one, which as any lawyer will tell you, is one of the signs that a person probably does. She denied all knowledge of how the blanket came to be in her car, although she did recognize it as one that had been given to the Clarks a few Christmases earlier. The blanket had been placed in storage in the attic because Colleen didn't like it and would permit it to be put on display only when she knew the gifters might be coming to visit.

Even this little detail was added to the testimony being used to damn her in the popular imagination: her husband's family had presented her with a nice blanket – expensive, too, not just a reject from the closeout shelves at Marshalls – but, ungrateful hypocrite that she was, she kept it hidden away from all eyes but theirs. Anonymous sources muttered disapprovingly about Colleen keeping herself to herself, of her failure to participate in joint community endeavors and her reluctance to join other young mothers for coffee, shopping trips, and stroller pushes at the Maine Mall. Thus a quiet, shy woman with better taste in furnishings than her in-laws, and with no fondness for the smell of mall disinfectant or Yankee Candle, was slowly transformed into a cold bitch capable of killing her son before concealing the body and concocting a fairy tale of infant-snatching.

But Colleen stuck to her story, even as the police set about picking it apart, and the media reported on it, with the result that she was virtually single-handedly keeping the Maine newspaper industry afloat. In addition, vloggers, amateur detectives, web sleuths, and would-be podcasters, along with protesters of various

3

stripes and sympathies, continued to haunt her neighborhood. If some entrepreneur had set up a stall selling pitchforks and flaming torches, the picture would have been complete.

'You think she's guilty?' asked Moxie, as he progressed to the French toast.

'I don't have an opinion either way,' I said. 'I only know what I've read.'

'So why the long face about adding her to the client list?'

'She's a mother suspected of killing her child. Whoever represents her is in for a world of pain – which is not to say you're wrong to take the case, just that it'll bring the crazies down on you. But my understanding is that she hasn't yet been charged with any crime.'

'She hasn't,' said Moxie, 'but she's about to be: criminal restraint of a child younger than eight, a class C felony; kidnapping, a class A felony; and manslaughter, another class A felony. If convicted, she's looking at thirty years on the class A charges, and that's assuming she receives concurrent sentences; consecutive, and Christ will have returned to claim his kingdom before she gets out.'

'Why not murder?'

'I wouldn't put it past the state, but they'd have to prove malice aforethought. They're on safer waters with manslaughter, and the additional charges for ballast.'

'Difficult to prove all that without a body.'

'Difficult, but not impossible. They have the bloodstained blanket, the absence of an alibi, and public opinion is against her, which counts for something in a case like this. Justice may be blind, but it's not deaf. Jury selection will be like picking daisies in a minefield.'

'Are you the first lawyer she's consulted?'

'Does that tone suggest I should have been the last?'

By now Moxie's plate was more than half-empty, while I'd still barely touched my toast. I'd only ordered it so Moxie wouldn't feel bad, but then I remembered that it took a lot to make Moxie feel bad.

'I think you're becoming more sensitive to criticism as you get older,' I said. 'Admittedly you couldn't become any more insensitive, but it's still troubling.'

Moxie speared the remaining sausage link.

'You know I broke up with Sylvia, right?'

Moxie had been seeing a woman named Sylvia Drake for a couple of months. She was an attractive older brunette, but if she ever met a bottle of booze she didn't like, she'd buried the evidence deep. She wasn't an alcoholic, though she tended to cease drinking at least one glass after she should have, and possessed only two voice settings: loud and too loud. I'd spent an evening with both of them a while back. It had been a testing experience.

Moxie had a string of ex-wives and never wanted for female company, even if none of the girlfriends ever remained on his books for long. Sylvia Drake would soon be replaced by another glamorous figure in her middle years, with some easily identifiable flaw that Moxie would later use to justify casting her aside, albeit with murmurs of regret. Interestingly, these women never held grudges against him, and a few even met up regularly for dinner and drinks, like an informal support group. Moxie would sometimes join them for a late cocktail. If I claimed to understand any of this, I'd be lying.

'I'm sorry to hear it,' I said.

'No, you're not. I saw the look on your face when she fondled your ear at dinner.'

'Well, sorry in general terms. Insincere sorry.'

Moxie nibbled the final sausage, making it last.

'I have to admit, Sylvia ran to extremes,' he said.

This was true. Her idea of redecorating was probably to blow up the house.

'Are you comfort-eating to ease your pain?'

'I was,' said Moxie, as the sausage gave up the ghost, 'but I stopped.'

'Thank God.'

'You were asking about Colleen Clark and lawyers. In answer to your question, no, she didn't have legal representation before now because she says she's innocent.'

'And innocent people don't go to prison.'

'That's right,' said Moxie. 'I explained to her that anyone who thought like her would never be short of company, especially in prison.'

I held up my mug for a refill of coffee.

'Who told you that charges were coming down the track?'

'Doug Isles, through a third party.'

Isles was a retired prosecutor in Androscoggin County. He'd run unsuccessfully for higher office on a number of occasions – including pitches for district attorney and the state senate – before giving up to snipe from the sidelines in a weekly newspaper column. He wrote well, but didn't admire anyone half as much as himself, and viewed the electorate's failure to acknowledge his finer qualities as a political offense on par with the murder of Julius Caesar.

'Any particular reason why he felt compelled to do that?' I asked.

'For one thing, he's a friend of Colleen's mother. They went to school together.'

'Sweet of him,' I said, 'and therefore out of character. I've read his columns.'

'Then you know he doesn't like Becker or Nowak, and the whisper is that Becker will prosecute. So that's the other thing.'

Erin Becker was the state's assistant attorney general and a protégée of Paul Nowak, the current attorney general. Nowak was preparing a run for governor and grooming Becker to succeed him as AG. A case like Colleen Clark's would garner a great deal of publicity for them both, but would only benefit them if she was convicted. If they were to lose, it would damage their reputations and hamper their ambitions, thus making Doug Isles happier on his pedestal.

'Who advised Colleen Clark to contact you?'

'Isles provided Colleen and her mother with a list of names. Mine was on it.'

'Did you have to pitch hard?'

'I was the only one Colleen called. She wasn't interested in the others.'

'Why is that?'

'Because of you,' said Moxie.

It was widely known that I did some work for Moxie. I occasionally accepted employment from other lawyers, but the difference with Moxie was that I both liked and trusted him, and had yet to refuse him my help.

'When will she be charged?'

'Isles thinks they'll come for her tomorrow. Becker's people have quietly been laying the groundwork because Nowak doesn't want any mistakes. They'll offer Colleen a plea deal, but it won't be generous, and there'll be no room for negotiation. If they don't get what they want, they'll push for a speedy trial.'

'How does your client feel about that?'

'She won't cop a plea,' said Moxie. 'She says she didn't harm her child.'

'Is this where I ask if you believe her?'

'It can be, and I'll reply that I'm here to defend her, whatever she may or may not have done. Between us, I really don't know for sure. My gut instinct is that she's innocent, but I'd still be concerned about putting her on the stand. She's not cold, exactly, but she is reserved. I think her reaction to pain is to internalize it before donning a mask to hide any stray feelings that might slip through.'

'What about her husband?'

'He's convinced she did it, or he's not convinced that she *didn't* do it, which is nearly as bad.'

'Have you spoken to him?'

'Not yet, but she's told me as much. Even if she hadn't, his body language and attitude in front of the media would have given it away. They're no longer living together, and Stephen Clark, or someone close to him, has been feeding details about their marriage to the press, although the scuttlebutt has dried up noticeably over the last few days.'

'Becker?'

'That would be my view. She probably told Stephen to stop courting the peanut gallery in case the defense starts hollering about the Sixth Amendment, for all the good that would do.'

The Sixth Amendment guarantees the right to a speedy and

public trial, which theoretically includes being defended from prejudicial information that might bias prospective jurors against the defendant, the media being more inclined to publish material leaked by the prosecution and law enforcement. In practice, sensationalized pretrial descriptions of crimes and defendants, even the publication of legally excludable material, rarely led to a change of venue or affected the decisions of trial courts, but most legal professionals agreed that these factors could work against an impartial jury. If the case went to trial, the best Moxie could hope for would be to raise with the judge the issue of what had previously been said or published about his client, and use it on appeal in the event of a conviction.

'Erin Becker doesn't like me,' I said. 'Nowak isn't a fan either.'

I'd learned from my contacts at the Special Investigations Unit, the Maine State Police's licensing division, that renewed pressure had been applied to rescind my PI's license. The source of that pressure was dual: the AG's office and the Cumberland County DA. To its credit, the division hadn't buckled so far, because I continued to fulfill the minimum requirements and my check always cleared. I had been forced to seek a new insurer for my obligatory general liability policy, but that was a consequence of bad publicity as much as anything else, or so I liked to believe. My new insurers had already been required to pay out for damage to the Braycott Arms, a dive hotel in town, in the course of a previous investigation. My broker told the insurers they were getting off lightly, although the words 'so far' remained unspoken in the background.

'Neither Becker nor Nowak was liable to be helpful anyway,' said Moxie, 'so don't take it personally in the current instance. Anyway, your involvement may encourage them to behave properly. If they try to be clever, I have faith in your ability to spot it; and if they've missed something, you'll find it.'

'I haven't said that I'll accept the job.'

'Haven't you? I'm sure I heard differently. If you're genuinely vacillating, take a ride by the Clark house and see what's been done to it. I can give you the address.'

My earlier comments to Moxie were returning to haunt me.

Whoever took Colleen Clark's side was likely to suffer, if only in the short term, and sometimes I grew tired of looking at unfriendly faces. But a child was missing, and his mother was about to be dragged into the machinery of the law. It chewed people up, the innocent as well as the guilty, and called the result justice, but only a fool would accept that as true.

'I'll take the address,' I said, 'and the job.'

'There you go, repeating yourself.'

'What about the boy?'

'That blanket was drenched in his blood. It's not inconceivable that he's still alive, but it is improbable.' Moxie waved for the check. 'Whatever the truth, we need to work on Colleen's defense. If she didn't do it – and like I said, my feeling is that she's innocent – then someone has probably killed her son and is trying to destroy her into the bargain. That's your territory, but it'll have to sit alongside trial prep.'

The check arrived. Moxie paid in cash, and tipped generously.

'Does she have funds?'

'Colleen doesn't have enough to pay for long-term legal representation, so her mother is picking up the tab. There's still a mortgage on the house, and Colleen's share from any sale won't come to more than thirty or forty thousand. But her father was a gas executive, and left his wife in clover when he died. She doesn't have a problem spending whatever is necessary to save her daughter, and perhaps find out what happened to her grandchild along the way.'

'Because one feeds into the other,' I said.

'If I can't prove her innocent,' said Moxie, 'proving someone else guilty will serve nearly as well.'

We stood to go. Moxie pulled a mask from his pocket and put it on to pass through the queue of people by the door. The mask was black, with the words CALL MOXIE written on it in white, along with his number.

'I got a trunk full of these,' he said. 'I'm determined to get some use out of them – and fuck what that CDC says about COVID, because I still wouldn't want anyone north of Bangor coughing on me. And mark my words, there'll be something else along soon

9

enough. You know, if COVID had given people warts or facial blisters, every fucking person in this state would have been fighting up for a jab and a hazmat suit. You want a box of these masks, just in case?'

'It's tempting, but I think I'll pass.'

'Well, if you change your mind, just ask. I'd offer to get some made up for you as well, because it pays to advertise, but they might make you look kind of conspicuous on a stakeout.'

The morning mist had matured to drizzle as we stepped outside. The lowering sky was the color of factory smoke, distant birds like charred fragments ascending.

'When can I talk to her?' I said.

'Whenever you want. She's home. I told her she ought to move away for a while, but she refused. Not only is she quiet, she's also stubborn as all hell. Takes after her mother. Colleen says she's not going to let anyone drive her out.'

He looked sorrowful for a moment, even with his face partly obscured.

'Is that all there is to it?'

'No,' said Moxie. 'She told me she sleeps on the floor of her son's room. I think she's tormenting herself.'

A container ship made its way along the Fore River toward the Casco Bay Bridge. A solitary sailor stood on deck, but I couldn't tell if he was looking forward or back, and the vessel was otherwise devoid of obvious crew. I glanced away for a moment, and when I turned back the sailor was gone. Had the ship then plowed untended into the riverbank, I wouldn't have been surprised.

'I take it you've already spoken with her at length?'

'I have, and my secretary has typed up the preliminary record. You can read it before you visit, if you think it'll help.'

'I'll wait,' I said.

Moxie's notes would be useful, but the most interesting observations would be stored in his brain. We could compare notes later.

'Do you want me to come along with you?' said Moxie.

'No, I'll speak with her alone first, if that's okay with you.'

'If I had an issue with how you operate, we wouldn't be having this conversation.'

We had reached Moxie's car. I waited while he tried to locate the fob, the cut of all his suits long since ruined by years of storing keys, notebooks, and cell phones in pockets that were never meant to house anything thicker than a credit card. Moxie didn't care. Even these aspects of his appearance, which seemingly spoke of a lack of attention, were carefully cultivated. Moxie's whole existence was one long strategic play.

I thought about Colleen Clark and what was to come. I felt what I always did at such moments: the temptation to walk away, except I knew that if I did, I would never be able to retrieve what I'd lost.

'It's going to be a bad one, isn't it?' I said.

'I don't think that boy is coming back,' said Moxie, 'so it already is.'

Chapter II

Colleen Clark lived in the Rosemont area of Portland, not far from Dougherty Field. It was a locale in which one might have expected to find a prosperous young family, with all the advantages of suburban living while still being close to the center of the city. The Clark residence wouldn't have been hard to identify even if Moxie hadn't given me the street number: someone had daubed the words BABY KILLER on the front of the house in red paint. An attempt had been made to obscure it with whitewash, but the letters persisted. The drapes were drawn, no car stood in the driveway, and the garage door was closed. The front door was on the eastern side, away from the street. It was a peculiar arrangement, as though the plans had been misread, or the house had been dropped randomly on its plot from the air.

I parked a short distance away, but couldn't see any sign of reporters. Perhaps the warning to Stephen Clark against engaging with the media had become a general advisory to the press and TV people themselves, now that a prosecution was imminent. It wouldn't stop online trolls from posting their bile, but they preferred to operate from the safety and anonymity of their caves, and anyone who gave them attention deserved to have their electricity shut off. I was old-fashioned about reporting: if it wasn't worth paying for, it wasn't worth reading.

I spotted the patrol car just seconds before the officer at the wheel got out. His presence explained why the street was so quiet. Someone, possibly a resident with influence, had complained about the mob, and anyone who didn't belong was now being sent on their way. Also, it wouldn't look good if someone took it into their head to assault Colleen Clark, or not before a jury had the chance to find her guilty. I showed the cop my ID and explained that I'd been engaged by Colleen's lawyer. I was now working on her behalf, so he'd be seeing a lot of me from here on out. He told me to wait while he confirmed this with Moxie and ran it by his superiors, before giving me the all clear.

'When did that happen?' I asked, pointing to the ghost of the words on the wall.

'Two nights ago, before a car was assigned. We just started keeping an eye on the place this morning.'

'I may bring in someone of my own, no offense meant.'

'None taken.'

I thanked him and headed for the house. I could, of course, have arranged to meet Colleen at Moxie's office, but I wanted to observe her in her own environment and view the room from which her son had vanished. I didn't expect to learn anything more than the police, but it was an important first step in understanding what might have taken place.

Moxie had supplied me with contact details for Colleen, including her new cell phone number, and promised to let her know that I was on my way. Regardless, I decided to call before knocking, because in her situation I'd have been cautious about opening my door to strangers. She picked up on the second ring. Her voice was very small, and I could almost see her preparing to flinch. New number or not, she'd probably received enough abuse to last two lifetimes. Whatever might happen in the future, it would be years before she heard a knock on the door, or the ringing of a phone, without her stomach tightening.

'My name is Parker,' I said. 'I believe Moxie Castin told you I'd be calling.'

'Where are you?'

'Outside. I can be on your doorstep in ten seconds, if that's not inconvenient.'

'It's not inconvenient at all. I'll be waiting.'

As I set foot on the Clark driveway, an elderly woman appeared on the doorstep of the house next door, her arms folded and her face set like a sulky child's. Her silver hair was cut close to the skull, revealing a hearing aid behind each ear.

'You from the police?' she said.

'No, I'm not.'
'Huh?'
'I said—'
'Huh?'
'I said, "I'm not the police!"'
It came out louder than I'd intended. The pilots of planes coming in to land at Portland Jetport now probably knew I wasn't a cop.
'Who are you, then?'
I could have lied, or told her to mind her own business, but the police would already have spoken with her, which meant that I'd need to speak with her, too. As part of the preparation for a possible trial, I'd be following in the footsteps of the law like a delayed shadow.
'I'm a private investigator,' I said.
'Huh?'
I walked to the boundary hedge, where I could strike some balance between volume and mutual comprehension.
'I'm a private investigator.' I showed her my ID.
'I can't read that,' she said. 'I don't have my glasses.'
'How about you just take my word for it?'
'I'll just take your word for it,' she said.
If the situation hadn't been so serious, I'd have been searching for a hidden camera.
'That's very good of you.'
'You working for the Clark girl?' she asked. Seen up close, she had shrewd eyes, and the wiriness of a long-lived hound.
'I'm working for a lawyer,' I said neutrally.
'Her lawyer?'
I had to admire her persistence.
'Would that be a problem?'
'Not for me.'
'Then would you mind if I spoke with you later?'
'I wouldn't mind at all. I'm not going anywhere. My name is Livonia Gammett, but you can call me Mrs Gammett. If I get to know you, and decide I like you, I'll consent to answering to Livvy.'
She prepared to go back into her house.

'And mind how you step,' she called over her shoulder. 'They threw bags of excrement at her door during the night. I cleaned up most of it, but I can't guarantee I got it all.'

Now I saw the stains on the driveway and the doorstep, although the door itself had been wiped clean. I could also smell disinfectant, and what it had been used to disguise. You didn't have to look very hard to be disappointed by human beings. We were not all bad, just enough of us, although the rest had to work very hard to make up for that minority.

The door to the Clark house opened before I could ring the bell. The interior was dim and quiet. A woman's pale face peered out at me, and I saw something familiar in it, like the spirit of someone I'd once known passing briefly through the body of another. Grief calls to grief, pain will find its echo, and sorrow, for all its idioms, is a universal language.

'Please come in,' said Colleen Clark.

I hesitated. The sense of loss was suffocating.

'Thank you,' I said, and joined her in the shadows.

Chapter III

Deep in the Maine woods, and distant from memory, if not quite forgotten, stands a house. It had been built back in 1912 from Sears Kit No. 174, at a cost of just under $1,500, or $300 less than the company's estimate, in large part because no laborers needed to be hired, the family responsible for its purchase taking care of the construction. The excavated basement had never been finished, and the plasterwork had always been rudimentary at best, while the brick mantel and fireplace in the dining room began to crumble shortly after the house was completed, for reasons that were never satisfactorily established. The cedar shingles on the roof and porch had lasted well into the 1970s, when they finally began to surrender to moisture and the decay that came with it. Even then, the deterioration was gradual, and might still have been arrested with proper maintenance. But nobody arrived to address the issue of preservation, and just enough was done to keep it standing and secure. No one had ever spent long in it – or no one had ever survived in it for long, which is not the same thing. No, not the same thing at all.

Kit No. 174 had originally been designed with a narrow lot in mind: twenty-four feet in width and fifty in length, give or take, which included the front porch. The kitchen was a ten-foot-square box and the two bedrooms on the second floor were not much larger. The parlor was grim, and the dining room was barely adequate for a standard table and chairs. It was, therefore, an odd choice of model for a woodland site, particularly on a large acreage owned by those who would be assembling the kit house. Only marginal effort would have been required to cut down some trees to facilitate a larger footprint, which would also have allowed more light to penetrate, any dwelling being otherwise destined to exist in an umbrous zone. Yet that option had not been explored, and so, for over a century, a slender house had occupied an attenuated lot in a woodland hollow upon which the sun shone only reluctantly, as though electing to be frugal about the expenditure of its rays on such a poor object.

A traveler coming across the house unexpectedly might have wondered why it had been constructed at all, so unwelcoming an aspect did it present. This traveler, in passing, might also have noted how, the lichen on the shingles apart, nature appeared to be keeping its distance from the habitation. No ivy climbed the walls, and no briars enmeshed the banisters and steps of the porch. Even the growth patterns of the surrounding trees had accommodated themselves to the intruder, adopting stratagems to avoid touching it with their branches, their extremities taking abnormal turns back upon themselves like broken limbs poorly set.

And while the house spoke of neglect, it was no ruin. The windows were dirty but unbroken, obscured by wooden boards on the lower floor, and the beveled plate glass in the oak front door remained in place, if now hidden behind reinforced steel. Inside, the original yellow pine flooring had been repaired in spots, but was otherwise intact. The ceilings' poor plaster hung on only in places, but whatever fell had been swept up and disposed of. Enough: always, just enough.

Would our traveler have been tempted to explore it further? No, they would not. Some places discourage curiosity. They trigger an ancient response, one that advises us not to linger, and perhaps not even to mention what we might have discovered. *Pretend you were never here*, a voice whispers, and it takes us a moment to realize that it is not our own. *Be on your way. If you forget me, I might forget you in turn.*

But there is no traveler, or if there ever was – an incautious person, or an inquisitive one – the ground has long since swallowed them up, and their grave lies unmarked. This is private land, and has been since early in the nineteenth century. Its trails are not for hikers or snowmobiles. Admonitions against trespass are posted on the nearest roads, both public and private, and nailed to trees. No local resident takes amiss this desire to be left alone. It is not uncommon in these parts. If the stewards of this realm wanted company, they would have situated themselves closer to people. They do not interfere with others, and others do not interfere with them. They give aid when it is sought, but do not offer it unless asked. They watch, but their gaze does not extend beyond the borders of their own land. They do not ask for credit, and always pay in cash. They do not trouble the law, and the law does not trouble them. For these reasons they pass, if not unnoticed, then at least unremarked, or mostly so.

True, some in the area know about Kit No. 174, or have heard tell of it, even if they have never themselves set eyes on it. There is a story of a daughter who died, or maybe it was a niece: the tale varies according to the teller. The house was to have been hers and was left empty after she passed, bearing faint traces of intentions never to be fulfilled, like fingerprints on a glass of untasted wine. For a house cursed by ill luck to remain unlived in is not unknown, even after so much time has gone by. After all, ghosts may not be real, but no one has told the ghosts.

So this particular incarnation of Kit No. 174 occupies a liminal space: it is both finished and unfinished; remembered and forgotten; concealed and in plain sight. Like all borderlands, it is disputed territory, but an accommodation has been reached, one that is satisfactory for most, if not all, concerned. No person has ever dwelt in it, but people have died there, and Kit No. 174 holds them in its memory.

Sometimes, it holds them so tightly that they scream.

Chapter IV

I had seen Colleen Clark only in newspaper photos and on television, always surrounded by taller men and women, but I was still surprised by how tiny she was. I doubted she could have nudged five feet, even in shoes, and she was thin in a brittle way that made me fear for her should she take a fall. I doubted she was eating very much, but then I doubted she ever ate a lot, and whatever calories she did consume were burned up just in keeping her alive, if barely. Her eyes were an unusually dark brown and sunk into her skull, as though the pith of her had retreated still deeper into itself for protection. She wore her long auburn hair in a pair of loose plaits that hung over her shoulders, and her feet were bare. Even in the dimness, I could see the veins standing out against the pallor of her skin, like the tributaries of a river in winter.

I followed her into the kitchen. She offered me coffee, but warned that she wasn't sure how old the jar was; she and Stephen usually drank fruit tea. I told her either would be fine. She didn't pause or stumble as she spoke her estranged husband's name, and had a calmness about her that I might have mistaken for narcotically induced had Moxie Castin not assured me that she had declined all offers of sedatives. I watched her boil a kettle of water to prepare two cups of tea. They smelled vaguely of strawberries, and not in a pleasant way. The scent was too strong, overripe. As she placed one cup in front of me, my stomach rebelled, but I drank nonetheless. She had gone to the trouble of making it, and I hoped that sharing it might alleviate the awkwardness of the situation.

'Mr Castin told me you'd agreed to help,' she said.

'He asked, and I make a point of trying not to refuse him.'

19

She was gripping the handle of her cup so firmly that her knuckles looked set to erupt from her right hand.

'Why is that?'

'Because otherwise, I'd have to hang out with him for free.'

A smile flickered like a dying bulb and was gone.

'Did he say I'd approached him because of his connection to you?'

'He mentioned it.'

'I've read about you. You lost a child. I thought you might understand.'

The quiet of the house was unnerving. Not even a clock ticked. It was, I'd found, one of death's traits: it muffled the sound in a place of loss, just as it rendered movements awkward and sluggish, and made an inconsequence of time. Of course, the boy might still be alive. But, as Moxie had intimated, it felt as though he was gone.

Colleen looked at me, expecting some response, but I was not about to give her access to my pain. It would not benefit either of us.

'I'd like you to tell me about the night your son went missing.'

'I was sleeping. I don't remember much at all.'

'Nevertheless, if you wouldn't mind.'

She sipped her tea, lifting the cup to her lips with both hands. She was dressed in an oversized Patriots' sweatshirt that might have been her husband's – the sleeves pushed above her elbows, the hem hanging to thigh level – and a pair of jeans rolled up at the cuffs. Her mode of dress accentuated that sense of withdrawal, of shrinkage, as though these clothes might once have fitted her, but no longer, just as the terms 'mother' and 'wife' were also becoming incompatible with her essence.

'Stephen left on business that afternoon. He's away from home a lot. He's trying to get a promotion. He's very ambitious.' She peered at me over the rim of her cup. 'Will you be speaking with him?'

'I'd like to, but he'll be under no obligation to talk to me.'

'If you do, be gentle. He's in a lot of pain.'

I searched for traces of anger in her, but could pick up none.

Something must have shown on my face, because she added: 'We've both lost a son, and we both want him back. Stephen's trying to cope with what's happened in his own way, but he's not very good at coping.'

'With life in general?'

'With emotions. Little things get on top of him, so big things . . .'

She let the implication hang.

'Mr Castin informed me that you and your husband are temporarily estranged,' I said. 'He also suggested that your husband might be holding you responsible for whatever happened to Henry.'

I was choosing my words carefully. There were layers of blame, justified or otherwise, to be mediated here, and many steps between Stephen Clark being confusedly angry at his wife for sleeping too soundly, or failing to check the window in their child's room, and believing her capable of abduction and killing. A memory came to me, unbidden: my mother having her change purse stolen in a restaurant, and my father slapping her hard on the cheek for what he regarded as her part in its loss, even though, as a policeman, he must have dealt with hundreds of such incidents over the years. My mother had not been unduly careless, nor had she conspired with the thieves to deprive her family of money. On one level, she was simply unfortunate, but she was also targeted by individuals who were accomplished at what they did: in this case, a couple who had seated themselves behind her at the restaurant, slipping a hand into the bag between her feet and then leaving before ordering. The combination of one's own bad luck and the resolve of others can undo even the best of us.

'He thinks I murdered our son,' she said, and again her voice was very even, without recrimination or regret. She might have been communicating her husband's views on a game in which she had no interest or stake. 'Aren't you going to ask me if I did?'

'No.'

'Why?'

'Because your answer would be the same either way.'

'Yes,' she said, 'I suppose it would. And you'll make your own determination, won't you?'

'That's not the reason Mr Castin has engaged my services. My main responsibility is to ensure that all relevant information to aid your defense has been uncovered or discovered. That means gathering evidence and witness statements, among other tasks.'

'But there are no witnesses,' said Colleen, 'and the only evidence is the blanket.'

'So far.'

'I didn't do this, Mr Parker. I didn't hurt Henry. I never would.'

'I understand that. Now our job may be to prove that to a jury.'

'If I didn't take him, someone else did.'

'Yes.'

'Are you going to look for that person? Because if you do, you might find Henry.'

'That may be part of my role,' I said neutrally, 'but I can't let it distract from trial preparation. We don't want to see you put behind bars, Mrs Clark, because once you're there, it'll be very hard to get you out again. Now, can we return to the night in question?'

She set the cup down. Some of the hot tea spilled on her hand, but she didn't seem to notice, even as I watched the skin redden.

'I fed Henry before putting him down at about eight. I watched some TV, but I couldn't keep my eyes open, so I went to bed. I mean, I brushed my teeth, if that's important, but I didn't do a very good job of it, because I still had toothpaste stains on my chin and nightshirt when I woke up. That's not unusual. I can't recall the last time I took off clothes that weren't stained. Like weariness and worry, it comes with motherhood.'

'Did you eat or drink anything before you turned in for the night?'

'I reheated some pasta and drank a glass of red wine.'

'Large or small?'

'Small. The police asked me that, too. I wasn't drunk, Mr Parker, only tired. I told you: I'm tired all the time. People warned me that parenting would be exhausting, but I didn't really understand what that meant until Henry arrived.' For the first time, she looked doubtful. 'I don't want you to think any of that would make me want to harm him.'

'Take that as given.'

'I was just grateful when he slept and the house was calm.' She raised her right hand and waved her long, thin fingers vaguely, like the conjuration of a spell. 'But not like this. This is wrong. It's too final.'

'Do you usually drink alcohol in the evenings?' I asked.

'Is that relevant?'

'It might be. Should this go to trial, and you testify, you may find yourself being forced to reply to questions you consider troubling or hurtful, or that are designed to paint you in the worst possible light. Consider this practice.'

'I have a glass of wine most evenings,' she said. 'I don't smoke, don't drink coffee, and don't eat candy. A glass of wine is my reward for getting through the day, but often I'm too exhausted to finish it.'

'Did you check on Henry before you went to bed?'

'Yes.'

'The window in the room, was it open or closed?'

'Open less than an inch, with the security cable in place. It was a stuffy night, uncommonly so for the time of year, and I prefer fresh air to the AC.'

'Did you wake at all?'

'No.'

'Is that normal for you?'

She frowned.

'No. I don't often sleep so soundly, but Henry is still teething, and he's had a couple of bad nights recently. I think my body was waiting to go into shutdown. I do recall feeling uncommonly heavy as I went to bed. I could barely lift my feet, and I was out cold as soon as my head touched the pillow.'

'Tell me about waking.'

'I woke at seven, but it took me a while to get going. I didn't want to leave my bed, but somehow I managed.'

'Did you head straight to Henry's room?'

'Yes. I didn't go to the bathroom first, even though I kind of needed to.'

'Why was that?'

23

'I suppose I was worried, as Henry wasn't making any noise. And it was cool, cooler than it should have been. I could feel the breeze. I went to his room. The bed was empty, and the window was open. I remember not being able to move. I kept thinking I was dreaming, and if I realized that I was, I'd wake up, and everything would be okay. But I wasn't, and it isn't.'

'What did you do next?'

'I ran outside. I didn't even stop to put on a robe. For some strange reason, I thought Henry might somehow have managed to open the window and climb out, even if there was no way he could have done that, none at all. I was calling his name, and Livvy came out to see what was happening.'

'Mrs Gammett, the woman who lives in the house on the left? I've met her.'

'She's a kind soul, but deaf, so I must have been shouting loudly for her to notice. She asked me what was wrong, and I told her Henry was gone. She said I should call the police, but I called Stephen first.'

'Why?'

'I don't know. Well, I do, but you'll think it's foolish.'

'Nothing concerning what took place here is foolish.'

That smile ghosted across her face again, one wraith visiting another.

'I rely on Stephen a lot,' she said. 'I've battled eating disorders over the years, and I suffered badly from postpartum depression until just a few months ago, when it finally began to ease. Stephen has been very patient with me, and considerate in his way. My instinct is to turn to him whenever there's a problem. Not very feminist of me, is it?'

'I wasn't aware that suffering was a feminist issue,' I said.

'I can offer you some books if you care to read up on it.'

I suspected she was serious.

'Thanks,' I said, 'but I'll pass.'

We went through the rest of what occurred that morning: the arrival of the police; her husband's return from New York within hours; the evidential statements taken from her and Stephen; the subsequent appeals via the media; and the support from neighbors and the larger community, followed by its gradual diminution because of the perceived deficiencies in Colleen Clark's response to the trauma of her son's disappearance.

'There was – *is* – this numbness,' she said. 'I can't explain it, except to guess that the pain was so great, my mind wanted to shield me from it. It felt like everything was happening to someone else. Obviously, I knew it was happening to me, and Stephen, and Henry, but it seemed both real and unreal at the same time. Even though it's all recent, I struggle to remember details. Hours, even days, are missing. It's a blur of absence, with Henry at its heart. And then the blanket was found.'

'By your husband.'

'Yes. I had a flat tire, and as you can imagine' – she raised one slender arm – 'I struggle with lug nuts. Stephen went outside to change the tire, and when he came back a few minutes later he was so ashen, I was sure he was going to faint. I went to help him, but he put up his hands to ward me off. I thought at first that he'd heard some news about Henry, bad news, but I couldn't see any police, and thought they'd have come in person if anything had changed. I asked Stephen what was wrong, but he couldn't speak. It took him three tries before he was able to produce any words.'

'What did he say?'

'He said, "I found the blanket." Naturally, I asked him what he was talking about, and he told me what he'd discovered in the trunk. I asked to see it, and he said we should wait for the police. I tried to get by him. I wanted to take a look for myself, but he made me go into the living room. Initially, I believed he was trying to protect me from the sight of blood, and possibly there was a part of that to it, even then. I hope so.'

'What did you do while he made the call?'

'I waited. I didn't have much choice. He locked me in. I figure he didn't know what else to do with me. It's not like it was a situation with which he had a great deal of experience.'

'Didn't he ask for your side of the story?'

'He didn't, but he got it anyway.'

'Through the locked door?'

'No, later, when the police came.'

'Mr Castin told me that you agreed to speak to them without a lawyer present.'

'I didn't have anything to hide,' she said. 'Stephen and I both talked to them.'

She wouldn't have been Mirandized, of course, because she hadn't been under arrest, yet every statement she made was now part of the record. We'd find out at the discovery stage how the recording officer had chosen to parse her testimony. Once again, I was struck by her solicitousness toward her husband. In her position, I might have been less forgiving of someone who had locked me in a room before throwing me to the police, not to mention his subsequent determination of my guilt. The benefit of the doubt might have been polite, at the minimum.

'May I ask, Mrs Clark—'

'Call me Colleen, please. Right now, the only people who call me "Mrs Clark" mean me some harm.'

'Colleen, then. I'm not going to sugarcoat this pill, but it strikes me that your husband has very quickly assumed an antagonistic position in this case, even allowing for the circumstances. It raises questions about the state of your marriage.'

She took a long time to answer. The gloom of the house drew tighter around us. She couldn't keep living like this, surrounded by loss and mired in adumbration. Before too long, her sanity would begin to crumble.

'Stephen had an affair,' she said at last, 'shortly after I became pregnant. It was a woman he met through work. It didn't last very long – it was barely more than a one-night stand – but not surprisingly, it's hung over us ever since.'

'How did you feel about that?'

She laughed for the first time. It wasn't a pleasant sound.

'Angry. Betrayed. And then, weirdly, sorry for him. It was a difficult pregnancy from the beginning, and I can't have been easy to live with. Stephen was working too hard, and drinking too much in hotel bars far from home. He faltered. It hurt – it hurt a lot – but it happens.'

'And after?'

'I told him I forgave him. I haven't, of course. I never will, not completely, but I wasn't about to let it destroy our marriage, not with a baby on the way. I suppose you think I'm an idiot for doing that. My mother certainly does.'

'I'm not here to judge you,' I said.

'Aren't you? I don't believe that. You wouldn't be human if you didn't.'

'You might be surprised.'

'I'm hard to surprise. The worst has already happened. There's not a whole lot left.'

I had to resist the urge to reach out to her, to tell her that I had some inkling of what she was going through. Grief is like cancer: near-universal in its reach, but specific in its grasp. No two people experience it alike, so to claim I knew how she was feeling would have been a lie, yet some aspect of it had also taken root in me, triggering a transformation both visible and unseen. That process did not end, merely ebbed and flowed. If her child was gone, the loss would define her for the rest of her days, just as my losses defined me.

'Do you know the name of the woman with whom your husband had his affair?'

'Mara,' she said. 'Mara Teller.'

Chapter V

We heard the sound of sirens approaching, and Colleen tensed. The noise passed on, but she didn't speak again until it had faded away entirely.

'If they come bringing news,' I said, 'it won't be with lights and sirens.'

'I'm afraid that someday I'll answer the door to find police officers standing on the step with their caps in their hands, looking like they'd rather be anywhere else. I think I might prefer some warning.'

I said nothing. I'd made those calls, and knew the procedure: always bring another officer; try to get inside and have the recipient seated before delivering bad tidings; and avoid platitudes, even at the risk of seeming uncaring. Disengagement was important, because there was still information to be sought. In a homicide, one might even be sharing intelligence with the killer. Should Henry Clark's body be found, that would be on the minds of the police who came to inform Colleen.

'We were talking about Mara Teller,' I said.

'Stephen didn't give me her last name, only her first. I had to find the rest out for myself.'

'How did you do that?'

'He met her at a conference in Boston. I looked up the names of the other attendees. There was only one Mara, so I knew it was her.'

'What was the conference?'

'The National Gas and Petrochemicals Forum,' she said. 'No doubt it was as boring as it sounds, the affair apart.'

'What was Mara Teller's role?'

'She was listed as an independent consultant on the website. I googled her, of course, but nothing came up, apart from a link to the consultancy. When I tried the link, it went to a homepage that said the site was still under construction. I returned to it a couple of times after, but the message remained the same, and then the homepage disappeared and the link went dead.'

'Do you recall the name of the consultancy?'

'AlterRealm Consulting, but AlterRealm is an anagram of Mara Teller, so it may have been a one-woman operation. There was some bullshit slogan about "a new world of business opportunities", but that was all.'

'What about a phone number or an email address?'

'There was neither.' She watched me writing all this down. 'Wouldn't it be easier to use a recording device?'

'Easier,' I said, 'but harder to recall. Writing helps keep things fresh in my mind. Also, some people might become alarmed if I started recording them. Not everyone wants their comments preserved in that way.'

The only sound for a time was the whispering of my pen against paper.

'Do you think Mara Teller could have taken Henry?' said Colleen.

I stopped writing.

'Do you have any reason to believe she might?'

'No, but you're going to talk to her anyway, aren't you?'

'I will, if I can find her, but I wouldn't go reading anything into that.' I put down my pen. 'I don't know how familiar you are with my background, but I was a detective with the NYPD before I became a private investigator. When a serious crime is committed, a machine clicks into operation. It has established processes, and those processes require a great deal of manpower to complete. Huge numbers of people may have to be interviewed, and while virtually none of them will have anything useful to offer, they have to be spoken with anyway, if only to cross off a name and prevent any more time being wasted on lines of inquiry that go nowhere. The rest, that very small group of individuals with something worthwhile to contribute, have to be found through those same processes.'

29

'Needles in haystacks,' said Colleen.

'It's not quite that bad, but it's close.'

'And you're just one man.'

'I can call on others for help if necessary, but I prefer not to. Reading someone else's account of an interview isn't the same as conducting it myself. Individuals are books to be interpreted, but their words are only part of the story. Right now, my resources are limited, and I only have so much time to read. That's why I made it clear to you earlier that I have to be careful not to become distracted from my primary role, which is to aid your defense. The resources of the police and prosecutors are greater than mine, but they also have their limitations. One of them is that they believe they now have a culprit for your son's disappearance. Their focus has shifted from searching to proving, and their attention will be fixed on you. I have more latitude.'

'But given the choice,' said Colleen, 'I'd still prefer you to be looking for my son.'

'If it's any consolation, he will be in my thoughts at all times. If I find anything that might reveal the truth, I'll follow it to the end.'

'Thank you.' She scratched at the hair on her arms, the evidence of her body's efforts to compensate for her fragility by keeping itself warm. She blinked hard and said, 'There was so much blood on the blanket.'

'I haven't seen it.'

'But you'll want to.'

'Not "want", I'll need to – the pictures, at least.'

'One of the detectives told Stephen that, with all the blood, there wasn't much hope for Henry. Being found alive, I mean.'

Her voice didn't tremble. She fixed her gaze on me, and I saw near-unfathomable pain.

'And your husband shared that information with you?'

'"Shared" might be too kind a way to put it.'

A flash of anger at last. *Good*, I thought.

'The police may be operating on the basis that Henry is no longer alive,' I said, 'but we aren't.'

'I have to hold on to hope,' she said. 'If I don't, I may as well crawl off and die.'

30

'If there wasn't hope of some kind,' I said, 'I wouldn't be here.'

'Okay,' she said, before repeating the word, as much to reassure herself as to indicate agreement. 'Okay.'

'Can we talk about relations between you and your husband after Henry was born?' I said. 'You mentioned depression.'

'Yes. It started out as post-partum, then turned into something longer-term. It was miserable, just awful. I even resented Henry.'

'Did you mention those feelings to anyone else?'

'My physician, and the therapist I've been seeing.'

'A trained psychologist?'

'Yes.'

The conversations with her doctor would be subject to the rule of doctor–patient confidentiality, unless Colleen chose to waive that entitlement. The therapist might be more vulnerable to legal pressure, although that would be a matter for Moxie. I'd have to talk to him about it later, but doubtless, he was already considering the angles.

'What about your husband?' I said.

'Stephen knew how hard I was finding motherhood. I hid nothing from him.'

This wasn't good. A husband couldn't be compelled to testify against his wife, but from what I was learning about Stephen Clark, duress wasn't set to be an issue. I couldn't claim to be an expert on how the judicial system treated women alleged to have committed an offense while suffering from depression, but if it bore any resemblance to the way it treated women generally, especially those accused of a violent crime, Colleen could expect to be hauled over hot coals.

'I have to ask this,' I said, 'but were you ever unfaithful to Stephen?'

'No, never. He's the only man I've ever slept with.'

We spent a few more minutes revisiting her movements on the day of Henry's disappearance, and what transpired after, but it didn't seem as though Colleen had a great deal more to add. With her assistance, I compiled a list of her neighbors, along with any reflections she had on their attitude toward her. The Clarks weren't close to any of them, and only Mrs Gammett had displayed actual solicitude since the finding of the bloodstained blanket. The rest were either keeping their distance or – by look, gesture, and intimation – communicating their hostility. I'd have to talk to all of them, chasing, like some sad dog, the trail left by the police.

'So what happens now?' asked Colleen.

'I know you were scheduled to speak with Mr Castin – Moxie – later today,' I said. 'If neither of you objects, I'd like to be present for that meeting. We can do it here, or I can drive you to the office and back, whichever you prefer.'

Her unease was obvious.

'Pictures are taken of me when I go out,' she said. 'They turn up online, and then people write bad things about me under them.'

'I didn't notice anyone hanging around when I arrived,' I said. 'The police presence will discourage them. That doesn't mean they're not out there somewhere, but I think we can get you wherever you want to go without too much difficulty. You should also stop reading what people say about you and the case, online or anywhere else. It's not helpful, it won't tell you anything you don't already know, and it won't affect the outcome.'

'I haven't been beyond the house in days,' she said. 'Is it cold out?'

'Not so much, but I'd bring a coat if I were you.' If I were her, I'd have worn a coat in summer.

I'd have to call Moxie first. He would have an opinion on a venue for the meeting. By now, word might have filtered out that he was representing Colleen, which meant his office would become another site of interest. There was always the Great Lost Bear. Dave Evans would find us somewhere private to talk. Dave's instinct was to avoid condemnation – being judgmental didn't help when it came to owning a bar – and if Moxie and I were working for Colleen, he'd instinctively take our side. I was still patting myself on the back for my choice when I considered the optics of a young mother, about to be charged with the abduction and killing of her child, emerging from one of Portland's best-loved bars. I couldn't take a chance on her being seen there because it would do her cause no good at all. Yet it still seemed beneficial to get her out of the house, not only for the sake of her own psychological and emotional well-being, but also because location influenced tone and response, and I now wanted a glimpse of Colleen Clark outside her home environment. Perhaps new surroundings would jog her memory, or stimulate a fresh perspective on events.

'I don't know,' she said.

'It might do you good to take some air,' I said.

She stared at me.

'But what if Henry comes back and I'm not here?'

Then she started to cry.

Chapter VI

Colleen Clark eventually stopped crying, though it took a while. Afterward she went to freshen up while I contacted Moxie. As it turned out, his secretary had already spotted two local reporters hanging around the parking lot behind his office. Once Colleen had been formally charged, and Moxie officially confirmed as her attorney, there'd be little point in trying to conceal their connection, but for now it made sense to take advantage while we could. Moxie suggested a small diner over in Stroudwater, which didn't stay open beyond noon. Moxie, it transpired, was a silent partner in the venture, even if he never ate there as the food was terrible. He had a key, and we could bring our own coffee, because the house blend tasted like a rat had drowned in it.

'Why,' I asked him, 'are you a partner in a bad restaurant?'

'Because that way,' Moxie replied, 'I can make it a better one.'

Which was a good answer, if vaguely reminiscent of something Christ might have said on the way to the cross.

While Colleen got ready to leave, I took a look at her son's bedroom. One wall was painted cerulean blue with white clouds, but the rest was a delicate eggshell already displaying signs of a child's occupancy: stains, scuff marks, scratches. The room had built-in closets and shelves, all neatly filled with a young boy's clothes and possessions, and a toy box stood by the door. The bed was positioned equidistant from the wall on the left and the window on the right. A white teddy bear sat slumped against the bed's safety bars like a prisoner. On the floor lay a mattress, a comforter, and a pillow, along with a brown-and-white stuffed dog. As Moxie had indicated, Colleen was sleeping in her son's room.

I checked the window. It had a standard latch, but also an

34

adjustable window restrictor to prevent it being opened more than two inches. The restrictor's cable had been neatly severed, but otherwise there was no sign of damage. Outside, a paved path ran along the wall of the house, so the police wouldn't have been able to find footprints. I took a tape measure from my pocket, ran it over the wall and the room, and made a note of the figures.

'It's already beginning to smell less like him.'

Colleen was standing in the doorway. She had changed into dark trousers and a long-sleeved white shirt. A blue casual jacket was draped over her left arm, and a purse hung from her right shoulder. She had put on some makeup, but her heart wasn't in it, causing her to resemble an unfinished doll.

'I thought about sleeping on his pillow,' she continued, 'but I was afraid that my scent would erase what was left of his.'

I said nothing, because nothing I had to say would help. I don't think she even wanted me to speak, only listen. I watched her straighten a pile of T-shirts and smooth the topmost.

'Whoever took him knew about the restrictor,' I said. 'A standard box cutter wouldn't have been enough to sever it. They brought along a cable cutter.'

'The police asked if we had one in the house.'

'When?'

She thought about the question.

'After Stephen found the blanket.'

That made sense. Following the discovery of the blanket, the police had been seeking evidence of a setup.

'What did you say?' I said.

'I told them I didn't know. Stephen has a tool set, but he doesn't use it much. He's not very good at that kind of thing.'

I was beginning to wonder what exactly Stephen Clark might have been good at. Whatever it was, it wouldn't make for a long inventory.

'Did your husband show them the set?'

'Yes, I remember him going to look for it.'

'And?'

'I believe the police have it now.'

'Did it contain a cable cutter?'

35

'I'm sorry, I couldn't say.'

I took one last look around the room, but there was only the evidence of absence.

'If you're ready,' I said, 'we can go.'

Chapter VII

In the Maine woods, unseen by man, a fly crawled across the basement floor of the house built from Kit No. 174. The surface was dirt, lately disturbed, and the fly could sense that there was something hidden in the cool dark, something worth finding.

The insect began to burrow, pushing aside loose soil, the taste organs on its tarsi growing increasingly stimulated. After a few seconds of activity, it paused as though alert to a new threat. Its body jerked, the shock sending it onto its back. It waved its legs in the air and tried to right itself, but the fight was over before it had begun. The legs curled in on the abdomen, and all movement ceased.

Whatever dwelt in Kit No. 174, whatever moved through its confines and stalked the surrounding forest, did not like to share its food.

Chapter VIII

We drove from Colleen Clark's house without incident, apart from a trio of neighbors – one man, two women – who watched us go, their expressions shading from neutral to passing unfriendly. Colleen was wearing sunglasses, so I couldn't tell if she was aware of their scrutiny. I kept an eye on them in the rearview mirror and thought I saw one of the women produce her cell phone and use it to take a photo of my license plate. Only when we were out of their sight did Colleen exhale.

'Do you know them?' I said.

'The Robacks,' said Colleen, 'and Alison Piucci. She's the blonde.'

It was Piucci who had taken the picture. All three were on the list of names Colleen had provided, each marked with the letter X to indicate a potentially hostile status.

'Alison has a daughter Henry's age,' said Colleen. 'The Robacks have no kids of their own, but they've been trying. They're on the third round of IVF. If this one doesn't work, they may consider adopting, but he doesn't think it'll be the same and blames her for not being able to conceive. Then again, he's an idiot. He once tried to feel me up at a party, and believes only Blacks commit serious crimes – well, Blacks, and now me.'

The Clark residence was looking less and less like the kind of place Colleen should be staying, because she was already barely one step above being a prisoner in her own home. The ignorant were writing graffiti on her walls and throwing excrement at her door, and the situation wasn't going to improve after she was arrested.

'Moxie said that he'd spoken to you about moving out temporarily.'

'He raised the possibility, but I told him that I can't, not until

I know what's happened to Henry.' She chewed at a hangnail. 'And maybe I don't want to give them the satisfaction. In any case, my picture is already out there, so it's not like I can relocate to a new street and become anonymous. It doesn't matter where I go, I'll still be recognized, so I may as well stay where I am. My mom has offered to move in, so at least I won't be alone there.'

'Do you two get along?'

Colleen didn't need to add parental complications to her burdens.

'Sure. I mean, in an ideal world we wouldn't be under the same roof for days or weeks on end, but beggars can't be choosers, right?'

'If you elect to stay,' I said, 'we may have to put someone outside the house, and possibly inside as well. I have candidates in mind.'

The Fulci brothers would be happy to do it and earn money into the bargain. They might have to adjust their new medication to ensure that one was awake while the other slept, the latest thinking on their condition – the current professional tendency was to avoid using the word psychosis, because it sounded pejorative – being that if they couldn't be cured, they could at least be encouraged to sleep more, as there was only so much trouble they could cause from their beds. Dave Evans, for one, didn't agree. He'd confessed to me that the Fulcis regularly showed up in his dreams. This might have been regarded merely as a sign of stress on Dave's part had Paulie Fulci not remarked, during Dave's waking hours, that he ought to consider repainting his bedroom ceiling because it was starting to flake. Paulie, as far as Dave was aware, had never been inside Dave's home, never mind his bedroom. When Dave asked him how he had come by this opinion, Paulie couldn't remember. The strange thing was, the paint on Dave's bedroom ceiling *was* flaking. As a result, Dave was now having trouble sleeping in his own bed, or doing very much else there. It might have been one of the reasons why he had quietly indicated his intention of retiring, with the bar being passed on to Mike and Byrd Dickson, and Andy Pillsbury, all of whom had long associations with the Bear. The Fulcis had not yet been informed, no one being quite willing to grasp that particular nettle.

'Now that I think of it,' said Colleen, 'it might be a good idea to have someone watch the house. Whatever about me, I'd hate to have something bad happen to my mom. How conspicuous will they be, these candidates of yours?'

I thought of the Fulcis' monster truck, and the brothers' undeniable physical presence, reminiscent of a pair of bank safes dressed in casual wear.

'After a while,' I assured her, 'you'll hardly notice them at all.'

The diner was called Twitchy's, but I couldn't say I'd ever darkened its door before Moxie revealed his interest in it. I'd passed by occasionally over the years, but never felt the urge to give it a try. Twitchy's looked like the kind of place where only the chef's sandwich was made from scratch, and that was prepared before he left home in the morning, possibly by his wife. Either Moxie was a dreamer, or he was laundering money.

I parked in the lot beside Moxie's Mercedes, and Colleen and I entered through the open back door, once I was sure nobody had followed us there. Moxie was in the kitchen, regarding a clogged grease trap from a safe distance. He nodded at me, and greeted Colleen more formally before directing her to take a seat in a booth away from the windows, while signaling me to stay where I was.

'I bet you think I've lost my mind,' he said, 'taking a piece of a dump like this.'

'Not really,' I said. 'Having seen the size of your breakfast, I just figured the next step up was to buy a diner of your own.'

'You know, when we open under new management, you won't be allowed to eat here.'

'Unless it's being managed by the CDC, I'll swallow my pain. It'll be less risky than swallowing the food.'

Moxie pointed out the door, to a vacant lot beyond.

'You see that land? It's zoned R-3, and the planning board is meeting to approve a new development of apartments and condos next week. By the time the first residents move in, you won't recognize this place.'

'I'm hoping I won't even remember it. Are you going to keep the name?'

'Nah, Twitchy died.'

'Food poisoning?'

'Stroke. If I didn't know better, I'd say you were working for the competition.'

It was hard to conceive of Twitchy's having competition, or not for any prize it might want to win. On the other hand, Moxie was wealthier than I was ever going to be, and his instincts were sound. I didn't doubt that, in a year or two, Twitchy's, or whatever its new incarnation was called, would be making a lot of coin.

Moxie had brought along sandwiches, pastries and beverages from the Big Sky Bread Company. Colleen Clark picked at her tomato, mozzarella and pesto on rye, and drank a soda. I listened and ate while Moxie went over details of paperwork and formalities before he cut to the chase.

'The police are going to come for you early tomorrow morning,' he said. 'The media will be informed in advance, since that's how the AG's office wants to play it. You're an electoral tool, Colleen, which means every step taken has to appeal to voters. The more public the arrest, the better, or so the reasoning goes in Augusta, so they'll want you to do the perp walk. Sorry for being so blunt, but that's what it's called.'

Colleen pulled a piece of bread from her sandwich and rolled it into a ball between her fingers.

'Perp – for perpetrator, right?'

'Yes.'

'So I'm already guilty?'

'It's a question of perception for now, but that's open to manipulation – by both sides.'

'What do you mean?'

Moxie gestured for me to step in.

'Some people have prejudged you,' I said. 'Others will be keeping a more open mind, and they may be troubled by seeing a young mother, worried for her missing child, railroaded on the basis of a single piece of evidence. But if we let the police arrest you at your home, in front of the cameras, we hand the prosecution an advantage. It will confirm the suspicions of those who believe you belong behind bars, and may also sway some of the neutrals in that direction.'

'What options do I have?' said Colleen. 'Chain myself to my door? Go on the run?'

'Let's call those plans B and C,' I said. 'Plan A is that you present yourself for arrest.'

'Wait,' she said, 'won't that be like an admission of guilt?'

'Not the way we're going to play it,' said Moxie. 'Instead of a suspect being arrested, it'll be a mother demanding that the circus leave town before it has a chance to set up its tents. She knows she's innocent, regards the police and prosecutor as being in error, and believes any investigation and proceedings will not only vindicate her but also force the police to follow other lines of inquiry that may currently lie unexamined. She wants to know what happened to her child. If handing herself over to the police will help, she's prepared to make the sacrifice.'

Even by Moxie's singular standards, this was an unusual gambit.

'Will that work?' said Colleen.

'It'll work better than letting them lead you from your home in handcuffs, running a gauntlet of cameras and cell phones.'

'What then?'

'Maine law prevents a defendant from being held for more than forty-eight hours without arraignment or an initial hearing,' said Moxie, 'but we'll push for twenty-four on the basis that you presented yourself, thus saving the police time and trouble.'

In Maine, a felony case required the accused and their attorney to appear before a judge for an initial hearing to ensure that the former was aware of both their constitutional rights and the nature of the charges against them, and to address the issue of bail. Following that appearance, the prosecutor would seek a grand jury indictment prior to an arraignment, at which the accused would be asked to enter a plea.

'Because we're talking about felony charges involving a child,' Moxie continued, 'bail will have to be set by a state judge, assuming it's decided that there's probable cause for proceeding. I'll meet with the prosecutor before the hearing to hammer out bail terms acceptable to both of us, just in case we're assigned a judge who's a teeth-grinder, but it's likely that you'll have to spend a night at Cumberland County Jail. I'll do my damnedest to ensure it's not two, but I'm not making any promises.'

Colleen put her face in her hands.

'But I didn't do this' she said, 'and I shouldn't have to go to jail to prove it.'

'I don't deny it,' said Moxie. 'The only consolation I can offer is that we will take care of you, and we will win this.'

'How can you be so sure?' she said.

'Because I don't like losing,' said Moxie. 'It becomes habit-forming.'

'And my son?'

She looked to me as she spoke, and I knew what she needed to hear. It would no longer be enough to relegate or abrogate any duty toward her son.

'You can be Moxie's priority,' I said. 'Henry can be mine.'

Chapter IX

Before leaving Twitchy's, I raised with Moxie the possibility of the Fulci brothers keeping an eye on Colleen Clark, both at home and when, or if, she chose to venture out. To my surprise, he made no objection, but perhaps he could see what was coming down the line and regarded the Fulcis as apt to discourage all but the most committed or foolhardy from attempting to interfere with or intimidate our client.

The afternoon sky remained gray, shading to white and black at the extremes, like being trapped under a pigeon's wing. I opened the car door for Colleen, and then spoke briefly and quietly to Moxie once she was safely inside.

'Learn anything interesting?' said Moxie.

'She has few friends, and we should ask the Fulcis to drop her husband on his head.'

Moxie shrugged. 'He thinks his wife killed their son. I'm prepared to allow him some leeway for trauma, if not for being an asshole.'

'He doesn't seem in any hurry to consider other possibilities. If they put him on the stand, he won't help her cause.'

'Let's hope it doesn't come to that. Did she tell you about his affair?'

'We discussed it. I imagine you'll also bring it up if he testifies against her.'

'I can hear the cries of "Objection!" already,' said Moxie. 'They're like music to my ears. What about the woman he slept with, Mara Teller?'

'I'll find her,' I said.

'I don't doubt it. I can't see too many loose threads yet, but she looks like one.'

Moxie hummed to himself as he yanked a weed from a crack

in the concrete. If someone had handed him a broom, he'd have begun sweeping the lot clean.

'If you don't mind me saying so,' I said, 'you're very relaxed.'

'This is what I do,' said Moxie, 'and I like it. The more difficult the case, the happier I am. We may have that in common.'

'It depends on how you define "happy".'

Colleen Clark was sitting stiffly in the passenger seat, her sunglasses once again concealing her eyes. I wondered how much longer she would be able to hold herself together, because my sense was that she was close to breaking. Her imminent incarceration, even if only for a night or two, might do it. I'd seen it happen before. At least Moxie and I both had contacts in the Department of Corrections and the Cumberland County Sheriff's Office, and could make sure she was kept safe.

'You haven't told me whether you think she's innocent,' said Moxie.

'I still don't know enough about her, or what happened.'

'But first impression?'

'She didn't do it.'

Although she couldn't have heard me, Colleen peered in our direction at that moment. Of course, she was aware that we were talking about her. What else could it have been? Her fate was now in the hands of two men she barely knew, but I doubted that was the main focus of her attention, not when her every breath contained the whisper of her son's name.

'Discovery might produce some surprises,' said Moxie, 'but for now it looks like the physical evidence against her amounts to a bloodied blanket that could easily have been planted in her car, and not much else. If I can't shoot that down, I ought to find another line of employment. The rest is circumstantial, but it worries me more. It introduces an unpredictable element.'

I knew what he meant. We were back to Colleen's depression and the conflicted feelings she had expressed about her son while enduring the worst of it. Many states had proven resistant to limiting charges against women alleged to have committed crimes while suffering from depression or psychosis. Other countries, recognizing these conditions as a form of mental illness, had introduced infanticide laws that permitted more lenient penalties for new or recent mothers convicted of killing their children, including probation, hospital orders, and supervision. In the United States, depending on the jurisdiction, a new mother convicted of killing her child, even if suffering from postpartum psychosis, could be jailed for anything up to life, or even face the death penalty. Like the rest of the judicial system, it was a lottery, and like all lotteries, it was loaded in favor of the house.

'Take Colleen home,' said Moxie. 'Tell her to use the bathroom, have a shower, and freshen up. I wrapped her sandwich' – he handed me a brown paper bag, stained slightly with grease – 'so see if you can get her to eat some more of it. I can't vouch for the food she'll be given in jail. It's a pity we can't wait until morning before bringing her in, but they're sure to come for her at first light and there's no percentage in waking her before dawn. It's not as if she's going to sleep soundly tonight either way, but better to get the stay behind bars over with.'

He checked his watch.

'I'll give you two hours,' he said, 'but don't worry if she needs more time. I'll park as close to the Portland PD as I can get. Call me when you leave, and I'll be ready and waiting.'

'Nowak and Becker are going to be angry at you for spoiling their show,' I said.

They might yet get some coverage out of Colleen's transfer to jail, but it wouldn't be the same. They would lose the impact of a home arrest, which would rankle. Meanwhile, Moxie would be priming his contacts in the media to ensure that the right message got out.

'They'll be pissed at both of us,' said Moxie. 'If Nowak is elected governor, and Becker makes AG, we should think about relocating to Cuba. They'll have a long list of scores to settle once they come into their kingdom, but we'll shoot right to the top of the list.'

I'd never met either Nowak or Becker, though I'd glimpsed both of them from a safe distance. It was enough to know that they didn't like me, and therefore it would be better if I stayed out of their way. That luxury was about to be denied me.

'I don't want to live in Cuba,' I said. 'I don't like heat.'

'Stock up on sunscreen,' said Moxie, 'just in case.'

Chapter X

I made some calls from Colleen Clark's kitchen while she showered. The first was to Paulie Fulci, informing him that I would require the brothers' services. Paulie didn't ask if I thought Colleen Clark was innocent or guilty – he just didn't like seeing a woman being railroaded – but I gave him my opinion anyway. I figured it was for the best. It was one thing to ask someone to look after a woman on a point of principle, but another to do so because you thought she was blameless.

Paulie offered to come by Portland PD headquarters later with Tony, on the off chance of any trouble, but I advised him to stay away. We wouldn't be announcing Colleen's arrival, the police would be able to take care of her once she got there, and I didn't care to see the Fulcis in cuffs because some concerned citizen started spitting at our client. Instead, I asked that one or both of them head over to the Clark house as soon as possible. I didn't want it standing empty while Colleen was in custody.

The remaining calls involved tidying up some loose ends on other cases and heading off prospective clients. Colleen would be consuming all my resources for the foreseeable future. She appeared in the doorway while I was finishing up.

'My mom's on her way here,' she said. 'Can we wait for her? She won't be very long.'

'Sure, we have time.'

Colleen had tied her hair back, put on a plain blue dress, and reapplied her makeup with more care than before. She held a matching blue purse in her hands, which she caught me looking at. Her shoulders sank as she realized why.

'I can't bring anything with me, can I?'

'You can, but it'll be taken from you when you're processed.'

'Processed,' she said. 'What a horrible word. It makes me sound like a slab of meat.'

She set the bag aside.

'I've never been inside a jail,' she said. 'I've only ever seen one on TV.'

'Moxie and I will make sure you're well looked after,' I said.

'Are you going to share my cell?'

But she wasn't smiling. She was scared, and I didn't blame her.

'Believe me,' I said, 'if I could, I would. In the absence of that, we have other ways of making sure you'll be kept out of harm's way.'

I didn't tell her that it would be easier for us to do that if she was held at Cumberland County Jail, which was smaller and, as places of incarceration went, kinder. If she were to be sent to Maine Correctional in Windham, or the state prison in Warren, our task would be made more difficult. We didn't have the same contacts in those institutions, and some of the inmates would be of a different degree of unpleasantness from CCJ's residents. But both Windham and Warren were overcrowded and might not have space to accommodate her anyway.

The doorbell rang. Colleen stood to get it, but I waved her down.

'From now on,' I said, 'this is how it will be. You don't answer the door or the phone, and you don't go anywhere unless I, or one of my colleagues, is with you. Okay?'

'Okay.'

I thought we might also get some surveillance cameras installed, and a video doorbell for the door. It would act as a deterrent, as well as helping the Fulcis with their duties. I went to the door and checked the peephole. A woman in her early sixties was standing on the step. I spotted the resemblance and let her in.

'Mrs Miller?' I said. 'My name is Parker. I'm working on your daughter's behalf, aiding her attorney.'

Evelyn Miller waited until the door had closed behind her before speaking. Her daughter might have acquired some of her looks, but not her demeanor. The mother radiated energy and purpose, and right now she was also being fueled by a rage so hot it had turned her face red. She dispensed with the niceties and cut to the chase.

'Seriously, you've advised her to hand herself over to the police?'

'Mom, please—' said Colleen from the kitchen.

'I didn't argue against it,' I said. 'I believed it was the correct decision.'

'I thought your job was to keep her *out* of jail.'

'This is a long game, Mrs Miller,' I said. 'Don't judge it by the first move.'

'Oh, that's very clever. Did you keep the fortune cookie it came in?'

'*Mom!*'

This time, Colleen Clark's voice was very loud. Even her mother was so surprised by the force of the interjection that it took her a few moments to react. After she did, her manner was more conciliatory.

'I'm just worried for you,' she said, advancing to the kitchen, where she took her daughter in her arms.

'I know,' said Colleen, 'but I told you: they were going to arrest me anyway, and try to make me look as bad as they could. This way I get to decide. I have the power. It's not much, but it's something. Mr Parker and Mr Castin aren't asking me to do anything I don't want to.'

Which wasn't completely true, because nobody really wants to go to jail. Nevertheless, it was kind of her to say. Her mother glanced back at me.

'I apologize,' she said.

'That's not necessary.'

Despite the front, Evelyn, like her daughter, was no more than two steps from crumbling to pieces.

'Is Mr Castin here?' she asked.

'We're going to meet him at Middle Street,' I said.

'You know, I was warned against allowing my daughter to hire him. I was told that he sometimes behaves in a manner unwise for a Maine lawyer – unwise for any lawyer, for that matter.'

'I'll concede that he's unconventional, but then this is hardly a conventional case. Speaking of which, Colleen, we ought to get going. Before we leave, I was wondering if you have a spare set of keys to the house?'

Colleen retrieved a leather keyholder from a hook inside one of the kitchen cabinets and handed it over.

49

'For you?' she asked.

'For the men who are going to be keeping an eye on you and your home. We'll have copies made, and return the originals to their spot.'

'Do you want the alarm codes and password, too?'

'Can't hurt, but it's not going to be standing empty.'

She wrote the information on a piece of paper, drew a deep breath, and took in her kitchen as though for the last time.

'Well, then,' she said. 'I suppose we'd better get this done.'

The Fulci brothers pulled up in their truck just as we were locking the front door. Colleen and her mother looked understandably alarmed, which was the effect the Fulcis had on strangers, and occasionally even on close acquaintances. Evelyn Miller reached into her bag, possibly for a can of Mace.

'These are the men who'll be taking care of you and your property,' I told Colleen. 'Let me introduce Paulie Fulci and his brother, Tony.'

The Fulcis had dressed to impress in pressed tan chinos and white shirts. They looked like massive vanilla ice cream cones.

'I've made up the bed in the spare room,' said Colleen, once the pleasantries were out of the way, 'and there's food in the refrigerator, but not much. I'm sorry, I haven't really been able to shop.'

Paulie thanked her and assured her that they could feed themselves, which was never in any doubt. I gave him the keys and the alarm details, and left it up to the brothers to decide how to divide their responsibilities, but I didn't anticipate any more problems with graffiti and excrement. I also asked them to pick up a video doorbell and a couple of cheap motion-activated cameras that could be accessed from cell phones.

The presence of the Fulcis appeared to have impressed Evelyn sufficiently to thaw her attitude still more.

'You know some threatening people, Mr Parker,' she said, as she joined her daughter in the back of my car.

'I do,' I said. 'Someday, you may even get to meet them.'

Chapter XI

As anticipated, Colleen Clark's arrival provoked a burst of surprised activity at Portland PD headquarters, which eventually concluded, after some hurried telephone calls, with her arrest on charges of criminal restraint by a parent, endangering the welfare of a child, and the manslaughter of a child under the age of six. An hour later, Erin Becker sailed in wearing a cocktail dress and heels, having been forced to leave a campaign fundraising dinner in Brunswick to deal with the consequences of Colleen's presentation of herself to the authorities. Even without the heels, Becker would have been taller than Moxie or me, and it was interesting that when she and Paul Nowak appeared together, the latter arranged for them to remain seated, or found a way to stand one step higher than her. Ultimately, he'd be forced to resort to lifts in his shoes.

Becker was a striking brunette, happily married to a business executive husband – as far as anyone could tell – with three children under the age of ten whom she sensibly didn't parade for photo opportunities, because criminals had a habit of taking it amiss when prosecutions went against them. She was clever, too, walking a political tightrope between the liberal east of the state and the more conservative interior, but she had little kindness to her, and no mercy. Those with ambition in the AG's office didn't progress by not putting people behind bars, and there were few votes in leniency.

That she was unhappy with the current turn of events was clear from the look she shot Moxie, and she didn't demonstrate any greater delight at the sight of me. She cornered Moxie outside the interview room in which Colleen was being held and asked him just how smart he thought he was. Moxie, as he told me later,

51

was tempted to reply that it depended on the company, but common sense prevailed. In the game being played, he had sacrificed a pawn in the hope of gaining an advantage elsewhere on the board, but Becker still had it in her power to punish him for what he'd done. She made this instantly clear when she announced that Colleen would be transferred not to Cumberland County Jail, but to Maine Correctional Center in Windham. It was a vindictive move and nothing more, and potentially placed Colleen in danger. The MCC was overpopulated to such a degree that some of the women were incarcerated in temporary buildings with male inmates, and accommodations originally designed for two or four female prisoners routinely housed twice those numbers. With staff overstretched already, Colleen's safety couldn't be guaranteed, even if she was kept in isolation, not with the charges leveled against her.

'Why would you do that?' said Moxie. 'What's the benefit?'

'She's a suspected child killer,' said Becker. 'Maybe you'd prefer to have her put up at the Regency?'

'I checked with Cumberland County Jail,' said Moxie. 'They're not even at capacity, and they've only one female inmate right now: a repeat DUI awaiting trial because she couldn't make bail. The Cumberland County DA isn't going to kick up a fuss if she's sent on her way so my client can have their exclusive attention.'

'You really think I'm going to make life easier for her, after the stunt you just pulled?'

'She's been charged, not convicted,' said Moxie, 'and the TV cameras aren't going anywhere. You'll get your exposure, but without my client's home address being advertised on every TV in the Northeast. If you put her in MCC to get stabbed by a junkie, you're going to look bad at the bail hearing for deliberately endangering the safety of a prisoner when you had options, and placing her far from counsel.'

Becker stewed, but it was obvious that her better judgment would have to prevail over baser emotions. Moxie wasn't some public defender she could browbeat into submission. He'd been handling murder cases back when Becker was still rigging elections to the student council.

'Fine,' she said. 'Let Cumberland take her, but you just blew all my goodwill, and then some.'

She stalked off, but not before pausing in front of me.

'What the fuck are you smiling at?'

'I'm just naturally buoyant.'

'When the ship goes down, you'll drown with the rest,' said Becker. 'Let's see how buoyant you are then.'

Moxie and I watched her depart. She was already making a call from her cell phone. I'd have bet good money that she was about to speak with her boss, Nowak.

'That went well,' I said to Moxie. 'You got your way twice already this evening, and Becker barely drew blood.'

'She'll try to kill us on bail. That's how she works.'

'You think Cuba will be far enough away for us?'

'Mars won't be far enough.'

He walked to a window and looked down on Middle Street. The news vans had gathered outside, the crews waiting to grab footage of Colleen being taken to jail.

'When will you make your statement?' I said.

'As soon as she's on her way. I have transcripts ready to hand out. I hate being misquoted.'

'And your every word a pearl. If you don't need me, I'd like to get going before you make your speech.'

'Sure,' said Moxie. 'It's been a long day. I know you don't like early starts, but I'd appreciate it if maybe you could come by the office before noon tomorrow. I'll order in lunch, if you like.'

'Let's see how things go. If I make it, coffee will be fine.'

'You're going to fade away,' said Moxie, 'and then none of your clothes will fit right.'

'You and me both.'

'Yeah, but I'm growing into mine. I plan ahead.'

'Well, that's why they pay you the big bucks,' I said, and left him to consign Colleen Clark to the cells.

Chapter XII

As it happened, I didn't escape from Middle Street unnoticed. The media were at both the front and the rear doors, and the camera lights came on as soon as I exited. Perhaps they'd already figured out that if Moxie Castin was representing Colleen Clark, I might be involved on the investigative side, but it was equally possible that Erin Becker's people had made some calls in the hope of muddying the waters. I had overstepped the line in the past, so it wasn't hard to predict the spin: if Colleen Clark was resorting to such dubious company to aid her defense, she really did have something to hide. The implication would have to be subtle to avoid trouble with a judge, but Becker was an operator. If anyone could carry it off, she could.

A couple of questions were shouted in my direction as I walked to my car, but I ignored them. Dealing with the media was Moxie's job. I already had a long list of people I needed to approach, and the first name on it was that of Colleen's husband, Stephen. But I'd also have to canvass her neighbors, and speak with her physician and therapist, since Colleen had given Moxie permission in writing to approach them and obtain any and all information pertinent to the case. Mostly, though, our job would be to confirm that the two professionals were aware of the extent and limitations of privilege, and make certain they contacted us in the event of being served with a subpoena by the prosecution.

Becker would move fast. She needed a speedy trial because a long delay wouldn't help her election chances, or Nowak's. Moxie, by contrast, would angle for as much time as he could get, but he couldn't apply the same pressure to the system as the AG's office. Colleen had agreed to be guided by Moxie, which was always beneficial, but she'd made it plain that she didn't want the trial hanging over her head for too long, not unless a delay helped the investigation into her son's disappearance: my territory. The more I considered it, the more her fate was coming to rest on my shoulders. Angel and Louis would have said it was my martyr complex manifesting itself. If so, they permanently occupied the crosses on either side of me, because whenever I looked around, there they were.

I hadn't eaten since Twitchy's, and even then I'd left three-quarters of a sandwich untouched. I drove down to Local 188 on Congress, parked on the street, and ordered a bowl of pasta and a glass of wine at the bar. A woman smiled at me, and I smiled back. She tried to strike up a conversation, but it never went beyond politeness on my part, and she soon found someone more sociable with whom to pass the evening.

And on a blank page of my notebook, I wrote a name: *Mara Teller*.

Chapter XIII

Far to the northwest, the wind whistled around Kit No. 174, and dead leaves skittered across the ground. Had anyone been present to witness it, they might have thought that a shadow passed across the window of one of the upper rooms, but as like as not, it was the reflection of a branch buffeted by the breeze.

In another universe, this particular iteration of Kit No. 174 might have been regarded as blighted from the start, fundamentally flawed by a series of incidents during its manufacture, each unconnected to the last but all ultimately contributing to a structure that should never have been permitted to leave the warehouse, or would have been better off returned to Sears as soon as its faults became apparent to the purchasers. Its undeniable oddness, its sense of elemental deficiency, would then have had a logical explanation. But the house conformed to every basic standard, and so had been permitted to stand. Its abnormality was not inherent, but acquired.

Yet the house was not haunted, whatever some locals might have suggested – although none had ventured out lately to check, because even the rowdier kids from the district paid heed to the NO TRESPASSING signs posted on the property. It was just a house, distinct from the ground on which it stood in the same way that a tombstone is not the same as a grave.

What did it mark, this structure? Nothing, nothing at all.

And everything.

The woman who had briefly gone by the name of Mara Teller was examining the coverage of Colleen Clark's arrest on her laptop, replaying the media footage that had been posted of her transfer to Cumberland County Jail. A beer stood by her right hand, and a cigarette was burning in an ashtray, its column of ash growing longer and longer like a gray worm being birthed, because the woman was entirely absorbed by the screen.

She watched, for a third time, the film of Clark being escorted from the Portland PD building. Her hands were cuffed, and she had a police officer at either side of her, but she held her head high, even as bright lights shone in her eyes and questions and abuse were shouted at her from the margins. The woman felt a degree of admiration, even sympathy, but not enough of either to hope that Clark got off. It was important she be convicted. If she were not, the inquiry into her son's disappearance would take a different direction, which would be unfortunate.

Behind Clark walked the lawyer Castin, who had later made a statement to the media declaring his client's innocence and expressing confidence that she would be exonerated. The woman thought Castin looked like a shyster. He talked too fast for her liking, and wore the kind of suit favored by hucksters who were trying to sell you something you didn't want to buy.

Finally, she reached a short section of reportage headed by footage of a man of slightly-above-average height leaving Portland PD headquarters. He wasn't trying to flee the cameras, but gave the impression that, while he was aware of their presence, they were of no consequence to him. She listened to the commentary, even though she was already familiar with his name and reputation, before freezing the video on the private investigator's face. Footsteps sounded behind her. She tapped the screen.

'I think,' she said, 'that we may have a complication.'

Chapter XIV

Colleen Clark had informed me that her estranged husband was currently staying with his brother, Michael, in Dayton, about a half hour south of Portland. He was, she said, avoiding unnecessary travel for the present, and working remotely from a makeshift office in his brother's home. Colleen and her husband had spoken only once since the revelation of the blanket in her car. In the course of the conversation, he had informed her that he never wished to see her again. According to a mutual acquaintance, he had consulted a divorce attorney and requested that papers be served on his wife as soon as she was released on bail.

I drove to Dayton the following morning in the first proper sunlight for a week, even if it hadn't brought much warmth. Michael Clark lived on Ruel Lane, almost halfway between Dayton and Union Falls. There wasn't much to Dayton, but that was true of a lot of small Maine towns. This region was once lumber and dairy country, but the lumber now came largely from up north and pasture had given way to industrial and housing developments, or warehouses with indefinable purposes, which counted as progress only if one was answerable to shareholders.

Michael Clark lived in a new family home surrounded by young pines, with three cars in the drive, two of which – a white Kia Stinger and a red Ford Fusion – were registered to the address. The third vehicle, a black Lexus coupe, I knew to be Stephen's. I parked behind it, got out, and repositioned a child's tricycle that was lying too close to one of the Stinger's rear tires. It would have been just the right size for Henry Clark in a year or so, I thought. I wondered who owned it, given that, per Colleen, the family was childless. A neighbor's kid, perhaps.

I rang the doorbell and waited. I'd spotted a drape move in

one of the upper front windows as I parked, so I knew my arrival had been noted. If the Clarks had been watching the news, or reading the papers – and it was almost certain they had – they'd know who I was and why I was at their door. With luck, I could convince Stephen Clark to talk to me, but a hostile reception was more probable. I was working on behalf of his wife, whom he believed to have killed their son.

A woman in her early thirties answered the call of the bell. She was wearing a gold wedding band and a diamond engagement ring that, judging by the number of small stones, had been bought for quantity, not quality. She reminded me of Colleen: same hair color, same height, and a similar build, although this woman was toned where Colleen was thin, and tanned where she was pale. Regardless, if this was Michael's wife, it appeared the Clark brothers shared a type.

'Mrs Clark?' I said.

'That's right.'

She wasn't opening the door very far, and was blocking the gap with her body as though to protect whomever was inside.

I showed her my ID. 'My name is Parker. I'm a private investigator. I was hoping to speak with your brother-in-law.'

'Why?'

But I could tell from her face that, as anticipated, she already knew why I was there.

'I'm involved in his wife's case,' I told her. 'I've been engaged by her lawyer to assist with the pretrial investigation.'

She stared at me for a good ten seconds without speaking.

'I meant why are you working for her?' she said at last. 'Why would you do that? You're taking money from a woman who murdered her own child.'

I didn't answer because there was no answer to give, or none that would have satisfied this woman. She wasn't the first to have asked me questions like that, and she wouldn't be the last. I could have told her that my actions had nothing to do with any presumptions of innocence or guilt, which would have been only partly true, but she still wouldn't have accepted the answer, and I wouldn't have blamed her for it.

'Stephen Clark,' I said. 'If he's available.'

A man's voice spoke from the shadows.

'It's okay, Donna. I'll talk to him.'

'Then you'll do it outside,' she said, as she stepped back to let the man come forward, 'because he's not setting foot in this house.'

I'd seen enough images of Stephen Clark in the newspapers and on TV to recognize him, but his height still surprised me. He must have been six six or six seven, but he probably weighed no more than 170 pounds, which caused me to wonder if anyone in the extended Clark family had ever said yes to dessert. This was not the striking gauntness of his wife, though, or even the carefully tended appearance of his sister-in-law. Colleen had told me that her husband was an obsessive runner who competed annually in the Boston, New York, and Chicago marathons, in addition to shorter races fit in around work and family commitments. The stripping of the fat from his body made his head appear too large for his frame, and a pair of oversized spectacles magnified his weak eyes, lending him a peculiarly buglike appearance. He wouldn't have been out of place lying semi-camouflaged on a stick.

'There's a table and some chairs in the yard,' he said. 'We can speak there, if the temperature doesn't bother you.'

'It doesn't bother me at all.'

Clark removed a green canvas jacket from the hallstand and stepped outside, pulling the door closed behind him. I followed him to where a white metal table and matching chairs stood on a patch of lawn. He brushed a few dead leaves from one of the chairs and folded himself into it, his knees ending up at an acute angle. He buried his hands deep in the pockets of his jacket.

'I'd offer you coffee,' he said, 'but—'

He gestured in the direction of the house. Through the kitchen window, I could see his sister-in-law removing breakfast dishes from the table and placing them noisily in a dishwasher. Her rage was obvious.

'Donna and my brother don't have any children of their own, so she doted on Henry.'

'Who owns the tricycle?'

'Donna's sister's kid. Donna takes care of her a couple days a week, while her mom is at work.'

Which answered that question, but I thought I might check the alibis for the brother and sister-in-law on the night of Henry's disappearance, just to be sure.

'This is a difficult time,' I said, 'and I'm sorry for what you're going through.'

'Thank you. I know it's your job, and Colleen is entitled to a defense, whatever she may have done.'

There was no hint of reservation in his voice. Either Stephen knew more about his wife than I did, or he didn't know her at all.

'She's also entitled to the presumption of innocence.'

'So they say, but you didn't find a blanket stained with your missing son's blood in the trunk of your wife's car. You didn't hear her talk about how sorry she was that she'd ever had a child, or how she sometimes wanted to smother him just to stop him from crying. I accept that my wife was depressed. She may even have been mentally disturbed. But that doesn't excuse her from murdering our boy and hiding his remains.'

'You have no doubts about her guilt?'

'None.' He relented slightly. 'Look, I know how that sounds, and I appreciate that under the circumstances a lot remains unknown, including Henry's whereabouts. But I've been living with my wife's strangeness since before Henry was born, because I don't think she even wanted a child, not really. Her health has never been great, and she's always had issues with body image. She didn't enjoy pregnancy and struggled with motherhood. In the event of a divorce, I'm not sure she'd have sought custody of Henry. I believe our marriage was already dying, but this, unsurprisingly, has killed it.'

He huddled deeper into his jacket, pupate in his misery.

'Was Colleen ever violent toward Henry?' I asked.

'I never saw her strike him, but then I was at work a lot of the time. He did have bruises, though, which had begun to worry me. I mentioned them to the police.'

Ouch, I thought. I had an image of Stephen Clark on the stand.

61

The prosecution wouldn't even have to coach him for long. He was already a gift to them.

'I think Colleen may simply have snapped,' he continued. 'Perhaps if I'd been more available to her and Henry, it wouldn't have happened.'

His voice almost broke. He took a breath before resuming.

'That's what I come back to,' he said, 'over and over. I wasn't there, and I should have been.'

'Does your job require you to travel a great deal?'

'I chose to travel more than was strictly necessary.'

'Why?'

'Because, like I said, my home life was unhappy – both before and after Henry was born.'

'Did you consider couples therapy?'

'Colleen suggested it, but I thought the trouble would pass, or I hoped it would.'

'That sounds like you're contradicting yourself,' I said, as mildly as I could, 'given what you said earlier about a divorce.'

'To be honest, I didn't want to sit with a stranger and talk about my feelings.'

To be honest: the liar's crutch.

'You're doing okay at it now.'

He gave me a death's-head grin.

'Circumstances have changed.'

'Yes,' I said, 'they have. Could your aversion to couples therapy also be related to the fact that you felt your marriage couldn't be saved, and you were unwilling to prolong the inevitable?'

He didn't immediately reply. He was smart enough to be able to spot someone trying to outsmart him, but not smart enough to protect himself by not talking.

'That's very perceptive,' he said. 'I wouldn't argue with the diagnosis. By the way, I'm waiting.'

'For what?'

'For you to ask me about the affair, if you want to dignify it with that name.'

'What would you call it?'

'A fling. A drunken mistake.'

'So you regretted it?'

'Of course. I take no pride in having cheated on my wife, whatever our difficulties. I erred once, but it was still a lousy way to behave.'

'My information is that it was more than a one-night stand.'

'You don't beat around the bush, do you?'

'With respect,' I said, 'you brought it up.'

'I suppose I did. You think I'll get asked about this if I'm called to give evidence?'

'It's conceivable.'

'I'd better get over my shame, then,' said Clark.

'If it helps, I'm not here to judge you, and you won't be the one on trial.'

'But her lawyer might try to make me look bad so Colleen will look better.'

'Your wife has been charged with killing her child,' I said. 'Your brief affair may represent a moral failing in some eyes, but not a criminal one.'

'Then I don't have to answer any questions about it?'

'Are you asking about mine, or anticipating those that may arise during the trial?'

'Let's say both.'

'You don't have to talk to me,' I said, 'but the fact that we're here suggests you don't mind, and you have nothing to hide beyond a certain level of discomfort with your failings.' I let that hook hang in the water. I didn't even twitch the line. 'If you're called as a witness, it's conceivable that the subject of your affair may be raised, most likely by the defense. The prosecution will object, but sustaining or overruling that objection will be a matter for the judge. So, in your position, I'd be preparing answers.'

'That's very forthright of you,' said Clark, 'seeing as how you're working for my wife.'

'I have no interest in tricking or misleading you, Mr Clark. My job is to ensure that the defense has any and all information that may be relevant to the case. I sometimes think I ought to have a clipboard for these occasions, with a series of forms to be filled in. It's procedure, that's all.'

Sometimes, I surprised even myself when it came to dissimulation.

A small brown mongrel dog ran from the front of the house and bounced over to us. Clark tickled it behind the ear, and it responded by trying to climb onto his lap. I wished it luck. Given its size, it would have required a rope and climbing gear to ascend Mount Clark. The effort left mud stains on his pants, so he sent it on its way. The dog peered at me, wagged its tail uncertainly, and retreated. Perhaps its mistress had told it about me. If so, I was lucky it hadn't bitten my ankle.

'I met Mara Teller at a conference in Boston,' said Clark. 'She was at the bar late on the second night, we got to talking, and one thing led to another. We had sex in my room, after which she returned to hers. We didn't see each other again at the event.'

'Did you exchange numbers?'

'No.'

'Why?'

'It was a one-shot deal for both of us. I wasn't looking for anything more, and I don't think she was either. Plus, I felt bad about it later. Despite appearances, I cared about my wife. I still do. It doesn't mean I can forgive her, but I don't want her to suffer.'

I didn't bother to congratulate him on his magnanimity.

'But you did meet Mara Teller subsequently,' I said.

'Yes, about a month later. I had business in Boston, and our paths crossed at Faneuil Hall.'

'Unplanned?'

'Yes.'

'That's quite a coincidence.'

'Maybe it was fated.'

'Maybe it was. Fate can be accommodating that way.'

'And, you know—'

'One thing led to another,' I said. 'Again.'

'Something like that. Things had grown worse between Colleen and me. The second time with Mara, I didn't feel so bad about it. In fact, I didn't feel bad at all.'

'Did you arrange to continue the relationship?'

'We talked about it,' said Clark, 'and this time we did exchange numbers. We spoke regularly on the phone, and hooked up once or twice more.'

'Which was it, out of curiosity?'

'What?'

'Once or twice?'

'Twice. The novelty was already fading for both of us, and Henry had been born. Then Colleen discovered the calls, along with the text messages, and confronted me with them. I didn't try to lie, and admitted everything. By then, I was convinced our marriage was heading for the rocks, child or no child, and I recognize that I was seeking to accelerate the collision. Colleen and I had a pretty miserable couple of weeks until things started to level out, or they did for me because I was moving toward a decision. I was looking for an exit, but Colleen wanted us to stay together.'

'Did you tell her you felt differently?'

'Not at first. I tried to go along with her way of seeing the marriage – as one that still had some hope of survival – but my heart wasn't in it. I was doing it for Henry's sake more than anything, but Colleen and I being unhappy wasn't going to help my son in the long run. I don't know how it dragged on, but somehow it did.'

'Do you still have Mara Teller's number?'

'It's not hers anymore. The number went out of service for a while, and now it's someone else's.'

'So you tried getting in touch with her?'

'I did, mainly to explain what was happening in my marriage.'

'Mainly?'

A half shrug this time, with a half grin to match. I mirrored it. We were guys together. I knew how it was.

'Call it one for the road,' he said. 'She was an attractive woman, and it wasn't as though Colleen wanted me in her bed. Her desire for reconciliation wasn't immediately reflected by a desire for more than that.'

'And did you get your "one for the road"?'

'No, Mara was gone.'

'Have you had any communication with her since?'

'None.'

'Do you still have those text messages?'

'I deleted all of them. Call it shame.'

I decided not to call it anything at all, although 'shame' still wouldn't have been the first word that sprang to mind.

'What do you know about her?' I asked.

'Next to nothing: her name, and the name of her consultancy service, which is, or was, a work in progress, and doesn't exist any longer. It might have been that not even her name was real. Who knows?'

'She didn't share anything of her background, or where she lived?'

'I didn't ask her to draw a family tree or a map. That stuff just gets in the way.'

'But you didn't find the absence of personal details odd?' I persisted.

'Welcome to the twenty-first century, Mr Parker. I know men who would regard a first name as surplus to requirements for a hookup.'

I didn't doubt it. On occasion, the modern world made me feel old and staid.

'Do you disapprove?' he asked.

'It strikes me as risky behavior for a married man.'

'Isn't that part of the appeal?'

'I don't know,' I said. 'Is it?'

'I think it was for me. No strings attached, just sex.'

'So what did you and Mara talk about?'

He laughed. It wasn't a pleasant laugh, but the sort one directs at an innocent, or a fool.

'We didn't talk,' he said, 'or not much. Again, that was a lot of the fun of it.'

I waited until the laughter stopped. There are better ways to spend one's time than waiting for someone to stop laughing. The sound quickly begins to grate.

'But you had telephone conversations,' I said. 'What did you discuss during those?'

'I don't recall. What we'd done, I suppose, and when we might do it again.'

66

'Did you speak about your home life?'

'I might have.'

'And the pregnancy? Or your son, after he was born?'

'I could have mentioned him. I don't remember.'

'So you were in touch with Mara Teller both before and after Henry's birth?'

'Largely before, but yes.' He removed his hands from his pockets and placed them flat on the table. 'Are you trying to suggest that Mara might have been responsible for what happened to Henry?'

'I'm just curious about her. Did you mention her to the police after Henry was taken?'

'No, Colleen did.'

'Why didn't you?'

'It didn't strike me as important at the time. As it happens, it still doesn't seem relevant. It was an affair. They happen. It seems spurious to attempt to connect it to my son's disappearance.'

'Did you ever cheat on your wife with anyone else?'

He recoiled as though struck.

'What kind of question is that?' he said.

'A natural one.'

'Well, I don't care for that word.'

'"Cheat"?'

'Yes.'

'Would you care to pick another?'

'Not off the top of my head.'

'Well, then. And you still haven't answered the question.'

'No, I haven't been with anyone else during my marriage.'

Strangely, I believed him, but I went on squeezing.

'Only Mara Teller?'

'That's right, and when the police eventually asked me about her, I told them what I've told you.'

'Did they follow up on the information?'

'I don't know. Is that what you and her lawyer are going to do, try to convince a jury that Mara might have abducted Henry so Colleen will get off?'

He was growing angry. It wasn't surprising. Being forced to admit to an affair is always humiliating, and Stephen Clark's unfaithfulness was certain to be made public in the event of a trial, which would add to the indignity. Then there was the fate of his son . . .

'What if Mara Teller did harm Henry?' I said. 'Wouldn't you want to know?'

'Are you implying that I don't care about my child?'

I was tired of him now. I'd gotten more out of him than anticipated, but it hadn't made me feel any better about humanity.

'I think you want someone to be punished for whatever befell him,' I said. 'You've decided that person should be your wife.'

'I didn't pull her name out of thin air.' He was close to shouting now. 'There's evidence: a blanket soaked with his blood, found in the trunk of her car, her depression, her whole damn attitude. She was never a fit mother for him.'

I heard a door open and close, and moments later his sister-in-law was standing nearby with her arms folded, the little brown dog circling her legs anxiously.

'That's circumstantial evidence,' I said. 'It would take more than a blanket to convince me of your wife's guilt.'

And, by implication, to convince me of my own wife's guilt in a similar situation.

'They'll find more.'

He spoke with absolute conviction.

'We'll see,' I said. It was time to leave. 'Thank you for your candor. If I have any further questions, I'll be in touch.'

'Save them,' said Clark. 'You won't be welcome here again.'

'I understand. I hope your son is found safe and well, for everyone's sake.'

I was walking away when he spoke again. Donna Clark was by his side, one arm curled protectively around him as he got to his feet.

'Do you really understand?' he said. 'I thought you might, which was why I decided to speak with you, but now I'm not so sure. I know all about you, Parker. You buried your child and hunted down her killer, yet you want to deny justice to me and my son. It's one law for you and another for everyone else. You're nothing but a hypocrite, trading on pain and misery, carrying your history like a cross for all to see. You're the one who ought to be ashamed. Go crawl back under your rock, you fuck.' He stormed away, but Donna continued to stare after me, and her hostility was almost triumphant. The dog advanced, barking to send me about my business.

And somewhere, a lie was hiding.

Chapter XV

I called Moxie on my way back to Portland. He told me that Colleen had spent as good a night as could be expected at Cumberland County Jail, and her initial court appearance was scheduled for that afternoon. Moxie would sit down with Erin Becker before the hearing in the hope of hammering out a bail agreement acceptable not only to both sides but also to the judge. Becker might have been nursing a grievance over Colleen's surrender, but if she tried to indulge it before an unsympathetic bench, she'd do herself more harm than good. Moxie was up for some horse-trading.

'Did you speak to the husband?'

I told him how it had gone.

'I'm surprised you got even that much out of him,' said Moxie. 'Impression?'

'He's already decided that his wife is guilty, but you knew that. If he was ever really in love with her, he might have started falling out of it before their son was born. But something about the Mara Teller affair doesn't ring true.'

'You think he cheated on his wife before?'

'He denies it. I'm inclined to accept his word because the accusation stung. Based on minimal acquaintance, he has a thin skin combined with an elevated opinion of himself. He doesn't like to be thought ill of, but the world may not view him as highly as he views himself, and he's smart enough to recognize it.'

'Does he still have feelings for the Teller woman?'

'He claims it was strictly a fling, and he wasn't overly troubled by the fact that he could no longer contact her, or said he couldn't.'

'So what's he hiding?'

'Possibly some personal or business details they shared. He was a little vague on what he and Teller might have spoken about when they weren't knocking boots.'

'Ever had an affair?' said Moxie.

'No.'

'Well I have. When you have an affair, mostly you talk about the affair. Bitching about a husband or wife casts a pall over proceedings. The best affairs are just about sex. It's the other stuff that causes all the problems.'

'Should I be taking notes?'

'Who knew you were such a tenderfoot?'

'I like to think I'm still pure on the inside. Returning to Stephen Clark, it was strange that he rejected out of hand any possibility of Teller's involvement in whatever happened to his son. It was as though he'd bet everything on his wife's guilt and couldn't countenance losing.'

'But to what end?' said Moxie.

'A conclusion to his marriage?'

'I handle divorces. Give him my card. There are simpler ways to get out of a bad relationship than trying to have your spouse jailed for murder. Speaking of which, the hearing is scheduled for four p.m. Think you can be at the courthouse by three thirty?'

'Whenever you need me.'

'Don't make it sound creepy. So what next?'

'I'm going to talk to some of Colleen's neighbors,' I said, 'but I might start with the friendlies and neutrals to ease myself in. It'll mean skipping our meeting in person later this morning, but since we're already speaking, ringing doorbells might be a better use of my resources. I'm also of a mind to begin following up on Mara Teller, if I have time. Stephen Clark says he discussed the affair with the police, but either they didn't feel it was a lead worth chasing down, or they didn't make any headway when they tried. I'd like to find out what happened there.'

'Will they share?'

'I can ask. They can only say no. But that's the official route. There are other ways.'

'I wish you luck,' he said. 'By the way, professional loyalties aside, you didn't much like our friend Stephen, did you?'

'He's callous and vain. That's a poor combination, although without the latter he probably wouldn't have talked to me.'

'So he wanted to match wits?' said Moxie. 'God bless his patience. Are you cutting him any slack for being a father who's lost his child?'

'I would,' I said, 'had he mentioned that child more often.'

Moxie was silent for so long that I thought the connection might have been lost.

'Let's keep your opinion of him between us for now,' he said at last.

'I wasn't planning on advertising it.'

'I meant keeping it from Colleen.'

'My lips are sealed. I'll see you at three thirty.'

Chapter XVI

Far from the broodings of Kit No. 174 – and those who guarded its secrets – a woman sat at the breakfast nook in her little cottage outside Haynesville, in the southeast corner of Aroostook County. The windows in the house were too small, so the rooms were always dim, but she didn't mind. She had never courted sunlight and didn't entertain visitors. In fact, for more than a decade she had been a virtual recluse, rarely venturing farther than the boundaries of her own town, unless health or business requirements dictated otherwise. Her name was Sabine Drew, and it had once, for a time, been known to many.

Sabine Drew's kitchen looked out on the Haynesville Woods by Route 2A, long regarded as one of the most dangerous roads in the county. During icy weather, drivers unfamiliar with its reputation often took the hairpin turns too fast. If they were lucky, they ended up in a ditch; if they were unlucky, they ended up in a cemetery. Dick Curless, the Tumbleweed Kid – a son of Aroostook, and the state's most famous country singer – even sang about Route 2A, 'A Tombstone Every Mile'. Dick would have known the road, since he'd resorted to driving a lumber truck for a while when the music business wasn't paying so well. Dick had probably taken those corners gently, though, what with him only having poor vision and all. They took out most of Dick's stomach in '75, a year after he stopped drinking and a year before he found Jesus, but the cancer got him anyway. Old Death was like that, Sabine had found. You could dodge him, even skip ahead for a while, and Death would never hold it against you. He knew he'd cross paths with you again, and it wasn't as though he didn't have enough custom to keep him occupied in the meantime.

All sorts of stories were told about Route 2A: tales of phantom girls walking the stretch of road where they'd died under the wheels of a truck, and dead women screaming for lost husbands, but they were nonsense. Sabine had lived in Haynesville all her life, and she'd never seen a single phantom girl or solitary dead woman on that road. Different ghosts, certainly, but not those.

Not that she spoke of specters to anyone these days. She'd left all that behind. Occasionally, folk still sought her out, either from curiosity or because they needed help, but she sent them off as politely as she could. It was always harder with the latter than the former, since she might have been able to assist them if she tried. But it was better not to; it would only bring trouble, and more knocks at the door.

So she lived with ghosts – her own, and those of others – while trying not to pay them too much notice. They were always seeking attention, and if they got it, like the callers at her door, they'd never go away. In that sense, they also resembled children, which was perhaps why Sabine had never wished for any kids of her own, not that anyone had ever seriously raised the possibility of making some with her. She'd never entertained any illusions about her attractiveness. Her mother had advised Sabine that she was 'homely', the kindest word she could find, so even without her peculiarity, Sabine might have struggled to interest a man for the long haul, which was like saying that with a different head, she might have been enticing. Her strangeness was as much a part of her as her looks, so she figured she'd die unmarried, but not alone. If she ever wanted for company, she could just alter her gaze and a ghost would come.

But as had been established, it was better not to do that. She'd learned to excise them from her consciousness; or more correctly, to accommodate her consciousness to their presence, like an alarm that had been ringing for so long that it became part of the soundscape, and one ceased to be unduly bothered by it. Lately, though, something had changed. A child was crying, and wouldn't stop.

Which was why Sabine, for the first time in many years, was

opening herself up to one of the dead. In silence, in shadow, she reached out and waited for the connection to be made. When it came, she listened and consoled as best she could, before getting in her car and driving toward the source of the cries.

Chapter XVII

I spent a couple of fruitless hours approaching as many of Colleen Clark's neighbors as I could, starting – as I'd told Moxie – with the ones who didn't appear to bear her any outright malice. Colleen had provided me with a comprehensive list of associates, casual acquaintances, and friends, but the latter were few, and far outnumbered by those she believed bore her some antipathy. Inevitably, I questioned some of the hostiles, too, because they couldn't be ignored, and received responses varying from 'Nothing to say' and 'I already told the police all I know', to 'Get lost' and 'You ought to be ashamed of yourself'.

Unfortunately, the obliging ones had little to share other than that Colleen and her husband were always polite but kept mainly to themselves, and none of them had ever spent longer inside the Clark home than it took to conduct a brief conversation, sometimes over coffee but more often not. After Henry's birth, Colleen had joined the younger mothers at Dougherty Field if the weather was good, and would sometimes take part in the weekly Mom & Kids breakfasts at the Crooked Mile Cafe on Milk Street, but she was an irregular attendee, and more of a listener than a talker.

'I liked her, though,' said a woman named Piper Hudson, who lived one street over from the Clarks on Bolton. 'Once you got to know her, she was really sweet. I think she was just lacking in confidence. My sister struggles with an eating disorder, and I thought I saw some of that in Colleen, though we never discussed it in depth.'

Hudson was bouncing a one-year-old girl named Isabella in her arms. She had two other children, with a Colombian nanny to help take care of them, which struck me as a full-time job given the noise that was coming from inside the house. Their mother left me alone for a moment to hand Isabella over to the nanny before returning to the porch. She hadn't asked me to step into the hall because she said it was quieter outside. From behind the door, I now heard the sound of three children competing to see who could scream loudest, should confirmation have been required.

'If you'd told me before the first one was born that I'd get tired of the weight of a child in my arms, I'd have scolded you,' she said. 'That novelty wore off the first time I went to bed with aching muscles and woke up the same way.'

We watched a squirrel forage for black walnuts beneath the mature ornamental tree in her yard. Black walnuts were not native to Maine, but squirrels loved them. The rodent would earn its meal, though: it would have to gnaw its way through the hard green husk to get at the nut inside. I knew fishermen who would pay good money for those discarded husks: to be crushed, cast on the water, and used to poison fish. It was odd the information one picked up as the years went by – or more correctly, the details one remembered. That knowledge about black walnuts and fishermen had probably displaced something useful from my brain, like how to avoid drowning.

'Did you and Colleen ever talk about her son?'

I could see her turning the question over in her mind, like a package of which she had grown suspicious halfway through the unwrapping of it.

'Of course.'

'My job isn't to undermine Colleen, Mrs Hudson,' I said. 'I'm only interested in helping her.'

I could tell she was still wary. I was glad. It would make me trust what she said that little bit more, especially as she was the first person I'd interviewed who'd offered me a seat.

'What do you know about Colleen's relationship with Henry?' she asked.

'I know that Colleen suffered from depression, struggling with the first years of motherhood, and then some,' I said. 'She told me she'd been seeing a therapist, which helped, and was emerging from that dark period. Her husband said she'd displayed feelings of resentment toward Henry, which she doesn't deny.'

77

'They'll use that against her, though, won't they?' asked Hudson. 'In court, I mean.'

'They'll certainly try,' I said.

'A bunch of men in suits, with no understanding of what it means to go through pregnancy, childbirth, or caring for an infant day and night, and no idea of what that does to a woman's body and mind.'

'I imagine it's one of the reasons why they've gone for a female prosecutor. They're aware of the optics.'

'Then maybe Colleen should have chosen a female lawyer,' said Hudson.

'Instead she chose the best one.'

'You're saying there isn't a female attorney in the state of Maine as good as Moxie Castin?'

'There isn't an attorney in the state who can compare with him,' I said. 'Colleen is in superlative hands.'

'What about you? Where do you fit in?'

'I bask in Mr Castin's reflected glory. So what can you tell me that I don't already know about Colleen and her son?'

She squinted at me. She had kind, shrewd eyes. Her husband was a lucky man.

'She loved Henry,' said Hudson. 'I mean, she always loved him, even when she was frustrated by him, or bored – because they don't tell you just how uninteresting babies can be – or floundering for lack of sleep. But loving and liking aren't the same thing, and I doubt there's a mother out there who hasn't at some point wanted to shake her baby to make them stop crying. You don't do it, but that doesn't mean you haven't considered it, and desperation and depression can make you think the worst things about your child and yourself. I speak from experience.

'But however low she felt, I don't think Colleen ever so much as raised her voice to that boy. It's not in her nature. Her instinct is to internalize and suffer quietly. But I could see the toll motherhood was taking on her, and glimpsed myself in her. I got her to open up about it. I was the one who persuaded her to go to therapy, and recommended she consider my therapist. I know Colleen resisted medication, though. She tried it for a while, but didn't like the way it deadened her, so she ended up with something less heavy that she could take when things got too much. But foremost she needed someone who would listen and empathize, because she couldn't manage alone.'

'What about her husband?'

'The cheater? He wanted to be a corporate big shot Monday to Friday, and a dad for a couple of hours on weekends, if it suited, but I don't think he was much of a husband or father at all toward the end. Colleen didn't want a divorce, though she suspected he did. Eventually, he'd have gotten his way.'

'I spoke to him earlier today,' I said. 'He was convinced that Colleen would have surrendered custody of Henry to him.'

'He told you that? What an asshole. And just who was supposed to look after Henry if that came to pass? Because he sure as hell wasn't going to be the one. He'd probably have handed him off to his brother and his wife, and they'd have been happy to take Henry, not having children of their own.'

'You and Colleen seem to have shared a lot.'

'Not everything, but enough. I told you, I liked her. I mean, I *like* her. I don't know why I'm talking about her in the past tense. Her life isn't over, no matter what others might say.'

'And Colleen's mother?'

'Evelyn's okay, I think,' said Hudson. 'She's a widow and Colleen's her only child, so Evelyn is very protective of her. She tried to help out as best she could, but she and Stephen didn't get along, especially after he cheated on her daughter.'

'Did Colleen talk to you about the other woman involved?'

'Mara? She mentioned her, but she wasn't able to find out a whole lot, and I bet Stephen didn't share even half of what he knew. What man would? It's weird, but it's almost as though Mara Teller didn't really exist. It's like someone made her up, but couldn't be bothered to do it properly.'

I whistled softly.

'What do you do for a living?' I asked.

'I'm a forensic accountant, but I've taken time off to raise my kids. I plan to return to work, though, as soon as they're all old enough for school. Why?'

'Your view of Mara Teller is remarkably acute.'

'So you agree?'

'Let's just say that if I ever need the services of a forensic accountant, I'll know where to turn. As for Mara Teller, there's no shortage of false identities on the internet. It was made for fake lives and alternative existences.'

'If Colleen isn't responsible for whatever happened to Henry – and I don't believe she is – then someone else must have taken him,' said Hudson, 'so why not this Mara Teller? But then, you're already thinking that way, aren't you?'

'I'm not ruling it out.'

I wasn't ruling out Stephen's brother and sister-in-law either, but I kept that to myself. The bloodstained blanket didn't fit with them, though. If they had somehow contrived to abduct Henry Clark because they couldn't have a child of their own, why would they then harm him? Something might have gone wrong, of course, but if it had not, and by some miracle Henry was still alive, where could they be keeping him? After all, his father was currently sharing their home, so how could they have hoped to hide Henry from Stephen? I still wanted to test their alibi, but logic said they weren't involved.

Inside the house, one of Hudson's children began wailing for her.

'Time for me to put on my mommy pants,' she said. 'There is another thing, although it doesn't mean much. I just considered it odd. Colleen told me she was surprised that Stephen bothered to have an affair. He'd never been very interested in sex, not even when they first began seeing each other. She used to worry it was her, a sign that he didn't find her attractive, but he admitted it early on. He liked running, and wanted to be a success in business, and it might be that getting married and having a family were things he felt he was supposed to do because it was what regular people did. I always thought he was a cold fish, but I guess he proved me wrong by cheating on her.'

'And this absence of a sexual component to the marriage didn't bother Colleen?'

'I'm not saying they never slept together, but it wasn't as though they were doing it more than a couple of times a month, even as newlyweds. Colleen had confidence issues, so it might have suited her to pursue a less physical relationship with her husband, or maybe the absence of sex compounded those difficulties. Who knows? That's not one I'd like to judge, and there was a limit to how far I was prepared to explore the subject with her.'

'People change,' I said, 'or so I've been told.'

'Some do but most don't, or not so you'd notice.'

The wailing increased in volume.

'I have to go, or the nanny will quit,' she said. 'Feel free to get in touch if I can be of any more help. Will Colleen make bail?'

'Today, with luck.'

'Then I'll go see her later this week. Don't let them put her back behind bars again, Mr Parker. If you do, I'll be disappointed.'

She went into her home and closed the door. I experienced a brief flash of a life with her, decided it wouldn't be so bad, and let it float away. I saw that the squirrel had bitten through the husk to the nut inside and took it as a good omen. We find them where we can. I checked my watch. I had enough time for a couple more calls and so, strengthened by Piper Hudson's cooperation, and the success of the squirrel, I headed back to the Clark house.

By good or bad fortune, Alison Piucci was once again out on the Clarks' street as I pulled up. She was in conversation with Kirk Roback, the man with the wandering hands. They were standing quite close to each other, their body language open and relaxed, even mildly intimate. Had Mrs Roback witnessed their interaction, her husband might have had some explaining to do. They stopped talking as I approached, the pair of them radiating nothing resembling good cheer.

'We haven't met,' I said, showing my ID. 'My name is Parker. I'm a private investigator.'

'We saw you on TV,' said Piucci. 'You're working for Colleen Clark.'

'Technically, I'm employed by her attorney, but let's not split hairs.'

Roback spoke up. 'We have nothing to say,' which was the day's echo. His voice was high for a man's, but soft, too. He was soft all over, like a figure made from marshmallows. Beside him, the slim Piucci resembled the first digit in the number 10. If anything was going on between them, Roback was pitching way out of his league.

'I haven't asked you anything yet,' I said.

'We're not going to help her get off,' said Piucci.

'We should let justice run its course,' added Roback.

'That's where I come in,' I said. 'We've moved on from witch dunking and trial by ordeal as proof of guilt or innocence. I just have a few questions—'

'I told you,' said Roback. 'We have nothing to say.'

He took a step forward, but when I didn't take a step back in response, he was left looking awkward, though in his mind it might have played well for Piucci.

'If she's a killer,' said Piucci, 'she should pay, but I have nothing against her personally.'

Her tone suggested that she did.

'The key word there,' I said, 'is "if".'

'We're not interested,' said Roback. 'Try your patter someplace else.'

'I'll do that,' I said. 'Thank you for your time.'

Before I went on my way, I waggled a finger at Roback, as though a half-forgotten detail about him had just returned to mind. All those episodes of *Columbo* that I'd watched as a boy hadn't gone to waste.

'I remember you now,' I said. 'You're the guy who tried to grope Colleen at a party.'

Roback reddened.

'That's slander,' he said. Piucci, meanwhile, was staring at him like he'd just begun picking his nose.

'Not if it's true,' I said. 'And if it's put to you on the stand, and you deny it, that would be perjury.'

'What do you mean, "on the stand"? Why should I be put on the stand?'

'Anyone could be called as a witness in this trial. You know

Colleen. You had interactions with her, at least one of which she claims was unwelcome. Think about that. We'll be in touch.'

I gave them both my best farewell smile, then crossed the street to the Clark house.

Chapter XVIII

Paulie Fulci was sitting in the brothers' monster truck when I tapped on the window. He was listening to a Harry Potter audiobook on the stereo. The bass was so low that Jim Dale's voice sounded like that of God Himself.

'Anything out of the ordinary?' I asked, as he lowered the window and paused the book.

'A couple of thrill-seekers. I told them to take a hike, and they did.'

This was hardly a surprise. Had Paulie told me to take a hike, I'd immediately have done so, conceivably to the Himalayas.

'Media?'

'A TV truck. I told them to take a hike too.'

'Did they object?'

'Not for long.'

When the mood struck him, Paulie could be kind of droll.

'And the police?'

'The patrol car left shortly after we got here. They drive by every couple of hours.'

'I hope you wave.'

'Not with more than one finger.'

I left him to Harry and rang the new video doorbell. The brothers had worked fast. I saw one camera mounted on the front of the house, covering the yard, and assumed its twin was monitoring the rear. Paulie's brother, Tony, opened the door and led me to the kitchen, where he and Evelyn Miller were working on a jigsaw puzzle of a Degas painting. Once I'd managed to get my mind around Tony Fulci and ballet dancers, I asked Evelyn how she was doing.

'Getting by,' she said. 'They allowed Colleen a phone call. She didn't sleep well last night, but otherwise, she's okay.'

'Nobody sleeps well on their first night in jail.'

'Let's make sure she doesn't have to experience a second. I have money ready to cover her bail. I disposed of some shares and consolidated accounts. I also have a line of credit open with my bank.' She stared hard at me. 'She *will* be granted bail, right?'

'There are no guarantees,' I told her, 'but Moxie is quietly confident. I only worry when he's loudly so.'

I suggested that Tony get some air, or take the opportunity to go listen to Harry Potter with his brother. I wanted a few minutes alone with Evelyn. Tony didn't mind. Among the Fulcis' many finer qualities was their ability to take a hint without taking offense as well.

'How are you finding the company?' I asked.

'Remarkably polite, and very attentive. Not excessively bright, perhaps, but I'll take kind over clever anytime.'

'You do speak your mind, don't you?'

'I can keep my mouth shut, too, when the situation requires, but I don't see any merit in being diplomatic right now.'

Or ever, I thought.

'And what have you been doing today?' she continued, in the tone of the schoolmistress she had once been. I had to resist the urge to check that my shirt wasn't untucked.

'Interviewing your daughter's neighbors and friends, or as many of them as I could get to. I also talked with her husband.'

'I hope you showered after.'

'I cleaned my hands. Like everyone else, I keep sanitizer in the car – but then, I always have.'

'For dirty work?'

'It's the nature of the business.'

'Yours more than most. I've been reading up on you, Mr Parker. You have violent tendencies.'

She didn't say it to wound. If anything, she sounded amused.

'It's more that trouble finds me.'

'It will if you leave a welcome mat out for it.'

'Are you having second thoughts about my involvement?'

'Not at all. I'd rather have you on our side than theirs.' She allowed some of the tension to leach from her. 'Sorry – not for the first time. That was blunt, even for me. I'm more fractious than usual. I didn't sleep well either.'

Now that we were done with the preliminaries, I took a seat across from her. I found a piece of a dancer's ballet slipper on the table and added it to the emerging picture. 'I have some questions for you, if you're up to trying to answer.'

'I'd welcome the mental exercise.'

'How much do you dislike your son-in-law?'

'Now, or how much did I dislike him before all this happened?'

'Let's accept "now" as a given.'

'I never took to him. Once, after too many glasses of wine, I even advised my daughter against marrying him. I sometimes wonder if she went ahead and did it out of spite. Colleen may act like a shrinking violet, but given the choice between doing the right thing at someone else's instigation, and the wrong thing of her own volition, she has a habit of picking the second option. She was always a headstrong child, in her disassociated way.'

'What about your late husband? Did he share your view of Stephen?'

'Thomas was a poor judge of character,' she said. 'No, that's not fair: my husband was simply better with numbers than people. He was more comfortable working in the abstract, but he doted on Colleen. He was happy she'd found someone she wanted to be with, and who wanted to be with her, too, insofar as Thomas understood the concept. He was never more at home with anyone than he was with himself.

'Also, he liked the fact that Stephen was ambitious and could talk stocks and bonds. Thomas knew that Colleen would always be financially secure, thanks to his own efforts, but in Stephen he saw someone who would work hard to convert comfort into actual wealth. For Thomas, love was secondary and overrated. "Like" was sufficient – he wasn't utterly devoid of emotion – but he'd grown up poor and had no illusions about it. Better, in his view, to be moderately happy and more than moderately wealthy, than to be very happy and moderately poor. He didn't link contentment with love, only with the absence of financial worry. He wasn't right, but neither was he completely wrong.'

'Did he love you?' I asked.

'In his way, and I loved him. We were fortunate in our union; our daughter less so in hers.'

I found a piece of the dancer's leg, or thought I had, but it didn't fit.

'I never liked jigsaws,' I said.

'Really? I'm surprised. I thought you were about to use it as a clumsy metaphor for your vocation.'

I had to hand it to her: Evelyn Miller was a piece of work.

'My grandfather was a policeman,' I said. 'He read every day, all his life. He never went anywhere without a book, and could discourse on literature like a professor. When he died, I laid the novel he'd left unfinished in the casket with him. He was a literate, literary man, but he couldn't play Scrabble worth a damn and didn't enjoy crossword puzzles.'

She took the errant piece from me, substituting it with the correct one.

'I feel you're circling me,' she said. 'Why don't you ask me straight out what you want to know?'

'Because I'm not certain you can be objective and without objectivity what you have to say will be of less value.'

'You might be surprised at my capacity for objectivity.'

I had listened to her description of her late husband, so perhaps she was right.

'Your daughter admits that she struggled with depression, and feelings of anger toward her son, but she says all that was mostly behind her by the time Henry went missing,' I said. 'Even during it, she claims she never stopped loving him, which I don't dispute. Her husband told me he didn't believe she ever wanted to be a mother, and in the event of a divorce would have ceded custody of Henry to him. Today, one of Colleen's friends said it was Stephen who was both emotionally and physically distant from the child, to the extent of displaying minimal interest in him. Not all those statements can be correct.'

'They aren't,' said Evelyn. 'Stephen's lying.'

'Remember what I said about objectivity.'

'This is me being objective. I didn't precede Stephen's name with the words "that cocksucker".'

I wasn't sure that would work as a dictionary definition of impartiality.

'Go on,' I said.

'Stephen is like some kind of alien building a simulacrum of a human life,' said Evelyn. 'He has a wife, a family, and hobbies, but only because he read somewhere that they're the components of a regular existence. None of them engages him, not on any deep level.'

That chimed with what Piper Hudson had observed about Mara Teller: a version of a life, as opposed to an actual one.

'Then what does?'

'Success, and how other people perceive him, which equate to the same thing for him. He wants to be envied and admired, but more the first than the second. He chose a wife who wouldn't embarrass him by drinking too much, talking out of turn, or getting fat. If he ever truly wished for a child, it was only to complete the picture. His image of married life came from cheap wedding catalogs and vintage reruns of *Leave It to Beaver*.'

I waited for her to pause for breath.

'Are we still being objective?' I asked.

'Not so much.'

'I didn't think so, but I wanted to be sure. I have a few more questions.'

'I'm listening.'

'Did Colleen ever speak to you about her physical relationship with her husband?'

'No, but I could read between the lines. She spoke about Stephen being tired a lot, working too hard, or traveling. I know those euphemisms because I used them myself over the years. I got the impression that it wasn't a make-or-break issue for either of them. Some couples are like that.'

This brought us to the issue of why Stephen Clark had become involved, however briefly, with Mara Teller. Maybe she had ignited a dormant fire in him, but this particular flame bothered me.

'And the next question?'

'Do you think Stephen was capable of hurting Henry?'

'By "hurt", do you mean physical abuse? Hitting?'

'No, I mean worse than that.'

She stared at me for what felt like a very long time. I didn't look away, but allowed her to consider the question in silence.

'No,' she said at last. 'I may dislike him intensely, but I don't think he has murder in him.'

'What about his brother and sister-in-law?'

She pursed her lips and thought hard before she answered.

'I liked them better than Stephen, and their longing for a child is real and profound. They fussed over Henry like he was their own, so I don't think they'd ever have done anything to harm him. If you're looking at them as possible abductors, I'd have to conclude you were on the wrong track. Which is not to conclude that I couldn't be mistaken, but I'd be very, very surprised.'

'Thank you,' I said. 'That's all for now. If you'd like, I'll give you a ride to the courthouse. If not, one of the Fulcis can keep you company.'

'I don't think either of them would fit in my car,' she replied, 'so I'd better go with you.'

Meanwhile, as I learned later, Moxie wasn't enjoying the company of Erin Becker at the courthouse, but at least the feeling was mutual. Becker was digging in on bail, which didn't surprise Moxie, even if the extent of her animosity toward Colleen Clark did. As anticipated, Becker rejected outright personal recognizance – release without bail – and neither would she countenance unsecured bail. Instead, she initially set the line at $250,000 secured and precluded Colleen from using her share in the family property as that security.

Moxie couldn't help but laugh. In Maine, $50,000 was a ball-park figure for bail on a murder charge, and usually required a body. For now, Henry Clark remained missing, if quietly presumed dead, and the most serious charge against Colleen was manslaughter, not murder.

'If you're actively seeking to alienate Pam Jedry,' Moxie told Becker, 'you could just try burning down her house or calling her kids ugly.'

Because the charges against Colleen involved not only felonies but also felonies alleged to have been committed against a family member, a bail commissioner was prohibited from setting bail, leaving the judge to make the determination. The initial hearing would therefore be held before Judge Pam Jedry, who was no soft touch but had worked closely with the Maine Women's Lobby before becoming one of Governor John Baldacci's first nominations to the bench back in 2003. It was fair to say that she wouldn't have been Becker's first choice for any stage of the Clark proceedings. There was also rumored to be bad blood between her and Nowak, the animosity being as much personal as political.

'I don't think you've been paying attention, Mr Castin. Perhaps you need to look again at the list of charges.'

'And perhaps you need to look again at a calendar, Ms Becker. This isn't the nineteenth century. Bail isn't prohibited on these charges, and you can't try to conjure a version of such a prohibition by pulling figures from thin air. You know you'll just be asking for a bad-tempered sidebar with Pam Jedry.'

'Or a Harnish,' said Becker. 'Would that be preferable?'

A Harnish bail proceeding determines whether a crime was a 'formerly capital offense' as identified by the Maine Supreme Judicial Court. Those offenses were limited to murder, rape, arson of a dwelling at nighttime, armed robbery, armed burglary of a dwelling at nighttime, and treason. In such cases, the defendant's constitutional right to bail is extinguished.

'Again,' said Moxie, 'I refer you to the manslaughter charge.'

'It's manslaughter for the present, but I'm becoming more optimistic about securing a murder conviction. Maine Revised Statute 17-A, Section 201: a person is guilty of murder if that person "engages in conduct that manifests a depraved indifference to the value of human life and that in fact causes the death of another human being". I'm open to adding or revisiting charges should any new evidence justify it. I'm willing to bet on that evidence emerging before too long. The investigation into Henry Clark's disappearance is ongoing, and I'm confident that the police will ultimately establish the truth about what happened to him. With that in mind, I have no difficulty announcing at our preliminary hearing that we're contemplating raising the main charge to murder.'

Moxie hid his unhappiness well, but Becker knew she'd scored a hit. If she went with a murder charge, a Harnish hearing was subsequently requested, and the judge sided with the prosecution, and Colleen would be left behind bars while her case wound its way to trial. She'd also be transferred to a less amenable environment than Cumberland County Jail, where a woman accused of killing her child would be a prime target for putative avengers.

Becker sat placidly, like an alligator watching a fawn cautiously approaching water, and said nothing while Moxie ran through a range of potential outcomes in his head. It could, he knew, all be a bluff, because he wasn't convinced that Becker was prepared to go with a murder charge. She needed a win, and manslaughter offered a better prospect.

'You won't get the judge to sign off on a quarter of a million,' he said finally, 'and I very much doubt that Jedry will look favorably on your Harnish play, not after I've had my say.'

Becker, having made Moxie squirm for a while, eased off.

'We always have the option of parking the request,' she said, 'and seeking revocation of bail at a later date based on a new charge. Who knows which judge might be required to make that decision?'

Moxie decided that he really, *really* didn't like Erin Becker. She possessed the vindictiveness of a despot, but also the conceit.

'You could go down that route,' said Moxie, 'but your friends in the media won't be able to get any good shots of my client if she's locked up. Out of sight, out of mind and all that, because there's always some new scandal to occupy the masses. It's a long journey to trial, even if you do manage to accelerate proceedings, and I'll do my best to stymie you every step of the way. I think you and your boss want Colleen Clark in the public eye, or else she's no use to you as an electoral tool.'

He waited for Becker to blink. It took a while, but she did.

'You're preying on my magnanimity,' she said.

'Is that what you call it?' said Moxie. 'I never would have guessed.'

'One hundred and fifty thousand dollars, unsecured.'

'One hundred thousand dollars,' countered Moxie, 'with half secured on her share of the family property.'

'Her husband won't permit any use of the family home. He'll fight it.'

'Let him.'

'Really? Then your client might want to consider how she wants to decorate her cell, because it'll be her domicile until the issue is resolved.'

This time it was Moxie who backed down.

'One hundred thousand dollars,' he said, 'half in cash, the remainder secured against her mother's property.'

Becker made a show of appearing unhappy, but Moxie knew she and Nowak would be content with $100,000. It was a nice round figure that would look good in the headlines.

'Okay,' she said, 'let's put that to the judge.'

Chapter XIX

Sabine Drew sat in her car by the side of the road outside the town of Gretton. The welcome sign stood fifty feet in front of her – GRETTON – HAPPY TO VISIT, SORRY TO LEAVE – but she made no effort to investigate the truth of this claim. The crying of the child was louder and more persistent now. If she were to enter Gretton, she was afraid the noise might become painful, even deafening. It was, she thought, as though the boy, aware that someone had heard him, was increasingly desperate to be found. It had been a long time since she'd heard a child cry that way.

She could try to pinpoint the source, but knew it would be difficult. That was one of the problems with her gift (or talent, curse, affliction – delete as appropriate, because it made no difference to her): it was often general, not specific, and trying to interpret what she was seeing or hearing was like attempting to unlock meaning from an abstract painting or photograph. If one got too close, it deteriorated into a collection of daubs or pixels; too far away, and one couldn't perceive anything at all. It was about finding a balance at the start before slowly, carefully, focusing on details.

Or so she told herself as she gripped the steering wheel, her eyes fixed on the sign. The truth was that she was frightened. She wanted no part of this. It had cost her so much before; she didn't want to risk bringing ignominy on herself again. But there was such a tormented edge to the child's wails. Wherever he was, he was suffering, and that suffering had to be brought to a close, except—

Except that Gretton felt bad: bad the way Toul Svay Prey High School in Phnom Penh, Cambodia, had felt when she'd visited it as a Peace Corps worker, back when she was still willing to travel beyond the boundaries of her home state. The Khmer Rouge had renamed the school S-21 and used it to systematically torture and exterminate their enemies. The official figure was eighteen thousand prisoners incarcerated; of them, only fourteen inmates were said to have survived. Sabine didn't know if her presence had woken the dead, like a high-pitched sound rousing dogs, or whether they were always screaming and she was just one of the few who could hear them, but it had taken all her strength to remain in the precincts of the old school, even as the tumult increased in volume. She had recognized an obligation to stay and listen, and she was convinced that when at last she had been able to take no more and fled from that place, there were fewer screams. Some were just waiting to be heard, and having been heard, were gone. Toul Svay, or Tuol Sleng as it was also known, was a monument to human malevolence, a physical manifestation of the depths to which men and women were capable of descending. Gretton was not on that level – few places could be – but it had something of the same stink to it, as well as an edge that Tuol Sleng had lacked.

Because the malevolence here wasn't human alone.

A presence at her window startled her from her reverie. A uniformed officer was standing by the glass, one hand resting lightly on the butt of his gun, though more out of habit and training than any fear of her. He looked to be in his forties and could have done with taking some exercise, she thought.

She glanced in the rearview mirror and saw an unmarked patrol car parked close behind her, its dashboard lights flashing. She hadn't even noticed its approach. *Fine psychic you are*, said a voice that might have been her mother's.

She hit the button to open the window.

'Is everything all right, Officer?'

His name badge read POULIN, and a crest on his jacket identified him as a constable. Sabine had a vague recollection that Gretton lacked a police force, so Poulin represented the law in town.

'I was about to ask you the same thing, ma'am.'

'I had a touch of migraine,' she said, 'so I decided to pull over until the worst of the nausea passed.'

It wasn't completely a lie. Her head hurt, and she did feel unwell. Gretton was responsible, or whatever had poisoned the town, but she wasn't about to share that with Officer Poulin. She didn't get any sense of ill will from him, only the tension that any encounter like this seemed to inspire in law enforcement, allied to a certain predilection in his case for the abuse of power. She didn't need her gift to be able to pick up on his insecurity. If he wasn't quite a bully, he possessed a bullying tendency, and wore his authority like a suit of armor.

Poulin showed no great sympathy for her condition. It wasn't that he didn't believe her: he just didn't care. Neither could she tell him she'd been drawn to his town by a child's cries, and that something foul had taken up residence there, because such talk was likely to invite the kind of attention that ended badly.

'License and registration, please.'

He stepped back as she rummaged in the glove compartment for the registration, followed by a search in her purse for her license. His palm, she noticed, remained on his gun. She found it interesting that he was left-handed. It reminded her of a film she'd seen as a child, with Paul Newman playing Billy the Kid as an overgrown juvenile delinquent, except Poulin was no Paul Newman. Even dead, Newman was better-looking than most of the men she knew. Poulin, by contrast, looked like someone had used his face to break rocks.

This town has corrupted you and you don't even realize it.

She handed over the documents.

'Turn off your engine,' said Poulin, and this time he didn't bother adding the 'please'.

She watched him waddle back to his car and begin tapping on the little computer by the dashboard. He wouldn't discover much of interest. She'd never even received a ticket. Unless—

Well, best not to think about that. She'd find out soon enough.

Poulin came back within a couple of minutes and returned her documents.

'Sorry about your headache,' he said, 'but you can't stay here.

You're too close to the corner. A truck coming round fast could rear-end you, and then you'd have more than nausea to worry about.'

But Sabine didn't want to go into Gretton: not yet, maybe not ever.

'You know,' she said, 'I'm feeling better already, so I may just go home. I was only driving for pleasure anyway.'

'Then you be careful. You'll see a deserted lot on the left just before the sign. Best use it to make the turn.'

She thanked him, started the car, and was soon heading back the way she'd come. Poulin remained in his vehicle, paying her no further attention as she passed. Her headache began to recede as soon as Gretton was out of sight.

But the child continued to cry.

Chapter XX

I sat next to Evelyn Miller for the short hearing. She looked shocked when the bail figure was announced, and even the judge displayed some surprise, but Moxie didn't object. His priority was getting Colleen out of jail, and he knew the money was available. Apart from the size of the surety, the conditions weren't onerous: for example, no prohibition sought on the possession of alcohol. During the hearing, Erin Becker had also briefly raised the possibility of prohibiting contact between Colleen and her husband, but the absurdity of this was made manifest by a single bark of what might have been laughter from Moxie, and the suggestion was quickly shelved.

It was, I supposed, another example of the incompatible positions involved in the case. The prosecution was basing its actions on the assumption that Henry Clark was dead and his mother was responsible. We, by contrast, were operating on the belief that Henry might yet be found alive, despite the evidence to the contrary, but more particularly that whatever had befallen him, it had not been at the hands of Colleen. From our perspective, there were two parents tormented by the disappearance of a child; from the prosecution's, only one.

Colleen was restored to the custody of the county sheriff while her mother made arrangements for the cash portion of the bail to be paid and signed the necessary documentation to secure the remainder against her home. Both Moxie and Becker made brief statements to the media, but avoided the full dog and pony show because the judge wouldn't have liked it. I stayed out of the way until Moxie indicated that he wanted to talk. We sat in my car and watched the media disperse.

'Officially,' said Moxie, 'the sheriff will release Colleen at eight.

Unofficially, as a personal favor, he'll show her the door at six thirty so we can avoid the cameras.'

'Do you want me to pick her up?'

'No, I'll get Matty to do it. The reporters know your face, and if someone spots you waiting in the jail lot, it won't take them long to put two and two together.'

Mattia Reggio was a retired guy who occasionally did driving and scut work for Moxie. In his prime, he'd been one of Cadillac Frank Salemme's bagmen, running deliveries across state lines for the New England outpost of the Office, the Providence mob. He'd begun having reservations about his vocation after Frank's son, the now-deceased Frank Jr, strangled the South Boston nightclub owner Steve DiSarro back in the early nineties to stop him from testifying against his silent partners, namely Cadillac Frank and Whitey Bulger. Reggio's qualms had hardened into resolve by the turn of the century: he wanted to throw in his hand. Not many people could get away with stepping away so easily, but Reggio and Cadillac Frank had walked the hard line together, and Reggio had never taken any shit from him – or from Whitey either, which irritated Whitey more than piles, though he had to suck it up like a big boy because of Cadillac Frank.

The ghost of DiSarro did eventually return to haunt Cadillac Frank, because the former's remains turned up in Rhode Island in 2016, and Cadillac Frank went to prison for the murder when he was in his eighties. By then, Reggio was long retired, an ex-mobster with a reasonably clear conscience and an absence of serious blood on his hands.

Or that was one version of the story. Another was that Reggio might have been involved in the disappearance of a rival mobster named Alessandro Angioni, a Genovese underboss who had operated out of Springfield, Massachusetts. Angioni wasn't well-liked, not even by his crew, but that didn't mean the Genoveses were prepared to let him drop off the map without making inquiries. Reggio had endured a bad night at the hands of the Genoveses' enforcers, but the bruises had healed and Angioni's fate remained a mystery, which was probably best for all concerned, Angioni excepted. Reggio had allowed an appropriate amount of time to go by before announcing that the whole experience had definitely soured him on the criminal lifestyle, and he wanted to cash out in favor of a less fraught means of earning a living. He'd ended up running a limo company out of Portland before retiring to tend to his garden and play with his grandchildren, but there was only so much of both he could do before he started getting bored, and he'd eventually found part-time employment with Moxie.

Reggio was reliable, though I still didn't like him. He might or might not have been a murderer, but he'd kept company with too many killers for me to feel secure in his company. He also had an irritating habit of noisily chewing gum, and in moments of stress was known to take the wad from his mouth and, seemingly unconsciously, stick it on the edges of tables and chairs. It was why I'd never allowed him past my front door, or was one more reason not to.

'By the way,' said Moxie, 'I've persuaded Colleen not to return home until things quiet down. I want to give her time to catch her breath.'

I knew what he meant. Colleen had just made her first court appearance, spent a night in jail, and was currently one of the most infamous women in the state. That would place additional strain on her, but home wasn't the place to deal with it right now. Eventually, she'd have to be allowed to go back, because she'd made it plain that those were her wishes, but it would be better to let the hounds disperse first.

'Do you have somewhere in mind?'

He waited for me to catch up, which didn't take long, especially when he was staring meaningfully at me.

'Really,' I said, 'my place?'

'It's secure and secluded. This will only be for a few nights.'

'The reporters will work it out soon enough.'

'Maybe not,' said Moxie. 'Her mother will stay at the Clark house and I'll run in Janice, my secretary's daughter, under a blanket to make the media and her neighbors believe it's Colleen. Janice can come out later, and as far as anyone will be able to tell, she was housesitting during the hearing, or stocking the refrigerator. We'll also leave the Fulcis where they are. It'll help keep up appearances.'

I wasn't happy, but conceded that it made sense. The media would grow weary of hanging around soon enough. Colleen wasn't going to be invited to many parties in the neighborhood, and would have to be wary about visiting the mall or eating out, but in time some superficial semblance of normality might return to her daily life until the trial commenced.

'Fine,' I said. 'Ask her mother to pack a bag for Janice to bring out with her. If Colleen needs anything else, you can arrange to have your secretary pick it up, or I can do it later.'

'Thanks,' said Moxie. 'Just add the expenses to your bill. Although,' he added, 'she probably won't cost much to feed.'

Chapter XXI

Because I had time on my hands and didn't like wasting it, I returned to Rosemont and rang the doorbell of Mrs Gammett, Colleen's neighbor. She answered almost before the bell stopped, which meant she'd probably been watching from the window. She invited me inside, but offered no hospitality beyond a chair. Unfortunately, she didn't have a lot to add to what I already knew, and I didn't know much. She was also, it was plain, not only deaf but profoundly deaf, yet it was her deafness that made one of her observations interesting.

'If Colleen took the child,' said Mrs Gammett, 'how did she get him away from the house?'

'Her car?' I suggested – shouted, actually.

'Mr Parker, I struggle to make conversation even with my hearing aids in place, and I don't sleep with them at night, but even I could hear Colleen's damn car start. I've been telling her and her fool husband for months that it needs a new muffler, but they never did get around to doing something about it, and now they have other things on their mind. The question stands: if Colleen took Henry – and I don't believe she did – then either she carried him from the house, or he's still on the property. If not, whoever took him didn't have a car with a busted exhaust.'

'What about her husband's vehicle?'

'That was parked out at the Jetport, as far as I'm aware.'

'Did you mention any of this to the police?'

'I told them I didn't hear Colleen's car start up, but I don't think they believed I could hear anything at all, so who knows how much got through to them. At least my deafness isn't selective.'

'And the neighbors?' I said. 'Can you tell me anything about them?'

101

'Any neighbors in particular?' She grinned crookedly. 'I saw you talking earlier with Alison Piucci and that doughboy Roback. Didn't look like you got very far with them.'

'I didn't get any distance at all. Is there something between them?'

'Roback wishes, but then he'd probably try to fuck me, given half a chance. Piucci plays along because she likes the attention, but if he ever got out of line with her, she'd cut his dick off and leave it in a box for the mailman, addressed to somewhere in Alaska.'

I think my jaw might have dropped open, but I managed to close it again before she noticed.

'And Roback's wife?'

'Come again?'

I tried once more, with better results.

'I feel sorry for her,' she said, 'and even him too, in moments of weakness. He's a lecher, but they want a child so badly. That may be why they've turned against Colleen with such a vengeance.'

Just like Stephen Clark's brother and sister-in-law, I thought.

'Which leaves Alison Piucci,' I said.

'Piucci is the local alpha female: chair of every committee, the first person to knock on your door if you forget to take in your trash container after collection. She regarded Colleen as weak and inconsequential. Having her locked up would be like thinning the herd of its runt, as far as Piucci is concerned.'

'Is that all?'

'Maybe she has her eye on Colleen's husband, too. They're both conceited, and both dull as a wet Tuesday in February. They'd make the perfect couple, but' – Mrs Gammett fixed me with her stare – 'I doubt either the Robacks or Alison Piucci hate one or both of the Clarks enough to hurt their child.'

She didn't have anything else to add, so I thanked her and prepared to leave. She walked me to the door and indicated the Fulcis, who were standing in Colleen's yard taking the late-afternoon air.

'Friends of yours?' she asked.

'Fortunately, yes. I wouldn't want them as enemies.'

'They must have hurt like hell coming out of their mother. I hope it was worth it for her.'

'She seems very fond of them.'

'Well, too late now, I guess,' said Mrs Gammett, as she closed the door. 'However much it hurt pushing them out, it would hurt a shitload more trying to push them back in . . .'

Chapter XXII

The pickup from the jail nearly went without a hitch, but nearly is never good enough.

Mattia Reggio arrived at the Cumberland County lockup ahead of time, was waiting by the door when Colleen Clark was released, and they were on the road before she even had the chance to take more than a few breaths of the evening air. Reggio, who had spent a lifetime looking in rearview mirrors, spotted immediately that they had been followed out of the lot by another vehicle – a blue Chrysler driven, he thought, by a woman. Reggio wasn't taking any chances, so instead of heading straight for the freeway, he lost his pursuer at the St John intersection before cutting back toward the river and continuing on to Scarborough. He tagged the would-be tail for a reporter with better-than-average contacts at the jail, and memorized the plate. Regrettably, he elected not to share that plate detail with either Moxie or me.

Reggio dropped Colleen at my door, and he and I exchanged a few words. Reggio was aware of how I felt about him, but I believed it was more cause for sadness than outright resentment on his part: he wanted me to like him, and I couldn't bring myself to do it, yet I wasn't above acknowledging my own hypocrisy where he was concerned. He might once have hurt men, or worse than hurt them, but I certainly had done so. Reggio could at least claim the benefit of the doubt.

I showed Colleen to her room. It was the one my daughter, Sam, used when she came to stay. She'd occupied it for all of her early childhood, before she and her mom moved to Vermont. Her belongings, including books, games, and even a couple of old dolls and soft toys, were on the shelves, and she still kept clothes in the closet and dresser. It was only as I stood on the threshold

104

with Colleen that I realized how inappropriate it might be to ask a woman with a missing son to sleep in the room of someone else's child. She must have seen something of this on my face, because she touched my arm and said, 'I'm happy to be here. In fact, I'll take comfort from it.'

'If you're sure.'

I left her to freshen up while I went to prepare dinner. It was a while since I'd had company for a meal at home, Angel and Louis excepted, so I made peperonata with rice, and prepared some flatbreads while Colleen showered. Moxie called as I was taking the bread from the griddle. He was making sure that Colleen was settling in as best she could.

'Did Matty tell you about being followed from the jail?' he said.

'That's the first I've heard. Is it something we should pursue?'

'There's no need. He lost the tail well before he left Portland, and the story is already on the net. The driver must have been Hazel Sloane. She's a reporter out of Bangor. Either she failed to read the memo about the release time, chose not to believe it if she had, or was tipped off by someone at the sheriff's office. Whatever the reason, it looks like she was cooling her heels a couple of vehicles away when Colleen Clark came out, because the footage is already on the website of the *Bangor Daily News*.'

This meant Moxie's ploy to convince everyone that Colleen was holed up in her home had failed. He went on to reveal that one of Sloane's colleagues had been waiting at the Clark house when a vehicle different from the one that had made the pickup arrived to disgorge a woman with her head covered by a jacket – a woman, what's more, dressed in clothing different from whatever Colleen had been wearing when she emerged from incarceration. On the other hand, no one had yet discovered where Colleen was currently sequestered. As long as she kept her head down, there was a chance we'd be okay. The local media knew better than to come knocking on my door asking questions, and Scarborough residents valued the privacy of others in return for their own being respected.

'Well, Reggio managed to lose Sloane,' I said, 'which is the main thing. I may not relish his company, but he knows how to drive.'

105

'Are you aware that you feel compelled to reiterate your dislike of him whenever his name comes up?'

'I feel you need reminding of my reservations.'

'You're not always around when I need you. Even if you were, donkeywork doesn't do justice to your particular skill set.'

'Then we'll have to agree to differ on Reggio's finer qualities.'

'If God judges sinners as harshly as you do,' said Moxie, 'we're all going to hell.'

Colleen Clark entered the kitchen. Her hair was wet from the shower, and she'd changed into a T-shirt and track pants. They made her appear even less substantial than ever, as though the night behind bars had contrived to shrink her still further.

'Colleen's here,' I said. 'Do you want to talk to her?'

'Sure.'

I told Colleen she should feel free to speak in the next room if she didn't want me to overhear her conversation.

'I've got nothing important to say,' she replied. 'And if I did, you'd need to hear it anyway.'

She made some small talk with Moxie while I put the food on the table. By the time she hung up, I'd opened a bottle of red wine and poured her a large glass, with a smaller one for myself out of politeness. I rarely drank at home, or alone.

'You made all this yourself?' she said, as she took in the spread.

'I have about four dishes in my repertoire. I was going to make chili, but it has unfortunate jailhouse connotations. This struck me as more elevated.'

I let her serve herself. She took barely enough food to fill half the plate, which wasn't large. She tried the peperonata and managed not to make the elaborate choking noises in which Angel liked to indulge when confronted by generous amounts of garlic and onion.

'Stephen wouldn't eat something like this,' she said.

'He doesn't like Italian food?'

'He doesn't like any food that doesn't include meat. His father was the same way, or so he says.'

'Was?'

'His parents died shortly after he graduated high school. I never got to meet them.'

'May I ask how they died?'

'They were overtaking a truck hauling logs somewhere up in the County. One of the support ropes broke. The rest you can picture for yourself.'

She drank some of the wine. When she put the glass back down, it was a lot emptier.

'I've spoken with your husband,' I said.

The fork paused at her lips.

'How was he?'

'Unyielding.'

She scowled in mock disapproval.

'I meant in general. Is he okay?'

'I'd say he remains . . . resilient, under the circumstances.'

'He was never very good at expressing his emotions. He keeps everything bottled up.'

I was tempted to inform her that he'd shown no difficulty with expressing his feelings about her, but I didn't think it would help, or be appreciated. The Clarks' relationship was both unsettling and peculiarly toxic. Colleen Clark's loyalty to her husband might have been considered admirable had he not been so committed to seeing her imprisoned, and had the fate of his child seemingly mattered less to him than the prospect of punishment for his wife.

I forced myself to recalibrate. I realized I had already evaluated both Colleen and Stephen, concluding that one was, in all likelihood, innocent, and the other guilty, if only of a deficit of character. Neither verdict was going to make my work any easier. It might even lead to the same errors that I felt had resulted in Colleen's arrest and impending trial.

The officers and detectives of the Portland PD were not foolish or venal, but there often comes a point in an investigation when locked-in errors begin to determine the course of inquiries. In the event of the death or disappearance of a child, the police will look first at the parents, because so many of these cases turn out to be instances of domestic harm. We typically hurt those we are closest to, and the young are particularly vulnerable. For the police, the discovery of the bloodied blanket in Colleen's car had confirmed a suspicion present from the start, and they were now fulfilling the role for which they believed they were being paid: to close cases and help secure convictions. If they were in error, the reasons were comprehensible.

Paul Nowak and Erin Becker represented a more nebulous proposition. They, too, were paid to close cases, but those cases would also determine their political futures. In the choice between a potentially unsafe conviction or no conviction at all, elected officials like Nowak and Becker were under pressure to pursue the former. It could take years for a wrongful verdict to be overturned, by which time they would have moved up the ladder, leaving to someone else the task of clearing up the mess. But a lack of convictions, especially in high-profile trials – of which Colleen Clark's was destined to be one – would damn them. It was the great flaw in a system that depended on elected officials to implement justice, because it would always be easier just to enforce the law.

Colleen was speaking again, but so lost was I in my own thoughts that I had to ask her to repeat herself.

'I said, "What now?"'

'For you or me?'

'For both of us.'

'I'll have to ask you to remain on the property for a few days,' I said. 'I'd prefer if you didn't go walking on the road or beach because it won't take much to connect a sighting of you to me. If you do go outside, stick to the back of the house, as it's not overlooked. I have books, music, and streaming services, but mostly you should take the opportunity to rest. You've been through a great deal, and the trauma is ongoing, though you don't need me to tell you that. Also, you may be surprised at what you remember upon reflection – anything, anything at all, you should feel free to share with me or Moxie, however minor. We can chase it down, and if it turns out to be a dead end, we'll cross it off the list.'

'But won't that be wasting your time?'

'If you recall our first conversation, that's not how an investigation works. Think of this as a grid that has to be searched, a finite series of possibilities to be explored. With every square we check, even if we find it empty, we're narrowing in on those that may contain something useful: in this case, the truth of what has happened to your son. Sometimes, you get lucky and hit the right square first time out, but that's very rare. Typically, you have to comb a lot of empty ground first.'

I didn't add that this was why investigations sometimes went on for years, or that finite could also mean near infinite.

'So that's what you'll be doing while I'm here?' she said.

'And also when you return home, because it could take a while. But as I told you before, Moxie hired me to ensure that he has all the information required should this case go to trial. I'll balance those duties – to you, to him, and to Henry – as best I can, but if they become overwhelming, and I require help, I won't hesitate to ask for it.'

She'd eaten about a third of the food on her plate, along with half a piece of flatbread, but had finished her glass of wine and was twisting the stem between the thumb and forefinger of her right hand.

'I'll trade you more wine for more eating,' I said.

'I don't have much of an appetite.'

'You're no good to us if you're tired and underfed. You have a role to play in this. We require you to be focused.'

She picked up her fork again.

'You're worse than my mother,' she said. 'How much do I have to eat?'

'Just what's on your plate, but if I find any food hidden in a napkin or the plant pot behind you, we'll have words.'

I waited for her to resume picking before I refilled her glass. To her credit, she finished the portion of peperonata – and, admittedly, most of the bottle – before she excused herself. She offered to help me clean up, but I told her not to worry about it. She still had wine left in her glass.

'Do you mind if I bring this upstairs with me?'

'I don't mind at all.'

She swirled the wine and watched spirals form.

'Do you think I drink too much?'

'For what you're going through,' I said, 'I'm not sure there's enough wine in the world.'

'Before—' She paused, drew a breath, began again. 'Before the blanket was found in my car, I was being criticized in the press for drinking with a child in the house, as if I were a bad mother for wanting to unwind while Henry slept.'

'And you wondered if they might be right?'

'More than that, I thought they were.'

'Whatever happened to your son didn't occur because you poured yourself a glass of wine.'

'Stephen told me to ignore it all,' she said. 'The stuff about my drinking, I mean. He didn't want me to ascribe any significance to it. At the start, he was so intent on protecting me, on telling me that it wasn't my fault. I don't think I remember him ever being kinder to me than he was in those first few days. He even poured the last of the wine down the sink and disposed of the bottle, just so I wouldn't have it to fixate on.'

'What would you like to happen between the two of you, when this is over?'

'If I don't go to prison, you mean?'

'We're operating on the assumption that you won't.'

She mulled over the question.

'I think I could forgive him for doubting me. I'd even be prepared for us to try again, except I don't think he'd accept that.'

'And Henry?'

'I feel Henry is dead. I want to believe differently. I want to believe he's coming back to me, but I feel he's gone. I felt it early on, like a sundering.'

She stepped into the hallway. She didn't want to try to explain further for fear she might not be able to speak the words.

'It was a very good meal,' she said, 'the best I've had in a while. Thank you – for the food, and for letting me stay here.'

'My pleasure.'

She showed no signs of unsteadiness as she went to her room. I hoped the wine might help her sleep, but when I went up to bed an hour later the light was shining under her door, and I could hear her weeping, weeping as though she might never stop.

Chapter XXIII

Sabine Drew woke to darkness. Mercifully, the child had ceased crying for the present, but the silence that had replaced it was unnerving. It was the quiet of watchfulness, of the prey hiding from the hunter, or the abused seeking to avoid attracting the attention of the abuser. Wherever he was, he was not alone.

Sabine closed her eyes, but not to sleep. She was trying to locate the boy, to draw closer and offer comfort. A song came to her, one her mother used to sing to lull her to sleep: 'The Old Oak Tree.' It was only in adulthood that Sabine had been struck by the oddness of a mother crooning a tale of murder and burial as a lullaby to her daughter, but all Sabine wanted was to hear her mother's voice.

> Dark was the night, cold blew the winds.
> And heavy fell the rain.
> Bessie left down by her mother's side,
> To never return again.

By then Sabine had already become aware of the immanence of the dead, and had even spoken of it to her mother. Maybelle Drew had shown no surprise, only sadness, for this was a burden she had hoped her daughter might be spared. Only later did Sabine learn that Maybelle's mother, Grandma Hattie, had endured presentiments of the death of others throughout her life, and Maybelle herself continued to hear the voice of her younger brother for years after his passing.

'Do they talk to you?' Maybelle had asked, after Sabine opened up to her.

'Not directly, I think they talk to themselves or to the ones who are still alive, even if the living can't hear them – or choose not to.'

Maybelle smoothed her daughter's hair.

'Well, don't go telling people about this, okay? Let's just keep it to ourselves.'

And Sabine did, or tried to, but as time went on, she often felt that she had no choice but to engage with the bereaved when the opportunity presented, because to do so might make them a little less sad.

'She says it weren't your fault, because you'd told her time and again not to go near the water . . .'

'He says he's sorry, that he should have said he loved you more often, but he did love you, loved you ever since that first day on the coaster in the Palace Playland back in 1948, right before it burned down . . .'

'They say they miss your bedtime stories . . .'

If she knew the family, or trusted the individual in question, she'd approach them directly. If in doubt, she'd write an anonymous letter. She had to be circumspect, because there was always a risk that people might feel they were being mocked or taken advantage of. On a few occasions, those she spoke with had become angry, while one or two grew desperate, trying to hold on to her, demanding that she open a channel of communication with the departed. Sabine grew better at handling those situations as she progressed from adolescence to adulthood, just as she learned to hold her tongue when required, because there were insights into both the living and the dead that were better kept to herself: accusations, threats. Such pain, such rage.

'You ought not to have done that to me . . .'

'I see now how you despised her. All those years, and I never knew . . .'

'I'll tear you apart, you motherfucker, fucking suck your eyes from the sockets and chew your fucking tongue from your mouth . . .'

In the worst cases, she'd send a letter to the police or social services, again anonymously, and she might subsequently gather through gossip, or read in the papers, that something had been done: an intervention, an arrest. But generally, her missives were ignored, or their contents dealt with privately.

Inevitably, word spread. The Drew girl, it was whispered, had a gift. They began coming to her: the distraught, the grief-stricken. She couldn't always tell them what they wanted to hear; her ability didn't work that way. The dead were not always capable of communicating with her, and death itself served to alter their speech, endowing them with a new language beyond the comprehension of the living. When that happened, Sabine tried to interpret feelings, the colors and textures of them. Mainly, though, the dead were absent, gone from this world. Their quietude, Sabine thought, was probably a blessing. They were at peace, or so she hoped.

Then she had made her big mistake, the one that had forced her into seclusion. She did not want to make the same error again.

But this child, this child . . .

In the stillness, Sabine began to sing, her voice crossing from the dusky regions of her bedroom to a still more shadowy realm.

> *Dark was the night, cold blew the winds,*
> *And heavy fell the rain.*

Through the song, she tried to offer solace to the boy. Her eye caught the newspaper by her bedside, and even in the dimness, the picture of a man exiting a police station in Portland. She set aside the song to speak directly to the little lost one.

'I know you're afraid,' she said, 'but I won't abandon you. I'm coming for you, do you hear? I'm coming to find you, but I won't be alone. I think I know someone who will help us, someone who will believe. So don't be frightened, because he won't be. Whatever is down there with you, that's what ought to be scared. You tell it, and you spit in its face when you do.

'You tell it that we're coming.'

Chapter XXIV

Amara Reggio woke to discover her husband's side of the bed empty. She listened for him in the bathroom, but could hear no sound. A chair scraped the floor in the kitchen downstairs. She got up, put on her robe, and went to see what was the matter.

Matty was seated at the kitchen table, a cup of green tea before him. This was unusual. Her husband never had any great difficulty sleeping, nocturnal trips to relieve his bladder apart. He liked to go to bed early, wake up with the dawn, and remember as little as possible of the hours that passed between. Now here he was in his T-shirt, slippers, and pajama bottoms, his robe hanging open, sitting in the quiet of the kitchen, staring into the dark.

She took the chair opposite.

'What's wrong?'

She loved many qualities in her husband, but among the best of them was his refusal to lie. If he didn't want to talk about something, he'd tell her as much, but would never try to deceive her, or brush off a worriment as 'nothing'. He had sometimes admitted acts she might have preferred him not to have committed, but she remained grateful that he was prepared to divulge them in her presence. She tried not to criticize him, even when it was hard, any successful marriage being an endless series of compromises.

Amara accepted that her husband had probably killed the man named Alessandro Angioni. Whether he'd planned to or not, she could not say. She had never asked him about it, and never would. Angioni was a thug who had been threatening to rape a young girl, a relative of Amara's on her mother's side. He would certainly have carried out that threat had he not been stopped. If killing him was the only way to prevent the girl's violation, Amara

114

believed God would not judge his murderer too harshly, while she elected not to judge him at all.

'It's the dumbest thing,' said Mattia.

'What is?'

'The way Parker looks at me, like he's just wiped me from his shoe. I've never done anything to him, never given him cause to distrust me, but I still feel the intensity of his dislike.'

'Do you know why that might be?'

'Why do you think? I have a past.'

'So does he, and it's blacker than yours.'

Amara was sufficiently familiar with Parker and his history to make her glad he kept his distance from her husband. He had the *maloik*, the evil eye. He had brought bad luck to those close to him – his wife, his child, his friends – so better that her husband did not number himself among his intimates.

'Who's to say that,' said Mattia, 'except for God?'

Amara always knew her husband was particularly melancholy when he mentioned God. If he ever prayed, he did so unspeakingly.

'And what does it matter if he likes you or not?' she asked. 'Are you so short of company that you need his so badly?'

Her husband reached for her hand. The sadness in his eyes made her tighten her grip on him for fear she might lose him to it.

'I want him to like me,' said Mattia. 'I want his respect.'

'But why?'

'Because one should be worthy of the respect of a man like him.'

Where had this come from, Amara pondered. Yes, Mattia had his pride. It came with his heritage, abetted by the circles in which he had once moved, where a man who allowed himself to stand belittled would find himself vulnerable. But the private investigator was nothing, a passing shadow.

'You *are* worthy of it,' she said, 'even if he does not recognize it.'

Mattia did not reply. He had lived too long not to realize how difficult it could be to change the opinion of others about oneself. It required the expenditure of time and effort for scant reward.

This was not the schoolyard and he was no longer a teenager requiring the affirmation of his peers. He was angry at Parker, but angry also at himself for allowing the opinion of a near stranger to assume such importance in his life. Yet it had hooked his heart and the barb would not easily be removed.

'Come to bed,' said Amara. 'Tomorrow we visit Stefano and Giulia. You'll need all your energy for them.'

Their grandchildren were the secondary lights of her husband's life, and in turn greeted his arrival as though he were Santa Claus, helped by the fact that he always brought gifts. Their daughter, Carla, and her husband would be glad to have the children taken off their hands, giving them an afternoon to themselves.

'I'll finish my tea,' said Mattia. 'It'll help me rest, maybe.'

Amara rose, kissed his forehead, and returned to bed, but she could not close her eyes. She loved him, her feral man, loved the strength of him, the sureness. She hated to see him this way, just as she winced to see him stumble, or pause to catch his breath, these signs of weakness reminding her that she might someday be deprived of him. This *ficcanaso* Parker was nothing like her husband, even if she could not declare him unfit to tie Mattia's shoes. There was no doubting his courage or his commitment to others, but to seek to emulate or impress him could only lead to trouble.

Her Matty was a good man. He might not always have been so, but he had tried to make recompense for his failings. He had altered the trajectory of his life and was a loyal husband and loving father; but when he saw himself reflected in Parker's eyes, he glimpsed only what he once had been, and perhaps what he feared he still might be.

At last he came back to bed, but she pretended to be dead to the world so he would not know that she continued to fret about him.

The next morning, nothing was said about their conversation. Mattia went out early, returning with fresh croissants from the bakery for their breakfast and sticker books for the grandchildren. She checked with her daughter that it was still okay for them to drop by and shortly after 2 p.m. they drove north to Bath, where they went walking with the kids at Lily Pond and ate an early dinner at Mateo's Hacienda. As usual on their visits to the restaurant, her husband joked that Mateo was his brother from Mexico, and the staff played along with the gag, calling Stefano and Giulia their *sobrino y sobrina*. If Mattia appeared subdued, only his wife noticed.

But as for his anger, well, that remained concealed, even from her.

Chapter XXV

Colleen Clark was already up and about when I woke. I could hear music playing in the kitchen, and pots and pans crashing, followed shortly after by the smell of frying bacon. I suppose I should have warned her I wasn't a morning person and rarely ate breakfast, but it was too late. I showered and went downstairs, thinking *A houseguest neither invite nor be.*

Colleen had made a pot of coffee, along with toast, bacon, and fried eggs. She was wearing jeans and a long-sleeved blue shirt, and her skin glistened with some recently applied cream, but her eyes were swollen and rimmed with red. Bright sunlight shone through the kitchen window. From it I could see a juvenile Little Blue Heron standing on a low branch of one of my red maples. It was watching the water, waiting. I pointed it out to Colleen.

'Why is it called blue when it's kind of white?'

'Because it's still young. They stay white for their first year before their feathers darken. My grandfather told me that one of the reasons was protection: the young herons hunt with snowy egrets, and the egrets protect them, but only as long as the herons are white. When they turn blue, the egrets don't want them around anymore.'

'That's rough.'

'I think herons are solitary by nature in adulthood,' I said. 'And they're good hunters.'

The heron, spotting prey in the shallows, disappeared from sight. I sat at the table to check my phone. Moxie, who had no objection to early mornings, only to those who objected to them in turn, had tried getting in touch twice already. Sometimes I think he liked to call just to remind me that the clock had a habit of turning seven twice a day.

'I hope you don't mind my preparing breakfast,' said Colleen. 'It was the least I could do after you made dinner last night.'

She put a plate in front of me. It held enough fried food to make me a poster boy for statins, and might even have given Moxie pause.

'I wasn't sure how you liked your eggs so I went for over medium.'

I steeled myself and tried to make some inroads into the stack. I noticed Colleen was sticking to coffee.

'Aren't you having anything?'

'I had an egg before you came down,' she said.

'Is this where I tell you again that you have to eat?'

'Only if this is where I ignore you.'

I remembered the wine she'd drunk the previous night. If I'd knocked back three-quarters of a bottle of red wine on a virtually empty stomach, I'd have been struggling the next morning, but she showed no ill effects. Her eyes were red from crying, not from a hangover. Yet on the night her son disappeared, she claimed that less than a single glass had left her sluggish.

I asked what she planned to do with her day. She told me she was going to watch TV, or sit in the backyard if the weather stayed fine.

'I've tried to read, but I struggle to concentrate since Henry went missing. I can't lose myself in anything because I always come back to him. It's gotten so that I'm almost afraid to forget him, even for a moment. If I do, the loss returns with greater force, just to punish me for letting him slip my mind. If I do it too often, he'll be gone forever, and I won't even be able to recall his face.'

She sipped her coffee.

'I know you don't want to talk about your own child,' she said, although she didn't look at me as she spoke, 'and I think I understand why. This is a job for you. It's business. It doesn't mean you don't care, but you have to maintain a distance. Am I right?'

'That's some of it,' I admitted.

'Just tell me one thing. How do you go on? Not just you: I mean how does *one* go on? Because every day I want to die, and the only thing stopping me is the desperation to know what's happened to Henry. Once I have an answer, and if it's the one I fear, I think I may kill myself.'

She wasn't being melodramatic, or seeking attention. I accepted the truth of what she was saying because I'd felt it myself. I'd lived through it, and continued to live through it. I endured, in both senses of the word.

'The pain grows duller,' I said. 'There are days you barely notice it.'

'And the guilt?'

'Some of that went away when I realized I couldn't have stopped what occurred. The man who killed my wife and child made the decision to hurt them, and that was beyond my control. Had I been there with them on the night he came, he might have tried to take us all; because of the mess I was back then, he'd have succeeded. But I think he'd have bided his time and waited for a better opportunity. For him, it was very personal.'

I set aside my silverware. I was done with eating.

'Somebody targeted your son, Colleen, and they came prepared. If you'd been standing watch over him that night, they'd have returned when your guard was down. Don't put that burden of guilt on yourself. Too many other people are already willing to do that. Our task is to prove them wrong.'

She pointed at my plate.

'You really don't eat breakfast, do you?'

'Not as a habit,' I said, 'but I appreciate the effort.'

I began to clear the table.

'Please don't,' she said. 'It'll give me something to do. Also, your washing dishes isn't going to bring us any closer to finding Henry.'

I had to concede that much. I told her I'd be gone for the day, but I'd bring back something for dinner. It all felt curiously domestic.

'If you can,' I said, 'I want you to reflect on the last few months, including anything odd, however trivial, that might have taken place: a conversation with a stranger in the supermarket, someone who stared at you and Henry for too long in a coffee shop, whatever you can remember.'

'The police asked Stephen and me to do all that already. I told them all I could.'

'You were under pressure, so there was no way you were thinking clearly. Start again, day by day. You may be surprised at what you can recall. Use routines to anchor your memories. I have a spare desk diary for this year in my office, every page blank. I'm going to leave it with you. Begin by writing down the things you habitually did: day care for Henry, weekly shopping, regular meetings with friends, whatever they might be. If you keep a record of appointments on your phone, add those as well. You'll find that recording regular occurrences will bring to mind irregular ones. We're back to patterns and grids: by detailing whatever fits, we have a chance of spotting what doesn't. Henry's abduction wasn't a crime of opportunity. You were being watched, Colleen, and it may be that some primitive part of your brain was alerted to it.'

She agreed to try.

'Can I ask what you're going to do?'

'I have one or two more interviews to conduct,' I replied. 'After that, I'm going to take a sharp stick and poke the undergrowth.'

'You're being deliberately vague,' she said.

'I am.'

'I imagine you were a frustrating man to be married to.'

'Yes,' I said, 'I imagine I was.'

Chapter XXVI

The National Gas and Petrochemicals Forum was the brainchild of an organization called the Gas and Petrochemical Energy Research Center, based in the Old Post Office Building in Lynn, Massachusetts. It was doubtful that asking for details about forum guests over the phone would yield positive results, so I decided it might be more productive to make the approach in person.

I hadn't been in Lynn in years, not since someone had blown up the business premises of an elderly lawyer named Eldritch. Since then, Eldritch had dropped from sight. For all I knew, he might be dead. If so, it could have come as a relief to him. He'd suffered his own losses over the years, too many and too deep for an old man to bear. He'd also kept some very bad company, terrifyingly so.

As I drove south, I touched base with Moxie. He was preparing his list of depositions, but Erin Becker was playing hard to get on discovery, including confirming whether Colleen's husband would be called as a witness.

'It's because Becker knows she's weak across the board,' said Moxie. 'We'll know more when we read the affidavit, but it'll come down to Stephen Clark's testimony, along with whatever corroborating expert opinions she can rustle up, backed by Colleen's subpoenaed medical and therapy records – assuming she can gain access to them, which we'll fight. After that, there's just the blanket from the car. Becker has nothing else.'

I hadn't seen the blanket, but Erin Becker, aware of its power, had been happy to share pictures with Moxie, and he'd passed them on to me. All that blood: the blanket, if displayed as evidence in court, would do Colleen no favors. It could only have been sourced from inside the house, and she and her son had been alone there on the night he disappeared. But if Colleen wasn't involved in Henry's abduction, how had the blanket come to be used?

'The police have obtained a warrant to search the Clark property,' said Moxie. 'They'll be looking for any traces of Henry's blood.'

This had been anticipated. It was only a surprise it had taken so long.

'They'll find them, too,' I said. 'He was a young boy, still getting the hang of walking, and we already know he had bumps and bruises.'

'There's a big difference between a cut that requires a Band-Aid and wounds that drench a blanket. But that won't stop them from adding anything that shows up to the evidence list. Have you spoken with Colleen's doctor and therapist yet?'

I told him I had appointments to meet each of them. 'I've also arranged to have a quiet conversation with Steady Freddy White,' I added.

Detective Frederick White was second lead on the Clark investigation. The lead was a suit called Furnish, but he and I had never seen eye to eye, and I couldn't expect any cooperation from that direction. Nobody liked Furnish, not within the Portland PD, and possibly not within his own family. The only reason he didn't own a dog was because it would undoubtedly have bitten him before leaving home forever. Freddy White, by contrast, was two years away from retirement with full benefits and had rarely met a boat he wanted to rock. He wouldn't do anything to screw up the Clark case, but neither would he object to being straight with me, especially if I was paying for the pleasure.

'Don't give away more than you get,' warned Moxie.

'And there I was hoping to work both sides against each other for personal gain,' I replied, before hanging up.

Lynn's Old Post Office Building was included on the National Register of Historic Places. With its copper domes, it looked like it belonged in another country, or at least another environment, but then Lynn had long endured a bad rap from the rest of

Massachusetts, although its architecture was more curious and interesting than its city-of-sin reputation suggested. Back in the day, Lynn's hookers had worked out of some pretty nice buildings.

The Gas and Petrochemical Energy Research Center might have evoked images of men and women in white coats laboring over test tubes, but it more closely resembled an insurance office, one that was superficially slick but wouldn't pay out on a policy until it had been dragged kicking and screaming to the courthouse steps. It occupied a suite of corner rooms, the lobby walls decorated with glossy photographs of pristine valleys and mighty flowing rivers, suggesting that the land could have asked for no better stewards than the people responsible for Louisiana's Cancer Alley, or closer to home, violating the Clean Air Act in South Portland, where, on a bad day, the smell from the petroleum storage tanks was enough to make the eyes water.

I'd called in advance to let the center know I was on my way. Nobody had objected, or threatened to barricade the doors against me, but that might have been because I hadn't specified the purpose of my visit. A secretary showed me straight to the office of the Director of Public Affairs, a woman named Delaney Duhamel with the face of one of the sadder Botticelli angels. She offered me coffee before setting her phone to record our conversation.

'Just a precaution,' she said.

'Against what?'

Her slightly downturned mouth dipped further, as though there was no end to the sorrows an unjust world might be prepared to inflict on a well-meaning shill for the gas industry.

'Future litigation. You're a private investigator and were noticeably reluctant to specify the nature of your inquiry over the phone. Naturally, we have to protect ourselves – and you, of course.'

'Of course,' I said. 'God forbid we should start off on the wrong foot.'

'That,' she agreed, 'would be bad.'

If Delaney Duhamel had ever encountered irony before, either the experience hadn't registered or she was even more comfortable with it than I was. The coffee arrived, along with some dinky little cookies that would stick between one's teeth for the rest of the day.

I let Delaney Duhamel pour. Someone laughed shrilly in an adjoining office, and she winced at the sound.

'So, what are you investigating, Mr Parker?'

'The disappearance of a child.'

'Henry Clark?'

Sensibly, she'd googled me before I arrived. The most recent results would have related to the Clark case.

'That's right.'

'How interesting,' she said, which was itself an interesting choice of word to use about a missing, possibly murdered boy. 'I had initially assumed it might be something else, until I googled your name.'

'Something else such as—?'

'When private investigators come our way, it's usually in relation to environmental issues. I don't think we've ever had one ask about a missing person, or not since I've been here.'

'And how long have you been here, Ms Duhamel?'

'Two years – actually, closer to three.'

'Were you involved with the most recent forum?'

'Deeply. Why?'

'Stephen Clark, the father of the missing boy, was an attendee.'

'But you're working for the mother, right? Or so I read.'

'That's correct.'

'How interesting,' she said again. Perhaps she just found everything interesting, which wasn't much different from finding nothing interesting at all. 'And what, apart from his attendance, connects the forum to your case?'

'He had an affair with another participant because nothing screams romance like oil and gas. I'd like to talk to the woman involved. The name under which she registered was Mara Teller.'

'We can't give out those details.'

'I haven't told you the kind of details I'm looking for.'

'Nevertheless, we have certain obligations when it comes to protecting the privacy of attendees.'

'Ms Duhamel,' I said, 'I went online. The forum guide included contact information for all the attendees: job titles, company names, websites, even some email addresses. Short of their sexual preferences and how they like their martinis, I'm not sure what's left to hide.'

'But if that information is freely available why are you here?'

'Because the woman I'm looking for may have registered under a false name. Her consultancy business consisted of a placeholder site and nothing more. The phone number she gave to Stephen Clark has since been reassigned to another user, and the email address came from a Swiss-based startup that provides anonymous accounts to users. That address, too, is now defunct. I can find no Mara Teller with a background corresponding to the woman who attended your forum. It makes me curious about who she really was, and why she was there.'

Delaney Duhamel, visibly unhappy, played with her engagement ring. The stone was blue and looked artificial, which made it doubly apt for her.

'We operate on trust,' she said. 'We can't contact every attendee to ensure that the particulars they've submitted are accurate. It simply wouldn't be feasible.'

'Just as long as the check clears. What was the attendance fee, five hundred dollars?'

'It included coffee,' she said icily.

'Unlimited, I hope. I'm not criticizing your registration policy, just making a point. You have no obligation to protect someone who has provided false information.'

'But I only have your word for that.'

I'd have tried to look hurt if I thought it might have helped. Instead, I shrugged and made heavy work of getting to my feet.

'Well then, the next step is for me to return to Portland and inform Mrs Clark's attorney of your reluctance to divulge material that may be germane to the defense's case, and your unwillingness to assist in an investigation into the whereabouts of a missing child. He will relay that intelligence to a judge as the basis for a subpoena, which will become a matter of public record. It never looks good for a company to appear to be hiding something, especially when it comes to the abduction of a little boy. I wouldn't want to be forced to explain that position to the press.'

I didn't bother pointing out to Delaney Duhamel that since she was the spokesperson for a branch of the oil and gas industries, she was already mired in dirty waters as far as any question of reputation was concerned, though that didn't mean her life couldn't be made more awkward. But I was also aware that she was recording our interaction, and blackmail always sounded worse when played back in court.

Delaney Duhamel regarded me with disappointment. *Men*, that look seemed to say. *First, they stiff you with a bum stone . . .*

She killed the recording.

'Everything from this moment on is off the record,' she said.

'With respect, I wasn't the one recording the conversation to begin with.'

She conceded this with a wave of a hand, like a dowager duchess wafting away the smell of poverty.

'Other issues have arisen out of recent forums,' she said.

'What kind of issues?'

'Two sexual harassment suits, and one allegation of serious sexual assault, which is under police investigation. Some of these men are little better than animals in suits. The harassment allegations should be settled quietly, but the sexual assault case may go the distance.'

'In other words, you don't need any more bad publicity.'

'It would be unwelcome. It might also cost me my position.'

'I can't help but detect a note of ambivalence about the second part.'

Delaney Duhamel tilted her head, as though examining me from a different angle might explain this previously unsuspected level of perspicacity on my part.

'Protecting would-be rapists wasn't part of the job description,' she said.

'In my experience, companies prefer to leave that bit out. It discourages the better candidates, although it also helps to winnow out the ones with a conscience.'

'You're representing a woman accused of killing her child. How do you square that with your conscience?'

'Mine is very evolved,' I said. 'Also, she didn't do it.'

'You would say that.'

'Not if I didn't believe it.'

'And do you suspect Mara Teller may be connected to the disappearance of the Clark boy?'

'Her consultancy could have hit the rocks before it even got started,' I said. 'She might have decided to pursue an alternative vocation. She might even have found Jesus, or got sick and died. But none of those would explain why Mara Teller, to my eyes, may never have existed.'

Delaney Duhamel took in her office. Through the glass partition wall, she regarded the staff at their desks and the pictures of unsullied rivers, mountains, and valleys on the walls. Two older men in shirtsleeves passed through the lobby. Their shirts were pink and light blue respectively, but each had a white collar. Depending on one's perspective, this was what passed for individuality in the corporate world, was nature's way of marking the wearer as a complete jackass, or both.

'If the details she gave were false,' she said, 'then what we have won't be of much use to you.'

'Perhaps so, but what about her attendance fee? She must have paid it somehow, unless she just turned up with cash on the day.'

'Preregistration was obligatory. We were oversubscribed.'

'So there's either an electronic or a paper trail for the payment,' I said. 'What about confirmation of identity?'

'We asked for proof, but a company ID, even self-produced, would have been enough. We didn't make photocopies, or take cell phone pictures, because that's a whole other can of privacy worms. Proof of payment was sufficient to gain access, and each participant received a welcome pack and badge on arrival. It wasn't as though we had anything to hide. We're not the Bilderberg Group.'

'Did the badges have to be worn at all times?'

'Yes, on a lanyard. The hotel insisted, for security reasons.'

'Did attendees have to sign up for particular sessions?'

'Not for the main events, but they did have to register for roundtable discussions, workshops, and special presentations.'

'Is there a record of those registrations?'

'Only of the ones who put their names down in advance. If there was room, people could just show up and grab a seat.

Theoretically, they were supposed to add their names to a list. In practice, that fell by the wayside after the first hour.'

'It's still worth checking, in case anyone can recall her.'

Delaney Duhamel folded her arms and legs simultaneously.

'I'm sorry, but I'm very uncomfortable with giving you access to other attendees beyond what may be publicly available, and I'm not going to reach out to them on your behalf. In fact, I'd much prefer it if you didn't go contacting registrants. We partly rely on membership subscriptions and forum registration to fund our endeavors. If we're perceived, however wrongly, to have sent a private investigator to participants' doors, we're going to suffer financially and reputationally.'

'And that's before the sexual assault case goes to trial,' I said. 'It only goes to prove that a bad situation can always be made worse.'

Sometimes it's advisable to beat a strategic retreat. I still had the option of knocking on doors, with or without Delaney Duhamel's cooperation.

'Look, I understand your position,' I continued. 'All I ask is that, if you do find a record of Teller's attendance as part of a smaller group, you set it aside. If there's anyone on the list of other participants whom you feel could be amenable to talking to me without compromising you or your employer, you might consider sharing that name.'

'I guess I can do that.'

'Lastly, did you have a photographer present?'

'We use a woman named Courtney Wasser. She's a local free-lancer.'

'Did she send you all the pictures she took?'

'She cherry-picked the best ones.'

'Maybe you could ask her to forward the entire file, and pass it on to me.'

Delaney Duhamel was taking notes.

'I'll need time to do all that,' she said at last. 'I can call you, or email whatever I think might be helpful.'

Experience had taught me that distance impacted negatively on commitment, and absence didn't necessarily make the heart grow fonder. I didn't want to leave Lynn without the information I'd come for.

'I can wait,' I said, 'unless you'd prefer that I didn't.'

'I think not waiting might be preferable, or not here. If you have an hour or two to spare, there's a place called the Walnut Street Café about a mile and a half away. I'll come by with whatever I pull together.'

There were probably coffee shops closer to the office than Walnut Street, but I couldn't blame her for being cautious. Delaney Duhamel might have been entertaining doubts about her vocation, but if she was going to leave, she wanted it to be of her own volition, preferably with references that didn't denounce her as a snitch.

I thanked her for her help and went to find the Walnut Street Café. I thought about leaving my car behind and walking, just to spite the oil and gas guys in the white-collared shirts, but the three-mile round trip on foot didn't appeal, so I drove. Which was the world's climate problem in a nutshell.

Chapter XXVII

Sabine Drew made sure her cell phone was charged and she had sufficient water, nuts, and fruit in the car to keep her alive in case she somehow broke down in the wilderness between her home and Portland – not that there was a great deal of wilderness heading south, but one never knew. Cars quit, people became disoriented and stumbled into the woods looking for shelter or help, and the next thing anyone knew, their bones were being carried out in a bag.

By now Sabine was convinced that the crying child was the missing Henry Clark, because the tenor of the wailing altered when she spoke his name. That was the only response he offered, but she was neither surprised nor disappointed by this. The years had taught her that this residue of the dead, or the aspect of it to which she was most sensitive, was less a personality than a vessel of emotion; sometimes one above all others – rage, fear, sorrow, love – but more often an assemblage of different feelings. Henry Clark, though, definitely fell into the former category: he was pure fear.

She started the car and steeled herself for the longest ride she'd taken in a decade. She tuned out Henry. She felt bad about it, but she needed to be able to concentrate to drive, and his terror was a distraction that, with constant exposure, could easily mutate into pain for her, and pain might leave her in a tangle of metal by the side of the road. She turned the old radio to WMEH out of Bangor. She only ever listened to Maine Public Radio and could hopscotch from WMEH to WMEW or WMEP once the coverage began to give out, and from there to WMEA as she drew nearer to Portland.

But as she prepared to turn south out of her driveway, she was assailed by a wave of doubt. Somehow, she had convinced herself that the private investigator would accept whatever she had to say, and act on it. Now, with the road about to stretch before her, she saw herself through his eyes: a reclusive woman of late middle age, with poor dress sense and a home dye job to match, carrying the weight of a reputation that was perhaps better not recalled at all; a sad virgin who kept tropical fish for company, and who claimed to be able to hear the dead. Didn't every disappearance draw similarly troubled souls, some of them attention-seekers, malicious or otherwise, but others whose lunacy had convinced them of the reality of their gifts?

'He'll laugh at me,' she said aloud. 'Worse, he'll listen sympathetically while checking his watch, and I'll be able to see the pity in his eyes.'

When you lived alone, you got used to the sound of your own voice: at least it was a conversation with someone who understood you. Similarly, when you lived with the reality of the lingering dead, you accommodated yourself to speaking without necessarily receiving a response, or not one that would have been audible even to the most sensitive of recording equipment.

'Stupid woman,' she said, and it was all she could do not to bang her forehead against the steering wheel. 'Stupid, deluded—'

An image flashed in her mind, like a night landscape briefly illuminated by lightning. The force of it was so strong that it pushed her into her seat, before the view through her windshield was transformed. It was no longer her own front yard that she saw, but a lagoon, or a lake; a bench; a girl –

And the dead, all of the dead.

'Oh my God,' said Sabine, as the scene flashed again, stronger this time, and now the girl was with her, both by the lake and in the car, but the two versions were not the same. The girl by the lake possessed beautiful, delicate features framed by long blond hair, but the girl in the car kept her head down, concealing her face, and her hair was dark with blood. Sabine could smell it, could smell *her*, in all her desolation.

if he doubts you, whispered the girl, *speak to him of me make him listen you have to make him listen*

'Who are you?' asked Sabine. But even as she spoke, she knew, for who else could it be? Beside her, the girl touched Sabine's hand.

say my name

'Jennifer Parker. Your name is Jennifer Parker.'

And for the first time in many years, Sabine felt afraid in the presence of the dead.

Chapter XXVIII

True to her word, Delaney Duhamel arrived at the Walnut Street Café just over an hour later. I saw her take a moment to look around before she entered, checking that no one else from her firm was present. I had a coffee in front of me, but I'd barely touched it. There was only so much coffee a person could drink, especially in middle age, and with a ninety-minute ride home ahead of them.

'Can I get you anything?' I said.

'I won't be staying.'

She sat on the edge of a chair, produced a flash drive from her purse, and slid it under my copy of the *New York Times*.

'It contains Mara Teller's registration details, copies of all the photographs taken by the freelancer during the forum, and details of the attendees at individual sessions. I figured in for a dime, but I couldn't find her name on those lists. If she attended, she did so on the spur of the moment.'

I put the drive in my pocket.

'Any images we used,' she continued, 'had to be with the consent of those pictured, so most of the publicity shots are grip-and-grins, though there are some general ones. But at first glance, I didn't see Stephen Clark or Mara Teller identified in any of the captions.'

'What about Teller's registration fee?'

'It was paid by USPS money order. I included a PDF of that, too. She originally tried to use one of those prepaid credit cards, but a glitch in the system meant it was rejected. Our registrants don't tend to rely on prepaid cards.'

'Or money orders.'

'Yes, a money order is unusual. Can it be traced?'

'I should be able to find out where it was purchased,' I said.

'That'll be a start. Thank you, by the way. I'll do my best not to bother you again, and I won't let this blow back on you.'

'Two years and change is long enough to spend in the same position. It's about time I started looking for a new challenge.'

It struck me then how young she was: late twenties, at most. She was of a different generation. My father had drummed into me the importance of finding a job for life, one with a strong union behind it, good health care and benefits, and from which you couldn't easily be dismissed, short of setting fire to your place of employment and giggling while it burned. That hadn't really worked out for me, but I doubt it had ever even crossed Delaney Duhamel's mind.

Before she left, I gave her my card.

'In case I'm ever in trouble?' she said.

'It's your favor to call in.'

She placed the card in her purse.

'Are you sure Colleen Clark didn't hurt her son?'

'Yes.'

'What if you found out otherwise?'

'I'd be under a legal obligation to share that information with the police, not to mention a moral one.'

'And would you tell them?'

'Yes, I would.'

'Okay, then. Goodbye, Mr Parker. It's been—'

'Interesting?'

For the first time since we'd met, she brightened. Had he been present, Botticelli might have embarked on a new sketch.

'Yes,' she said, 'that's just the word I was looking for.'

Chapter XXIX

As I drove back to Portland, Steady Freddy White got in touch to let me know he couldn't make it for lunch the next day, as his wife was insisting they head down to Exeter, New Hampshire to see her mother. Judging by his tone, his wife might have encountered resistance to the suggestion that they cross the street to see her mother, never mind traverse the state line but we bear our burdens with fortitude. I was buying gas in Portsmouth at the time, and could probably have dropped in on Steady Freddy's mother-in-law as a favor thus saving him a trip. As it happened, he texted again moments later to let me know that, alternatively, he was free in an hour or so, if I still wanted to talk.

Picking a venue was the only issue. While it wasn't uncommon for police and private investigators to discuss cases, even those where the PI might be working for the defense, the Colleen Clark affair was unusually high-profile. Were Steady Freddy and I to be seen together, it could get back to Erin Becker or her boss. That ruled out places like the Great Lost Bear or Ruski's, bars where cops liked to congregate. In the end, I settled for LFK on State Street, which had the additional benefit of being dimly lit.

Steady Freddy was already waiting for me when I got there, sticking out like a priest at an orgy. No one had ever looked more like a detective than Steady Freddy White. Perhaps there was a section at Nordstrom Rack devoted entirely to the budget-conscious plainclothes policeman: sensible shoes, comfortable pants, jackets that already resembled pre-owned before the label came off, and shirts and ties that came as a set with a free hand-kerchief. If so, Steady Freddy haunted it like a ghost. He was seated at a table near the back of the bar, with a lager and a menu before him, casting a skeptical eye over the clientele while wincing at the music.

'What kind of joint is this?' he asked.

'A young person's one. You remember young people, even if you were never one yourself.'

Steady Freddy tapped the menu accusingly.

'They serve a burger with avocado, and I don't even know what the fuck dill tahini might be. This,' he concluded solemnly, 'is why we need to bring back conscription.'

He ordered a signature burger, having been assured by the server that it wouldn't even share prep space with an avocado, never mind tahini. Steady Freddy gave the server a parting glance that suggested he'd better make sure of it. Otherwise, should he ever have the misfortune to be arrested, he would rue the day he had disappointed a hungry Steady Freddy White.

The server brought me an alcohol-free beer that wasn't an O'Doul's, which confirmed Steady Freddy in the opinion that LFK represented the world going to hell in a handbasket, and we circled each other with small talk before alighting at last on our reason for being there.

'It's a rotten business,' said Steady Freddy. 'For the kid, the husband, even her. But you're going to tell me she didn't do it, right?'

It was the second time in a matter of hours that I'd been asked a version of the old question. I gave a version of the old answer, but one tailored to the questioner.

'I'm uneasy about some aspects,' I offered, 'enough to make me think she's probably innocent.'

'Are you planning on sharing your doubts, or do I have to guess?'

Before I could reply, the burgers arrived. Steady Freddy inspected his as though the chef might personally have shat it onto the plate, but his first taste caused him to brighten considerably, loaded as it was with pimento cheese.

'You know, my wife wouldn't let me eat a hamburger like this,' he said.

He was already leaving enough evidence on his tie in the form of juices and cheese to convict him without hope of appeal when he got home.

'Maybe you should have married me.'

'You didn't ask,' said Steady Freddy, 'which saved me the trouble of having to shoot you.'

He wiped his mouth with a napkin.

'So,' he said, 'tell me about the innocence mission.'

Chapter XXX

Sabine Drew reached Portland without incident, apart from a small detour to Easy Aquariums in Gorham, where she permitted herself some purchases for her tanks at home. She liked to keep the fish stimulated with novelties.

It had been many years since she'd visited Portland, and the changes took her by surprise. Stores and restaurants once familiar to her were either altered beyond easy recognition or had vanished completely; whole blocks of offices and condos looked to have been dropped from space; and she counted enough hotels to make Commercial Street resemble a section of midtown Manhattan. She parked at a meter, inserted four quarters to cover her until after 6 p.m., and went exploring. Down in the Old Port, she found stores that didn't offer anything she might have wanted to buy, the contents of a couple of bookstores excepted, and the prices on the restaurant menus, allied to the pervasive smell of weed, made her feel faint.

She wandered by the waterfront, enjoying the smell of salt air and the sight of some of the older structures on Custom House Wharf, which reminded her of the Portland she used to know. She would have walked for longer, but she glimpsed a boy emerge naked and dripping from the water to stand by one of the docks. His skin was blue, and the sea creatures had blinded him, but his sightlessness didn't prevent him from glancing left and right, searching in his awful blackness for the signal transmitted by Sabine's gift. She walked quickly back to Exchange Street, trusting in distance and the noise of crowds to hide her from the boy. She suffered an intense burst of sorrow, but she lacked the energy to spare for him. Anyway, he had spent too long in the water. He belonged to the sea now.

She did not have an address for the private investigator, but remembered from an article she had read that he maintained a connection with the Great Lost Bear on Forest Avenue. She thought she might ask after him there. She had a telephone number for him, but didn't want to use it. Whatever she had to say, she needed to communicate in person, but it was also the case that she avoided phones unless she had no choice. She owned only a primitive cell phone, seldom used, and let an ancient answering machine screen her landline calls. For Sabine, the phrase 'ghosts in the wire' had come to possess a literal meaning – specters inhabited the ether – and any conversation conducted by phone inevitably involved some uninvited third party only she could hear. But she was also afraid that if she told Parker who she was in advance, he might find a reason not to meet with her. If necessary, she would spend a night in town and try again the following day. She had researched places to stay and made a list of those she could afford. They wouldn't be anything fancy, but a couple offered premium cable and complimentary breakfast. It would be a treat to herself.

She headed back to her car along Fore Street, the bars buzzing with early-evening drinkers. Some of the groups of young men were very loud. They made her nervous, even though she was virtually invisible to them, a plain woman over forty having no place or purpose in their lives. Two police cars were parked in anticipation of potential trouble later, but then this part of town had always enjoyed a reputation for wildness. Back in the day, when she was much younger, a man had come on to her at one of its bars, a rare occurrence even then. He kissed her at the end of the night, smoke and whiskey on his breath, and she kissed him back. He lived in the West End, and invited her to return with him to his lodgings, but she turned him down. He asked for her number, and she gave it, but he never called. Sometimes she wondered what might have happened had she gone with him – indeed, had she gone with any of the handful of men who had shown a passing sexual interest in her. She might have been married by now, or a mother. Alex Mazur: that was the name of the man who had kissed her, the surname a relic of his great-grandparents' emigration from Poland during the nineteenth century. He was dead now, burned to death before he was thirty, lost in a fire in that same West End apartment building, the one to which he had so wanted to bring her. He had come to her in the aftermath because he was single and solitary, an only child long estranged from his father, his mother having predeceased him. Sabine had calmed him and sent him onward to his mom, but the smell of his charred flesh had stayed with her for weeks after.

She drove to the Great Lost Bear, the lot so full that she had to park on the street. The bar area was crammed for a beer promotion, so she found a seat in one of the quieter dining sections and ordered a glass of white wine and a portobello mushroom sandwich.

'I'm looking for someone,' she told the waitress, 'a man who sometimes comes here. His name is Charlie Parker. He's a private detective.'

'I don't think he's been in tonight,' said the waitress. 'I'm sure we have a number for him, if you need to call, or we can make sure he gets a message. He's pretty good about responding fast.'

Sabine thanked her, and said she might try the number she had for him after she'd eaten. She needed to reconsider. Of course, he wouldn't have been there when she arrived; that would have been too much of a coincidence. It struck her that she wasn't thinking straight. It might be best if she accepted the waitress's offer and asked her to pass on a message. But what to say without revealing too much, while also revealing just enough?

Her wine arrived. In a bar like this, she should probably have ordered a beer, but beer always smelled better to her than it tasted. Her sandwich followed not long after, along with a massive shadow that cast itself across her table. She looked up to see, standing before her, a man almost as wide as he was tall. He was wearing a golf shirt stretched taut over his arms and torso – she had no idea how he'd managed to get into it, but was convinced he'd have to be cut out – and the sort of tan pants favored by construction workers, the ones with pockets everywhere.

'Pardon me for intruding,' he said, and his voice was gentler

141

than she might have expected, 'but the server mentioned you were asking after Mr Parker.'

'Yes, I was.'

'My name is Paulie Fulci. I'm proud to call myself his friend. Are you in some kind of trouble?'

'No,' said Sabine, 'but a child is.'

Chapter XXXI

Steady Freddy listened while I told him of my conversation with Stephen Clark and my interest in the woman who called herself Mara Teller. I neglected to mention my earlier meeting with Delaney Duhamel, or the material she had provided. I didn't want Steady Freddy – or, God forbid, his colleague Furnish – turning up on Duhamel's doorstep, not yet. If I was in possession of information that the police did not yet have, I wanted to remain ahead of them until it suited me to share it.

'I got to admit,' said Steady Freddy, 'that the Teller woman is kind of interesting – or was, until we found the blanket in Colleen Clark's car. After that, Teller and anyone else, ceased to be of much relevance as far as Erin Becker was concerned. She didn't want anything muddying the waters. If Becker was a guy, I'd have said she had a hard-on for your client, but in the worst possible way. Out of due diligence, I did the basics on Teller. I came up with the website and not much else. She's a splinter under a fingernail for me, but I'm learning to ignore the irritation.'

'What about Furnish?'

'Furnish!' said Steady Freddy, and I was surprised at just how much scorn could be poured into two syllables. 'You ever read any John Sandford novels?'

'I've read all of them,' I said. 'Sandford's as good as they come.'

'Yeah, I save them for my vacation. You know how in the books they call Virgil "that Fuckin Flowers"? Well, you can't spend more than a day at Middle Street without someone talking about "Fuckin Furnish", and not with any affection, not like Virgil. I bet Furnish is already writing up the chapter about Colleen Clark for his memoirs, and hoping Becker will remember him when she comes into her kingdom. For him, the case is done and dusted.'

'And for you?'

'I'm just trying to go along to get along, that splinter excepted.'

'Which is why you're here, obviously, eating a hamburger on my dime.'

'A very good hamburger, too, though I remain troubled by that avocado business and may have to remonstrate with the management about it.'

He finished his beer before peering into the glass to trace the hole in the bottom. I ordered another round.

'Where were we?' he asked, once a server had been dispatched in the direction of the bar.

'We were talking about how you were inclined to go along to get along, splinters notwithstanding.'

'Which I am but I do like neatness, and in a fundamentally uncertain world, I crave surety. Unlike you, I think Clark probably did harm her son. She may have been depressed, or driven crazy by not getting enough sleep, but sometimes the simplest answer is the right one. At the same time, I don't want to be dragged from my retirement in a few years to explain how I fucked up a case through negligence, or because of pressure from suits in Augusta, thus helping to put the wrong woman behind bars – and worse, leaving whoever took her boy free to do the same to another child. So ask your questions, and I'll do my best to answer them.'

'Straightforward ones first. Do you have any camera footage from the night Henry Clark disappeared?'

'We have a window of almost nine hours, so that's a lot of traffic going through the area,' said Steady Freddy. 'Also, the residents have an association, and together they decided to discourage the use of security cameras with a range beyond the edge of anyone's yard. Even then, a few of the homes, including the Clarks', lack any kind of camera at all. We appealed for dashcam footage early in the investigation, and checked on business premises with external cameras. What we got didn't amount to much – or amounted to too much, depending on your point of view – and hasn't resulted in any useful leads. Moxie can ask for what we have during discovery, but I think you'll be wasting your time unless you already know what it is you're looking for, which I'm guessing you don't.

'Now, with Colleen Clark being charged, we'll be searching closer to her home. The working assumption is that she killed the boy in the house and immediately got rid of the body by burying it nearby; that, or she held on to it to dispose of later. Either way, trawling through license plates from the night in question won't help us. We have her phone, and that's under forensic examination. She says she kept it with her at all times. If true, we'll soon know everywhere she went, and how long she stayed there. But unless she's dumb, she'd have left the phone elsewhere when she was interring her son's remains.'

I let it go. We were back to assumptions of guilt and innocence. If Colleen was innocent, the police weren't going to find anything on the phone to prove otherwise. I was operating on the basis that she wasn't responsible for Henry's disappearance, but nevertheless, he had been removed from the area somehow. Unless he had been taken away on foot, which would have been risky, a vehicle must have been used, as the neighbor, Mrs Gammett, had noted: a quiet one, well-maintained, so it wouldn't draw attention or break down at an inopportune moment.

'What about Stephen Clark's brother and his wife?' I asked.

'What about them?'

'Do they have an alibi for the night Henry went missing?'

'Jesus, you are clutching at straws. I may have misjudged you, and Moxie ought to cut a plea deal.'

'Indulge me.'

'They were out of town: tickets to a music concert in Boston, and a hotel bed to go with them.'

'A gift, or their own purchase?'

'A birthday gift for the brother.'

'From?'

'Stephen Clark.'

'Huh.'

'Don't go jumping to conclusions, though in your case that's like telling a dog not to chase a rabbit.'

'It's just curious, that's all.'

'An alibi for when they needed one, you mean? Alternatively, it's what's known to regular people as life. Take your pick, but they're off the hook.'

'And Stephen Clark was in New York. Do we know if he was alone?'

'Hotel security footage has him entering his room unaccompanied shortly after ten p.m. Nobody joined him subsequently, so the answer is probably yes. No hookers, and no mistress.'

'No Mara Teller.'

'Not unless she climbed in through a tenth-story window.'

'When did Stephen Clark tell you about the affair?'

'He didn't, not at first. His wife did. It was during the second interview on the day the boy went missing. We had trouble getting anything out of her during the first run-through because, understandably, she was distraught. A physician subsequently gave her something to take away the edge, but not so much that she wasn't coherent or able to concentrate.'

'How did the subject come up?'

The fresh beers arrived, and we paused until the server was out of earshot.

'We asked about the state of the marriage,' said Steady Freddy. 'You know the drill. If a child disappears, you start with the parents and work outward. She told us that her husband had cheated on her, but they were getting through it.'

'So he wasn't present when you spoke with Colleen?'

'No. The procedure in these situations is first to interview the parents separately, then compare notes.'

'Was this interview conducted at the house or the station?'

'The house. The husband was in the kitchen, with an officer keeping him company, and she was in the living room. Then we switched them around.'

'Did you ask Stephen Clark directly about the affair?'

'He said they'd had some ups and downs, just like any married couple. Furnish then asked if it had ever been more than that, and Clark responded by demanding to know what his wife had said.'

'Did you tell him?'

'I told him we were interested in what he had to say first, so he squirmed for a while before admitting to an affair that arose out of a conference. He didn't use the word "affair", though. He called it a "two- or three-night stand", which I hadn't heard before, and gave us Teller's name, along with whatever contact details he had for her.'

'The dormant website, and a cell phone number that no longer worked?'

'So it was hinky,' conceded Steady Freddy, 'but not off the scale. I've never had an affair – I find it hard enough to keep one woman happy, and the stress of trying to satisfy two might kill me – but if I got involved with someone and then thought better of it, the first thing I'd do would be to get myself a new cell phone number.'

'What about the website?'

'Some business ideas never get beyond a wish and a name. Or it might be that she no longer wanted Stephen Clark in her life after spending a few nights in his company, and simultaneously decided to find alternative employment.'

'Those theories might be plausible,' I said, 'if the website wasn't the only indication that Mara Teller was anything other than a shadow identity. It's not a particularly common name, and someone in her profession shouldn't be so hard to find.'

'That's the part that itches,' said Steady Freddy. 'Even Furnish wasn't rushing to sign off on it. We had marked her, but then the blanket turned up, followed by word from Nowak's office that they were going to proceed against Colleen Clark with what they had. But I had intended to talk to the organizers of the forum to set my mind at rest. I might find the time when my wife and I head south tomorrow. It'll give me an excuse to do something other than drink Earl Grey tea while basking in her mother's disapproval.'

I decided to play the Delaney Duhamel card. There was no point in holding on to it, not if Steady Freddy was going to contact her anyway. If I didn't mention her, it would leave bad blood between us.

'I already did,' I said. 'Talk to the forum people, I mean, not bask in your mother-in-law's disapproval.'

'And?'

'Mara Teller paid her registration fee with a money order, so I might be able to trace that back to the post office where it was bought. She would have been asked for ID at the forum registration table. In theory, that should have required her to produce a driver's license or similar. In practice, a company ID would also have been acceptable and she could have run one of those off on her home printer. Whatever ID she used, no copy of it was kept, so that's a dead end.'

Steady Freddy took all this in, fed it through the machinery of his brain, and waited for a result. Whatever emerged didn't impress him.

'I'm still struggling to make the leap from bed-hopping to abduction and murder,' he said. 'Why would Teller be so angry with Stephen Clark that she'd want to harm his son? After all, Clark claimed it was Teller who cut off contact with him, not the other way round.'

'He could be lying about how the affair ended. Or—'

'Is this the part in a Sherlock Holmes story where Watson looks shocked by Holmes's powers of deduction?' asked Steady Freddy.

'I think you'd have to play Lestrade, but the principle is the same.'

'Happy to oblige.'

'What if Mara Teller attended the forum with the express purpose of targeting someone? Suppose she wasn't looking for an affair.'

'So if not for business or sex, why was she there?'

'What,' I said, 'if she was looking for a victim?'

Chapter XXXII

After some time spent digging Mattia Reggio obtained a cell phone number and an address for Hazel Sloane, the reporter who had written the eyewitness piece about Colleen Clark being picked up from Cumberland County Jail. Reggio called Sloane, explained who he was, and asked, in the politest possible way, if it was chance that had led her to be present when he arrived early to collect Moxie Castin's client after her release. Sloane, being smart enough to recognize that she might now have an in with the defense, didn't tell Reggio to take a hike, but admitted that she herself had not been at the jail, and the tip-off had come from a source in Portland.

'What source?' said Reggio.

'I can't tell you that on a point of principle,' said Sloane, 'but I couldn't even if I wanted to. The pictures were sent via email, with a message detailing where and when they were taken. We assumed they must have come from a woman, since the message was signed "A Concerned Mother". A call to the Cumberland County Sheriff's Office confirmed that Colleen Clark had been released at that time.'

Reggio decided not to mention the car that had followed him from the parking lot. He had assumed, based on information received from Moxie Castin, that it was Sloane's vehicle, but now it seemed Moxie had been mistaken, incorrectly linking the car to the reporter once the pictures of Colleen leaving jail appeared on the newspaper's website. Moxie had then immediately lost interest.

'What about the email address used to send the pictures?' said Reggio. 'Do you still have it?'

'I'm not giving that to you,' said Sloane, 'but again, it wouldn't be much use. I sent a couple of messages in reply but they bounced back. Whoever provided those pictures doesn't want to be identified down, which is another reason to think it might be someone who could lose their job for what they did.'

Reggio wasn't sure what he could have done with the email address even if she'd shared it with him. He didn't have that type of expertise – didn't have much expertise at all, really, and what he did have was criminal.

'You've been very helpful,' he told Sloane. 'Thank you.'

'I'm hoping it might be a two-way street. After all, you—'

But Reggio had already hung up. He had no interest in being a source – no, call it what it was: a rat – for a reporter. If she wanted information, she could get in touch with Moxie Castin, who would know how to roll those dice so they came up sixes for him.

Reggio heard a soft knock on the door of his den. This was his personal fiefdom and Amara never entered without asking first. It was a holdover from the old days, when it was better if she didn't know what might be stored in the drawers of the old metal desk that had accompanied them to Maine. She never even cleaned the space, leaving the care of it to him. He did vacuum the floor occasionally, but only when he could no longer see his feet for dust and debris.

Reggio told her to come in. Amara was carrying his nightly caffè corretto on a tray: a shot of espresso with a small glass of brandy on the side. She placed the tray on his desk and stroked his hair.

'I didn't want to disturb you while you were on the phone,' she said. 'Anything I should be worried about?'

'Nothing,' said Reggio. He took her right hand in his and kissed it softly. 'It's all good.'

Chapter XXXIII

I prepared to leave LFK little wiser than I had been when I arrived, a pattern that was becoming uncomfortably familiar. I hadn't managed to get a lot out of Steady Freddy, but I might have succeeded in sowing a few seeds of uncertainty regarding Colleen Clark's guilt. Also, from what he was willing to share toward the end of our conversation, any earth-shattering revelations from the prosecution were unlikely. As Moxie had anticipated, Erin Becker was relying on the evidence of the bloodied blanket and the absence of an alibi as the basis for her case, along with testimony from Stephen Clark regarding his wife's supposedly hostile feelings toward their son, and – if Becker could swing it – evidence from Colleen's physician and therapist that the accused had been suffering from severe depression and had admitted to feelings of anger toward her child.

'Becker's good,' said Steady Freddy, as he ordered one more for the road on my tab, 'but my guess is that it's still sixty-forty in favor of a conviction, at best. We're under pressure to locate a body.'

'Meaning?' I said.

'Meaning we finally start digging at the Clark property tomorrow morning.'

Becker and Nowak had been hoping that Colleen would break down and confess, thereby avoiding the necessity of a blind excavation, but frustratingly for them – and their ambitions – she continued to protest her innocence, even with the prosecution mooting a shorter sentence in return for a guilty plea and a burial site.

'I heard you were looking for a warrant. Has Becker alerted the media to the search?'

'Won't make much difference one way or the other. As soon as we arrive with spades and a cadaver dog, we'll have coverage up the wazoo. Wherever you've stashed Colleen Clark, you'd be advised to keep her there until we're done, because the carnival is about to set up again in her part of town.'

'What about the house itself?'

'That was searched thoroughly with the Clarks' consent as soon as the child went missing, and so far no one has suggested we should take up the floorboards. If Henry Clark's body was somewhere inside, we'd know about it by now. You can hide a body, but hiding a smell is harder. Still, I don't doubt they'll run the dog through there as well. They'll also be looking for traces of blood, obviously. If there was a cleanup, however thorough, it'll show.'

I thanked Steady Freddy for his time, paid the tab, and put on my coat.

'That money order could be smart thinking,' he said, 'if there's mileage in the Teller lead.'

'It was luck, but it might come to nothing. As you said, I may just be chasing after a woman who had an affair she regretted and is now covering her tracks.'

'But you don't believe that, do you?'

'No, I don't. And do you want to hear something else?'

He raised his fresh glass of beer. 'You pay the piper,' he said, 'you call the tune.'

'I think Stephen Clark hasn't been straight about his relationship with Teller, whoever she really is: not with you, not with me, and not with his wife. By being unfaithful, he's demonstrated that he's capable of deceit. He may even have become habituated to it.'

Steady Freddy sipped his beer.

'I've revised those odds,' he said.

'Already?'

'Yeah. I think I was mistaken earlier: seventy-thirty in favor of a conviction.'

'And there I was about to congratulate myself for changing your mind.'

Neither of us had to stress that our meeting should stay between ourselves, even though nothing major had been conceded or revealed on either side. Discretion was understood.

'I'll see you around, Freddy.'

'That you will.'

As the server arrived to pick up the credit card receipt and his tip, Steady Freddy tapped him on the arm.

'Son,' he said, 'I'd like you to send a manager my way. We need to have a conversation about avocado . . .'

Paulie Fulci called as I started my car.

'I was at the Bear,' he said. 'I drove over to get takeout for Evelyn and Tony. You know how my brother likes the Angry Bird.'

The Angry Bird was a fried chicken sandwich loaded with Hellfire sauce, jalapeños, and blue cheese. Tony Fulci's version was customized for him with a few added drops of something called Chilli Pepper Pete's Dragon's Blood Mega Hot Sauce. Moxie had tried it once, and spent the whole of the following day afraid to leave the house.

'Is there a problem?' I said. 'If they've run out of hot sauce, I can't help.'

'There's a woman here,' said Paulie. 'She was asking after you. She says she knows something about Henry Clark. She's—'

He struggled to find the right description before settling for 'strange'.

'Crazy strange?'

Just as I had expected the police to get around to a more extensive examination of the Clark property, I had also been anticipating the emergence of lunatics and self-promoters. Missing persons cases drew them like flies, but particularly those involving children. Paulie Fulci might not have been a trained psychiatrist, but he'd been around enough of them in his life, along with the folk they treated, to be able to spot signs of disturbance in others.

'I don't think so,' said Paulie. 'Or if she is, it's the mellow sort.'

I heard a muffled voice from nearby.

'Wait a minute,' said Paulie. 'Dave wants to speak to you.'

Moments later, Dave Evans came on the phone.

'It took me a while to figure out who she is, the woman waiting for you,' he said. 'I knew the face was familiar, but it's been a few years.'

'Well?' I said.

'It's Sabine Drew.'

II

I shall not commit the fashionable stupidity of regarding
everything I cannot explain as a fraud.

C. G. Jung, Address to the Society for Psychical Research, 1919

Chapter XXXIV

Five-year-old Verona Walters went missing from Mill Park in Augusta, Maine, on a bright July day in 2015. She and her father, Chris, had been playing hide-and-seek among the bushes and trees, and Chris had turned his back on her while he counted down from ten to one. In reality, he'd been peeking, unwilling to let his daughter out of his sight, but she caught him looking and instructed him to cover his eyes properly. Later, he would tell detectives that he couldn't have had his back to her for more than three or four seconds, five tops, before he went searching. By then, she was already gone.

What followed was one of the most high-profile missing persons cases in the Northeast's living memory, extending first statewide and subsequently into the contiguous regions. The police conducted hundreds of interviews and followed up every possible lead and sighting, however tenuous or improbable. Dogs searched the banks of the Kennebec, boats worked their way up and down its length, and divers explored its depths. Known sex offenders were made to account for their movements. Weeks went by, then months, but no trace of Verona Walters was found.

Inevitably, a number of self-proclaimed mediums came forward, claiming to have received messages either from Verona or from spirits with insights into her fate. Interventions of this kind presented problems for police because they had to be treated with seriousness, even at the risk of investigators being mocked. Leads came in all forms, and who was to say that a 'vision' might not be a buried memory, a minor detail witnessed and then forgotten, only to resurface in an altered form?

But there was also the fear that a lead dismissed because of its source might turn out to be accurate, even if only accidentally:

the medium who claims a child is in a river, weeks before a body is pulled from the muddy bed; or the psychic who talks of glimpsing a wood or glade in winter, only for the spring thaw to reveal infant bones among pine roots. The result, if those reports had been ignored, was that the police might end up being hauled over hot coals for their narrow-mindedness, and upbraided for prolonging a family's agony. At the same time, to follow up such claims too quickly or publicly risked appearing desperate or excessively credulous.

Sabine Drew didn't call the line dedicated to the Verona Walters case. Neither did she send a note or an email, but instead turned up at Augusta PD headquarters on Union Street and asked to speak with Ronnie Pascal, the lead detective on the case. Pascal was off duty when Drew arrived, so Drew was asked if she'd care to deal with one of the other officers involved. She refused. She would, she said, talk only with Pascal.

Ronnie Pascal lived a ten-minute drive from the center of Augusta and wasn't doing a whole lot that day, so he agreed to come in. Sabine Drew asked if they could sit somewhere private, and he showed her to an empty interview room. He offered her coffee, but she requested water instead. By the time Pascal returned with the bottle, Drew had placed a hand-drawn map on the table.

'What's this?' asked Pascal.

'A map, obviously,' said Drew. 'It's where Verona Walters is buried.'

A reply of that sort might lead any detective worth his salt to wonder if he should begin recording the conversation after asking the person sitting opposite if they were waiving the right to an attorney. Ronnie Pascal did none of those things, not yet, because he'd spent too long dealing with a great many people who professed to have intelligence relating to the whereabouts of Verona Walters, a not inconsiderable proportion of whom had been wrong, deluded, or actively mischief-making.

'And how do you know that?'

'Because she told me,' Drew replied.

'Told you how?'

But Drew answered a different question.

'In my kitchen yesterday morning, shortly after breakfast.'

Ronnie Pascal was tempted to ask Drew what she'd been cooking, and how strong the fumes might have been. He was a confirmed atheist who made a point of walking under ladders, and was proud to have been born on the thirteenth day of the month. For this reason, he tried to leave the interviews with mediums and similar wingnuts to his colleagues, liberating him from having to mask a skepticism that curdled too quickly into contempt. Now he realized that here was time he could happily have been whiling away at home.

'You don't believe me, do you?'

'I'm happy to listen to whatever you have to say,' Pascal lied, 'but I also have to warn you against wasting police time.'

'She told me to ask for you specifically.'

'Why? Because she saw me on TV?'

'No, because she met you once.'

Pascal had been tapping his pen on his notebook – nib first, then top, twisting it between his fingers, distracting himself with the pattern. Now he stopped. This was not common knowledge. Two years previously, he had called by the Walters house to take a witness statement from the father about an armed robbery at a bank on Senator Way. Verona Walters was then three years old. She'd shown him one of her dolls.

'Where did you hear that?'

'From Verona,' said Drew. 'You handled one of her dolls. She told you the doll's name. Do you remember it?'

'Yes.'

'Carly, right?'

Ronnie Pascal had heard of people getting chills down their spines. He'd even experienced it himself once or twice, but only in the company of violent, unrepentant men. He had never before felt it while sitting across from a mild-mannered, unexceptional-looking woman with a hole in the right elbow of her cardigan.

'Yes, that was the doll's name,' he said. 'But with respect, there are other ways you could have found it out.'

'Yes, I suppose there are.' She didn't sound remotely offended. 'I might be a friend of the family, although I'm not. I could have

159

heard about it from one of your fellow officers, but I have no intimates in the Augusta PD. I only know the police in Haynesville, where I live.'

She concentrated, assembling her thoughts.

'Verona stated that she'd had oatmeal for breakfast the morning she died. She doesn't like oatmeal, but she agreed to eat it twice a week – except not on weekends – because her mother said it was good for her. That morning, she couldn't finish the bowl because she accidentally put too much salt on it. Well, she told her mother it was accidental, but in reality she loosened the top of the saltcellar so the contents would spill out. Her mother asked her if that's what she'd done, but Verona denied it. I think she's sorry that the final thing she told her mother was a lie.'

Pascal had no idea if this was true or not. The subject of Verona Walters's last meal with her parents had not previously come up.

'Why don't you check that with her family?' said Drew. 'It might help to convince you of the truth of what I have to say. I don't mind waiting. I've set aside the afternoon.'

Pascal still remained hopeful of finding a rational explanation for this woman's knowledge of events. He tried to recall if the little girl's doll had been mentioned in any of the briefings or news reports, and decided it hadn't. The doll wasn't in Verona's possession when she vanished, but in her bedroom at home. He knew because he'd seen it there himself when they'd searched, in case the room revealed any previous contact between Verona and her abductor, and therefore clues as to where she might have been taken.

'I'll do that,' he said. 'I have to warn you again: there are penalties for wasting police time. If for any reason you've been in touch with the Walters family in the past, or have some insight into their routines through friends or associates, it would be better if you told me now.'

'I've never met the rest of the family in my life,' said Drew. 'Just their daughter, and then only in a manner of speaking.'

Pascal asked a female officer to sit with her while he went to call the Walterses. He couldn't have said why he wanted Drew to have company. It wasn't that he thought she might damage police

160

property, or harm herself out of some further derangement. Perhaps he was afraid she might begin levitating, or walking through walls.

He made the call from his desk. Larraine Walters was at home with their infant son while her husband was at work. He was a supervisor at the city's Public Works Department, and had been offered extended compassionate leave with full pay while the search for his daughter continued. He was inclined to accept, but his wife advised him to return to his post. She loved him, but he was driving her nuts, and she was close enough to madness as things stood.

'This may sound like an odd question,' said Pascal to Larraine Walters, 'but would you happen to remember what your daughter had for breakfast the day she went missing?'

Even as the last words emerged from his mouth, he was already regretting them. Dumb, so dumb. Thanks to all the forensics-led shows on TV, and the mystery section in the local Barnes & Noble, everyone was now an expert on autopsies. But the Drew woman had thrown him. It was her calmness.

'Have you found a body?' asked Larraine. 'My God, you have, haven't you?'

'No, Mrs Walters, we haven't. I can't even explain right now why this might be important, but I'd be obliged if you'd answer the question.'

'She had oatmeal, just a spoonful or two,' said Larraine. 'She doesn't like oatmeal, but we try to encourage her to eat it a couple of times a week. She can be fussy about food, and that's a slippery slope. Next thing you know, she'll be refusing to eat her greens and subsisting on fried food and Butterfingers.'

He noted her use of the present tense and wondered how often she now found herself lapsing into the past when speaking of Verona.

'Did she refuse to eat her oatmeal that morning only because she doesn't like it?' he asked.

'No, she claimed the top had come off the saltcellar and doused the bowl, but I suspect she might have tampered with it. Verona has more tricks up her sleeve than David Copperfield. Now, can you please give me some idea of what this is about?'

Pascal contemplated just how much he should share with her: a little, and no more.

'Are you or your husband acquainted with a woman named Sabine Drew?'

There was silence while Larraine Clark rummaged through her memory.

'I don't recognize the name. Have you spoken to Chris? She might be someone he knows from work.'

'I'll ask him, but I wanted to talk to you first. The name doesn't ring any bells at all? That's Sabine Drew.' Pascal spelled it out for her.

'Definitely not. Who is she? Do you think she had something to do with Verona's disappearance?'

'No, that's not why I'm asking about her.'

Pascal wasn't sure if this was true. He knew certain types of killers liked to circle a case, even involving themselves as potential witnesses. They returned to the scenes of their kills to relive the experience. They drew pictures. Maps.

'Then why *are* you asking about her?'

'Because she wants to help,' said Pascal, 'and before I engage with her further, I thought I'd try to find out more. Oh, and another thing.' It had just struck him. 'Your daughter had a doll: Carly.'

'She still does,' said Larraine, and he experienced the correction as a slap.

Dumb again. Three strikes and you're out.

'Of course. I apologize. Did you ever take Carly to be repaired? You know, to a doll's hospital, or a seamstress?'

'No.'

'Did Verona ever lose Carly, only to have her returned by someone: a stranger, a woman?'

'No. These are odd questions, Detective.'

'I did warn you. If I send you a picture of this woman by email, will you look at it and tell me if she appears familiar?'

'Sure, I'll get right back to you.'

He could hear the eagerness in her voice. After so many dead ends, here might be something resembling progress at last.

Pascal hung up, called Chris Walters, and asked him much the same questions, with much the same replies. Pascal ended the conversation and returned to Sabine Drew. She was speaking with the female officer about lasagne recipes. It helped, said Drew, to spread pesto over the top just before the lasagne goes into the oven.

'It makes it smell like Italy. Or what I always imagine Italy smells like, never having been.'

She gave her attention to Pascal.

'Well?'

'With your consent,' he said, 'I'd like to send a photograph of you to Verona's parents.'

She frowned, but not without amusement.

'You still think I might have met them.'

'I'm a rationalist, Ms Drew.'

'And a Holmesian?'

He frowned.

'I don't know what you mean.'

'"When you have eliminated the impossible, whatever remains, however improbable, must be the truth."'

'Oliver Wendell?' offered Pascal.

'Sherlock,' said Drew.

'I don't read mysteries.'

'That's understandable, given your line of work. I presume the plots stretch your credulity. And no, I don't mind your taking my picture.'

Pascal used his cell phone to snap three shots of Drew before emailing them to Larraine and Chris Walters. He sat at his desk to wait for their replies. Minutes later, both came back to confirm that they'd never seen the woman in the pictures.

Pascal went back to the interview room, thanked the female officer for her help, and sat alone with Sabine Drew. From now on, he informed her, he would be recording their exchanges. He surveyed again the map she'd drawn. It showed paths through trees, and a road to the west. There were also two houses, although he couldn't tell the distance between them because the map wasn't drawn to scale.

'Explain to me again how you knew about the oatmeal and the doll,' he said.

'Verona told me.'

163

'Verona Walters.'

'Yes.'

'Did you see as well as hear her?'

'Yes, briefly.'

'How did she look?'

'I'm not being facetious,' said Drew, 'but she looked dead.'

'Can you elaborate?'

'I could see bruising to her neck. That was how she died. He strangled her.'

'He?'

'She couldn't see his face, but she could hear and smell him. It was a man. She wasn't sure if he meant to kill her. He was trying to get her out of the car and she fought him. He pressed his hands hard on her neck and she felt something break inside. Then she was gone.'

'Why couldn't she see him?'

'He put a bag or hood over her head when he abducted her.'

Pascal was taking notes. If, by some wild stretch of the imagination, there was a shred of truth to what he was hearing, the man who had abducted Verona Walters didn't want her to see his face. Either he didn't wish to look at his victim as he killed her – and some killers preferred not to – or he intended to release her, possibly after sexually assaulting her or following the payment of a ransom. But the Walterses weren't wealthy, which hardly made them an attractive target for a kidnapper.

'So you say he killed her?'

'I don't,' said Drew. 'Verona does.'

'And then?'

'He buried her.'

'If she's underground, how could she have helped you to create a map?'

'Is that supposed to be a clever question, Detective Pascal?'

For the first time, she expressed irritation.

'Just a logical one,' he said.

'Her body is down there, but another part of her isn't.'

'Her soul? Her ghost?'

'Call it what you like. I don't have a name for it, or any of them, not beyond "the dead",'

'Them? You mean there's more than one?'

'Not with Verona. I'm speaking in general terms. She's not the first for me.'

'And do they all speak to you?'

'Only some. The rest talk to themselves, or to the people they've left behind. I'm not convinced all of them can see me. If they do, it may be that I'm present as a specter, a flickering in the dark, much like they sometimes are to me. The majority don't stay very long anyway. I blink, and they're gone.'

'Gone where?'

'Since they don't come back, I've never had a chance to ask. Nor would I wish to, even given the opportunity. I try not to have unnecessary discourse with them. I find it's best to ignore them unless they're insistent, or I can be of help.'

'Why is that?'

'Because, Detective, the dead are very dull, and the ones that aren't dull are frightened, angry, or sad. That's not company anyone would willingly keep.'

'Yet you say Verona Walters spoke to you.'

'And I to her.'

'Why?'

'Because,' said Drew, 'I went looking for her.'

Chapter XXXV

It was odd, Sabine Drew reflected, how the extraordinary could so quickly come to seem quotidian. In the beginning, once she'd stopped being frightened of the figures that drifted through the shadow landscape of her life, she became, quite naturally, fascinated by them. It was like watching some rare, pale species of fish inhabiting, however briefly, a dark exorheic region, destined to remain in place only for as long as it took to locate the egress stream leading to the sea. Like fish, the dead had to be approached carefully. They were similarly alert to observation, though unlike fish, they favored approaching the observer in turn. The departed, in addition to being dull, were easily distracted.

But having them draw close was an unpleasant experience. They didn't smell bad, or not usually, but there was an undeniable miasma about them, a fog of confusion, even despair. Sabine found extended exposure to it debilitating, as though they were draining some of the life from her to compensate for their own absence of vitality; and it was worse when they tried to touch her, because even a gentle stroke from one of them was painful, though it left no visible mark.

And they had such *need*: for answers, reassurance, companionship. The younger they were, the more profound it was. She learned that early on when, without thinking, she reached out to comfort a boy of three or four with burns along the entire right side of his body. His face was such a mask of misery and remembered agony that she had felt compelled to offer succor.

Five days later, he was still there. He followed her to school and church. He was the first sight to greet her in the morning and the last she took with her when she closed her eyes at night. She never even discovered his name, because he never spoke. She felt sorry for him for the first day or two, but then he grew annoying. She

166

began to worry that he might never leave and she would be stuck with him unto the grave and beyond, because she had no doubt that he'd be waiting for her on the other side as well. Finally, in a fit of desperation, she had called out to a middle-aged woman leading two little girls by the hand. All three were wet, and the left side of the woman's face was caved in, but none gave any sign of being troubled. The woman paused when Sabine spoke, and her one good eye drifted in confusion from the boy to Sabine before she realized what was being asked of her. The younger of the girls tried to run to Sabine and the boy, but her mother held on tight to her.

Thank goodness, thought Sabine. *I already have enough problems with one lost child. I don't need another.*

The girl, recognizing that she was not about to be released, extended her hand to the burnt boy, but he would not move.

'Go on,' said Sabine. 'They'll take care of you.'

The boy raised his arms to her.

'No,' she said. 'I don't want to play with you anymore.'

She didn't feel bad about rejecting him. It was for his own good, and she really was tired of having him around. For an instant, tiny fires of rage ignited in his eyes, and Sabine could have sworn that the burn marks on his body glowed red. Then he dropped his arms, turned away, and went to join the woman and her daughters. He took the younger girl's hand and the quartet faded from view. The boy did not once look back.

'Well,' Sabine said aloud, as he vanished, 'there's gratitude.'

Still, it was a lesson she took to heart. She grew adept at surveying the dead, at regarding without being noticed. She aided them when and where she could, but kept her distance unless her sense of disorder, of wrongness, became too acute. In those situations, her appetite and sleep patterns would become affected. Her skin would grow dry and itchy. She might even get ulcers in her mouth. It was no surprise that she preferred not to involve herself, but the Verona Walters case was one instance where she felt she had no option but to help.

Sabine had seated herself at the kitchen table, the newspaper photograph of Verona before her, and asked her mother not to disturb her for an hour or two. The latter, by now familiar with her daughter's ways, left her alone, even going so far as to turn off the radio in the living room and temporarily halting her never-ending cleaning of the old house. In the stillness that followed, Sabine had reached out to the dead girl.

Ronnie Pascal shifted in his chair. He was trying to find a comfortable position, but was beginning to fear that he never would, not while he was in the company of this woman.

'You appreciate how unlikely all this sounds?' he said.

'Of course. Do you really think I wanted to come here just to have you look at me like I'm insane? I could have stayed home and kept all this to myself.'

'Why didn't you?'

'Is that a serious question?'

'No,' said Pascal, 'I guess not.'

He examined again the notes he'd made and came to a decision. It went against all his beliefs, but not, oddly, against his instincts. He would treat this woman as a potential witness, and approach her testimony as he had that of the others who had come forward to help with the case. After all, what harm could it do? Pascal took off his jacket and told her to call him Ronnie. She, in turn, asked him to call her by her first name.

'Sabine, you say that Verona told you that the man who abducted her smelled. Did she mention how? You know, was he sweaty or unwashed?'

'She said he smelled of garbage.'

'Garbage?'

'Like the inside of a trash can.'

Something tickled Pascal unpleasantly, like a bug on his skin preparing to bite.

'What else did she notice? What about his hands?'

'He wore gloves. She saw them when he took her. He smothered her mouth to stop her from screaming.'

'What kind of gloves?'

Sabine didn't even pause.

'Green, but a dirty green. Hard-wearing, with padded fingers. A workman's gloves. They, too, smelled bad.'

'You're very sure of that,' said Pascal.

'Not I. Verona.'

'Well, someone has good recall, down to small details.'

'Aren't small details important in a case like this?'

'All details are important.'

'Well, there you are. I remember everything Verona told me. Don't you think you'd remember all that a dead girl said to you?'

'I can't say I've ever had the experience.'

'You should count yourself lucky.'

Sabine rummaged in her purse, produced a packet of tissues, and blew her nose noisily.

'Excuse me,' she said. 'Allergies.'

When she was done, she carefully placed the used tissue in a plastic Ziploc bag before sanitizing her hands. Years later, with the coming of COVID-19, such actions would become unremarkable. To Pascal, at this time, they only added to the woman's eccentricity.

'You still doubt me,' she said. 'I don't blame you – honestly, I don't – but it will become very tedious before too long. So why don't we just take it as given that you'll treat everything I say with a degree of skepticism, and therefore you won't have to keep expressing it aloud or by grimacing?'

If she was a fruit loop, as Pascal remained tempted to believe, she was at least a self-possessed, self-aware one. And there was that business about the abductor's odor—

'What else did she tell you?' he asked. 'Did she see a vehicle?'

'Verona thinks it was a cream car, or perhaps yellow. She was panicking, so she can't be sure. He put her face down in the trunk and covered her head. When she kept struggling, he hit her – not too hard, but enough to subdue her. Then he tied her hands behind her back and bound her legs.'

'And in all that time, she didn't get a look at his face?'

'He was wearing sunglasses, and a scarf wrapped across his mouth. Then the hood went on.'

'Anything else about the car?'

'It smelled much the way he did.'

'Like garbage?'

'Yes, like garbage.'

Pascal made another note, although it wasn't necessary. He knew he was procrastinating. He didn't yet want to progress to the next stage: the death of the girl. He was a father himself, of two daughters. One could not be both empathic and objective, and only the latter would serve any purpose here.

'You're hesitant to ask about what happened next, aren't you?' Sabine asked. 'Even though we need to talk more about how she died, or what happened after.'

'You ought to be a psychologist.'

'Maybe I am, in my small way.'

'For the living, I mean.'

'Oh, generally the living are even less interesting than the dead,' she said. 'Who'd want to listen to their problems, even at payment by the hour? Leastways, the dead have real cause for complaint.'

That, thought Pascal, was undeniable.

'You know you share your name with a philosopher?'

'Yeah, the wager guy.'

'Our lives are a bet on the existence or nonexistence of God,' said Sabine, 'or so he posited. I take you as a batter for the nonexistence team.'

'You take me right.'

'Have you ever heard of Pyrrho?'

'Can't say that I have. Was he Pascal's older brother?'

'Hardly, not unless he was unusually long-lived. He was a Greek philosopher, among the earliest skeptics – although one unlike yourself, skepticism being an oft-misused term.'

Pascal realized he'd just been given a ticking-off, even if he couldn't have said exactly how or why.

'Pyrrho,' continued Sabine, 'believed that one should suspend judgment on nonevident propositions – the existence of gods, for instance, or ghosts – because there can be no truth to them, only arguments for and against. You should consider my testimony as an argument "for".'

'And what do I set against it?'

'Whatever you choose.'

'Results?'

She thought about this.

'Results might do it, though you could ascribe them to coincidence if it made you feel better about the whole business.' She sniffed, and rummaged for another tissue. 'I ought to read more philosophy, but there are only so many hours in the day. I was more invested when I was younger, in the hope that it might assist me in understanding my responsibilities, but either I wasn't smart enough or the philosophers weren't. Then again, it may be that we were equally at fault.'

She stopped talking and waited expectantly for him to resume, as though their exchange should have put an end to any reasons he might have had for further hesitation.

'You said—' He corrected himself. '*Verona* said that he choked her to death.'

'Once more, she doesn't think it was his intention, but that's what it amounts to. She managed to get her hands free while she was in the trunk and attacked him when he unlocked the lid. He took hold of her throat to restrain her and fractured something inside. There's a little bone—'

'The hyoid,' said Pascal.

'Yes, that's it. I had to read up on it, but you just knew. That's impressive, although it bespeaks experience I'm glad I don't have. It seems the hyoid is very delicate, especially in children, or am I mistaken?'

'No, you're correct.'

'Then that may be what he broke inside her. Afterward, he buried her.'

'Was his face still obscured when he popped the trunk?'

'Yes, but in the moment before he could react, Verona caught sight of those aspects of the landscape that I've reproduced on paper for you.'

'Which brings us to the map.'

It resembled a sketch a child might have created, and Pascal experienced an absurd temptation to ask Sabine if, in fact, Verona herself might have been responsible. He saw a pen moving of its own volition while Sabine watched. He waited until the image had passed before continuing, even as he wondered if exposure to this woman was somehow polluting his rationalism. He was also, he had to admit, still smarting about that Pyrrho crack.

171

'I concede,' said Drew, 'that my artistic skills leave much to be desired.'

'Did Verona describe this scene to you?'

'Not exactly. Some of it she described, and some she . . . showed me.'

'Showed?'

'It's like a camera flash going off in a dark space, except the image is blurred. Like so much else, it's hard to explain.'

'So what did you see in this flash?'

'Trees. Dirt. Sky. Parts of those two buildings or houses, but only briefly.'

'Do you remember anything about them, anything that might distinguish them: numbers, a name on a mailbox?'

Sabine closed her eyes. Pascal waited, the second hand on his watch counting off almost a minute.

'A blue door on one,' she said at last, 'the one to the left. Junk in the yard, but I can't be sure what kind. And—'

She frowned in concentration.

'There was a shape hanging from one of the trees, like someone had strung up a deer to be skinned, but it wasn't that.'

Pascal did not speak. What she was telling him could not possibly be true, but he wished it to be so. He wanted desperately for her not to be a fake or a crazy, while at the same time needing her to be wrong – not only for the sake of his own convictions about the nature of this world but also for the Walters family.

Because if Sabine Drew was right, their daughter was dead.

'Look harder,' said Pascal. 'Take your time.'

She opened her eyes again.

'You know what it is, don't you?'

'I just want to be clear about everything,' he replied neutrally.

She huffed at his intransigence before reclosing her eyes. Her body relaxed, even as Pascal grew tenser. Was this some kind of psychic trance? Was she summoning the spirit of Verona Walters here, to this interview room? Would the air turn cold? Would Pascal hear his dead great-grandmother tell him where she'd hidden the family treasure transported from France by her ancestors, a running joke in the clan since it certainly amounted to no more than a couple of silver spoons and a bag of centimes? Was Ronnie Pascal, for the first time to his knowledge, about to be exposed to the presence of the uncanny?

Sabine unlidded one eye.

'In case you're wondering, this isn't a séance. It's just easier to concentrate without visual or auditory distractions.'

'The thought hadn't even crossed my mind.'

'Liar.'

Pascal could hear someone speaking outside the interview room door, and the ringing of a cell phone. He found that he was forcing himself not to think of the yard, like a gambler at a carnival sideshow who'd wagered a dollar that the mind reader couldn't guess the nature of the animal he'd been told to visualize. But even as he tried, the trees became clearer to him, and he saw what had been suspended from the lowest branch of an oak, the weight keeping it unmoving despite the breeze.

'It's a punching bag,' said Sabine Drew, her eyes still shut, 'a brown leather punching bag. It's been there for a long time: the grass beneath has been worn away by the movement of feet. There's a strap around the branch, then a carabiner hook, and finally a chain leading to the bag itself. The links are a bit rusty, but still solid.'

She opened her eyes.

'You've seen it,' she said. 'You know where it is. You know who *he* is, the one who took her.'

Pascal released the breath he'd been holding.

'Ms Drew—' he began.

'Sabine.'

'Sabine. Again, I'm obliged to advise you that if you've come by this information through some means other than those you're claiming, you should tell me now. Similarly, if this is some vendetta against a neighbor, or a guy who cut you off in the parking lot at Hannaford's, and you're manufacturing a story out of spite, I guarantee I'll have you jailed.'

She did not reply, and her eyes never left his face. It was so quiet that he could hear the gentle ticking of his watch.

'Well?' he said.

'Sorry I thought you were done, and had already figured out for yourself that I wasn't about to dignify it with a response.'

Pascal gathered up his notes, adding the map to them.

'If you don't mind staying here a while longer,' he said.

'Not at all. I do need to use the restroom, though, after which I will take you up on the offer of a coffee, and something sweet to go with it, if you can oblige me. My blood sugar is getting low.'

'I'll send Officer Loscarso back in,' said Pascal. 'She'll show you to the restroom, and ensure that you're fed and watered.'

'You make me sound like a horse.'

'A thoroughbred, I hope.'

'I hope so too. However unlikely it may sound, I'm telling you the truth.'

She stood and smoothed her skirt, a gesture more habitual than practical. Pascal didn't even want to guess when the skirt had last seen an iron. She placed a hand on his arm, the intimacy of the gesture the final step in his disarmament.

'Have you met him, the man who owns that punching bag?'

'Yes.'

'What does he look like?'

'He looks like a regular guy.'

'When you arrest him, remember that he didn't mean to kill Verona.'

'But he did kill her.'

'Yes,' she said. She looked desperately sad. 'A regular guy.'

'You sound almost sorry for him.'

'I suppose I am.'

'Why?'

She blew her nose, and added the used tissue to the others in her Ziploc bag.

'Because,' she said, 'I have some inkling of what's waiting for him on the other side.'

Chapter XXXVI

Ronnie Pascal had a problem, one he had to work through alone. He left the station house, and Sabine Drew, and walked by the banks of the Kennebec, heading south instead of north so that he would not be forced even to glimpse Mill Park, however distant it was from Union Street.

The man with the punching bag in his yard was named Lester Boulier. He lived with his mother at a two-building property in Sidney, about twelve miles north of Augusta. He had been interviewed about Verona Walters's disappearance because, some weeks previously, he'd been involved in an altercation with her father, who was one of his bosses at the Public Works Department. Boulier worked in sanitation, and had been accused of theft by a woman on one of his routes. Walters had been prepared to give Boulier the benefit of the doubt – sometimes good stuff was left out as garbage, either deliberately or accidentally, and one man's trash was another man's treasure – but that was before a pattern of such complaints began to emerge, all of them linked to routes Boulier worked. He had narrowly avoided losing his job, but was taken off the trucks, which he loved, and sent instead to the Hatch Hill Solid Waste Disposal and Recycling Facility out on Route 105.

When interviewed by Pascal and his partner, Erik McCard, Boulier maintained that he wasn't too bothered by his transfer, ascribing the whole affair to a series of misunderstandings. He was sorry he'd raised his voice to Chris Walters, he said, because he knew his boss was only doing his job. As for the day of Verona's disappearance, Boulier's alibi came from his mother Estelle, who declared he'd been home with her all morning and afternoon. But, as McCard pointed out when they left the property, Mrs Boulier wasn't too confident about what day today was, never mind any other day that her son might or might not have been at home. She was very elderly, and claimed to be able to hear better with her glasses on.

So Lester Boulier had remained a person of interest, but no more than that, given his alibi and a complete dearth of witnesses to the abduction. He'd since been reinterviewed by McCard, but he and his mother were sticking to their stories, Mrs Boulier being, if anything, still more insistent on her son's presence at home on the day in question. In light of what Sabine Drew had told him, Pascal was now considering the possibility that Lester Boulier could have coached his mother, or convinced her that a falsehood might be the truth.

After leaving Sabine, Pascal made a call to the Kennebec County Registry of Deeds, to be told that the Boulier family owned a total of forty acres around Sidney, largely planted with pine to be sold for Christmas trees. That constituted plenty of acreage in which to dispose of a body, although Pascal now had a crude map with a grave marked on it.

That brought him back to his main problem: he couldn't approach a judge or justice of the peace for a search warrant based on the evidence of a woman who claimed to be psychic, a medium, or whatever. Pascal couldn't say in what world that might constitute probable cause, but it wasn't this one. He could ask for Boulier's consent to search the property, though that was unlikely to be forthcoming if Verona Walters really was buried on it.

Except . . .

Lester Boulier wasn't the registered owner. That was his mother, who had inherited the land following the death of her husband in 1999. Of course, the old lady might be sharper than she acted, in which case she'd send them on their way before they could get their spades dirty, but not before calling her son, a lawyer, or both. On the other hand, if she really believed that spectacles improved her hearing, and refused to accept a Black man was president, they had a chance.

Pascal returned to Union Street and the interview room, where Sabine Drew and Officer Loscarso were now speaking about books from childhood. Pascal requested that Loscarso join him outside. What he was about to ask of her didn't necessarily make him feel good about himself, but potentially allowing Verona Walters's disappearance to remain unsolved would make him feel a whole lot worse.

'Your mom has Alzheimer's, right?'

'Yes,' said Loscarso. 'She has good and bad days, but lately she's started thinking I'm her sister. So far it's harder for my pop, my brother, and me than it is for her. My mom doesn't show any signs of being disturbed by it.'

'Long may that continue, for her sake.'

'Amen.'

'Here's the thing. I might need your help on the Alzheimer's front.'

'You mean, help you talk to someone who has it?'

'No,' said Pascal, 'I was thinking more along the lines of taking advantage of them.'

Minutes later, Pascal was thanking Sabine Drew for her time and help, and telling her that she could go.

'What are you planning to do?' she asked.

'We're going to attempt to search this man's property.'

'Attempt?'

'What you've shared with me isn't even close to enough for a warrant. We'll have to find another way, but you've given us information that may prove crucial.'

Sabine remained seated.

'Lou,' she said.

'What?'

'That's the only detail I've kept back. Verona thought his first name might be Lou. Someone called him on the phone, while she was in the trunk. It came over the speaker in the car, and she heard the caller use that name.'

Pascal experienced the sharp, familiar pain of disappointment. All his doubts threatened to flood back. He was about to expend a great deal of effort, and possibly endanger his career, by pursuing an elderly, vulnerable woman and her son on the evidence of a psychic. Sure, the names Lester and Lou both started with the letter L, but—

Ah, Jesus.

'Boo,' he said.

'Excuse me?'

'Boo,' Pascal repeated. 'That's what his friends call him. He told us, back when we first spoke to him.'

'Not Mr Boulier. Just Boo.'

Sabine Drew buttoned her cardigan and put on her coat.

'Boo,' she said. 'You clever girl, Verona.'

Chapter XXXVII

The discussion about how best to handle Lester Boulier and his mother took place behind closed doors; officially, it never took place at all. Present were Pascal; his partner McCard; Loren Noyes, deputy chief of the Augusta PD; and Rodd Turin, the commander of the Bureau of Criminal Investigations, who had served as Pascal's mentor when he first joined the force. Pascal shared with them exactly what Sabine had told him, leaving nothing out, not even his own qualms, including the possibility that he was interpreting what he had heard in a manner that would justify targeting Lester Boulier. He wanted Boulier to be the culprit, he knew, because he, as much as the Walters family, needed closure.

When Pascal was done, Turin turned to McCard.

'What do you think of all this?'

'I only just got here,' said McCard.

'You brought your ears. I can see them on the sides of your head.'

McCard jerked a thumb at Pascal. 'Then whatever he said.'

'You know how many psychics contact us for major cases?' asked Noyes. 'We could open a touring show, we got so many of them on the books.'

'I don't even believe in God,' said Pascal, 'so I can't figure out if psychics represent an easier or harder sell.'

Noyes addressed Turin.

'If this gets out, we'll be inundated with crystal gazers, not to mention being made to look a laughing stock.'

'Only if Sabine Drew is wrong,' said Pascal.

'And maybe not even then,' said McCard. 'We've had no solid leads so far. To be seen to be doing something is better than to be perceived as not doing enough.'

'We've been working flat out on this,' said Turin, 'you and Pascal as much as anyone.'

'Yeah, I know that, and you know that, but tell the public.'

'Boulier fits,' said Pascal.

'Fits how?' asked Turin.

'We were looking at known pedophiles, as well as men with previous criminal records involving harm to children, but Boulier was clean. Either he'd been careful in the past, or this was his first time. I'm now leaning toward the latter. Again, assuming Drew is correct, and we take at face value what she's telling us, Boulier panicked when Verona lashed out at him. If he'd been practiced at abduction, a young girl wouldn't have managed to get the better of him, however briefly; and if he'd planned the snatch, he'd have come better equipped. He'd have used cable ties, not rope, and brought along a proper gag to keep Verona quiet.'

'You're thinking crime of opportunity?'

'Yes,' said Pascal, 'if it's him.'

'If.'

Noyes spoke again.

'Suppose you do find something,' he said to Pascal. 'How will you explain it to the press or a judge?'

'I'll tell the truth.'

'And if we find nothing?'

'Then we've lost nothing.'

Noyes let it play out in his head, taking time to explore each divergent path, following it to its end.

'How do you want to play it?' he said at last. 'We ought to inform the state police and the Kennebec County Sheriff's Office, out of courtesy.'

'If we go in heavy,' warned McCard, 'we might spook the old woman.'

'And if too many people know that we're looking at Boulier,' said Pascal, 'it'll send vibrations down the wire, the kind he might pick up.'

'Gotta tell them,' said Turin. 'You know how it is.'

'Then the less notice they receive, the better.'

'I can live with that,' said Noyes. 'When do you want to start?'

'Tomorrow morning,' said Pascal, 'after Boulier leaves for work.

He's at Hatch Hill right now, but won't be for much longer. Doesn't give us enough time to work on the mother.'

'What about monitoring Boulier in the interim?' asked Turin.

'He clocks off in an hour. We can stay with him until he enters his property, then put two men in the woods across from the entrance for the night. It won't be comfortable, but the overtime is always welcome. It's one route in and out, so we'll spot him if he leaves. There's a self-storage place on Middle Road. We can station a second car out back of it in case he heads north, and keep another behind Annie's Variety if he goes south.'

'Can't do that and not inform the other agencies,' said Turin. 'If someone makes a call about strangers in cars, you'll have twitchy state troopers shining lights in their eyes.'

'My brother uses that self-storage,' said Pascal. 'No one goes there after dark, and even if they do, you'd need X-ray vision to spot a car among the trees. Same for Annie's. It closes at eight p.m., and after that it's deader than dirt. Worse comes to worst, we'll show our badges to the troopers and ask them to forget they ever saw us.'

'If Estelle Boulier refuses to allow a search,' said Noyes, 'we'll have tipped our hand to her son. We can't keep eyes on him all the time, not over forty acres of private woodland. If Verona is buried there, he'll have ample opportunity to dispose of the body. Lord knows what kind of chemical crap he has access to out at Hatch Hill. He could probably dissolve her in a barrel.'

'Then,' said Pascal, 'we have to make sure that Estelle Boulier doesn't turn us down.'

The night was uneventful. Lester Boulier was followed to his home and did not leave it until morning, except for half an hour spent hitting the punching bag before dark. The next day, he was tailed all the way to Hatch Hill. As soon as he commenced work, Pascal and Loscarso drove to the Boulier property and parked in the yard shared by the two houses. Estelle Boulier lived in the main one, while her son occupied the smaller, permitting each of them privacy and independence while allowing Lester to keep a close eye on his mother.

Estelle answered her door on the third ring.

'Been waiting long?'

'Not at all,' said Pascal.

'I must have missed the bell,' she said. 'I didn't have my glasses on. What can I do for you? My son's not here, if you're looking for him. He's at work.'

They identified themselves and displayed their badges. Pascal reminded Estelle that they'd met before, but she didn't recall him.

'Would you mind if we came in?' he said. 'We'd like to talk with you about something.'

'I ought to call Lester,' she replied. 'He looks after my affairs.'

'Do you really want to do that?' said Loscarso. 'He's probably very busy, and this won't take long.'

Pascal knew that Loscarso was ambivalent about what they were doing. She hadn't signed up as a police officer to manipulate confused seniors. Pascal had been forced to remind her that Verona Walters was five years old, and potentially buried on this woman's land.

Estelle Boulier winced at the idea of her son being disturbed. Conceivably, Lester had a temper, or simply suffered from the occasional moments of frustration that were an inevitable consequence of dealing with a parent whose memory was failing. Whatever the reason, his mother had no desire to irritate him further.

They sat with her in a living room with faded wallpaper and scuffed boards, in which only the TV was modern. Loscarso asked Estelle about her late husband, and the two officers were shown faded wedding photos over bad coffee. Estelle could remember her wedding day, and the names of everyone in the pictures, but when Pascal tried to turn the conversation to their previous meeting, she again regarded him blankly, even though he'd reminded her of the circumstances of it on the doorstep only a short time before. He was conscious of time passing. They'd made discreet inquiries about Lester Boulier's routines, and established that he took his lunch at Hatch Hill, but Pascal had been a detective for long enough – had been alive long enough – to know that the last thing you wanted to happen was generally the first thing that did.

'Mrs Boulier,' said Loscarso, sensing Pascal's growing impatience, 'we were hoping to take a look around your property – if it's okay with you.'

'Why would you want to do that?'

'We've lost something, and we think it might be here.'

'What did you lose?'

'A little girl. Her name is Verona.'

Estelle scratched at her bony hands, which resembled the claws of a bird. 'I haven't seen a little girl.'

'That's a lot of land you own, most of it planted with evergreens,' said Pascal. 'Hard to see much, trees excepted.'

'I ought to call Lester,' said Estelle. 'He looks after my affairs.'

'I know,' said Loscarso, 'but you didn't want to bother him, remember, in case he was busy. I bet he works hard.'

'He does. He's a good boy. He looks after my affairs.'

'We can always call him later to explain. No sense in hauling him from his place of work without cause.'

'I guess. He won't be mad, will he? Because he looks after my affairs.'

'We'll make sure he understands,' said Loscarso. 'Do we have your permission to search the property?'

'As long as Lester won't be mad.'

Pascal didn't want to interrupt, but they needed more than that. He tapped his right foot against Loscarso's left and set his phone to record.

'Is that a yes?' asked Loscarso.

Estelle Boulier's eyes went blank and Pascal was convinced their moment had passed. Then Estelle spoke again:

'Yes,' she said, 'you can take a look around the property. But don't leave a mess.'

It was decided that Loscarso should stay with Estelle. They didn't want her to reconsider and try calling her son. While they had her permission to enter and conduct a search, a smart lawyer could seize on her mental condition to seek an emergency court order preventing them from proceeding. Loscarso, therefore, was forced to make more coffee and look at further photos of the dead before Estelle eventually fell asleep in her chair.

By then, the cadaver dogs were already yapping.

*

183

At her home in Haynesville, Sabine Drew sat in the kitchen, a newspaper open to the crossword. Her mother was nearby, clearing up after breakfast. She turned at the sound of a cup shattering on the floor, to see her daughter stretch out her right hand to caress empty air.

'Oh, honey,' said Sabine. 'Yes, I hear the dogs too. They're coming to get you. They're coming to set you free.'

Pine trees spread their roots thinly, and there were only so many clear patches of ground in which Lester Boulier could have interred Verona Walters.

They found her within the hour.

Chapter XXXVIII

Lester Boulier was operating a forklift when the convoy of police cars arrived at Hatch Hill and pulled up outside the main building. He killed the engine, climbed out, and wiped his brow on his sleeve as Pascal and Loscarso walked toward him. Pascal had wanted Loscarso to be present. Without her, they couldn't have talked Estelle Boulier into allowing them onto her property. Loscarso deserved to be there at the finish. If nothing else, it would help ease her conscience about what she'd been asked to do.

Boulier didn't try to run. He didn't even look especially unhappy to see them coming. Around them all work ceased, and they advanced on Boulier to a chorus of gulls.

'Lester Boulier,' said Pascal, 'I'm arresting you for the abduction and murder of Verona Walters.'

He Mirandized Boulier while Loscarso cuffed him. Boulier reeked of trash, the same stink of which Verona Walters had spoken to Sabine Drew. He probably always smelled of it, thought Pascal, even after a shower. You worked with something long enough and it became part of you, changed you. Dangling from Boulier's belt was a pair of green work gloves, but Pascal saw that they were comparatively new. He'd surely burned the others, the ones he was wearing when he killed the child.

Boulier had said nothing so far, barely acknowledging Pascal and Loscarso beyond turning his back for the cuffs. His gaze was drawn to the surrounding hills of garbage, as though this was a landscape he wished to fix in his memory before being deprived of it forever. Only when they began to lead him to the car did he speak.

'I just wanted to frighten her father some,' he said. 'I was going to let her go after a couple of hours.'

It might even have been true; if it was, the pointlessness somehow made everything worse. But it didn't much matter one way or the other, not to Verona Walters and not to her family, so Pascal didn't bother replying. They put Boulier in the car and closed the door on him. Pascal looked at Loscarso. She was pale and her hands were shaking. She walked to the front of the car and sat on the hood. Pascal joined her as two officers went to search Boulier's locker.

'I thought it would feel different,' she said softly, 'like some kind of victory, but it doesn't, not at all.'

'The worse the crime, the less it feels that way,' said Pascal. 'But it's an ending. That will have to do.'

'I want to be with you when you inform the parents.'

'Okay.'

He thought he understood why. Some suffering was so great that a failure to assume even a fraction of its burden was a sin. He took his cell phone from his pocket.

'I should call Sabine Drew to let her know what's happened.'

'She probably already knows,' said Loscarso.

Pascal expected to catch her smiling, but she wasn't.

'Nevertheless,' he said, 'it would be polite.'

'Yes, it would.'

Loscarso stared at her feet.

'Do you really think a dead girl spoke to her?' she asked.

'I don't know,' said Pascal, 'but I hope not, truly. The difficulty is, I don't have an alternative explanation that makes any sense.'

'Are you afraid of ghosts?'

'No,' said Pascal, 'I just don't want to have to believe in them, because once that starts, there'll be no end to it. Next thing you know, I'll have an angel bumper sticker on my car, or turn vegan.'

'I'm vegan,' said Loscarso. She sounded mildly affronted.

Pascal eased himself from the hood of the car.

'You don't say? And I was just beginning to like you.'

III

There must have been a moment, at the beginning, where we could have said – no. But somehow we missed it.

Tom Stoppard, *Rosencrantz & Guildenstern Are Dead*

Chapter XXXIX

M attia Reggio had made a few more calls since his conversation with the journalist Hazel Sloane. Some of them required him to renew old acquaintances, which Reggio generally preferred not to do, but he didn't have any personal contacts at the Maine Bureau of Motor Vehicles who might have been able to help him trace the owner of a car. The difficulty in reaching out – or, more particularly, in extending a hand into the past – was that any help came with a price attached, the bill to be paid now or in the future. You asked a favor, you owed a favor, that was how it worked. But if anyone came looking for something especially awkward in return – meaning a service that might conceivably land Reggio in trouble with the law – he would try to work around it. At worst, a couple of people still owed *him*, and he'd find a way to pass the debt to them. This was one of the reasons Reggio had abjured criminality: it was so damn hard to keep track of one's obligations, and the debit and credit columns never balanced the way they should.

After a lot of how-you-doin', Reggio was now in possession of a name and address for the owner of the vehicle that had attempted to follow him from Cumberland County Jail: Ellar Michaud, 56, a resident of Gretton, up in Piscataquis County. Reggio had never been to Gretton, and hadn't even been aware of the town's existence before the information came through. He located it on Google Maps, but there wasn't much to locate: a few bars, a gas station, a diner or two, and stores that either sold only what people needed or resold what some of them no longer did. If there was anything worth seeing in the place, it was well hidden.

Michaud lived some way out of town on Private Road 7, an address that suggested holding parties for the neighborhood kids

189

wasn't high on the owner's list of priorities. Reggio pulled up a satellite image of the area – nothing was secret anymore, he reflected: a man could run but he couldn't hide – and spotted what had to be the Michaud residence, given the absence of much else resembling a home in the vicinity. The trees were so thick that Reggio could barely make out the turnoff from the main road; then, farther on, was the roof of the house itself, so that it seemed a dwelling unreachable, unless one elected to trek through the forest on foot. But somewhere under that foliage was undoubtedly an access trail, even as its actual course was open to speculation.

Reggio zoomed in on the house and thought he could discern what might have been a figure in the yard: a blue shape with a pale blur for a face, one arm raised to shield the eyes, as though the man – Reggio was pretty sure it was a man – had somehow sensed surveillance and emerged to determine the source, before realizing it was coming from somewhere far above his head. Of course, Reggio knew better. He was just projecting oddness where he had no cause to find it. Yet he couldn't shake the feeling that this man was looking, not at some satellite invisible to the naked eye, but at *him*; that it was Reggio's interest of which he was aware, and not some high-tech lens. Abruptly, Reggio killed the screen and had the strangest premonition that, were he to return in a few minutes, the figure in the yard would be gone, as in some lost episode of *The Twilight Zone*, with Rod Serling promising only bad luck and misery to anyone foolish enough to trespass on 'Private Road 7'.

Reggio shifted his attention to the official Piscataquis County website, where he located the link to the Maine Registry of Deeds. It required him to make a user account, which he did after first determining that it wouldn't cost him anything. He could have logged in as a guest, but he wouldn't have been given printing privileges, and he might as well have documentary evidence of any useful information he came across in the form of maps, plans, or land records. He hadn't yet decided what he was going to do with whatever he collated, or so he told himself. He could pass it on to Moxie Castin, or Parker, and let one of them figure out what it all meant. Then again, he was open to taking a little road trip, because it was always good for a man to explore new vistas. And he had a point to prove, to Parker and himself.

The county land records dated from 1948, but some of the plans came from as far back as 1812, although only those from 1970 onward included images. Michaud was a common enough name in Maine, and the region around Gretton had more than a few of them. It took Reggio some time, because he had to open and read each document, but with patience he weeded out the ones that weren't pertinent, whether they were ultimately related to the object of his interest or not, to be left with index data from the start of the nineteenth century relating to 'Michaud, Jotham T.', registered owner of fifty acres that roughly corresponded to the relevant area off Private Road 7, then referred to only as 'a certain lot or parcel of land westerly of Sullivan Creek'.

Jotham T. Michaud, already in situ at the time of the earliest records, had begun extending his family's initial holding by purchasing tracts of adjoining territory. Reggio worked through them all, printing off each item of paperwork and making note of any new names that were mentioned, until he had amassed a pile of deeds, probates, leases, liens, wills, and death affidavits forming an official history of the Michaud family's presence in Gretton. Among them was evidence of a second house on the land in the form of plans lodged. But when he returned to the Google satellite image – the figure in the yard thankfully still present, so in your face, Rod Serling – he could see no trace of it. Perhaps, he thought, it had rotted away or been demolished.

He glanced at the clock and saw that he'd been at his computer for the best part of three hours. He couldn't remember the last time he'd spent so long staring at its screen. In the main, it was useful for looking up solutions to baffling crossword clues, or watching videos of old shows and ball games on YouTube. He rarely even bothered with email. Yet he'd surprised himself by how much he'd found out, up to and including Ellar Michaud's status as the current owner of the property on Private Road 7, having inherited it following the death of his father, Normand, in 1996.

But one pressing question remained: Why should Ellar Michaud, scion of a family that seemed to have put down roots in Piscataquis back when God was a boy, be interested in the movements of Colleen Clark, a young mother accused of abducting and killing her child?

Before switching off his computer, Reggio ensured that his browsing history was deleted. Force of habit: never leave a trail. He then went to his office closet and recovered a lockbox from the highest shelf, far beyond the reach of even the most determined grandchild. From it, he took a snubnose Smith & Wesson Model 10. The gun was nearly fifty years old, the same one he'd carried back when he was running with Cadillac Frank. Model 10s had more than a century of reliability behind them, were easy to carry concealed, and, unlike a pistol, would never jam. A man needed nothing more from a gun.

Reggio had never taken a life with his Model 10 – he'd fired it a couple of times, but he didn't think he'd ever hit anyone, or not that he'd heard about later. He'd whipped a few heads with the muzzle and the butt, if only when all attempts at reasoning had failed, but he'd never signed up to put someone's lights out permanently. Every guy he knew who'd killed for the Office ended up either dead or in jail, every single one of them, but he might just have hung out with some very unlucky people. If so, he'd done his best to make sure their bad luck didn't rub off on him, which was why he was currently at liberty, despite having secret blood on his hands. He very much intended for that state of affairs to continue until he expired of some cause that didn't involve a bullet. He'd take the revolver along on his road trip, though, because you never knew just how the Ellar Michauds of this world might take it into their heads to respond to an unexpected visitor.

In Reggio's experience, every man who truly valued his privacy had something to hide.

Chapter XL

Sabine Drew watched the private investigator enter the Great Lost Bear: one could tell a lot from the way a man occupied a public space. (Women were different, less prone to imposing themselves, or annexing territory.) The detective held the door for the older couple walking in behind him, but she noticed that he used it as an opportunity to survey the area immediately around and then beyond him, his attention briefly alighting on customers and staff alike. She wondered if he was aware of doing it, so ingrained had the behavior become. She didn't detect any fear in his movements, even though, from what she knew, some apprehension would have been justified. A man who has been shot once will do his best to avoid being shot again, but a man who has been shot multiple times will wake from his sleep to the fading sound of bullets fired, unable ever to be fully at ease for the rest of his days. But in the investigator's face, Sabine saw only a preparedness, an alertness. He'd grown used to danger, she thought, and his psychological processes, both conscious and unconscious, had adapted themselves to it. He was simultaneously hard prey and evolved predator.

The bar owner intercepted him near the door and they exchanged a few words. Sabine adjusted the front of her shirt, and picked food crumbs from her old jeans. She found herself wishing she'd put in more effort when selecting her outfit, before realizing that it wouldn't have made any difference. Her entire wardrobe was uniformly functional, down to the sole nice black dress she kept for funerals. Most of the time it didn't matter, but suddenly, in this bar, with the investigator approaching, it did.

Now here he was, his shadow and hers uniting briefly in intimacy.

'Ms Drew?' he said, as she got to her feet. 'My name is Parker.'

He extended a hand, an instinctive gesture. Sabine hadn't shaken hands with anyone in a long time, certainly not since before the pandemic, but she accepted his – and was instantly among the dead.

Chapter XLI

A series of trails cut through the woods from both sides of Private Road 7, like branches growing from a tree trunk, narrowing the farther they extended from the parent limb. Some had become desire paths for deer, and Ellar Michaud could smell their spoor as he walked. The animals roamed unhindered on Michaud territory. Ellar did not hunt on this land, and no others were permitted to hunt there either. This was, in its way, sacred ground, although the Michaud prohibition on hunting had not prevented Ellar from arming himself, before leaving home, with a Tikka T3x Superlite bolt-action rifle loaded with a ten-round magazine.

He carried a flashlight, but had not turned it on. The moon was full and bright, illuminating the way, yet even without it he would not have struggled. These were his woods and he knew them well. He had walked them with his father and mother as they tested him on the names and properties of trees, bushes, leaves, and berries until there was none he could not identify. He had no respect for those unable to do likewise, even if all they owned was a single small garden. If a man was not intimately familiar with his environment and respectful of it, how could he position himself securely in the world? The answer was that he could not, and so nature would not help him when he needed help, and in time would rid itself of him. This Ellar firmly believed. One just had to look at the fires that raged each summer, the flooded subways, the proliferating viruses, to see the truth of it.

Only when he left the trail did he use the flashlight. Any paths that had once existed here had since been reclaimed by low foliage, while the tree canopy shadowed the ground by day and left it fully dark at night. After five minutes of walking, the lineaments of Kit No. 174 were revealed to him against the night sky. He paused before the steel door at the front. He had always been aware of the building's power, but sensed it more profoundly in the dark. What lay within grew sensate and active only once dusk fell.

Even after all this time, Ellar still marveled at its existence, although it had, until recently, been dormant – dead, he might have hoped, if not aloud. Its cycles were irregular: at least one whole generation of Michauds had been born, lived out their lives, and died without ever being called upon to witness its reemergence. But they had remained cognizant of its presence, as one might of a bear in hibernation on one's land. To stand before Kit No. 174 was to be aware that this was no empty house, and once inside, the basement floor seemed always about to rise and fall with the inhalations and exhalations of its secret occupant.

Ellar carried a spade over his shoulder and a sack tucked into his belt. He unlocked the door, entered the house, and went straight to the basement. With his knowledge of the occupant, he would have preferred to have completed his task in daylight, but any activities concerning Kit No. 174 were better carried out under cover of night, particularly ones as delicate as this.

He took the stairs carefully. While they were well maintained, he had suffered a misstep halfway down only a few weeks earlier and wrenched his ankle. Had he broken it, he would have been forced to hobble all the way home with a branch for support, because no cell phone worked out here. It was a dead zone, in every sense.

Finally, he reached the bottom step and stared at the empty dirt floor. He should have been looking at a small set of human remains, but something had gone wrong. He ran the flashlight a second time, as though expecting limbs to reveal themselves in a corner, extruded from the earth like pale fungi sprouting in the gloom.

Ellar sat on the step to wait. Minutes went by. He tapped the blade rhythmically against the dirt, as though that might help, with no result. After fifteen minutes he stood. It was clear: he would not be getting anything of the child back, not tonight. The occupant was not done with it, and like a dog gnawing on a rotten bone, it could not be made to understand the necessity of surrendering its prize.

For the first time in many years, Ellar Michaud was worried.

Chapter XLII

What I knew about Sabine Drew came from the pair of missing persons cases on which she'd worked, those of Verona Walters and Edie Brook. Both had ended badly, if in different ways, the second of them so traumatically that it had transformed Drew into a recluse. But between those two investigations came a brief period during which she was one of the most conspicuous people in the state, and among the best-known mediums in the Northeast, assuming you accepted the reality of psychic phenomena. If you didn't, then you were probably of the opinion that Drew had come lucky once, but struck out a second time when it mattered.

I wasn't sure what I believed. I knew Ronnie Pascal, because Maine was a big state but a small society, and the law enforcement community was smaller still. Pascal had been perfectly straight with everyone about how the Augusta PD had come to unearth the remains of Verona Walters, although the more peculiar details – Sabine Drew's awareness of what the girl had for breakfast on the morning she disappeared, or her abductor's smell – he retained for private distribution, and the discussions that took place where only police were gathered. Pascal was retired, but his opinion that Drew was the real deal had not altered. Coming to terms with this had cost him, shifting his view of existence in a manner that he struggled to articulate. As far as I was aware, he remained an agnostic, but willing to accept that something more than oblivion might await him after death. Even what happened subsequently with Edie Brook hadn't caused him to doubt her, but by then he was in the minority.

Sabine Drew was broadly unchanged. She had always come across as older than her years, but in seclusion the clock might almost have stopped for her. True, her hair showed more signs of gray, but her face was unlined and bore the ruddiness of a life lived largely in the open air. I put out a hand to her and she grasped it, but her grip immediately dropped away. She swayed, and some of the color faded from her cheeks. I thought she might be about to faint, but as I moved to help her, she waved me back, breaking contact.

'The wine must have gone to my head,' she said.

She sat, reached for the water glass on her table, and drank until it was empty. I waved a server over and asked for a refill, as well as a club soda for myself. I'd had enough beer, alcohol-free or otherwise, for the time being.

'They told you who I was, didn't they?' she asked, once the soda and water had arrived.

'Dave, the owner, recognized you. You could have saved him the trouble by just giving your name to Paulie.'

'I wasn't certain you'd come if I did,' she said, 'although the fact that I took the trip down here in the first place means I must have been hopeful. I hadn't necessarily thought the whole business through. I've fallen out of the habit of dealing with strangers. I don't have much of a social life.'

I noticed that she was unwilling to look directly at me. It made conversation awkward.

'Do I have something on my face?' I asked.

'Not that I can see. Why do you ask?'

'You're having trouble maintaining eye contact. If you're not incurably shy, or trying to conceal some deception, then I must need a better mirror.'

She put down her glass, composed herself, and looked straight at me.

'Is that better?'

'Much,' I said.

'I've heard a lot about you.'

'Likewise.'

'What I've heard doesn't do you justice. Based on what I'd read, I assumed you to be a committed, if sometimes violent man, but you're more than that, much more. You see them, don't you?'

'Them?'

198

'The dead, some of them – and worse than the dead, even if the dead are bad enough. Forgive my bluntness, but I place a premium on honesty.'

I didn't reply. This was not a subject I was prepared to indulge. Sitting with a professed medium, as with a priest, presupposed some discussion of the numinous, but there were limits. As it turned out, Drew wasn't waiting for a response. This was less a conversation and closer to a reading.

'I heard that you died on the operating table after you were shot,' she continued. 'I can believe it now. When you crossed back, you left part of yourself behind.' She frowned. 'Or was it always missing? It's hard to be sure. Whatever the truth may be, there's a darkness inside you, like a spot on a lung, but impenetrable. And around you' – I could see her choosing her next words carefully – 'traces of the dead, trailing like gossamer.'

I sipped my soda.

'This,' I said, 'may be why you struggle to maintain a social circle.'

She laughed spontaneously. It was a lovely, bright sound. The action transformed her face and lit up her eyes, the best and liveliest part of her.

'Too much information?'

'You need to save something for the second date.'

The laughter faded slowly, leaving her puzzled by its unfamiliarity.

'I hope you see loved ones,' she said, 'and that you gain consolation from them. I've never been able to see those to whom I was close. I tried reaching out to my mother after she died because I missed her so, but she was gone. I like to think it was because her death was peaceful and natural. There was little pain to her passing, and no rage. The dead are not meant to vacillate. If they do, it's only because of anger and hurt. In my experience, there are no happy ghosts.'

'Do you still see them?'

'Oh yes, but I choose not to engage, for the most part.'

I tried to recall an odder recent conversation and failed.

'I was told,' I said, 'that you might have some information about the Clark case.'

199

'I think I know where Henry Clark can be found.'

'Alive?'

'Is that meant to be a trick? Because I doubt even his own parents believe he's still alive, not with all the blood, though I'm sure they're hoping.'

'I was hoping, too,' I said.

I meant it, and she saw that it was so.

'I'm sorry, but Henry Clark is dead. Whatever is left of him lies in the vicinity of the town of Gretton.'

'How do you know?'

'I hear him crying.'

'Why? Do you live near Gretton?'

It sounded sarcastic, which wasn't my intention.

'Are you trying to alienate me, Mr Parker? If so, you're doing a better job than most.'

'I don't know how these things work.'

'These "things"? Perhaps I've misjudged you in more ways than one. Whatever that black mass inside you is concealing, it's not a surfeit of common sense or good manners.'

She began gathering her things. I raised a conciliatory hand.

'I think you're hearing an insult where none was meant,' I said. 'I know it must have taken a great deal to bring you here, and it could be that you were primed for rejection. You may not like some of my questions, but I'm asking them only because I don't know the answers.'

She wasn't used to compromise. Those who live alone rarely are – I could speak from experience – but I saw that she was still inclined to depart.

'My daughter,' I said.

'What?'

'You asked about the ones I see. I see my dead daughter.' I lowered my hand. It suddenly felt very heavy. 'Among others.'

Chapter XLIII

Ellar Michaud left Kit No. 174, the sack still empty, the spade unused. So distracted was he that he failed to notice the man standing on the far side of Sullivan Creek. Only when he moved did Michaud react, dropping the spade and reaching for the hunting rifle. But he held the weapon low and did not raise it to his shoulder, not yet.

'Ho!' said the man by the water, raising his hands. 'I'm just taking a walk in the moonlight. I didn't mean to startle you.'

He stepped forward, emerging from the shadows so Ellar could see his face. Ellar thought his name might have been Ungar, Lars Ungar – not that it was of any importance. They would never be friends, because this man did not belong in the woods.

'You ought not to be there,' said Ellar.

'I'm on our side of the creek. I'm not trespassing.'

'Our' side, noticed Ellar. This, from an interloper.

'That's a matter of dispute,' said Ellar.

'Mr Hickman says otherwise.'

The Hickmans had owned the land east of the Michaud property for more than a century and a half, although their interests and those of the Michauds had not come into direct conflict until the 1970s, when Dennen Hickman – Den to his friends, or those who'd admit to it – was still in his early twenties. The Michauds had long been trying to induce the Hickmans to sell them a parcel of land that would act as a buffer to the east, extending far beyond Sullivan Creek, but the Hickmans had refused all reasonable offers. As a result, the two families fell into a state of cold enmity that had persisted for the best part of fifty years.

But over the last decade or so, the animosity between the Michauds and the Hickmans had descended into outright loathing.

The reason for the deterioration in relations was Sullivan Creek itself, which had, due to natural causes – principally the collapse of a promontory back in 1986 – begun to alter course until it flowed farther west than before. The Michauds believed it now moved through their property, but Den Hickman had argued that the original deed ceded to his family the territory east of Sullivan Creek – it was there in black and white for anyone to read – and the stream's new channel did not alter that fact.

All of which should have been incidental, a source of irritation to the Michauds but not much else, given the size of the affected terrain, but this would have been to ignore the attachment of families to their land, especially those with a lineage dating back centuries. In this case, Sullivan Creek's redirected meanderings also brought it close, at its westernmost point, to Kit No. 174 – so close, in fact, that from the far bank one could pick out the roof through a gap in the trees.

To compound the difficulty, Den Hickman, possibly as a means of further antagonizing his neighbors, had recently rented out a patch of clear ground to a group of men and women to form a semipermanent settlement. They varied in age from late teens to midforties, and a few were related to one another. According to local gossip, the ones who weren't related were sleeping with each other, and some of the ones who were related might have been sleeping with each other, too. A number of the men and women sported tattoos, among them the twin lightning bolts of the Schutzstaffel, along with the good old swastika, beloved of inbreds, peckerwoods, and general shitheads everywhere, as well as an Iron Cross or two. A few also had Russian flag bumper stickers on their vehicles, and one of their trucks had been sprayed with the letter Z, in the manner of the Russian tanks in Ukraine. Ungar was one of the old-school types, with a small jailhouse swastika tattooed at the corner of his left eye. It crinkled when he smiled.

Ellar Michaud didn't pay politics a lot of mind and had never voted in his life, but he knew enough about history to recognize that if the guy next to you was wearing a swastika, you were keeping the wrong kind of company; and if a whole such tribe moved onto the land adjoining your own, they presented a quandary that was moral as much as anything else. They could take their promises about keeping to their own side of Sullivan Creek and shove them up their asses, because that was what the Nazis had said about the Danube.

Den Hickman had recently hosted a brown bag lunch in Gretton for a speaker from the William Stonehurst Foundation for American Ideas, a political and social pressure group founded by the retired Portland businessman Bobby Stonehurst, better known as Bobby Ocean. As far as Ellar Michaud could tell, the Stonehurst Foundation didn't like Jews, Blacks, Asians, Mexicans, feminists, queers or Catholics. Ellar didn't know very many people in any of those categories personally, a few Catholics aside, and wasn't likely to lose sleep should something bad befall them, but he wasn't about to go out of his way to make that happen, either. Some of those living on Hickman's land had attended the lunch meeting, and one of them had apparently threatened to beat the shit out of a reporter from the *Bangor Daily News* in the parking lot afterward. It might even have been Ungar, currently hollering at Ellar Michaud over Sullivan Creek. Ellar reckoned that, sooner or later, these people were going to attract serious attention from the law, government agencies, protestors, or the media, none of which would be helpful to the Michauds. Ensuring the outsiders' departure from Hickman land was, therefore, an issue of some urgency.

'You'd better be on your way,' he told Ungar. 'I don't even like you looking at my property.'

Ungar grinned.

'See you got yourself a house back there,' he said. 'Anyone living in it?'

Ellar returned the gun to his shoulder and prepared to walk away. He was already done here.

'Maybe you ought to consider renting it out,' continued Ungar. 'Some of us are tired of trailers. We like it around here. We're contemplating a more substantial relocation. Isn't that right, fellas?'

More men were emerging from the trees. Ellar counted four, five, six of them, two with rifles at port arms and the rest with pistols in their belts. He wondered how long they'd been there, watching and listening. He should have spotted them earlier. He was growing careless, but he'd learn from this mistake.

'We should try to get along better,' said Ungar, 'seeing as how we're neighbors and all.'

'I don't think so,' said Ellar.

'That's just a shame. You don't want us as enemies, Ellar. We're here to defend the American way of life, and those who are not with us are against us.'

Ellar regarded him evenly.

'Boy,' he said, 'you ever call me by my given name again, and I'll hurt you.'

'Well then I guess that's just the way it's going to be. We'll be seeing you, *Ellar*.'

Ungar retreated into the woods, the others slowly joining him, until none were left in sight. Only then did Ellar Michaud continue on his way, but he did not turn his back on the creek, keeping it in sight until he, too, was taken by the trees.

Chapter XLIV

The Senzati Jet Sprinter was a luxury people carrier based on Mercedes-Benz technology, a lighter version of the original Sprinter. Its captain's chairs could be configured in club seating for meetings, and it boasted its own private bathroom. It was as close as one could get to a private jet while traveling by road, and was popular with discerning executives.

On Interstate 91 in Connecticut, just beyond the Meriden exit, one particular Senzati Jet Sprinter currently lay sprawled across two lanes of traffic. A truck had hit it side-on after the Senzati's driver appeared to lose control of the vehicle. Since the truck was traveling at almost 70 mph, and carrying a full load of home appliances, the effect on the Senzati and its passengers was catastrophic. All four men in the rear were either dead or dying, and the driver, although not fatally injured, had suffered a broken back. Blood and oil leaked from the main body of the vehicle, and glass and metal, caught by moonlight and headlights, spangled the highway.

The casualties in the rear were all senior executives at DavMatt-Hunter Industries, a modestly sized but highly regarded oil and gas consultancy based in New Hampshire. It specialized in digital and advanced analytics in the area of ethylene cracker investment, particularly liquid feedstocks: naphtha, gas oil, and heavier feeds. Just hours earlier, the four men had flown into LaGuardia from a scouting mission in Louisiana, where a Taiwanese plastics group was preparing to move forward on a $9.4 billion ethylene cracker complex by the Mississippi River, another addition to Cancer Alley. The quartet had been due to spend the night in Hartford in advance of a strategy meeting with core investors the following morning, and news of the accident immediately threw

DavMatt-Hunter into convulsions. Within minutes of the CEO being informed of what had happened, efforts were underway to reorganize the company, reposition staff, and – most important of all – reassure stakeholders. Emails were sent. Phones buzzed with messages and incoming calls.

One such call was made to a house in Dayton, Maine, the temporary home of Stephen Clark.

Chapter XLV

The crowd at the Bear was thinning out, and Dave Evans had gone home for the night. A woman was dancing close by her partner in the center of the floor, swaying in time to music I did not recognize. The man tried to pull the woman closer, but she slipped from his grasp. She wasn't dancing for him, only herself.

Sabine Drew had not asked me anything more about Jennifer, my dead daughter. Neither had I spoken to her of the others I had seen – Jennifer's mother, or some semblance of her, among them. It was enough for Drew that I had revealed myself to her.

'I wonder why they still come to you,' was all she said. 'I expect you'll find out, when the time is right.'

'I may have to die for that.'

'Then the revelation could be some way off, since you strike me as remarkably difficult to kill.'

'You make it sound like a character flaw.'

'I don't doubt there are some people who might see it that way.'

'More than I'd prefer.'

'Although you have reduced their number somewhat over the years.'

'There you go again,' I said, 'speaking your mind.'

'Consider it one of my character flaws.' She moved on. 'He cries so much – Henry, I mean. I get annoyed at him sometimes, but it's not his fault. He's hardly more than a baby, and doesn't understand what's happening to him. He stops only when I sing. That helps to quiet him. I imagine his mother sang to him. You might ask her, should the opportunity arise. I don't know many songs for children, and it feels inappropriate to lull him with murder ballads. If I knew what he liked to hear, I could add it to my repertoire.'

'And you're convinced he's in Gretton?'

'Or somewhere nearby,' she said. 'I can't be more specific. It's like putting an ear too close to the speaker on a radio: the music turns to noise and becomes unidentifiable. But I haven't ventured past the town line.'

'Why is that?'

'Because I'm frightened. He isn't alone in there. There's someone, or something, with him. I think it's feeding on Henry, victualing on his pain and confusion. It's taking its time with him.'

I tried to process what I was hearing.

'Are you talking about an animal?'

'No, not an animal, and not even a human being with an animal's nature. I can't tell you precisely what it is, because I'm not sure Henry knows. It's completely black where he's being kept. He can't see, only feel, so he may be underground: buried, perhaps. That's the reason it's taken me so long to come forward, and why I chose to approach you and not the police. You see, I think this presence is familiar. I've encountered it before.'

'When?' I asked.

'When I failed to find Edie Brook.'

Chapter XLVI

Moxie Castin lived in Deering Center, in a grand old house that once belonged to his uncle. How it had come to be in Moxie's possession remained unclear, since rumor had it that his uncle hated Moxie's guts and would have burned the place to the ground rather than see his nephew happily situated in it, but the ways of lawyers are not like those of other men. The uncle died, and after a suitable period had elapsed, the house became Moxie's.

Deering Center was formerly known simply as Deering, back in the 1800s when it was an independent entity. In the last year of that century, it was absorbed into Portland and the name was changed, but it still resembled a country town, aided by its proximity to the thirty acres and more of Baxter Woods, which Moxie's home abutted. As he parked his car, one of his neighbors, Phil Ferry, was picking a couple of pieces of windblown trash from his lawn while his dog, a near-blind terrier named Artie, went for its nighttime pee in the bushes. Ferry was an old coot with long white hair, and sideburns that connected to a mustache above his bare chin, a style once popularized by the Union general Ambrose Burnside, hero of the Siege of Knoxville, but rarely glimpsed since his passing.

'Saw you on TV,' said Ferry.

'How did I look?'

'I got to say, you looked like you were enjoying yourself.'

'It's what I was bred for.'

'Plus,' said Ferry, 'you got skin harder'n a jockey's ass. You'll need it, too, for what you're mixed up in. Half the state already has your client fitted for a jail suit.'

'Only half? That seems generous.'

'Not so much, since the other half wants to bring back hanging for her.'

Moxie juggled his paperwork while he tried to locate his house keys. He usually enjoyed shooting the breeze with Ferry, who had a distinctive view of the world and a gently combative relationship with his wife. As Ferry had once explained to Moxie, his wife was forever accusing him of failing to listen to what she was saying. 'But,' Ferry explained, 'she talks so much that if I start listening to everything she says, I'll never have time to do anything else.' That he had spoken while his wife was within striking distance indicated either a comfort born of a half-century of marriage or a death wish. Tonight, though, Moxie wasn't in the mood for conversation. He wanted to eat a sandwich, drink a glass of milk, and sleep without dreaming.

'Were you expecting company?' asked Ferry.

'Company?' Moxie found his house keys only to lose them again in the nether regions of his briefcase.

'Of the female persuasion.'

'I swear,' said Moxie, 'the most beautiful woman in the world could parade naked through my bedroom, and she'd have more hope of raising the dead than getting a response from me. Why do you ask?'

'Because I thought I saw a woman on your property, could be an hour ago. She went around back, which was how come I wondered if she might not have been expected, and knew where you kept a spare key. When I went out to check on her, she was gone.'

Moxie paused.

'Did you get a look at her?'

'No, sir. I could tell it was a woman, but no more than that.'

'What about a car?'

'I didn't see or hear a vehicle. I suppose she might have gone into the woods, but who'd be walking those trails in the dark? I took a look at your back door, for security's sake, but it was locked up tight.'

The dog finished its business. Dimly, it recognized Moxie and wagged its tail. Moxie patted it absently.

'If you see anyone around here again,' he said, 'I'd be obliged if you'd let me know. You have my number.'

'Or I could call nine-one-one, if you prefer.'

'I'm not anticipating that level of vexation on my doorstep.'

Ferry picked up his dog.

'With the Clark case, maybe you ought to be,' said Ferry. 'Because I am.'

Stephen Clark was smoking a cigarette at the table in his sister-in-law's yard. Before him was a glass of the sixteen-year-old Lagavulin he'd rescued from his marital home before leaving. It had been a gift from Gary Champine, senior vice president and personnel officer of DavMatt-Hunter – well, less a gift and more a consolation prize for missing out on a promotion for the second year running, albeit with a suggestion, however vague, that the next year could be his. Clark wasn't sure he believed it, though. He'd believed it the previous year, and the year before that, but wasn't disposed to be fooled three times in a row. He was sure that Champine didn't rate him highly, a view supported by restroom gossip.

But Gary Champine was now dead. He was among the men involved in the crash on I-91, along with one other senior vice president and two executive vice presidents, essentially annihilating the second tier of DavMatt-Hunter's management. A strained phone call from the company CEO, Kenny Knapp, had apprised Clark that he was now acting executive vice president for sales, an appointment that would be confirmed formally once the board of directors had an opportunity to convene. The subject of remuneration would be dealt with as soon as possible thereafter. For the present, it was crucial that the ship was steadied so key investors didn't take fright and run. The company would also have to find time to bury and mourn its dead, Knapp said, but Clark noted that burial and mourning qualified as marginally more than afterthoughts for Knapp, who'd have whored his daughters to add ten percent to DMH's share price. Clark had responded by assuring Knapp that he wasn't even thinking about money right now, only the future of the company and the relatives of their deceased colleagues and friends. That was how the call had ended, with both parties having made all the right noises, and sincerity left to the fancy of the beholder.

211

Now here was Clark, a cigarette in one hand, a glass of whisky in the other, and a better future stretching before him. His sister-in-law emerged from the house to stand at the edge of the cone of illumination cast by the porch light.

'What are you doing out here in the dark?' she asked. 'Are you okay?'

'I'm just reflecting.'

'On those poor men?'

'Yes.'

'What a terrible thing,' she said. 'Just awful.'

She came to him, and placed a hand on his shoulder. He reached for it, grasping it tightly. He'd always liked her. Sometimes he thought she might have married the wrong brother, and suspected she felt the same way.

'It is,' he said. 'One of them gave me this whisky.'

He raised the glass.

'Then it's an apt way to celebrate his life,' she said.

Clark took a sip of the Lagavulin and rolled it in his mouth. It brought to mind Gary Champine, with his too-white teeth and his too-tight suits, his $200 haircuts and his collection of showy watches. Champine had died in the ambulance, the last of the four to give up the ghost. Clark hoped he'd suffered.

'Celebrate,' he said. 'Yes, that's the word.'

Chapter XLVII

Sabine Drew had never wanted to be on TV or pointed at by strangers on the street. She didn't enjoy reporters calling so often that she and her mother were forced to contemplate changing their phone number and locking the gates to their home. Most of all, she had no desire to answer questions about the events that had led to the arrest of Lester Boulier, but the detective, Ronnie Pascal, had been forced to reveal her involvement in the case. Even though he'd done his best to obfuscate and withhold, he'd still shared more with the media than Sabine would have preferred.

And it wasn't only reporters and TV crews who had beaten a path to her door after Edie Brook's body was found. No, the oddballs arrived too, and the religious lunatics, the crazies who were convinced she had a personal hotline to God. A few had grown angry when she denied it, as though she were electing to hide matters of import that she had a divine obligation to share, while others whispered it was not from God that her gifts came, and the living had no business consorting with the dead.

But they weren't even the worst, not by a long shot. The sad and the desperate contacted her, some of them traveling hundreds of miles to plead for help. The poorest came by bus, their clothes wrinkled and bearing the marks of ablutions at rest stops and gas stations, their sustenance carried in vacuum flasks and Tupperware containers now empty after hard journeys. They brought with them photos, mementos, items of jewelry, single shoes, locks of hair – even, in one case, a glass eye, perhaps in the hope that she might be able to turn her gaze to the next world and identify its owner by an empty socket. They wished to be told that all was well, that they were remembered, loved, forgiven, and awaited. They sought the location of wills, cashboxes, and keys to safe deposit boxes. They asked why, where, with whom, by whom, and of whom. Their need was endless.

And then there were the ones who sought the missing, who were uncertain as to whether they should be searching among the living or the dead: husbands, wives, siblings, parents, and children who had vanished without explanation. Those left behind sought closure, an end to their own suffering and nightmares of the ongoing agonies of their loved ones. Those who had lost children endured greater depths of torment, being additionally burdened with guilt at their failure to protect them.

In the beginning, Sabine tried to assist as many as she could, but most went away disappointed. She couldn't make them understand that seeking answers from the dead was as hard as obtaining them from the living – harder, indeed, because the former far outnumbered the latter, and spoke in a different tongue. Even Verona Walters had become less intelligible to Sabine in the final moments before her body was revealed, and all communication between them ceased forever. Also, by questing, Sabine drew attention; when the dead saw her light and felt her presence, they were drawn like moths. If she foraged among them, she had to do so without revealing too much of herself. It was like exploring a deep darkness with the aid of a flashlight that could only be used intermittently.

But now and again, she had successes: a sighting, however partial; a reply, however imperfectly understood. There was never closure, because closure was a myth, but the sum of unhappiness was marginally decreased and the agony of unknowing lessened. Yet the cost to Sabine was considerable. She struggled to eat and sleep. Her mouth festered with ulcers. Her hair began to fall out. Finally, she collapsed and was taken, first to the local clinic, then to Millinocket Regional, but even there she was not safe. Patients and visitors came to her, as well as apologetic doctors and nurses. She woke one night to find a man with pancreatic cancer kneeling by her bedside. He had placed her hand on his head and was praying for her to heal him. He was still thanking her for what she could not do as the orderlies ushered him gently away.

After she was discharged, she put an end to the visits and the calls. A remote-locking system replaced the old gates. For a while, the more persistent still succeeded in overcoming these obstacles, but the local police were always available to escort them from the property, with a stern lecture about the consequences of trespassing.

But Sabine continued to aid investigators when she could. They contacted her circumspectly, some embarrassed at being forced to resort to such a measure, although she did not judge them for their discomfiture. To the police, as with the general public, she could not always be of much use, but again, there were small triumphs, little victories. Each involved a child. Children were easier to locate because their light shone brighter. Quietly, Sabine began to gain a reputation among law enforcement. One thing could be said of her: she did not lie.

And then came Edie Brook.

Chapter XLVIII

Edie Brook was eight years old when she disappeared from the Maine Mall in South Portland. Her mother, Andie, was in the men's section at Macy's, picking up some jeans on special for her husband, who swore he still wore 34x34 Levi's 501, if only in his dreams. Yes, he could fit into them, but barely, and had to wear his shirts untucked to disguise the resulting muffin top. To sit comfortably required him leaving open the top button for a time until the jeans bedded in or risk taking someone's eye out when it popped. Men, Andie Brook reflected, were just about the vainest creatures on earth this side of a peacock. Her husband hated the mall, so she'd offered to buy the jeans for him, with the ulterior motive of picking up 36x34 501s and slipping them into his closet. He was unlikely to check the size, but on the off chance that he did, she thought she might first obscure the measurements by defacing them with a pen or pin.

So these were her thoughts as she compared shades of blue in the artificial light of the store. She looked around and couldn't see her daughter. She didn't take fright, not immediately, because the store was a maze of racks and Edie liked playing hide-and-seek among them, or pretending she was Dora the Explorer trying to stop Swiper from stealing stuff. Lord knows, the folks at Macy's might even have been willing to pay her by the hour, the amount of merchandise that must have been shoplifted every day.

Jeans in hand, Andie had begun hunting for her daughter, even as a nasty feeling slowly began to take hold. She had an ache in her stomach, like she really needed to get to a restroom, and her mouth tasted sour. She called Edie's name, louder and louder, until finally she was screaming it, which brought staff and security running. The store was searched, the effort rippling outward to take in the mall and its parking lot. The police arrived, followed by her husband. He'd left their two older boys with his mom, but by then Andie was only just managing to hold it together. The sight of him, and his solicitude toward her, caused her to break. She folded slowly to the floor, taking a display of Florsheim shoes with her, and wanted to die.

No trace of Edie Brook could be found. Security footage showed her by the exit in the men's section, leaning out of the open door. She appeared to be talking to someone outside, although there was no external store camera covering that particular angle, and whomever she was conversing with might deliberately have chosen the spot, like a hunter picking the best stand from which to target prey. Finally, after a few seconds of conversation, Edie could be seen departing the store, her arms extended as though to hug someone. That was the final sighting of her.

An AMBER Alert was issued. The main external cameras in the mall parking lot, which ordinarily would have given a view of the doors, had been obscured by an illegally-parked truck at the time of Edie's disappearance, but three other vehicles, including a panel van, had stopped briefly during the window established for what was now being treated as an abduction. The drivers of the truck and the two cars were quickly traced, because all were still on mall property, but the van, a dark blue 1990 Ford Falcon XF, was not. The police started tracking it, using adjacent cameras to establish its exit route from the mall, and came up with a license number, but the plate and vehicle didn't match because the plate should have been attached to a silver Town & Country.

Twenty minutes later, a report was received of a vehicle on fire in a disused lot over in North Deering. The vehicle in question was a Ford panel van, its blue paint already almost completely scorched away by the heat of the flames. Hanging from a nearby tree was Edie Brook's yellow rain jacket.

After that, the trail went dead, despite repeated searches of the area, tearful appeals from Edie's parents, and a $75,000 reward from a local businessman for information leading to her safe return. The reward was as much a hindrance as a help, because the promise of easy money lured lowlifes and scoundrels, any number of psychics among them: some fake, others sincere, and all wrong.

One week after the vanishing of Edie Brook, Sabine Drew began hearing her voice. It came to her at the same time each day, just before 4 p.m., asking for a glass of grape juice and an Oreo. Sabine was still in mourning for her mother, who had passed away a few months earlier. The voice was, in its way, a welcome distraction from her grief. After three days of listening to it, and some tentative reaching out to the source, Sabine approached the South Portland PD, a force she had not previously assisted. Calls were made, one of them to Ronnie Pascal, and assurances received about Sabine's bona fides. She ended up sitting in another police interview room – different, but similar – and told them what she knew.

'I think Edie's alive,' she said.

'How do you know?' asked the lead detective, a man named Wilbert Sullivan whose attitude Sabine didn't care for, not one bit. She could tell he didn't trust her, and gave no credence to a word she had to say. Short of being marched into the interview room at gunpoint, he couldn't have looked unhappier at being there, but it wasn't as though he and his colleagues were doing so well without her help. Edie was still missing and parents in the area were one scare away from cuffing their kids to their wrists. Sullivan's demeanor probably caused Sabine to present herself more forcefully than was her norm.

'I can tell the difference between the living and the dead,' she snapped. 'Can't you?'

'We've had some experience of it, yes,' said the man seated next to Sullivan, another detective, this one named Cogan. He was less hostile than his partner, which wouldn't have been hard.

A woman, who had been standing in the shadows but not yet introduced, stepped forward.

'This is unfamiliar territory for us, Ms Drew,' she said. 'We try to treat all offers of assistance with respect, but we've already wasted a lot of time on false leads, some of them from individuals claiming to have certain . . . gifts.'

'You have the advantage of me,' said Sabine. 'You know my name, but I don't know yours.'

'My name is Detective Sharon Macy. This investigation involves the efforts of multiple branches of law enforcement across the state and beyond its borders. I'm the acting liaison officer between the Portland and South Portland PDs, but I also have experience coordinating multiagency operations in the state. I try to smooth the way when I can.'

Sullivan didn't look any happier at Macy's intervention. Sabine wondered if he didn't like women very much. He opened his mouth to regain control of proceedings, but Sabine continued to address herself to Macy, as much to annoy Sullivan as anything else.

'I try to smooth the way too,' said Sabine, 'so we have that much in common. And I'm not interested in any reward money, if that's what you're worried about. I don't need seventy-five thousand dollars. I already have enough to get by.'

'How do you earn a living,' said Macy, 'if you don't mind me asking?'

'I channel the numbers for the state lottery,' said Drew. 'I stick with Pick 3, though, so as not to draw attention. On straights and box three-ways, I can usually clear $600 a week, give or take.'

There was silence in the interview room. Sabine let it build, then said, 'Actually, I work part-time at Muller's grocery store in Haynesville, which helps pay the bills, but my mom and dad left me with enough investment income to support a frugal lifestyle, and I don't have a mortgage. You guys. I swear, it's a wonder nobody has swindled your watches and wallets from you before now.'

But rather than lighten the mood, this turned out to be the final straw for Detective Wilbert Sullivan.

'I don't have time for this,' he said, and left the room. Cogan and Macy stayed, the latter taking Sullivan's chair.

'Detective Sullivan hasn't enjoyed a good night's sleep since this began,' said Macy. 'No one involved in the case has, so patience is at a premium.'

'I think Edie Brook's parents give her grape juice and a cookie as a treat each afternoon, probably at around four o'clock,' said Sabine. 'She prefers Oreos. You might want to check that with them.'

'How do you know this?' asked Cogan.

'Because that's what I hear her asking for.'

Cogan looked at Macy.

'I'll do it,' he said.

He went away. Macy didn't try making small talk, which Sabine appreciated. Cogan returned after about five minutes, nodding once at Macy.

'Is it a trick?' Macy asked Sabine.

'It's no trick.'

Macy spun her cell phone on the table while she thought. She shared an unspoken exchange with Cogan, who shrugged.

'Okay,' said Macy, 'what else can you tell us about her?'

Sabine spent two days trying to establish a proper line of communication with Edie Brook. It was difficult, more difficult than anything she'd attempted before. Edie was oddly resistant, and the channel between them remained open for only a few minutes each day. Finally, though, Sabine managed to convince her to describe her surroundings, and what she could see, smell, and hear.

She was not blindfolded, Edie informed her, but the man who had taken her wore a wolf mask when he came to bring her meals or empty the bucket she used to go to the bathroom. She thought she was in a cellar or basement, with a single small window high up that she couldn't reach. She could hear vehicles passing, but not people. The man never spoke to her, but neither had he hurt her in any way. She had a TV to watch, and candy and water to consume from an old refrigerator. She heard the man go out once or twice every day, sometimes for long periods. His car made a racket as it drove away.

Cogan and Macy stayed in touch with Sabine throughout. Slowly, Edie Brook was opening up to Sabine, although she remained reluctant to engage for any length of time. Edie was, in most senses, a blank slate. Macy asked Sabine to find out from Edie what news channel she could see on the TV, and Edie told her it was WLBZ, which was the state's central and northern NBC affiliate. If Sabine really was in touch with Edie, she was being held somewhere in the top half of the state. It wasn't much to go on, but it was a start.

On the fourth day, Edie told Sabine that if she moved the refrigerator and climbed on top, she thought she might be able to see out the window. The refrigerator was heavy, she said, but if she put all her weight against one side, she could shift it a fraction. It was tough work, though, and any movement made a noise on the floor. Sabine advised her to wait until the man left before making a big effort.

Edie moved the refrigerator. Using the interior shelves, she managed to climb up and peer out the window. She could see a sign, she said, black on white, just above some trees. The sign read PATTEN. Patten was a small town in Penobscot County, at the intersections of Route 11 and State Route 159, which fit with the TV receiving WLBZ. By this time Cogan and Macy – Macy in particular – had invested a lot of faith in Sabine. They wanted to believe her.

The focus of the investigation shifted to Patten, although the source of the information – the noted psychic Sabine Drew – was not revealed. Law enforcement personnel descended on the town, quickly followed by a media pack. Houses and properties were searched both inside and beyond the town line. Cogan and Macy encouraged Sabine to reach out again to Edie and ask her if there was anything else, anything at all, she had seen that might help to narrow the search. But Edie Brook had gone silent.

'Is she dead?' Macy asked Sabine.

'I don't know,' said Sabine. 'I can't find her. It's almost as though—'

She stopped. She didn't want to say it.

'What?' said Macy.

But Sabine could not be dishonest with her.

'It's almost,' she said, 'as though she was never there.'

The search of Patten and the surrounding area continued: one day, two, three. Word leaked that the decision to devote so much manpower to Patten was the result of a tip-off, though police still declined to reveal the source. Sabine persisted in her efforts to restore contact with Edie, but it was only at night that she now heard her, and even then she could not be entirely sure she was not dreaming. In the dark, between sleeping and waking, Edie

221

told her that the man holding her captive had become anxious. She thought she'd heard sirens in the distance, as well as the shouts of men and the howling of dogs.

Then daylight would come, causing Edie to fall quiet again.

On the final day of the Patten search, and two hundred miles to the southeast, a woman named Myrna Liddie was rowing in Scarborough Marsh with her granddaughter Erika, Myrna's American water spaniel Chloe seated between them in the canoe. As they rounded a bend in the channel, Chloe, as was her wont, dove into the water and swam toward a clump of reeds. Myrna expected to see a duck ascend, quacking in panic, but no bird flew, and Chloe was content to circle the same spot. Unusually for her, she did not return when called, but instead began barking at her mistress. Myrna instructed her granddaughter to help steer the canoe toward the dog.

The clump of reeds lay close to the margin between high and low marsh. The areas of high marsh had been growing fewer and fewer each year due to rising sea levels. Soon, it was said, half the ecosystem would be underwater.

'Ugh!' said her granddaughter. The reeds were alive with European green crabs.

Myrna could see that Chloe had been drawn by what looked like the top of an old sack that had broken the surface of the water. It was crawling with crabs. Gingerly, Myrna touched it with the tip of her oar. It felt solid, and was shaped like a ball. Using the oar, she traced the lineaments of the form below the water until she could reach no farther.

'What is it, Grandma?' asked her granddaughter, but Myrna was already dialing 911.

'Get Chloe back in the canoe,' she said, as her emergency call was answered. 'My name is Myrna Liddie,' she told the dispatcher. 'I think I may have found a body in Scarborough Marsh.'

Edie Brook had been in the water for a couple of days, but dead for more than a week. She had been placed in a sack bound with a length of chain. The chain was padlocked to a concrete block before the whole was dumped. Had her killer taken the time to pierce the corpse, preventing the accumulation of gas, she might not have been found, or not so soon, but detectives speculated that whoever put her in the water had wanted her to be discovered: there were better places to hide the body of a young girl than a tidal marsh.

As soon as the remains were identified, questions were asked about the lead that had brought the police not to Scarborough, but to Patten. Sabine's involvement was made public, but by whom was never established. The denunciations came thick and fast. She was a fraud, an attention-seeker, an exploiter of the sorrow of others. Perhaps, some whispered, she might even have killed Edie Brook herself and used Patten as a diversion. Nobody involved in the case really believed this, but they didn't have to: Sabine's reputation and character lay in tatters within twenty-four hours of her being named in media reports. She was spat on in the street and her car was set alight. Her mailbox filled with abusive letters and boxes of dog excrement. Someone sent her a .30-06 Springfield bullet, on which her initials had been written in Wite-Out.

She stopped leaving the house. Her groceries arrived by special delivery. Neighbors grew reluctant to interact with her, and a handful would never speak to her again. Police no longer sought her help with investigations. She continued to receive missives from those looking for the lost, but only the most despairing. Sabine ignored them all, until, at last, they slowed to a trickle before drying up entirely.

She still saw the dead, though.

And sometimes, the dead saw her.

Chapter XLIX

The cups and glasses on the table before us stood empty. Much of Sabine Drew's story was already known to me, but some of it was unfamiliar. I had not known that Sharon Macy was involved in the Edie Brook case. After a false start some years earlier, she and I had begun seeing each other again. I wondered how she would take the news that Edie's specter had found its way to my door.

'Why are you telling me this?' I asked.

'Two reasons,' said Sabine. 'The first is that I want you to understand.'

'Understand what?'

'That I'm not a liar, whatever anyone might say. I've just shared with you the worst experience of my life. I failed Edie Brook, but not willfully. My flaw was arrogance, which was exploited.'

'By whom? The police?'

'No. By something else.'

'Something?' There was that word again.

She sighed in the manner of a schoolmistress faced with a slow child.

'Mr Parker, I was convinced that the voice I heard was Edie Brook's. Even now, I remain certain that it was she who spoke to me, at least in the beginning. I couldn't have manufactured that detail about the cookies and milk at four o'clock each afternoon, and it wasn't anything that had been shared with the media. But I believe something else was listening, something that didn't want me looking for lost children. It saw its chance to deal with the threat I posed and took it.'

'Are you saying that this entity imitated Edie Brook to disgrace you?'

'Yes, that's exactly what I'm saying. It may even be that this entity was not unknown to whoever took Edie, or was working through them. Then again, they may not have been aware of it. Whatever the truth, I'm convinced that it used Edie's disappearance to manipulate and, as you say, disgrace me.'

I had heard and witnessed a great many strange things in my life. I was a man whose dead daughter spoke not only to him but also to his living child. I had been present in a church in England when the boundaries between worlds grew thin enough to fracture, and had stared into the face of the God of Wasps. Why, then, was Sabine Drew's tale too rich for my blood? I could not have said, other than that it is one thing to accept the evidence of one's own eyes and ears – although even then, the mind may try to convince one otherwise – but another to embrace without reservation the convictions of another. I tried to keep my face neutral, but she could see that I was struggling to accept the truth of her claim.

'You think I'm deluded, don't you?'

'Frankly, I don't know what to think.'

'I usually hate that word "frankly", but I'm prepared to make an exception in your case because I don't doubt your essential probity.'

'Perhaps we can set all this aside for a moment,' I said. 'Does it matter if I need time to consider the implications of what you're telling me?'

'Actually, it does. It's pertinent to the second reason I came here, and the whereabouts of Henry Clark.'

'Go on,' I said. 'I'll try to keep an open mind.'

I could sense her frustration. She'd emerged from seclusion to present her case to someone she hoped might be willing to listen, but the more she spoke, the less likely it seemed that its substance might be accepted. Yet she had come this far, and no purpose would be served by stopping before the end.

'The presence,' she said, 'the intelligence that misled me about Edie Brook, I've felt it again, for the first time in years.'

'Where?'

'Gretton. I hear Henry Clark crying in the night, but behind it I can make out – well, I can only describe it as a sonic distortion,

225

with the echo of a voice, a murmur, buried deep in its patterns. The last time I heard that murmur was when I thought I was in contact with Edie Brook.'

'And for obvious reasons,' I said, 'you can't go to the police with this.'

'They'd have even less reason to believe me than you do.'

'And suppose I did believe you? I can tell you that I don't have the resources or the authority to go scouring Gretton for the body of a child. Even if you – or we – did manage to convince the police that Henry Clark might be there, based on whatever evidence was sufficient, any search would have to be narrowed to a manageable area.'

'I know,' she said. 'I've had to explain in the past how hard it is for me to do that.' She rubbed at her temples with her fingertips, her eyes squeezed closed as though enduring a headache. 'But that's not the only difficulty I have with Gretton. You see, I drove to the town line, but couldn't go any farther.'

'Why not?'

She looked up at me, her hands still cradling her head.

'I told you. I was afraid.'

'Of whatever you think is there?'

She nodded.

'It's old. I can apprehend its antiquity. I think it sleeps for years, decades, but it always wakes hungry and it likes the taste of children. It's feeding on Henry Clark now, eating his light, and when it's finally consumed the last of him, it'll hibernate again. This is a cycle, one that's persisted for a long, long time. When Henry succumbs, any hope we might have of locating it will be gone. By the time it wakes again, who knows, I could be dead. If I'm not, it may be that I won't hear the next child crying. Either way, the entity will survive, but the child won't.'

'How did it get to Henry?' I asked.

'With help, I assume. Evil finds its own. It forms clusters.'

She checked her watch.

'I'm tired,' she said. 'I don't often stay up this late, and I'm not used to people and bars. My brain feels as though it's being pricked with needles.'

She rose and put on her coat, before remembering the check. She rummaged in her purse, crumpling bills in her hand as she counted them out.

'I'll take care of it,' I said. 'You came all this way, so it's the least I can do.'

'You listened,' she replied, 'and that's the least you could have done, but I don't know what else I expected from you. To ride in like the cavalry with guns blazing, all on the word of a solitary woman who still claims to hear departed voices, even after she was denounced as a liar and a fraud? What was I thinking? Such foolishness.'

She tossed some bills on the table and moved past me.

'Do you need a ride?' I asked.

'My car is outside and I have a place to stay in town.' She paused, and her hand brushed my shoulder. 'I hope your daughter finds peace, Mr Parker. I hope you do, too. There just isn't enough of it – in this world or the next.'

And she gave herself to the night.

Chapter L

I decided it might be more straightforward to drop by Moxie's house than try to update him on developments over the phone. He invited me into the kitchen, where the table was spread with paperwork, some of it related to Colleen Clark, the rest involving other cases. The table was a dark oak monster that had come with the property. It didn't really suit the room, which Moxie had modernized, but I could see why he'd decided to hold on to it. Half a dozen lawyers could comfortably have worked from it without touching elbows. Then again, it might have been that Moxie couldn't figure out how to get the table out of the kitchen without sawing it into pieces. It looked like the room had been constructed around it.

'Would you care for a drink?' he asked.

'No, I'm good. I've taken in so much liquid today that my body is now probably eighty percent water instead of sixty – well, water, coffee, club soda, and alcohol-free beer.'

I went through the events of the day with him, from the meeting with Delaney Duhamel, through the conversation with Steady Freddy, and finally, my encounter with Sabine Drew.

'The phony psychic?' said Moxie. 'Jesus, next thing this case will be attracting fortune tellers and guess-your-weight hucksters.'

'I'm not sure that "phony" is the right word for her,' I said. 'Or "psychic" for that matter. Technically, she may be a medium.'

'If you prefer "fraud" or "fake", I have no objection.'

'She's sincere. I don't believe she's trying to deceive anyone.'

'Maybe you should talk to your girlfriend, Macy, see what she says, given she was among those who got stung over Edie Brook.'

Moxie had the memory of a dozen elephants, but it still bothered me slightly that he was familiar with aspects of Macy's past unknown to me until that evening.

'I might just do that. And she's not my girlfriend.'

'What do you mean, she's not your girlfriend? What are you, nine years old?'

Put like that, I had to admit I'd sounded like someone denying an accusation leveled in the schoolyard. Damn Moxie and his cunning lawyerly ways.

'I might hear what she has to say,' I conceded.

'Yeah, I'd do that before I started digging up half of Gretton. You might consider buying her some flowers as well before you go raking over old hurts. You can tell her they came from me, if that makes it easier.'

'Thanks, Moxie. You're the best.'

He flicked through some of the notes he'd made while I was talking.

'And the more I learn about Mara Teller,' he said, 'the less I like. There might be a way to light a fire under the police about her, if you think Furnish is dragging his heels.'

'If Nowak and Becker get elected, Furnish is convinced he'll be looked after, so he's got no reason to begin picking apart the case they're making against Colleen. At worst, if we set him on Teller, he may louse things up, either deliberately or through his own incompetence. I planted the seed with Steady Freddy. He's a plodder, but he's honest and has a conscience. If he can see substance behind the shadow, he'll do the right thing.'

'Speaking of shadows,' said Moxie, 'my neighbor told me that a woman might have been hanging around my house earlier this evening.'

'Let me remind you that I didn't laugh when you offered me relationship advice just now. How many women does one man need?'

'Too many, and never enough.'

'So what was it?'

'Probably nothing, but there are scratches on the lock of my back door.' Moxie jerked a thumb at the door behind him that opened into the yard. 'They look fresh.'

I examined the lock. He was right. When I rubbed a thumb over the marks, tiny flecks of brass came away.

'How's your alarm?'

'In need of service. I've been busy.'

'Weapons?'

'Only my rapier wit. I don't like guns. That's why I have you.'

I stared out into the dark, where Baxter Woods lay.

'Get the alarm up to spec,' I said. 'I'll make a call tomorrow about that money order from the forum. If I can find out where it was purchased, I might also be able to put a face on whoever bought it.'

I powered up my laptop and opened the file of photographs given to me by Delaney Duhamel. I hadn't yet gone through them in detail, but a cursory search had produced two pictures of Stephen Clark, although in both he was visible only in the background, distinguished by his height. In the first, he was accompanied by a much shorter woman. Her head was down, her face turned to her left to glance up at him. Even in profile, I could tell she was smiling. Around her neck hung a lanyard ID, partly obscured by the lapel of her jacket. Magnifying meant losing definition, but I thought the letters might have included at least one 'I'.

'You think this is her?' asked Moxie. 'Because Clark might have met any number of women at that event.'

'Look at his right hand,' I said. 'It's resting on the small of her back.'

'Could be, although there are women who might construe that as a friendly gesture instead of an intimate one.' Moxie magnified her face. 'Not enough to make a positive identification.'

'Not in a court of law, but I'd know her if I saw her.'

'Would Stephen Clark be willing to tell us who she is?'

'I doubt he'd confirm his own name if I asked. That door has closed.'

'Still, it might be useful if we get him on the stand. Send the image to me. I'll add it to the file. What else have you got on your schedule for tomorrow?'

'Appointments with both Colleen's physician and her therapist,' I said. 'If I have enough time, I'll knock on more doors, but according to Steady Freddy, the Portland PD's inquiries didn't turn up anything useful on that front. I'm not sure I'll do much better.'

'I'll leave it to you to decide the best use of your time. How's Colleen doing under sequestration?'

'Okay, last time I saw her, but there's a limit to how long I can keep her cooped up in Scarborough.'

'Have you told your girlfriend that you've taken in a female lodger?' said Moxie. 'Sorry, your *non*-girlfriend.'

He sniggered. He was a schoolkid at heart.

'I hope someone breaks into your house and steals your pencils,' I said.

Chapter LI

Colleen Clark was dozing in front of the television when I got home. I could see her through the living room window as I parked. She was a difficult woman to feel sorry for, although I still struggled to pinpoint why. It might have been the element of fatalism to her character, or her continued solicitude toward a husband who struck me as unworthy of it. But this was an observation more than a judgment: I'd lived too long with my own grief, and guilt for the harm it had caused, to admonish others for how they dealt with a sorrow unimaginable to anyone who had not experienced it for themselves. Nonetheless, her demeanor would have to be taken into account in the event of a trial. Whatever instructions it might receive from a judge, no jury made its decision on evidence alone. If justice was truly blind, a screen would be placed between jurors and the accused.

Colleen woke as I closed the car door, and came to meet me in the kitchen. She was wearing loose jeans and an old sweater. Her feet were bare, and I noticed that her toenails were freshly painted in different colors. She saw me looking at them.

'I was bored,' she said. 'I found the nail polish in your daughter's room.'

'As long as you're here, you can paint them any color that makes you happy. But when you do eventually go out again, keep them covered – or better still, remove the varnish and leave them plain. The same goes for your fingernails.'

'Should I wear a veil, too?'

'Whether you like it or not, you're in the public eye, and the jury will be drawn from people who read newspapers, watch TV, and gossip with their friends. How you act, how you hold yourself, the clothes you choose to wear, whether you smile or remain solemn, all carry potential consequences in court. It's harder for a woman accused of a crime than a man, but I'm sure you're already aware that women are held to a different standard in life, so forgive the mansplaining.'

I stood against the sink and stretched. My back ached from hours of sitting.

'I'm sorry,' I said. 'That sounded sharper than it was meant to.'

'Not at all. I hadn't even considered what you just told me. It's better to hear it, and from you. I'll get rid of the rainbow before I go to bed.'

I felt lousy. A little color wasn't going to bring about the end of the world, but on the other hand, it was for the best. Until the trial, Colleen would have to learn to live life as though a camera was trained on her every move.

She took a seat at the table.

'I went walking earlier, just by the back of the house where I wouldn't be seen,' she said. 'It's very beautiful here.'

She sniffed her hand.

'I can still smell salt on my skin.' The tip of her tongue touched her wrist. 'I can taste it too.'

There was nothing erotic or deliberately seductive about the gesture. She had the unselfconsciousness of a child.

'Did you make any progress?' she asked.

I elected not to tell her about Sabine Drew. No good could come of that. Neither did I wish to discuss the substance of my conversations with Delaney Duhamel or Steady Freddy. Colleen was Moxie's client, and technically I was working for him, not her. If she had any questions about the conduct of the case or my associated investigation, she could direct them to him.

'Small steps,' I said. 'And it's early days.'

'You really don't want to share anything with me, do you?'

'Everything should go through Moxie. It'll avoid confusion.'

'And prevent me getting my hopes up for the wrong reasons?'

'When there's more hope, Colleen, you'll be the first to know.'

'I should go back to bed,' she said. 'I only came downstairs because something woke me. After that, I didn't care to return to my room.'

'What woke you?'

'A feeling, or just the wind in the trees. The world sounds different out here. The noises are unfamiliar. I stood at the bedroom window, and for a moment I was sure I could see a figure between the trees by the road, looking toward the house. Then the wind changed direction, the shadows moved, and it was gone.'

I thought of Moxie and the scratches on his lock.

'Was it a man or a woman?'

I kept my voice neutral.

'I couldn't tell, and I might have been mistaken. Sorry, I didn't mean to cause a fuss.'

'There's no fuss,' I said, 'and you absolutely did the right thing by mentioning it. This property has a security system in place. I deactivated sections of it because you were here and I didn't want to make you feel like a prisoner, but any boundary breaches are automatically sent to my cell phone. You're quite safe, and the Scarborough police are just minutes away. If you're ever worried, and you can't get hold of me, call them.'

'Won't they tell people I'm staying here?'

'There's always that chance, but this is only a short-term solution. In a few days, I'll quietly drop you home. Your mom will be there, and we'll keep the Fulcis in place for the time being, or as long as you want them to stay. One of them will be happy to go with you to the store, or a movie if you need the distraction, although I'd advise against the latter.'

'Because people might take it amiss if I'm seen at a movie theater.'

'Or a play, or attending a concert. If a photographer catches you laughing, it'll be made to look bad.'

'I hate this.'

'I know, but attention fades. A time will come when you'll notice people struggling to recall your face, but by then you'll have moved on. Give it longer, and they won't remember you at all.'

'What about Henry?' she asked, 'Will they forget him as well?'

'We'll do our best to make sure that doesn't happen.'

She took a last look at her painted toenails.

'I think they already have, because none of this is about Henry, not anymore.'

She poured herself a glass of water to take to her room with her.

'Did you sing to your son?' I asked as she was turning off the faucet.

'What?'

'Did you sing to him,' I repeated, 'to lull him to sleep?'

She looked at me quizzically.

'Why would you ask that?'

'Curiosity.'

The answer appeared to satisfy her.

'Then yes,' she said. 'I did. I suppose most mothers do. It seems to come naturally, because I never sang much at all before I had Henry.'

'Do you remember what you sang?'

She thought about this. I could see her eyes were growing wet, but I didn't regret the line of questioning. I needed to be sure about Sabine Drew.

'Oh, I just held him to me and hummed, really. I wonder if it's something to do with the vibrations.'

'And did you gain comfort from it?'

'Yes, I think I did. Are you suggesting I should sing to my lost child?'

'I don't see why not. Wherever Henry is, he's listening for you.'

She wiped at her face.

'Then maybe I will. Goodnight.'

And as she ascended the stairs, I heard her start to hum.

Chapter LII

Colleen still hadn't surfaced when I called Maralou Burnham shortly after 8 the following morning. Maralou was the only real contact I had at the US Postal Service. She worked in administrative support up in Augusta and was always willing to help in return for a token bottle of wine, so long as it didn't require her to break any laws. I gave her the number of the money order that had been used by her near-namesake Mara Teller, and she confirmed it wouldn't be difficult to discover where it was purchased, along with the form of payment. As a wager to make things interesting, I told her I'd send a second bottle if the money order hadn't been paid for in cash, but suspected I was unlikely to have to come through for the extra bottle.

Colleen's physician was a woman named Lyra Shapleigh. She worked in the Libbytown area of Portland, based in a fancy medical center seemingly designed to make a person feel guilty about being ill, in case they bled and left a mark. Her sister, Molly, was the obstetrician who had delivered Colleen's son.

Dr. Lyra Shapleigh was in her late thirties, all soft curves hiding sharp, hard edges. She informed me that she'd treated Colleen Clark for postnatal depression, and although Colleen had struggled with motherhood early on, she had been managing better in recent months. Shapleigh had suggested therapy to help address the problem, and hadn't objected to the therapist recommended to Colleen by one of her friends, Piper Hudson. Shapleigh then sat back with the air of a woman who had completed an unpleasant task without vomiting. Her main concern, as she made no effort to hide, was less for her patient than her own reputation. She explained that she didn't want to be dragged into the case, for which I could hardly blame her. I asked if she'd been contacted by the prosecution, and she admitted that she had. A conversation with someone from Erin Becker's team was scheduled for later in the day, but so far there had been no suggestion of a subpoena being served.

'I've already consulted my lawyer,' she said, 'and he doubts I can be forced to testify – by either side.'

I didn't offer an alternative view. I wasn't a lawyer, and every night I promised on my knees to be good so God wouldn't turn me into one while I slept.

'Do you like Colleen?' I asked.

The question threw Shapleigh.

'Like?' she replied, as though it had never before struck her that a physician might have feelings for a patient, positive or otherwise. I assumed it wasn't always relevant to a practitioner, given the nature of the Hippocratic oath, and a doctor could find ways to relieve themselves of an unloved patient if they really tried. 'I – Well, sure. She was quiet at first, and very shy, but I found her sharp, self-aware, and drily funny when she wanted to be. Why do you ask?'

'I have an inquiring mind,' I said. 'Also, I'm wondering whether you were surprised when she was accused of harming her son.'

'If I said that it requires a lot to surprise me, would that constitute avoidance?'

'I'd take it as contextualization.'

Shapleigh permitted some warmth to melt her.

'Then, within that context, yes, I was surprised,' she said. 'Colleen had never demonstrated harmful ideation toward her son, not in my presence. A lot of young women have difficulty with motherhood, particularly with a first child in the early months – or years. It's not uncommon. But Colleen's case was more severe than most, and both psychologically and physically debilitating. It was important that the issue be addressed, for Henry's sake as well as her own.'

'Did she speak to you about her husband?'

'He came up in conversation.'

'And?'

'I'm not a marriage counselor, Mr Parker.'

'Did you suggest they ought to see one?'

'I might have indicated that it couldn't hurt, but her therapist may have a better insight into that aspect of her life.'

'Was there ever an intimation of violence in the relationship?'

'On the part of the husband? I saw no evidence of it, and Colleen never raised the subject. Have you reason to suspect him of it?'

'I've been spending a lot of time in Colleen's company,' I said. 'Something about her demeanor has been troubling me, and the closest point of reference I can find was in abused women I've met. She's been worn down. But then, there's more than one kind of abuse.'

'Her husband struck me as unsympathetic to her situation,' said Shapleigh, 'which would have affected Colleen emotionally and psychologically, but that's only based on what she shared with me. I met him a couple of times when he came to collect her. Colleen introduced us, but I had no interaction with him beyond that.'

'What about his attitude toward the child? Was he close to Henry, involved in his life?'

I already thought I knew the answer, but it never hurt to look for a professional opinion, especially when it came free of charge.

'Again,' said Shapleigh, 'from what Colleen told me, he wasn't particularly interested in Henry's day-to-day upbringing, but she did qualify that by emphasizing how hard her husband worked. He wasn't home a great deal, but he also possessed a somewhat old-fashioned attitude toward the patterns of child-rearing, in my opinion.'

'It was women's work.'

'Yes.'

Shapleigh removed her spectacles. It might have been meant to emphasize her sincerity. She leaned forward on her desk and gave me her best sympathetic look, possibly a variation on the one reserved for patients who were about to receive an unwelcome diagnosis and be advised to get their affairs in order.

'Look, Mr Parker,' she said, 'I have nothing to share with prosecutors that will reflect adversely on your client – and my patient – even if they succeed in subpoenaing records or forcing me to take the stand. I hope that's some reassurance. Otherwise, I wish I could be of more help, but I can't.'

She replaced her spectacles. We were done.

Chapter LIII

Mattia Reggio drove northwest in glorious sunshine. He had a bag of Swedish fish to nibble on, although he also intended to stop along the way for a snack and to use a restroom. He was no longer able to walk more than a mile without thinking about taking a leak, and if he had to get up only once during the night to empty his bladder, he felt like offering up a prayer of thanksgiving. His wife kept urging him to see a doctor to confirm that there was nothing amiss with his plumbing, but he assured her it was his advancing years. There was hardly a man who didn't make it beyond fifty without passing more water more often, and Reggio had exceeded that milestone by almost two decades.

But unbeknownst to his wife, he was worried, because he had a suspicion that there might well be something wrong down there. He experienced intermittent pain in his ass and groin, and sometimes he saw blood in the bowl, but he kept this to himself. One of his drinking buddies, Ed Nibloe, had consulted an internist about pain when he took a leak, and next thing the guy was whipping out Ed's prostate and hacking at tumors. Now the poor bastard couldn't even fuck his wife, and wore a bag or some such contraption to collect his piss. To Reggio, that sounded like the cure might be worse than the disease. Once you started allowing doctors to poke around your insides, they were bound to find cracks in the machinery. It stood to reason. But as any guy who'd ever tended an old house, car, or marriage would tell you, it was often better to ignore certain deficiencies and imperfections for fear that one might otherwise discover oneself stranded amid rubble, wreckage, or divorce lawyers. Leave well enough alone, that was Reggio's motto.

He ate another Swedish fish and checked that he was keeping

below the speed limit. He had a license for the gun in his pocket, the prohibition on possession of a firearm by a convicted criminal being five years in the state of Maine, and it had been many decades since Mattia Reggio last subsisted on prison food. But to be pulled over by cops would involve having his license run through the system, and being forced to answer questions about his affairs that he had no desire to answer, if only on a point of principle.

Amara had seen him stow away the gun; the woman was gifted with the eyesight of a hawk. She had always tolerated his old profession, but never approved of it. She loved him, she liked to say, despite her better judgment, but she loved him even more once he'd retired from the life.

'Where are you going?' she'd asked that morning, as he was checking the tire pressure with a pocket gauge. His father always used to do it before taking a trip, because he said you couldn't trust the ones in gas stations worth a shit. Now you were lucky if you could find a gas station that would even provide air, or not without charging you a buck or two for the pleasure, the clock ticking down as you scuttled like an idiot from tire to tire, praying your time wouldn't run out before you finished the job.

'Road trip,' he said.

'With a gun?'

'It's for my own peace of mind. I'm not expecting to use it. I just want to ask someone a few questions.'

Even as he answered, he realized that the three statements, when linked together, became drained of any sense or truth.

'Questions about what?'

'About the Colleen Clark thing.'

'Does Mr Castin know you're doing this?'

'Yes,' Reggio said, then caught the cold gleam in her eye. Jesus, the woman ought to have been a cop. 'Or no,' he relented, 'not as such, but I don't want him wasting his time on what might be nothing. If it pans out, it could be helpful, and if it doesn't, I'll have had myself a change of scenery.'

'Perhaps you should run it by him, just in case.'

'In case of what?'

'In case, you know, you—'

'Mess things up, is that what you were going to say?'

He was on the verge of shouting, and regretted it. He regarded raising one's voice, especially to a woman, as both a failure of courtesy and a sign of weakness. But for crying out loud, give a guy a break.

'No, that wasn't what I was going to say,' she replied evenly, but he could tell it probably was, or some version of the same. 'You've got nothing to prove, you know? Not to me, not to that detective, not to anyone.'

He finished checking the tires. She was following him as he knelt by each one, never letting him out of her sight, never giving him a chance to escape her attention. This was why he'd never had an affair. He could have gone to the North Pole and fucked an Eskimo in an igloo a half-mile from the cold heart of nowhere, and when he stepped outside to zip up his pants, she'd have been waiting for him in a pair of snowshoes, all disappointment – or chiefly disappointment, with a healthy shot of fury on the side. It was lucky that he loved her, too. Some of his former acquaintances, the ones who liked to screw around on their *mogli*, used to kid him about it, but he'd never minded. Why risk years of resentment for fleeting pleasure? Because if he'd ever had an affair, divorce wouldn't have entered into the equation. Amara wouldn't have given him the satisfaction, not when she could spend decades reminding him of his indiscretion instead. He'd never have known peace again.

'How long will you be gone?' she asked. She had spotted the overnight bag on the back seat.

'One night. Two at most.'

'Call me when you get there, wherever "there" is.'

'And when I wake, and before I go to sleep.'

'You'd better.' She gripped the lapels of his jacket and kissed him hard. 'You're an exasperating man, you know that?'

'Would you have me any other way?'

'Was it ever an option? If so, I don't recall it being mentioned.'

'Probably not,' said Reggio. 'But then, your father also warned me against marrying you because you couldn't be tamed.'

This was true. Amara's father had admitted it during his wedding speech. His wife had kicked him under the table after he said it, causing him to spill his champagne.

'He was right,' she said.

'Thankfully.'

She released him only reluctantly, and stayed in the yard to wave him off.

Once on the road, Reggio had felt a sense of liberation and purpose that was unfamiliar but welcome. The work he did for Moxie Castin contributed to his sense of self-worth, but it was often mundane. This was different. A little boy was missing, presumed dead, and his mother was about to face trial for his abduction and killing. Mr Castin didn't believe she was responsible, and Reggio trusted his judgment. Reggio had a chance to do something useful, to make a difference. That was all most men wanted and the desire did not diminish with age. He selected '50s Gold on Sirius and turned Connie Francis up loud. It was, he concluded, a good day to be alive.

Chapter LIV

I left Lyra Shapleigh's office no wiser, but with the knowledge that she might be unlikely to do or say anything that would strengthen the case against Colleen Clark, if only out of self-interest – and if one were being cynical about it, self-interest was a more reliable stimulus than altruism, particularly when it came to the law. I was pulling out of the medical center's parking lot when Dave Evans called from the Great Lost Bear.

'Do you know a guy called John Wayne Akers?'

'Seriously?' I said. 'After the serial killer, or the movie star?'

'The movie star, smartass.' Dave paused. 'Or I'm pretty sure it's the movie star. Still, I'll take that as a no. He drives a truck for Pine State, so he's in and out of here every couple of weeks.' Pine State Beverage was one of the biggest beer and wine distributors in the region. 'He's solid.'

I dodged a battle-scarred cat on the road and saw that I'd also missed a call from Tony Fulci while speaking with Shapleigh.

'What about John Wayne Akers,' I said, 'solidity apart?'

'He saw on the news that you were involved with the Colleen Clark case. He told me that a friend of his sister used to date Stephen Clark. Before he was married, obviously.'

'We all know that Clark cheated at least once on his wife,' I told him, 'so I wouldn't go rushing to qualify his behavior.'

'My grandmother used to say that every man looked like someone who'd cheat on his wife,' said Dave. 'I think she did it to get a rise out of my grandfather. Worked every time. Anyway, John Wayne says that Clark used his fists on the girl. She came close to pressing charges, before deciding it might be less trouble just to dump him.'

'Did John Wayne give you a name?'

'Beth Witham. He thinks it's Witham with an "i", but he couldn't swear to it. She lives in Topsham now. Last he heard, she was working weekdays at the Kopper Kettle. He said it might be worth your while talking to her.'

'That was helpful of him.'

'Do I detect a note of hesitation?'

'So far, helpfulness has been rare when it comes to Colleen Clark, for obvious reasons.'

'All the more cause to be open to breaks. John Wayne told me that no one who knew Stephen Clark from those days has any great fondness for him. John Wayne's sister is convinced she smells a rat. When she read about the case, the first thing she said to him was "Stephen did it", and even the appearance of that bloodied blanket hasn't altered her opinion.'

I thanked Dave and stopped to make a note of the two names – John Wayne Akers and Beth Witham – on the writing pad attached to the dashboard. Dave was right: under the current circumstances, I'd accept help, whatever the source.

Topsham was just shy of thirty miles north of Portland, but I'd still have to set aside a couple of hours to travel there and back to speak with Witham, assuming Akers was as solid as Dave maintained. The Kopper Kettle opened only for breakfast and lunch. I could aim to cross paths with her at her place of employment the next morning. Right now, I wanted to check in at the Clark house, and speak with Tony.

True to Steady Freddy's word, the police had begun a new search of the Clark property, this time using a cadaver dog. To offer some element of privacy to those inside, and also to ensure that no graphic images of human remains made their way onto the internet, a barrier tarp had been erected at the front of the property, and a no-fly zone for drones created by order of the court. That wouldn't necessarily stop people from trying to use them, but the police would have to act if they did.

I doubted the searchers would find anything beyond old squirrel bones under the Clark dirt, but the search had attracted a media presence, as well as assorted locals – the Robacks to the fore, though not Alison Piucci – and a handful of lookie-loos from farther afield. I wondered if Mara Teller might be among them, but a quick recce of the other faces turned up only hostile men and hard women.

Tony was on duty when I pulled up, the monster truck casting a literal pall over the lawn and a metaphorical one over the lives of the neighbors. That truck was hard to ignore. Tony jumped out to greet me, and the ground shook as he landed.

'I saw I missed some calls,' I said.

'Paulie had a problem last night.'

'What kind of problem?'

Tony led me past the cop in the yard, a patrolman who knew us both by sight and reputation. There were scorch marks under the living room window, and blackened flowers in the beds beneath. To my right, I saw two officers working a grid with the cadaver dog.

'A firebomb, lobbed from a passing car,' said Tony. 'Two guys: one driving, one throwing. Paulie used an extinguisher on the flames, but by then the car was gone.'

'Was Paulie in the truck?'

'No, I took the truck home. He was in the Explorer.'

That might have explained it. The Explorer was a lot less conspicuous.

'Did he get a license number or make of the vehicle?' I asked.

'He didn't get a look at the plate, though he thought he might know the car. It was a gray sedan, though the driver's door was black. He's seen it around the Old Port. He thinks it belongs to Antoine Pinette.'

Antoine Pinette was a racist and committed anti-Semite, but far from unintelligent, which made his shortcomings even more reprehensible. Lately, he'd been made responsible for what passed for security in the world of Bobby Ocean and his Stonehurst Foundation. Bobby and I had history. His son, Billy, had once burned out my car and nearly set fire to my home. The kid was now dead, and his father had compiled a long list of people he held responsible, me included. His son's passing had driven any semblance of humanity from Bobby, who was now mired in racial hatred and the politics of the far right. If Antoine Pinette was pitching firebombs at the Clark home as part of his deal with Bobby Ocean, it was as much an attack on me as on Colleen. Bobby was sending a message: he hadn't forgiven, or forgotten.

'Where's Paulie now?'

'At home, asleep.'

'You sure about that?'

'I wouldn't lie to you, Mr. Parker.'

'When he wakes up, you tell him to keep his distance from Pinette,' I said. 'That goes for you as well. If you see Pinette, cross the street to avoid him. I'll take care of this.'

'What if they try again?'

'I'll set things in motion today,' I said, but I couldn't hide my frustration. I had enough to keep me occupied without reentering the world of Bobby Ocean. Neither would Moxie be pleased to hear that Bobby had involved himself in the Clark affair, if only by proxy. I was becoming stretched, which wouldn't be helpful to Moxie or Colleen. Sometimes, you had to know when to ask for more help. I stepped aside from Tony and called New York. The conversation was brief and to the point. When I hung up, Tony's face had brightened considerably.

'Are they coming?'

'Yes, Tony,' I said, in the manner of Francis Pharcellus Church informing Virginia O'Hanlon that there was indeed a Santa Claus, 'they're coming. They'll be here by evening.'

Tony grinned.

'I like it better when they're around,' he said. 'They make everything more colorful.'

I doubted Bobby Ocean or Antoine Pinette would view this development in quite the same light, but that was the point.

'Colorful is one term for it,' I said.

'Yeah,' said Tony. He frowned for a moment as he thought. 'Wait, is "fucked up" the other?'

*

Inside the house, Evelyn Miller was reading a copy of the *Boston Globe* at the breakfast table. After the firebomb, her nerves were likely to be on edge, not helped by police looking for her grandson's body in the yard.

'Is everything okay?' she asked. 'With Colleen, I mean.'

'She might be going stir-crazy,' I said, 'but she's safe.'

'I just spoke to her,' said Evelyn, 'and she sounded so down. She says she keeps waiting for her phone to ring with news of Henry. She knows he's dead, she said, but she doesn't want him to be lost anymore.'

She put her hand to her mouth. I waited for her to compose herself.

'I'm sorry about what happened last night,' I said.

'The fire? There was nothing more that Paulie could have done, but if he hadn't been on watch, the whole house might have gone up.'

'We may have some idea of who was responsible,' I said. 'They'll be spoken to.'

'Will that be enough?'

'It depends on who's doing the talking.'

'I have confidence in your ability to select appropriate candidates.' She turned the newspaper toward me. 'Have you seen this?'

The story detailed the deaths of four men in a crash on I-91, all executives from the same company, DavMatt-Hunter.

'Your son-in-law's firm,' I said.

'I'd prefer not to hear him referred to in that way any longer,' she said, 'but yes.'

'What does this mean for him?'

'The last I heard, the company was poised to sign two or three big deals. If they've just lost four people, they'll have to consolidate, and present the best face possible. That could work out well for Stephen. He's good at what he does, but others at DavMatt-Hunter are better.'

'Any of them among the dead?'

'At least two.'

'So it's good news for him, once he gets over the shock.'

'I don't think shock will be much of a problem,' she said.

'Stephen always viewed those immediately above him as obstacles to what should have been his progress. I fear that was one of the reasons he chose my daughter: because she represented a means of ascension. Perhaps it was less a case of marrying her than her father and his influence.'

'And did your late husband oblige?'

'He put in a word or two where it mattered, and wasn't averse to introducing Stephen to the right people. Had he not, I don't believe DavMatt-Hunter would have hired him.' She reconsidered. 'No, that makes Stephen sound less competent than he is. It might be more accurate to say that his status as the son-in-law of Thomas Miller was enough to tip the scales in his favor. Once Stephen got a foot on the ladder, he became hard to dislodge, but I didn't think he'd rise much higher than his current position, for all his aspirations, not unless something changed dramatically. This accident means that an opportunity for advancement has presented itself, and you can be sure Stephen will grasp it.'

It wasn't an unfamiliar situation, and didn't necessarily make Stephen Clark a terrible person. Much depended on his level of self-awareness and his understanding of his strengths and weaknesses. In life, I often thought it was better to have twenty percent talent and eighty percent application than the opposite, because you'd get a lot more done. Ambition wasn't a vice: as Browning wrote, 'a man's reach should exceed his grasp, / Or what's a heaven for?', but the trick was to measure the gap and act accordingly. If someone didn't learn that lesson, they were likely to end up bitter, disappointed, or dead.

'How long will this go on?' she asked, as another pair of searchers joined the first set. We could see them through the kitchen window.

'It isn't a large area to search. They'll be done by the afternoon. The house will follow, but again, it won't take much time.'

Moxie hadn't bothered raising any objection to the search. Cooperating was another move in the game.

'I miss my own home and garden,' said Evelyn. 'Do you think Colleen could be persuaded to join me there until the trial? I know she's said that she wants to return here, but increasingly

249

it's starting to feel like a combination of a goldfish bowl and the waiting room of a funeral home. I'm sorry, but it's the truth.'

The legal system was a form of limbo, leaving accusers and accused, along with their families, suspended in an enervating existence as cases slowly wended their way to court. No wonder the case of Jarndyce and Jarndyce broke so many people in *Bleak House*, leaving bodies and madness in its wake. Evelyn Miller was getting her first taste of that now.

'Aside from the fact that we don't know when the trial might be, this is her home,' I replied. 'If it's where she wants to be, that has to be respected.'

'Even without Henry?'

'She'll be without Henry regardless of where she goes. Until he's found, Colleen is a ghost, and this is the place she'll have to haunt.'

Evelyn pointedly returned to her newspaper, ruffling the pages for good measure.

'I was warned you were a strange man,' she said.

'I try not to disappoint.'

Chapter LV

Maynard Vaughn had lived a peripatetic existence. He was born in the town of Dexter, Maine, but was always restless there. He left school at fifteen and joined the army at seventeen with the consent of his parents, who were happy to see him leave, Maynard qualifying as the definition of a difficult child. By eighteen, he was fighting in Vietnam, and his experiences there exacerbated the undiagnosed psychological conditions that had plagued his adolescence, including bipolar disorder and obsessive-compulsive behavior. Following a firefight at Lai Khe in December 1968, Maynard's company sergeant discovered him sitting in a deserted enemy bunker, arranging pebbles into a pyramid while holding between his teeth a grenade with the pin pulled. After a tense negotiation, the sergeant succeeded in restoring the pin to the grenade, and for the safety of multiple parties, Maynard was transferred to the care of the 98th Psychiatric Detachment – the KO team, as it was known – at the 8th Field Hospital in Nha Trang.

It wasn't obvious if Maynard had been actively trying to kill himself at Lai Khe, since his upper row of teeth was clamped down firmly on the strike lever when he was found. Later, during sessions with a civilian-trained psychiatrist, he admitted to a pattern of suicidal ideation since early adolescence, and confessed to passing idle evenings at home in Dexter by playing Russian roulette in the family barn with his father's Colt revolver. Maynard also revealed that he felt bad about shooting at the Vietnamese. Every time he fired his weapon in anger, he experienced a strong urge to turn it on himself immediately afterward. When asked why he had not done so, Maynard replied that having licked various bullets and grenades, he'd finally decided he preferred the taste of the latter. But he had detected subtle differences in flavor between individual devices and was determined to find one with a hint of licorice, this being a sign that he had located the ideal grenade with which to end his life. Following these revelations, it was decided that it might be best to ship Maynard Vaughn home.

In the years that followed, Maynard dipped in and out of employment, marriage, homelessness, and psychiatric care. With treatment, he ceased to contemplate suicide daily, not least because he was worried about leaving a mess for someone to clean up, and gained sufficient insight into his bipolar condition to recognize the importance of keeping up with his meds. In due course, he returned to Dexter, but any family he once had were long departed and few people remembered his name. Thanks to the combined efforts of social services, the National Coalition for Homeless Veterans, and the Bureau of Veterans' Services, subsidized housing was found for him in the area and modest benefits secured. For the first time in his life, Maynard knew a version of contentment.

Maynard was very grateful to everyone who helped him and never failed to say thank you for a kindness offered. There was a gentleness to him, and a simplicity. When he went into one of his periodic declines, when he became angry and weepy and craved the taste of licorice, he would be taken by an officer of the Dexter PD to the Hometown Health Center, where he would be looked after. If he was very ill, he would be referred to the Togus VA facility in Chelsea, but some bed rest at Hometown was usually sufficient to set him to rights.

Maynard spent most of his waking hours doing odd jobs around town, collecting bottles for redemption, watching TV, and reading old comic books. Sometimes, when the walls closed in on him, he would sleep rough for a night or two, but he always returned to his little apartment; and even the worst of the local kids, as bored and frustrated by their surroundings as he had once been, left Maynard unbothered.

On this particular afternoon, Maynard crossed Lake Wassookeag on Grove Street, hung a right onto Bugbee Road, and followed it down to the lakeshore. His pack contained two cans of soda and two wrapped slices of pizza – one regular, one pepperoni

– that had been handed to him as he passed the Dexter House of Pizza not long before. He also had in his possession a copy of that day's *Bangor Daily News*, rescued from a trash can, and a couple of Fantastic Four comics that he hadn't reread in a while, including a Marvel *Team-Up* from 1975 in which Wyatt Wingfoot and the entire Keewazi tribe become possessed by the demon Dryminextes, and have to be saved by Daimon Hellstrom, the Son of Satan, and Johnny Storm, the Human Torch. Except, of course, Daimon also briefly becomes possessed by Dryminextes, which indicated to Maynard that Dryminextes was really something: it wasn't just any old demon that could go around possessing the son of the Hell-Lord. So Maynard planned to become reacquainted with Wyatt Wingfoot over pizza and soda at a quiet spot by the lake. Afterward, he might have himself a nap before heading back to town, because a man who couldn't appreciate the pleasure of forty winks under God's own ceiling on a clement afternoon was an idiot.

Just as Maynard was about to leave the fire road for the lake, he heard a car slowing behind him. He'd seen it around town earlier in the day and waved a greeting at the driver, but hadn't received one in return. Maynard wasn't too troubled by this. Some people considered the driver odd, which in Maynard's opinion involved a heap of kettles calling the pot black, because it wasn't as though Dexter was going to run out of odd anytime soon, Maynard himself included. In addition, the driver's family had been known to put work Maynard's way. They were private folk who preferred not to have their business broadcast for the diversion of others. Maynard, by virtue of his condition and his place in the hierarchy of the town, could be trusted not to talk out of turn. Probably.

Maynard hadn't spoken with the driver in a while, but the last conversation had earned him twenty dollars for standing in line for a few minutes, which was about the best remuneration Maynard had ever received in his life.

The car drew up alongside him. The window rolled down.

'Hello, Maynard,' said the driver. 'You got a few minutes? Might be I can make it worth your while.'

Maynard shifted the pack on his left shoulder. He thought about the slices, the sodas, and the comic books. He recalled Wyatt Wingfoot and his battle against possession. He felt the breeze on his face. He had been anticipating an afternoon of leisure. On the other hand, he could do with another twenty right now. Maynard could always do with another twenty. He didn't know anyone who could not.

'I got time,' said Maynard.

The passenger door opened. Despite the sunlight, the interior was very dark.

'Then hop in.'

Maynard got in.

'Is it okay if I eat my pizza?' he asked. 'I won't make a mess.'

'Sure, you eat away.'

And Maynard Vaughn started the last meal he would consume.

Chapter LVI

I made contact with Moxie Castin on my way to my appointment with Colleen Clark's therapist. Moxie was unhappy to learn of the incident at the Clark house, and even less happy to learn that Antoine Pinette had probably been responsible, which also implicated Bobby Ocean.

'That fucking Ocean family,' said Moxie. 'The sooner the line dies out, the better.'

I'd been working on Moxie's dime when I first came into conflict with the Oceans, so we both had reason to be wary of any further involvement with its patriarch. Then again, Bobby was the one inviting renewed acquaintance through the use of firebombs.

'I'll have to beard him,' I said.

'Pinette or Bobby?'

'If Pinette's the monkey, Bobby is grinding the organ. But two separate conversations may be in order.'

'If Antoine Pinette's a monkey, it's one with sharp teeth,' said Moxie. 'No lawyer in town will touch him, and it takes a lot for a lawyer to turn down hard cash. I'm not sure your talking with him is going to do us a lot of good.'

I'd already begun asking around town about Pinette's latest rackets: to be forewarned was to be forearmed, which was an apt saying in this instance. I was hearing that Pinette's criminal interests now extended to illegal firearms, and not just discounted pistols from the trunk of a car. Pinette, it was said, might have a line on military-grade weaponry, for the right people and the right price.

'I wasn't planning on confronting him alone,' I said.

Moxie absorbed this information. He knew what it meant. Bobby Ocean might have hated me for what happened to his boy, and despised Moxie for his part in it – as well as for his bloodline, which wasn't pure enough for Bobby's liking – but he reserved most of his fury for the man he considered to be the primary instigator, the one who ignited the conflagration that ultimately consumed his son: Louis.

'If I didn't know better, I'd almost be tempted to hold off,' said Moxie. 'They may just be trying to stir up mischief.'

'This time,' I said. 'But later, who knows? Bobby holds us all responsible for his boy's death. He's not about to let that slide, which means he's always going to be looking for opportunities to come at us.'

I heard the sound of a soda can opening on the other end of the line: Moxie resorting, in a moment of stress, to his namesake drink of choice.

'Even if you meet with Bobby,' said Moxie, 'he'll deny all knowledge of the attack.'

'Let him. But if he has any sense, he'll back down. He won't want me nosing around in his affairs, and we don't need him as a distraction. I feel like I'm being pulled in ten different directions as it is.'

'You know,' said Moxie, 'you seem worryingly eager to renew acquaintance with Bobby.'

'It's going to happen one way or the other,' I said. 'And I don't like waiting.'

Chapter LVII

Colleen Clark's therapist, Blaise Veilleux, worked out of a neat cottage in Pownal, a small town north of Portland. Veilleux was a stern woman with features that didn't settle naturally into an expression of empathy, and the blazing eyes of a zealot. She showed me into the room in which she conducted her sessions: a small, studiedly neutral space with two chairs, a couch, and a console table on which stood a box of tissues and a bottle of hand sanitizer shaped like a dove. She offered me a glass of water or herbal tea. I stuck with water. I didn't want to ask for the wrong kind of tea for the time of day and come off like a rube.

If Lyra Shapleigh had demonstrated a marked reluctance to be called as a witness in the impending trial, Veilleux was the opposite. Even during the call to establish a time for our meeting, she told me she was marking likely trial dates in her diary. From my research, I knew that she worked with various women's support groups and family charities across Maine. She was frequently quoted in newspaper and magazine features about domestic abuse, coercive control, reproductive rights, and issues related to motherhood, including postnatal depression. I'd even caught her on a couple of news shows. If she wasn't quite a celebrity, she was becoming well-known, and gave every impression of relishing it.

As soon as I sat, she began asking when she might be required to provide a deposition and why Moxie Castin himself wasn't present to hear what she had to say.

'I mean,' she concluded, 'sending an employee suggests a possible lack of engagement on his part.'

Moxie, I thought, had dodged a bullet, and not only because he didn't drink a lot of water, or go in for herbal tea. Still, there was some element of truth to what Veilleux had said – in general terms, if not specific. By taking care of the preliminary interviews, I could save Moxie time that might otherwise have been wasted in recording statements from witnesses with nothing useful to offer, but my impressions would also help lay the groundwork for his own line of questioning. I tried to explain some of this to Veilleux, emphasizing the second part over the first, but she wasn't convinced. She poured me water from a jug, accompanied by a lot of sighing and frowning. I wouldn't have wanted her as my therapist. I wouldn't even have wanted her standing too close to me in line at the post office.

'How long have you been treating Colleen?' I asked, once she'd quietened down, and I'd made it apparent that I wasn't uncomfortable with silence.

'About a year,' said Veilleux. 'Colleen also gave me permission to consult with her physician.'

'Lyra Shapleigh.'

'That's right. Have you spoken to Lyra?'

'I have.'

'And?'

'She was helpful.'

Veilleux arched an eyebrow. 'Really?'

'Within certain limits,' I conceded.

'She doesn't want to get too involved.'

'Are you asking or telling me?'

'Both, if you wish.'

'Then, yes, I think that's a fair summary of her position.'

'Do you know why?'

'Regardless of the ultimate verdict, there'll be fallout from this case,' I said. 'I wouldn't condemn anyone for preferring not to be drawn into it.'

'Which isn't answering the question.'

'No, because I gather you may have an opinion of your own.'

'Not an opinion,' said Veilleux, 'but knowledge. Lyra's an admirer of Paul Nowak, and would like to see him elected governor. She's planning to make the maximum contribution to his campaign once he officially announces his candidacy. Her wife will do the same.'

That would amount to at least $3,900, which was a considerable financial commitment. But if what Veilleux was saying was true – and it could easily be checked – it also represented a potential conflict of interest should Shapleigh be required to testify, which was something on which Moxie would have to adjudicate. I was annoyed with Shapleigh. She was entitled to support whomever she liked. I just wished she'd been open about it from the start.

But Veilleux's information raised another question, which was why she had elected to share it with me at this early stage of our conversation. It might have been an issue of conscience, which would make her a better person than I was inclined to give her credit for; but in my experience, people didn't offer this kind of intelligence without an ulterior motive.

'How do you know this?' I asked.

'Lyra and I have mutual acquaintances. Her political affiliations are hardly worth keeping secret. It's not like she's joined the Klan.'

'What about you? Are you in the Nowak camp?'

'The two-party system has failed our country,' she said. 'I favor Hannah Russell.'

Russell routinely ran as an unenrolled candidate and was always quickly eliminated. I tried to keep abreast of politics, and regarded myself as reasonably well-informed, but even I struggled to figure out exactly what she stood for, apart from better holistic veterinary care for pets.

'She seems like' – I searched for the right words, and failed – 'a nice person,' I concluded lamely.

'She's a dog with three legs,' said Veilleux, 'but her heart is in the right place.'

'And Dr Shapleigh?'

'What about her?'

'Is her heart also in the right place?'

'That depends on what you can do for her. I've known Lyra for many years now. She's a pragmatic person, which makes her a pretty good physician. In the case of Colleen Clark, she wouldn't want to do or say anything that might damage Nowak's chances, but her preference would be to avoid saying anything at all. As you pointed out, there'll be blowback if it goes to trial, whatever the verdict. If Lyra were to testify, and that testimony aided the prosecution, a small but vocal community, some of whom she considers friends, might view her as perpetuating a system that penalizes psychologically troubled women. On the other hand, if she were to help Colleen get off, there'd be people prepared to throw bricks through her window, and it wouldn't help Nowak's cause either. So Lyra will try to stay out of it, even if she has to lawyer up. She won't go out of her way to assist you, but she'll do her damnedest not to damage your cause either.'

Which was what Shapleigh herself had told me, if without the political insights.

'Does she often refer patients to you?'

'Sometimes, and always women – though Colleen's initial referral came from another client, not Lyra. My base is almost entirely female, apart from a few couples.'

'Aren't you sympathetic to male problems?'

Her eyes narrowed.

'Are you trying to bait me, Mr Parker?'

'Perhaps I'm in the market for a therapist.'

'From what I've heard about you, that wouldn't surprise me. I might even be prepared to make an exception out of inquisitiveness.'

'I'll be sure to pick up a card on my way out. Tell me about Colleen.'

'There's a limit to what I'm prepared to divulge,' said Veilleux, 'even with her permission. She's in a vulnerable position right now, but I have to take the larger picture into account.'

'I appreciate that, so let's go with what you feel comfortable sharing. If you testify, much of the questioning is likely to revolve around whether Colleen displayed signs of hostile ideation toward her son.'

'She did not,' said Veilleux firmly.

'Never?'

'No. She was frustrated and depressed, and admitted to impatience with him, but on no occasion did she indicate that she had seriously contemplated hurting Henry. She worried that she wasn't a fit mother and would never be able to take care of him properly. She felt isolated – more so than usual, given that she's not naturally a sociable person – and believed her husband wasn't assuming anything resembling an appropriate share of responsibility for the child, especially as he was the one who wanted them to begin a family, perhaps before Colleen was ready.'

I was tempted to go straight to the subject of Stephen Clark, but instead spent some time going into more detail about Colleen's difficulties, or as much as Veilleux was willing to offer. As far as she could attest, Colleen loved her son, but lacked confidence in her own emotional, psychological, and even physical capacities for motherhood. This, said Veilleux, wasn't unusual, but each woman who endured this kind of difficulty experienced it in her own unique way.

'Like grief,' I said.

'Yes,' agreed Veilleux, 'like grief, like love, like despair. Like life.'

'Had Stephen stepped up to the plate, do you think that might have eased that pressure on Colleen?'

'Certainly, but her treatment primarily involved developing the skills and mindset to cope with what she was going through. Altering her husband's behavior was out of her hands, and would have involved a different form of therapy.'

'Couples therapy?'

'Yes.'

'Did you raise that possibility?'

'I indicated that it might be beneficial,' said Veilleux. 'I'm not saying her husband was unaware of her suffering – that would imply emotional blindness verging on sociopathy – but he might not have been cognizant of its depth, or even the simple steps he could have taken to alleviate it. Also, it was obvious that he was working long hours, and was very much engaged in his career. From what Colleen told me, he was intent on providing a certain quality of life for his family, but the emphasis was on financial security accrued from corporate success rather than emotional security arising from day-to-day engagement with his wife and child. Again, that's not uncommon, albeit, I think, a peculiarly male approach.'

'And the therapy?'

'He declined to become involved, on any level. This was his wife's problem, and he had enough difficulties of his own, which was his position as articulated by Colleen. I should emphasize that fact: whatever information or insights I may have about Stephen Clark are refracted through the prism of his wife's experience. Were he to sit in that chair, we might be given a very different tale.'

'Be careful what you wish for,' I said. 'I've met him.'

'You didn't like him?'

'He wants to see his wife imprisoned. He's not prepared to countenance any narrative that precludes her from having harmed their child.'

She turned her palms upward, like Christ displaying his wounds.

'I'm reluctant to condemn him for it,' she said. 'This is a terrible situation for any parent to find themselves in.'

'I may be less reluctant to condemn.'

'You find his certitude disconcerting?'

'Yes.'

'Well, that's why you're a detective. You're trained to respond with suspicion. I'm trained to understand.'

I wondered how many of her patients had been tempted to burn her house down. Not enough of them, I decided.

'Did Colleen speak to you about his affair with Mara Teller?' I asked.

'Yes.'

'What were her feelings about it?'

'Sorrow, and to a lesser degree anger and shame.'

'Why shame?'

'Because she blamed herself more than she blamed her husband,' said Veilleux. 'She felt that if she'd been enough for him, he would not have looked elsewhere to satisfy those needs. I mean, it's obviously more complicated than that, but as a bare précis of her position, it's adequate.'

Veilleux tugged at her bottom lip with the forefinger of her right hand, the first time she'd displayed anything resembling a nervous tic. I let a distant clock count the seconds.

'You're very patient, aren't you?' she said.

'It's born of necessity. I spend a lot of time sitting, watching. Not understanding.'

'Was that sarcasm?'

'Barely.'

'And listening, too?'

'Yes.'

'Then we may not be so dissimilar after all.'

'I never intimated that we were.'

'No, you didn't, did you?' She clasped her hands and leaned forward, like someone about to share a delicious secret. 'Did Colleen mention that she suspected Stephen of cheating on her previously?'

'It's a natural response to unfaithfulness, to suspect there may have been more than one instance of it.'

'With me, she was more specific,' said Veilleux. 'You see, she thought her husband might have met this Mara Teller person before.'

This I had not known.

'When?' I asked.

'At an earlier conference, before Colleen even became pregnant. She was convinced that she recalled the name, potentially from a document she'd seen, or notes made by her husband. She used to help Stephen with reports, because he was a lousy typist and a poor speller. Later, as she tried to keep her marriage together, she started to doubt herself, and ultimately she recanted. When I attempted to return to the subject a couple of months ago, she waved it off as a misapprehension brought on by the stress of all that had happened, and the name Mara Teller going round and round in her head, but I thought it was interesting. Our initial impressions are often correct: the first name that comes to mind upon renewing acquaintance with someone, for example, or the title of a film or song seemingly half-remembered.'

I would have to ask Colleen about this when I returned to Scarborough. More and more, I was finding aspects of her conduct disquieting, although I still did not believe she had killed her son. Instead, I was reminded of a novel I had first read in college, and to which I had returned many times since: Ford Madox Ford's *The Good Soldier*, a book as steeped in irony as any I'd encountered. Colleen reminded me of its narrator, John Dowell, a character to whom things happen yet who does very little himself, a figure existing in a curious state of enervation. Even his name was only a letter away from *dowel*, a joint of wood in a wall to which other pieces are nailed.

'Would it be fair to describe Colleen's disposition as passive?'

'I think it might,' said Veilleux. 'The hardest part of our therapy has been convincing her to be something more than an observer of her own life. Even the decision to become a mother could almost be regarded as one made for her by another.'

'Her husband?'

'Chiefly, but there was also some pressure from her mother, however well-intentioned. The main driver, though, was Stephen. He was very eager to be a father. It represented a change of heart for him, since he'd shown little interest in fatherhood for much of their relationship.'

'Why the transformation?'

'Colleen couldn't say, other than that a child was just something he'd suddenly decided he wanted. We could speculate, I suppose. The ethos in certain corporations requires men to present a set version of themselves, one that includes a stable family life, even if the burden of work, and the pressure to succeed, is destined to undermine that stability. Obviously, that doesn't apply to female executives, who are most definitely not encouraged to become pregnant and start families, but that's an argument for another day. And there's the simple biological imperative: Stephen might have wanted to pass on his genes, to leave something of himself in the world after he was gone. The truth, of course, may come down to some combination of the above, allied to motives of which we have no knowledge due to Stephen's reluctance to reveal himself, even to his wife.'

I looked at my notes. I'd circled the names of Mara Teller and Stephen Clark before enfolding them in a larger oval. I felt the urge to check my phone in case Maralou Burnham had gotten back to me with news about the money order used by Teller to pay for her attendance at the forum. If she hadn't, I'd nudge her.

I asked Blaise Veilleux if there was anything else she could think of that might be of assistance, but she skirted the question in order to return to the subject of her testimony. She wanted to be sure she'd have the opportunity to give evidence, and that zealot's gleam returned to her eyes. I phrased the next inquiry carefully, even disingenuously.

'It means a lot that you're so open to taking the stand,' I said. 'What you have to say could be important.'

'It *is* important,' said Veilleux. 'It's a chance to set out publicly the reality of postnatal depression, and the way it is dismissed or, as in the case of Colleen, used against women for evidential or political gain. People have to be told. They must be made aware.'

So there it was: Veilleux might have cared about Colleen as a patient, but she also viewed her as a resource, a weapon to be wielded. Veilleux was a crusader, and while I didn't doubt the righteousness of her cause, it wasn't for her to use Colleen to further it. Back in the fifteenth century, men and women not dissimilar to Blaise Veilleux had viewed Joan of Arc's immolation as collateral damage.

I thanked her for her time, and advised her that Moxie would be in touch to arrange a further meeting. But if she were to testify, I knew she'd need to be held in check. What she had to offer would be beneficial to Colleen's case, but only if it wasn't accompanied by grandstanding. It would be up to Moxie to convince Veilleux that clearing Colleen's name would aid the larger cause without the need for any additional finger-wagging in court. Whatever else Veilleux had to offer could be included in the feature articles and television appearances that might follow the verdict.

She walked me to the door and waited for me to drive off before closing it, as though fearful that I might otherwise take up residence in her yard and seek therapeutic assistance in return for light gardening duties. In one of the flower beds stood a weather-worn lawn sign advocating Hannah Russell's candidacy for governor. I hadn't spotted it before, but I expected that if I returned to Veilleux's home anytime between now and the election, the sign would still be there, and might even be standing come the next set of primaries. Blaise Veilleux didn't strike me as a person who gave up easily, which wasn't always a bad state of being. As she said, we might not have been so dissimilar after all.

Chapter LVIII

Mattia Reggio didn't drive directly to the Michaud property, but first took a run through Gretton, mainly with the intention of finding somewhere to take a leak. In the center of town was a local coffee shop and grocery store with a parking lot, so he ordered a coffee and scone to go before grabbing the restroom key. When he returned, lighter in spirit and bladder, his coffee and pastry were waiting for him. The skies opened as he prepared to leave, scouring the streets, so he took a seat by the window and watched what passed for life in Gretton. The town, he decided, wasn't much to look at it in the rain, not that it would have been anyone's idea of paradise in the sunlight either. Were he forced to spend his declining years here – he couldn't imagine settling in the place voluntarily – the general low-level melancholy he carried with him would certainly have deepened into outright misery.

The scone was dry and heavy, and he gave up on it halfway through. He was just wadding what remained of it in the paper bag when a man walking on the opposite side of the street caught his attention.

Lars Ungar, thought Reggio. *Just when you figured a place couldn't drop any lower, the Nazis move in.*

Through his work for Moxie Castin, Reggio was aware of all manner of malefactors, but he was particularly aware of those who orbited Bobby Ocean, because of the history between the Oceans and Charlie Parker. What distinguished Ocean's cohort from generic haters, the kind who infected the lower reaches of human interaction like a gonorrhea of the soul, was their relative intelligence. Lars Ungar might have been a bigot and a xenophobe, but he could string together a series of coherent sentences without lapsing into spittle-flecked abuse, and might even have passed for a regular human being were it not for the swastika tattooed on his face, a relic of youthful overenthusiasm during a two-year sentence in Maine State Prison for aggravated assault, if none that he saw a reason to disown. That was back when the MSP was still located in Thomaston, and prisoners occupied six-by-seven cells in a facility that had been modern when it was built in the 1920s, but hadn't aged well.

Reggio, as a much younger and more reckless man, had served time in Thomaston for wire fraud. It was only a six-month term, but enough to convince him of the error of his ways: in future, he would be more careful, and not get caught. Thomaston had burned down twice, once in 1850 and again in 1923, but no one had ever been able to tell Reggio for sure how many prisoners died in the fires. He supposed that nobody really cared, but he'd hated Thomaston, hated it as intensely as any institution in which he'd been imprisoned, and he'd seen the inside of a few in his early years. In the dead of night, he would wake to the smell of burning in his cell, and in those moments the torments of long-departed men touched his soul, taking him as close as he had ever come to worlds beyond this one.

Now here was Lars Ungar, a fellow alumnus, ambling toward a late-model Ford truck parked outside the Rite Aid, heedless of the rain, two bags of groceries in his arms and a pistol on open carry at his right side. The last Reggio had heard, Ungar was living north of Freeport in a house owned by one of Antoine Pinette's sisters. He might even have been sleeping with her, presumably with her brother's knowledge and assent, given that Antoine was staying there too.

Reggio took out his cell phone and clicked off a series of photographs of Ungar as he climbed into the passenger seat and the truck pulled away, passing the coffee shop as it headed south. Reggio didn't recognize the driver, but he took a picture of him as well.

Reggio felt a presence at his right shoulder. He glanced up to see one of the waitstaff also taking in the truck. She wore a full-face plastic shield and a blue surgical mask beneath. A rainbow flag pin was attached to the lapel of her shirt, above a second, larger pin that read IMMUNOCOMPROMISED AND TRYING TO STAY SAFE!

'You know those folks?' asked Reggio.

'I might.' She pointed a finger at the bag containing the remains of Reggio's scone, but didn't look directly at him. 'You finished with that, hon?'

'Yes, ma'am.' He decided to persist. 'Not a fan?'

'Of trash?' Her question could deliberately be taken two ways. 'No, sir.'

'Me neither,' he said. 'Would those particular pieces of trash be staying somewhere nearby?'

'Why do you ask?'

'Just curious.'

'Curious, huh?'

She didn't believe him, and he could see that she didn't, but she wasn't about to let the lie bother her. She appraised him, and decided he could be trusted.

'They have a camp outside of town,' she said, 'men and women both. The talk is that more are coming, but we don't want them here – or the majority don't, the ones who remember that we once fought a war to defeat people like them.'

'Do they own the property?'

'No, it's Hickman land. Den always did pull where others pushed, but I never took him for a bigot, not until they showed up.'

That name was familiar to Reggio.

'Is that the same Hickman whose holdings sit next to the Michaud place?'

'That's right.' She was peering at him with interest now. 'Are you a realtor – or a reporter, maybe?'

'Perish the thought,' said Reggio. 'I just drive, but I take an interest in local affairs.'

'Well, if you've any sense you'll keep driving, and let affairs in this locale take care of themselves.'

He thanked her for the advice and she moved on. Reggio waited until the rain stopped before returning to his car, but paused by the exit to ask some more questions of the woman with the rainbow flag pin, now that he was on a roll with her.

'How do the Michauds feel about those people living on the neighboring property?'

'Let's just say the Michauds and the Hickmans are neighbors without being neighborly,' she replied, 'so the Michauds probably don't feel very good about it at all.'

'Would the Michauds be willing to talk to me?'

'You sure you're not a reporter?'

'Cross my heart.'

'Whatever you are,' she said, 'I'd leave the Michauds be. Their land is posted, and they don't welcome visitors.'

'I can be very persuasive.'

'Nobody's that ingratiating,' she said, 'believe me.'

Reggio left the coffee shop. He'd tucked a few dollars extra under his cup because he thought she was a nice lady. His phone pinged as he got in the car: Amara, checking that he was safe. He replied with an OK, and added an X.

A screenshot of the message would be made public after his death.

Chapter LIX

I tried Maralou Burnham as I was driving back to Scarborough. My call went straight to voice mail, but she got back to me within minutes, and I pulled over so I could concentrate on what she had to say. It turned out that she'd just spoken to someone about the money order used by Mara Teller.

'I have good news' – she said.

I steeled myself for the worst, but was pleasantly surprised.

– 'and better news,' she finished. 'First, I know where the money order was purchased. It was bought at the post office in Dover-Foxcroft on April 8, paid for with cash.'

'Is that the good news or the better news?'

'That's just the good news,' said Maralou. 'The better news is that the clerk remembers who bought the money order, and it wasn't a woman. It was purchased – and this most assuredly did not come from me – by a man named Maynard Vaughn, who lives down in Dexter. The reason the clerk remembered is that Vaughn is sort of a local character around that neck of the woods. He's a veteran with psychological problems, but he's harmless. He's also not the kind of guy who usually buys money orders, or certainly not for oil and gas forums.'

'Did the clerk ask what the deal was?'

'The clerk might have made some remark, but Vaughn didn't bite. She just chalked it up to eccentricity, Vaughn not being immune to it.'

It sounded like Maynard Vaughn might have been paid a few bucks to pick up the money order for someone who didn't want to be caught on camera, which would be as bad as leaving a paper trail.

'Any idea if Vaughn owns a car?'

'He barely owns a second pair of shoes.'

Which raised the question of how he'd traveled the dozen miles, give or take, from Dexter to Dover-Foxcroft. There might be a local bus service, but I wasn't sure of it. I wondered if Mara Teller had driven Vaughn to the post office herself, in which case it might be worth seeking that court order to access any security footage from outside cameras. But if Teller was smart – and I was starting to think she was – she would have parked somewhere unmonitored to await Vaughn's return.

Now it was a matter of finding Vaughn and persuading him to tell me all he knew about Teller. She hadn't picked him at random, which would have been too risky. No, she'd chosen Vaughn because he could be trusted not to vanish with her money, or blab about what he'd been paid to do after the fact. I told Maralou that a whole case of wine was on its way to her, and if she wanted to share a bottle or two with the clerk at the Dover-Foxcroft post office, mentioning my name, I'd make up the difference next time.

I checked my watch. Angel and Louis would be in town in a couple of hours. They'd elected to drive up from New York to avoid two airports and the associated concerns about COVID, particularly given Angel's brush with cancer not so long before. By now, they'd probably stopped arguing over the choice of music for the trip and settled into companionable silence. I decided to wait until they arrived before tackling the problem of Antoine Pinette and Bobby Ocean. That was a wasps' nest, and it made no sense to poke it alone.

I took my *Maine Atlas and Gazetteer* from under the passenger seat, opened it to Map 32, and rested my smartphone on the page while I did a quick Google search. As anticipated, Dexter had its own post office, but Teller had decided not to have Maynard Vaughn buy the money order there: he would have been too well-known in town, which offered a greater likelihood of the purchase being flagged. Even though Dover-Foxcroft was only a fifteen-minute car ride away, it was in the next county, so taking Vaughn north to buy the money order must have seemed a safer bet. It would have been even better to have driven him to Bangor, since no one would have batted an eyelid in the city, but Teller might have been pressed for time, or had settled on a level of caution she regarded as appropriate but not excessive. She was covering her tracks because it was better than leaving them unconcealed, but she still probably considered any pursuit unlikely.

A more-or-less straight line north could be drawn between Dexter and Dover-Foxcroft, forming the base of a triangle. Virtually equidistant from both, on the border between Penobscot County to the south and Piscataquis County to the north, stood the town of Gretton, where Sabine Drew claimed to be able to hear Henry Clark crying. Gretton represented the apex of the triangle.

Soon, I thought, I'd be paying Gretton a visit.

Chapter LX

Mattia Reggio had printed off images of the Michaud land from Google Maps, and checked them one last time before heading out to the property while the light was still good. The first of the PRIVATE signs was posted by the main road, where a trail wide enough for a small truck led into heavy evergreens. A mailbox stood to the right of an open five-bar field gate, but Reggio saw no cameras or other security measures. He supposed that, if the server at the coffee shop was correct, the Michauds' reputation for unsociability was enough to dissuade locals from intruding, while the sign, and the general gloominess of the route through the trees, would have put off any desperate salesman who might have been tempted to make a cold call.

Reggio followed the trail, noting how well-maintained it was, even for a surface that was barely a step above dirt. He could see the places where depressions had been filled in with stones, and the foliage, although thick above, was cut back at the verge so as not to impede passage. But the trail took a couple of sharp turns along the way, and Reggio wouldn't have liked to be negotiating it at night. He passed two more signs advising against trespass before the house came in sight. It was wood-framed and painted a dull green, blending into its surroundings. A truck stood in the drive next to a garage with an open door, the interior well-ordered and filled with pegged tools, as well as what looked like boiler parts laid out on the cement floor. Male and female clothing hung from a line, stirring listlessly in the breeze. Reggio wondered if whoever was responsible for putting it out had bothered taking it in during the recent shower. At the first sign of a cloud, Amara was always fussing with a basket, even if the clothes were fresh out of the wash and so damp that Noah's own flood couldn't have made them any wetter.

Reggio pulled up behind the truck and got out. His gun was now tucked into the waistband of his pants, hidden by his jacket. He'd never owned a holster in his life, and if needed, the pistol could be in his right hand in seconds. Reggio was very much hoping he wouldn't have to use it, because he was out of practice, having fallen from the habit of traveling with a firearm now that he rarely did anything more exciting than drink an extra beer on Fridays or throw a ball too hard with his grandchildren. When he'd asked Moxie Castin if he might be required to carry a weapon as part of his duties, the lawyer told him that Parker took care of the rough stuff. Moxie said that he didn't want to have to lie awake nights worrying about the possibility of being forced to defend in court a second person who was on the payroll.

To Reggio's left was an extensive vegetable patch, with sticks set at regular intervals in the dirt. Amara grew some vegetables of her own, so Reggio knew that at this stage of the year the patch would be planted with broccoli and cabbage, some cauliflower too, and seeded with carrot and onion, along with peas, radishes, turnip, and spinach. The breeze caught coils of what might have been brown wire attached to each of the sticks. When Reggio squatted to take a closer look, he saw they were garlands of human hair.

The door of the house opened wide to reveal a man standing in the gap. He would easily have been six one or six two in his stocking feet, but the work boots he wore added extra inches. His shoulders were massive, but so too were his waist and gut, and Reggio thought that here was a guy not destined to be troubling Medicare for long. The weight he was carrying made it hard to tell his age, but if he was the man Reggio believed him to be, he was fifty-six. He wore coveralls over a half-buttoned collarless shirt, a mass of graying hair sprouting from the gap like a small mammal trying to make a break for freedom. He didn't appear armed, which was something. Reggio's nightmare was to have arrived at the Michaud place only to be confronted by some yokel with a shotgun.

275

'Can I help you?' asked the man, in a tone of unanticipated civility.

'I'm looking for Ellar Michaud,' said Reggio.

'Not any longer, although if you'd paid attention to all those signs you passed, you might still be. Must be a terrible burden, going through life not being able to read.'

'I saw them,' said Reggio, 'but they all started to blur into one after a while.' He gestured at the vegetable patch. 'What's with the hair?'

'Rabbits don't like the smell of it. They hate it more than they love what's buried beneath.'

Reggio felt the next question bubbling up, but forced it back unasked.

Yeah, but whose hair is it?

'My name's Mattia Reggio. I work for a lawyer down in Portland named Moxie Castin. I was hoping to speak with you for a few minutes.'

Michaud folded his arms and leaned against the doorframe. Reggio was surprised that the whole house didn't immediately tilt to the right.

'Speak away,' said Michaud, 'now you're here.'

Reggio might not have been experienced in matters of investigation, not like Parker, but he knew better than to go tackling a subject like a missing child head-on. He'd watched Michaud's face for a flicker of recognition at the mention of Castin's name, but spotted none. Nevertheless, everything about the Michaud property was making him wary, just as it had been since he'd first looked at those satellite images.

'I thought we might talk about those people holed up next door,' said Reggio.

This time Michaud's expression did change, and Reggio caught something that might have been relief.

'What are they to you?'

'To me? Nothing. I'm a live-and-let-live guy. Mr Castin, though, doesn't have any love for men of their stripe.'

'Their "stripe"?'

'He looks unfavorably on those who adorn their flesh with

relics of the Third Reich.' He tapped the corner of his left eye, roughly where Lars Ungar had his swastika tattoo. 'He views it as a weakness of character. I'm hoping you do too.'

'We can take care of our own disputes,' said Michaud. 'We don't have to resort to lawyers.'

'I don't doubt it,' said Reggio, 'if Lars Ungar was the sum of them. But it's not just him and one or two of his buddies setting up camp on Hickman land. They're the advance guard, with more to follow – and they've got money behind them.'

Reggio didn't know if this was true, but he considered it an educated guess. Lars Ungar equaled Antoine Pinette, who equaled Bobby Ocean, and Bobby was throwing cash at anyone with hatred to spare. All of which intelligence might just be sufficient to string the conversation with Michaud along for a while, assuming he was willing to countenance some extended parley. Reggio watched while Michaud did the math: a little of his time in return for what might be useful intelligence on the interlopers.

But the hair. What about the hair?

'Then you'd better come inside,' said Michaud, 'and we can find out what you know.'

Chapter LXI

Sabine Drew was reheating a slice of pizza when the boy, Henry Clark, started up again: not crying, but screaming, as whatever was holding him increased the pressure, clutching him tighter to itself. His captor was reacting to something, an outside stimulus – this it channeled through Henry – and its instinct was to draw the child close, because it feared his being taken away.

Which could only mean that, over in Gretton, someone was close to where the boy was buried, someone who represented a threat. Could the private detective have traveled there after all, following up quickly on whatever information she had been able to offer? She debated calling him, before deciding against it. If he was in Gretton, she'd find out about it soon enough.

Sabine set aside the pizza to sing a lullaby to the dead child.

Chapter LXII

Reggio sat at the pine table in Ellar Michaud's kitchen. The interior was cleaner than he'd expected, but gloomier than he would have been willing to tolerate in a home of his own. It was a consequence of the trees that crowded to the west of the house, blocking out the last of the evening sunlight; and the size of the windows, which were smaller than the room justified. The table was handcrafted, and the chairs too; they were rustic without being crude and their joinery, like the kitchen cabinetry, looked solid and true.

The two men passed through an uncluttered living room on the way to the kitchen, although the former was just as crepuscular as the latter. The couches and chairs were mismatched, while the wallpaper reminded Reggio of a funeral home. A small bookshelf held assorted hardcover volumes: *Reader's Digest* works on house-keeping, gardening, and cooking, along with a set of encyclopedias that looked old enough to have antedated the moon landings, or even the Second World War. There was no fiction, and no Bible, which was unusual in Reggio's experience of rural Maine. Neither could he see any religious iconography on the walls, only the kind of paintings and prints familiar from thrift stores: anonymous, bland depictions of landscapes and animals – art for those who either didn't like it or mistakenly believed that they did.

The kitchen reeked of stewed meat and boiled vegetables. Bare sanded boards formed the floor, and Reggio spotted flecks of blood and small white feathers on the chopping block beside the sink. He had deliberately positioned himself so he could see both the front door, via the living room, and the kitchen door that opened into the yard. Michaud took the seat opposite, his back to the window. Reggio had put a piece of fresh gum in his mouth before leaving the car, and was now rolling the foil into a ball with his fingertips. Fucking nervous tic: he'd have made a lousy poker player.

'Is this your handiwork?' he asked Michaud, indicating the kitchen cabinets and the furniture.

'The joinery is, but my father made the table and chairs. They're by way of being heirlooms now.'

'You live here alone?'

There had to be a woman around. The place had that feel, even had the laundry hanging on the line not confirmed it, but Michaud didn't reply to the question.

'You said you had something to tell me about those newcomers living over on Hickman's land.'

'I know Lars Ungar, or I know of him,' said Reggio. 'He's the one with the swastika by his eye.'

'I'm familiar with him,' said Michaud, 'and his taste in prettifications. What about him?'

This wasn't the speed or direction of conversation that Reggio favored. He'd come here to find out more about the driver of the car that had followed him from the county jail, but he was no Scheherazade, and there was only so long he could spin out a yarn. Even so, he didn't need Michaud trying to bring him directly to the point.

'Look, Mr Michaud, let's be clear on this: I want to help you, but I was also hoping that you might be able to help me. Whatever information I have to offer may require something in return.'

'I don't know nothing about those people,' said Michaud, 'beyond that I don't like them sharing my air.'

'Lars Ungar has done time,' said Reggio, 'but not for the things he ought to have. He raped a woman up in Winterville a couple of years back, and she wasn't the first, but nothing came of it.'

If Michaud considered this to be a grave moral or criminal error on Ungar's part, he hid his disapproval.

'So?'

'Are you comfortable with having a rapist living so close to your holding?'

Michaud shrugged. 'If I had a mind to, I could walk into the

Junco in Gretton and point out men I know for sure to have abused women. If I was to put it to them, they wouldn't even have the grace to look ashamed.'

Reggio made a mental note to give the Junco a miss, whatever the hell kind of establishment it was.

'There's a difference between knowing what acquaintances may be capable of,' he said, 'and leaving yourself and yours vulnerable to the predations of strangers.'

'Who says we're vulnerable?'

'You have guns?'

'This is rural Maine,' said Michaud. 'What do you think?'

'Well,' said Reggio, 'I understand how that might make you feel more secure, but here's the thing.' He leaned forward, as though to take Michaud into his confidence. 'Rumor has it that Lars Ungar and his people also have guns. *Lots* of guns. You could even say that, with them, it's by way of being an occupation.'

Chapter LXIII

Angel and Louis arrived in Portland shortly after 7 p.m., having become embroiled in snarls of traffic before and after Boston. They freshened up, and let some air into their apartment, but by then it was too late for us to pay a visit to Bobby Ocean at his place of business, and confronting him at his home after dark struck me as unwise. If Bobby was intent on stirring up trouble, he'd take any opportunity offered. I wouldn't have put it past him to summon the police and claim trespass or intimidation before we'd even managed to ring his doorbell, assuming he didn't decide to cut out the middle man by shooting us himself.

On the other hand, Antoine Pinette was a regular at a place called the Capital over in Thornton Heights. The Capital was known locally as the Murder Capital due to its reputation for violence, and rarely did a weekend go by without someone being carried out feet first by paramedics. With the closure of Sangillo's Tavern back in 2015, the Capital counted as one of the last of Cumberland County's true dive bars. The Fulcis had wept when Sangillo's Tavern lost its liquor license – Dave Evans had wept, too, but only because it meant that the Fulcis would be spending more time at the Great Lost Bear – but not even Tony and Paulie were sufficiently nostalgic for mayhem to darken the door of the Capital. Its interior smelled of dust, urine, and drain cleaner, the floor was permanently littered with fragments of shattered glass and broken dreams, and even the furniture had tattoos. In recent years it had also become a clubhouse for Pinette and his people, making it still less desirable as a hostelry for the masses, were such a thing possible.

If getting in Bobby Ocean's face on his home territory had been rejected as unnecessarily provocative, squaring up to his alpha dog in a bar notorious for its savagery might have been considered foolhardy in the extreme, but Pinette had to be dealt with. Even if we approached Bobby first, his natural reaction would be to summon Pinette soon after, with orders to salve his master's wounded pride by stirring the pot some more, maybe by taking another run at Colleen Clark's house. But by making Pinette aware of the consequences of his actions, we might be able to give him pause for thought and potentially defang Bobby along the way.

The Capital occupied the first floor of an old two-story brownstone that looked out of place amid modern warehouse stores and a couple of dilapidated strip malls, like the last surviving structure from an earlier settlement annihilated by aerial bombing. The windows had bars on the outside and wire mesh on the inside, while the main door was a slab of graffitied metal monitored by the kind of meathead who bought his T-shirts too small and his pants too large. This latest version was sitting on a high stool, immersed in his cell phone like a chump, so our shadows had fallen on him before he even registered our approach. From inside the Capital came the sound of raised voices competing with speed metal.

The doorman finally looked up. His eyes drifted over Angel and me before resting on Louis.

'I don't think this is your kind of place, fellas,' he said, addressing himself to one of us in particular. People of color didn't frequent the Capital, not unless they were lost or angling for an insurance settlement.

Angel looked momentarily confused, but then his face cleared.

'Wait a minute,' he said, 'this isn't one of those straight bars, is it? You know, with heterosexuals touching and kissing and all? We've heard about those kinds of places. I'd like to visit one myself, seeing as how I'm on vacation. It'll be something to tell the folks about back home.'

'We're from New York,' added Louis, as though this explained everything, which it possibly did.

'Then get the fuck back there,' said the doorman.

Here's the thing about stools: they have a tendency toward instability, especially if you've unwisely developed the bad habit of shifting your weight back to raise the front legs briefly from the ground, as the doorman had. That was why, seconds after advising Louis to head south for the duration, he found himself lying on his back with the sole of Louis's right shoe pressed hard against his neck. His eyes were now even duller than before because he'd banged his head hard.

'Like the man told you,' said Louis, 'we're on vacation.'

I picked up what was left of the stool and tossed it between two cars. God forbid we should have created a trip hazard.

'Why don't you introduce us to everyone inside?' I said to the doorman. He nodded once, before immediately regretting it. He struggled to rise, but if he expected any help, he was out of luck. We let him get vertical at his own pace before giving him time to stop swaying. He managed to get the door open and half fell into the bar, the three of us close behind.

The music was painfully loud. A dozen people were scattered around the room – three at the bar, two in a booth halfway down on the right, and the rest by the pool table at the rear – but the attention of nearly all, the bartender included, was fixed on two young women playing eight ball. One of them was wearing only a bra and denim shorts. She missed her shot, and the men whooped as she began to remove the bra.

'I warned you,' said Angel. 'It's a straight joint.'

'Classy too,' said Louis.

Only one man wasn't taking in the show, and that was Antoine Pinette. He was seated at the end of the bar farthest from the door, with a glass of orange juice in front of him. He barely reacted when I reached across and turned off the music, as though he'd long before tuned it out. Pinette was lean in the way of those who burned off calories at a higher rate than the average, consuming vast quantities of energy even in repose. He got his ash-blond hair cut at the same place in the Old Port frequented by a lot of the local cops, much to their disgust, so it was always short and neat. Unlike everyone else in the Capital, his skin was free of ink, and his white shirt was freshly laundered. Slowly, lazily, he turned toward us, revealing his strange symmetry. Pinette's features were unsettling in their regularity, resembling an image that had been created by placing a mirror down the center of a visage and transplanting the reflection. The absence of imperfection rendered him incongruous, turning what might have been a handsome man into a living mannequin. The effect was rendered more extreme by his eyes, which were a very vivid blue. They suggested a presence trapped behind a mask, like a ghost haunting itself.

Pinette looked after himself. He read books, worked out, ate a lot of protein, didn't screw around, and forged bonds of discipline among his people based on shared credos. He did not own a cell phone, not even one of the old flips that couldn't do more than make or receive calls, which, in addition to preserving his sanity and attention span, gave him a layer of deniability should the law come calling. Like Bobby Ocean, he had left conventional politics far behind. Republicans and Democratic elites were one and the same to Pinette, joint conspirators in a 'globohomo' pyramid scheme, a cancerous metastasis whose visible sores took the form of shopping malls, outlet stores, minimum-wage jobs without security, and despoiled nature. I might even have agreed with some of his conclusions, but not his solution: the consolidation of white power through the exploitation of the credulous; the victimization and terrorization of those who did not share his color or beliefs; and a conviction that the strong and powerful had no obligations to the weak and vulnerable, and the only earth destined to be inherited by the meek was the patch of ground in which they were finally interred. Men like Pinette had helped the aged and crippled climb down from the cattle cars at Auschwitz, and offered soft words of reassurance as they were led to the gas chambers.

A familiar brute in denim and leather, seated not far from Pinette, eased himself from his stool and waddled in our direction. His name was Noah Morin, and he came from a long line of welfare deadbeats who prided themselves on never having done an honest day's labor, not unless a prison guard was standing over them with a baton. Cumulatively, his people worked fewer hours each year than the Easter Bunny. If Morin had finished high school, he had no recollection of it, and if he'd ever learned anything, he'd done his best to forget that as well. But compared to the rest of his clan, Noah was quite the go-getter: he picked up jobs here and there, the majority dishonest and the rest actively crooked. His bulk meant he was rarely required to inflict or suffer harm, since his physicality alone was enough to encourage compliance. I wasn't surprised that he'd fallen in with Pinette and Bobby Ocean. Morin was a bully boy, cannon fodder. He was one of the reasons Bobby was so vehemently antiabortion, because it reduced the stock of foot soldiers for the battles to come. When that fighting was done, Morin's betters would step over his corpse without a second glance.

'I was listening to the music,' said Morin, to all and none of us.

He showed no sign of recognizing me. Then again, he had the retentive memory of a hamster.

'What music?' Louis replied. 'I didn't hear any music.'

Morin's head swiveled in Louis's direction.

'We heard noise, is what we heard,' Louis continued. 'We didn't like it, so we brought it to an end.'

Morin's brow furrowed so deeply that his face practically collapsed in on itself. He advanced a couple of steps to get in Louis's face. Flecks of spittle struck Louis's skin as he spoke again.

'Who the fuck are you to—?'

Louis had slowed up in recent years. In his prime, I wouldn't have seen the blow before it landed. Now, as he struck Morin in the throat with the rigid, outstretched fingers of his right hand, I caught the blur. Morin dropped to his knees and began to choke. Louis regarded the spectacle with mild interest.

'Who am I?' he said. 'I'm That Guy.'

Around us, the clientele were reacting to this assault on one of their own. I saw pool cues being taken from the rack, and I was sure that blades, and a gun or two, would also be available for selection. The woman in the denim shorts, her bra refastened, picked up the cue ball and hefted it, ready to throw.

Only then did Antoine Pinette intervene, the bodies nearest him parting like the Red Sea before Moses, although that analogy immediately ran aground on the rocks of Pinette's frequently expressed anti-Semitism.

'I'll take care of this,' he said. 'I'm sure it's just a misunderstanding.'

He stared hard at me. 'Right, Mr Parker?'

'No,' I said, 'I think we've understood everything so far, what with all the single syllables. But we'd like to use some longer words with you, Antoine.'

Pinette gestured to the empty stools.

'So sit.'

By Louis's feet, Noah Morin had turned a shade of puce.

'You mind if someone helps Noah?' said Pinette. 'Be unfortunate for everyone if he choked to death.'

Louis gave signs of being about to dispute this, before saving his breath.

'If they must,' he said.

We stepped back, allowing two men to hoist Morin to his feet and drag him to a chair. He managed to breathe again, which was something; and when he spoke in response to his buddies, he didn't sound too different, only wheezier. Perhaps Louis had pulled the blow at the last minute to avoid damaging Morin's carotid artery, since being ignorant shouldn't carry a death sentence. Eventually, after some consultation, it was decided to take Morin to the ER as a precaution. Given the probable state of his general health, he might have been at risk of a stroke.

'You could just have answered his question,' said Pinette, once Morin had been removed. His voice was very low, and he pronounced with precision every syllable of each word.

'I did,' said Louis.

'Without disabling him, I meant.'

'I doubt it would have been as effective.'

Pinette took in Louis, like one prizefighter sizing up another.

'I don't think we've met,' he said, 'but then, introductions are hardly necessary. You wouldn't be here if you didn't know who I was, and I've heard all about you from Bobby. You're Louis, the one who blew up his son's truck. Bobby thinks that incident might have led to the boy's death.'

Louis made no comment.

'Between ourselves,' Pinette continued, 'I reckon Billy's stupidity

287

was the main contributary factor, but don't tell his old man I said that. Can I buy you gentlemen a drink?'

'We won't be staying,' I said, 'so we'll pass.'

Pinette called for another juice, and settled himself more comfortably. We remained standing. I noticed a pack of cards beside him, and two blackjack hands lying face down. I took a look at the nearer: a pair of eights. I didn't see any upcard.

'Your hand?' I asked Pinette.

'Someone else's. Should I surrender?'

'I wouldn't.'

'You play?'

'Not me. I promised Mother.'

'Pity, I take Social Security checks. Well, what do you want to talk about?'

'Last night's attack on a house in Rosemont.'

'First I heard of it.'

It was always difficult to determine Antoine Pinette's thought processes, because that unsettlingly congruous face gave so little away. When confronted with someone of his genus, it was often best to assume he was being dishonest and act accordingly. But Pinette had a curious code of honor, preferring to stay silent rather than lie, which had resulted in prison terms that perjury might have avoided.

'I expected more of you, Antoine,' I said. 'It was a step down from beating up trans college kids or young mothers at Black Lives Matter protests, and that's saying a lot.'

'You're speaking a foreign tongue,' said Pinette. 'Try English.'

'Last night someone tried to firebomb the home of one of my clients.'

'And?'

'The firebomb was thrown from your vehicle.'

For the first time since our arrival, Pinette looked flustered.

'You must be mistaken,' he said.

'You have a distinctive two-tone car, Antoine. It was spotted fleeing the scene. There's no mistake.'

Pinette drank some juice before wiping his mouth with a napkin. His teeth were curiously small and gapped, causing his dentition to resemble a child's.

'Who's the client?'

'Colleen Clark.'

'The one whose kid disappeared?'

'The same.'

'I got no beef with her, whatever she might have done.'

'I never said you had, but you work for Bobby Ocean, and he has a beef with me. To be fair, Bobby has a beef with virtually everyone.'

'I don't work *for* Bobby,' said Pinette. 'We share certain perspectives on the world, but I'm strictly self-employed.'

'So either Bobby paid you to attack a woman's home, or you did it of your own volition. Regardless, we have an issue.'

'I give you my word,' he said. 'This isn't on me. I don't even know where she lives. What time did this happen?'

Frustratingly, I was starting to believe him. Like I said, Pinette was many things, but a liar wasn't among them.

'About one in the morning.'

'I was home in bed,' he said. 'My girl was with me.'

Pinette had long been involved with a woman named Jesse Waite, out of Saco. I knew Jesse because I'd gone to school in Scarborough with her and her older sister, Kristine. Their father had an issue with the Saco School Department, which led to an agreement that his kids could attend high school outside the district as long as he paid tuition and transportation. Then he died, rendering the disagreement moot and leaving Jesse and Kristine free to go to school closer to home, after which I fell out of touch with them. I remembered Jesse as being bright and charming, and if she'd ever said anything derogatory about people of color, she had not done so in my presence. She and Pinette might have reached an accommodation about leaving politics and race on the doorstep, but that was about as likely as marrying a preacher and keeping religion for Sundays only. Jesse Waite, therefore, had obviously changed a lot since her schooldays.

'And your car,' I said. 'Was that with you, too?'

Pinette's eyelids flickered. He might not have lobbed the firebomb at the Clark house, but he knew who did. He called out to one of the men by the pool table, addressing him as Olin.

'Where's Leo?' asked Pinette.

Leo was Antoine's younger brother. I'd seen him around, always in the company of a couple of wingmen who had mistaken him for an alpha male, or a beta with aspirations, and a bunch of generic young women who were too dim to be able to tell the difference. He was a weak man who coasted on Antoine's fumes, relying on his older brother's reputation in the absence of one of his own. It didn't shock me to learn that he might have been involved in the nighttime attack on the Clark house. It was his style, the only surprise being that he'd come at the place from the front instead of the back.

'He went to get a couple of slices at the market,' said Olin. 'He ought to be back any minute.'

'Go find him,' said Pinette. 'And Olin?'

'Yes?'

'You say nothing to him about our guests, you hear?'

Olin heard, and left through the rear door.

'Did you give your car to your brother last night?' I asked.

'His is in the shop,' said Pinette. 'He dropped me home at ten, and wanted to go watch some MMA shit with his buddies. I didn't see any harm in letting him use the car, because he only lives a block away from me, but it doesn't mean he then went on a drive-by. We'll talk to him, hear what he has to say. If he fucked up, I'll take care of it, not you and your friends.'

I told him I didn't have any difficulty with that. In fact, it was a relief to learn that Antoine hadn't been responsible as it de-escalated the situation. My priority was to ensure Colleen and her home remained safe. If that meant ceding retribution duties to Antoine, so be it.

Pinette played with a discarded ring pull. Around us conversation resumed, but at a lower level than before. The pool game had been abandoned and the women were now fully dressed. I noticed that Pinette's jeans were very new, and his black boots carefully polished. Even the laces were clean. There was a military precision to him, a discipline, even though he'd never served. When he delivered a beating, it was reputed to be with no more or less intensity than the misdeed required, carried out with the minimum

290

of exertion and without any great alteration in his demeanor. But that wasn't to say he didn't enjoy it.

Pinette's eyes were moving between Angel and Louis, sizing them up.

'Is it true what they say?' he asked.

'And what would that be?' answered Louis.

'That you're, you know, together.'

Louis's face remained deadpan.

'We're here,' he said, 'and you can count to two, so yeah, I'd describe that as a fair summation.'

'You know what I mean.'

'Yes, I know.'

Pinette shook his head at the ways of the world.

'Bobby Ocean really fucking hates you three guys.'

'Bobby has a long list of people he hates,' I replied, 'most of whom he's never met.'

'You're all right up there with the best of them.'

'And your feelings about us? Just to avoid any confusion.'

Pinette pointed at Angel and Louis.

'I hate those two for what they are' – his finger shifted toward me – 'and I hate you for the company you keep, among other things.'

His attention became fixed on Angel.

'You're very quiet,' he said.

'I'm trying not to breathe in too deep,' said Angel. 'This place smells of stale sperm.'

'I figure you'd know,' said Pinette, as the front door opened and Olin returned, trailed by two younger men. They were both eating greasy pizza from paper plates, but the first of them stopped chewing as soon as he saw me. Leo Pinette resembled a failed laboratory effort to replicate his older brother. The same looks were present, but clouded by physical indolence and intellectual sloth. He wore box-fresh white Nikes, a black Lonsdale tracksuit, and a UFC baseball cap with the holographic sticker still on the visor, which was nature's way of communicating that here, incontestably, was a dick. Leo was gym-heavy from hours spent in a mixed-martial-arts dump over by the Jetport, but a halfway decent boxer could have put him on the floor in minutes, if not seconds, because he lacked application and skill. The tougher competitors, those who could take the hits, might have hoped to make some money from MMA, but most of the meatheads who gravitated to it did so because they wanted to learn how to hurt someone weaker than themselves and got their kicks from watching others being hurt in turn. The sight of blood gave them a hard-on, as long as the blood wasn't their own. Leo Pinette would never set foot inside a ring for a fair fight and would never throw a punch outside one before first checking that his boys had his back. He was, I imagined, a grave disappointment to his brother, someday destined to land himself in a mess from which Antoine wouldn't be able to extricate him.

Leo was also an object lesson for those who didn't actively resist the encroachments of the far right. When the dust cleared, the local gauleiter would be someone like Leo: a petty tyrant, an abuser of men and women, and therefore the last person to whom authority should ever be ceded.

'I think you know Mr Parker,' said Antoine, as Olin leaned against the door, more to prevent anyone from entering than leaving. Leo might have been a coward, but he wouldn't want to lose face in front of his brother and his buddies, and calculated he was safe while they were nearby.

Behind Leo, the kid who'd entered with him was doing his best to make like a snowflake and melt, drifting toward the pool table as a prelude to vanishing.

'Did I tell you to go anywhere?' said Antoine.

The kid paused, a half-eaten slice still in his hand. He was afraid to set it down so it sat congealing in his hand, excess grease dripping to the floor. In another bar, or another life, I might have felt sorry for him.

'You borrowed my car last night,' said Antoine to Leo. 'Where did you go?'

His voice was mellow, even bored, like a father feigning curiosity in the activities of one of the more tedious of his teenage offspring.

'Around,' replied Leo.

'Around where?'

'Just around.'

'You told me you were going to Sonny's to watch TV.' Antoine's eyes flicked to Leo's associate. 'Is that what you did, Sonny?'

To his credit, Sonny was bright enough to know when he was screwed. We could see him assessing the risks involved in lying and the chances of being successful, before deciding that honesty was, if not the best policy, then marginally better than the alternative.

'We went back to my place after,' he said.

'After?'

Sonny looked to Leo, hoping he wouldn't have to commit to this path alone, but Leo, I guessed, had also run the odds and come up with a different outcome, which only proved he didn't have a future as a gambler.

'Don't look at him, Sonny,' said Antoine, 'look at me.'

'We took a ride by a house. Maybe we threw something at it.'

'Like what?'

'We were just trying to—'

'Like *what*?' Antoine repeated.

'A bottle, with gasoline in it, and some sugar.'

Sonny bowed his head.

'And why'd you do that?'

Again, Sonny's eyes flicked to Leo, but this time with more hostility. I got the impression that Sonny had been doing whatever Leo told him to do. Antoine had come to the same conclusion, likely long before the two men had returned to the bar, and he was now focused on Leo. The show was for our benefit, but Antoine would also grasp the opportunity to teach his brother a lesson by making his humiliation lengthy and public. I doubted it was the first such lesson Antoine had tried to teach him. If nothing else, one had to admire Antoine's perseverance, because Leo wasn't the learning type.

'Well,' said Antoine, 'you want to tell me?'

'We did it for Bobby O.'

Bobby O? I'd never heard Bobby Ocean called that before. Perhaps he was trying to be down with the kids.

'Bobby asked you to burn a woman's house?' said Antoine, not even trying to conceal his incredulity.

'Not in so many words,' said Leo.

293

'Not in so many words, huh? Then how about you tell me the words he did use, unless he sent the message by fucking Morse code.'

Leo licked his lips.

'He said someone ought to teach the bitch a lesson.'

'What bitch?'

'The Clark woman, the one who killed her kid.'

'When did he say this?'

'Yesterday. And not just her.' Leo jerked his chin in my direction. 'Him too, and his kike lawyer.'

Moxie wasn't Jewish, not that it mattered, but Antoine saw me react to the slur. He raised his hand.

'You do anything to my brother and this will become about us, not him.'

'He needs to modify his language,' I said. 'If he doesn't, I'll take my chances.'

Louis, meanwhile, was grinning at Leo. It wasn't a friendly grin, but resembled what a mouse might see moments before a cat got tired of watching it squirm beneath its paw.

'We have company, Leo,' said Antoine, 'so watch your mouth.'

Leo did some eye-rolling, but only for form's sake.

'And was Bobby pointing at you when he said this?' Antoine persisted. 'Did he suggest that *you* ought to be the one to do it, and direct *you* toward the matches and gasoline?'

But it was Sonny who answered.

'He wanted us to do something to her. He didn't tell us directly, but we knew. We got it.'

Antoine studied Sonny.

'I can believe that,' he said, before striking Sonny full in the face with the heel of his right hand. Sonny's nose crumpled under the impact, and he toppled backward as Antoine advanced, the steel toe of his booted right foot catching the boy in the side. Sonny curled up on the floor to protect himself, and the next kick struck the base of his spine. By the door, Olin opened his jacket to reveal the butt of the gun tucked into his belt, on the off chance that we, or anyone else, felt the urge to intervene. Leo didn't do anything except drop his pizza.

Eventually, Olin said 'Antoine' and the kicking ended so abruptly that a switch might have been thrown in Pinette's brain. He stepped back, ran his hands through his hair, and turned to his brother.

'Take Sonny to the emergency room,' he said. 'Get him seen to. You can pay the bill. Then I want you to put a thousand dollars – no, *two* thousand dollars – in an envelope and drop it off at his place. After that, I never want to see him around here again. The next time you feel the urge to show some initiative, you talk to me first, understand?'

Leo swallowed hard.

'Yes,' he said, but behind his eyes a dark shape scuttled, like a spider stalking the inside of his head, seeking an outlet for its venom. The atmosphere roiled with Leo's suppressed rage, the sediment disturbed from his depths dimming the very air around us.

'Sara,' said Antoine, 'give them a ride to the ER.'

The girl with the cue ball, who had kept it in her right hand throughout, tossed it on the pool table, buttoned her shirt, and dug her car keys from her shorts. The ER would be doing good business that night thanks to the Murder Capital, even by the usual standards. Leo and another man picked up Sonny and carried him out, Sara trailing behind. Puddles of blood marked Sonny's path.

'We good?' said Antoine to me.

'That's not the word I'd have used. I didn't like the performance.'

'Says the guy who leaves bodies in his wake. You want to be a judge, get some robes. We're done.'

'I'm going to have to talk to Bobby Ocean as well,' I said.

'You and me both. I prefer afternoons. You might want to bear that in mind for your diary, so our paths don't cross again. Now get the fuck out of here.'

We left without saying anything more. After all, what would have been the point? Olin, now returned, held the door so it didn't hit us in our asses on the way out.

'Well?' I said, as we walked to my car.

'Antoine's a step up from the norm in intellect,' observed Louis, 'but a step down in every other way.'

'What makes him dangerous,' I said, 'is that he knows exactly who he is, and has chosen his path after reflection. He's not deluded, or crazy, but he's definitely malign.'

'The way he dealt with that Sonny kid was impressively methodical,' said Louis. 'I'd be surprised if Pinette's heart rate went above sixty during the whole beating.'

Olin emerged from the Capital, watching us while he smoked a cigarette and spoke on his cell phone. We got in my car and I started the engine.

'I wonder who Olin's calling,' I said.

'Bobby Ocean?' suggested Angel.

'If it's Bobby, he's getting in touch with him at Antoine's instigation. Olin is Antoine's creature through and through.'

'As opposed to Leo,' said Angel. 'For a moment back there, I believe Leo wanted to kill his brother.'

'Antoine does cast a big shadow for someone with no light around him,' I said. 'Leo worships him, but that's not the same as liking.'

We drove off. I had hoped that as the Capital receded in the distance I might sense its miasma lifting from me, but I did not. Antoine Pinette and Bobby Ocean were part of a new ascendancy, but if you caught their reflection in a glass, they would appear dressed in an older raiment, one adorned with death's heads. They would have to be faced down and crushed because there could be no negotiation with them. If they were given free rein, they would trample goodness and morality into the dirt, and burn truth and decency to ash.

'What are you thinking?' asked Louis.

'That it never ends.'

'If so,' said Louis, 'it's not for want of us trying.'

Chapter LXIV

Mattia Reggio's conversation with Ellar Michaud was drawing to a close. Reggio hadn't learned much from it, other than that Michaud gave him the creeps and he'd be glad to quit his company. Before he did so, though, he was going to ask him one last question: namely why Michaud, or a car registered to him, had followed Colleen Clark from Cumberland County Jail. As preparation, Reggio's right hand now lay on his right thigh, the pad of his thumb touching the grip of his revolver. Reggio's heart was beating fast and the gum was gone from his mouth. He couldn't even remember getting rid of it.

'I want to thank you for your time, Mr Michaud,' said Reggio, 'even if I think you've learned more from me than I've learned from you. With that in mind, and before I go—'

A cool gust of air brushed the back of his head. Reggio hadn't even heard the door open behind him. What he had taken for a kitchen closet must have been another entrance. A woman's hand came to rest on his shoulder, and a gun barrel nudged his skull, just hard enough to let him know it was there.

Dumb. He was so fucking dumb.

'Put your hands flat on the table and keep your head down,' Michaud instructed.

Reggio did as he was told.

'Look,' he said, 'there's been some kind of misunderstanding.'

Footsteps descended from above, and another woman joined the first, although Reggio could see only plain brown shoes, tan tights, and the hem of a worn beige dress.

'He wears it on his right side,' said Michaud.

Reggio's gun was taken from him.

'If you're carrying another weapon, better tell us now,' said Michaud.

'I only ever needed one,' said Reggio. 'For peace of mind.'

'How's that working out for you?'

'Like I said, we have a misunderstanding.'

Reggio saw metal flash by his right eye as a carving knife was driven through the back of his right hand, impaling it on the table. Reggio screamed.

'Consider that,' said Michaud, 'a first step toward enlightenment.'

Chapter LXV

I dropped Angel and Louis at their place and left them to their own devices for the rest of the night. My plan for the following day was to head up to Dexter to look for the man named Maynard Vaughn, who had made the straw purchase of the money order used by Mara Teller. Along the way, I intended to call at the Kopper Kettle to speak with Beth Witham, the waitress who was said to have dated Stephen Clark, a relationship that might have involved domestic abuse. Finally, there was the matter of a conversation with Bobby Ocean. That would be the morning's first work.

I was due to meet Sharon Macy in an hour at The Grill Room, but only for drinks and appetizers, the Grill Room being nobody's idea of a venue for a cheap date. The bar mixed a good old-fashioned, which was Macy's cocktail of choice. Lately, Macy – she didn't like being called Sharon, even by me – had been cutting back on liquor and bar food for health reasons, so she preferred to order one decent old-fashioned and make it last.

Macy and I had dated casually a few years previously, but circumstances and timing had dictated that we never went further, and any intimacy was limited to some kissing and fumbling. It was like being back in high school, but with more bills and responsibilities. Subsequently, we drifted apart, but continued to exchange nods in passing, before coming together again after a couple of guys tried to blow up my car in the parking lot of the Great Lost Bear. Macy and I had even ended up in bed, breaking long dry spells for both of us. Since then, we'd been circling each other, if less cautiously than before, in a benign form of orbital decay.

A difficulty for Macy was her position in the Portland PD, notably her role as liaison with the governor's office and other state and federal law enforcement agencies, which made it inadvisable for her to be seen on the arm of a private investigator whom many of those same agencies would like to have seen deprived of his license or jailed. For that reason, we were discreet about where we met and avoided restaurants and bars frequented by police. No cop was likely to be eating at the Grill Room, not unless they were on the take, so we'd deemed it relatively safe, aided by dim lighting and a reserved space by the bar that allowed us to see first without being seen.

I had not yet had a chance to bring up with Macy the subject of Sabine Drew, and was wary of doing so. Apart from the fact that Macy undoubtedly held strong feelings about her due to the fallout from the Edie Brook case, both of us were mindful of trying to keep our private and professional lives separate, however futile this might ultimately prove. After all, I wasn't sure my personal and professional lives were separate even to myself, never mind the complicating factor of another human being operating in a sphere not far removed from my own. Macy was career police and unlikely to cash out after twenty-five years to open a bar. We were both in our respective vocations for the long haul.

Macy and I hadn't met since I'd agreed to work the Colleen Clark case for Moxie, but she couldn't but be aware of the problems posed for us by my involvement. I knew she respected Paul Nowak as AG, and relations between his office and the Portland PD were currently better than they'd ever been, thanks in part to Macy's efforts. She was also loyal to the force, but I needed to know more about the Edie Brook affair, and wanted to establish what, if anything, the oxygen thief Furnish, lead investigator on the Clark case, had accomplished in terms of proper legwork. Steady Freddy had shared that he wasn't a fan of Furnish. This wouldn't have troubled Furnish, since he was enough of a fan of himself for two people, but Freddy had also suggested that Furnish was willing to drag his heels to please the AG's office. I suppose I could have tried raising these subjects with Macy as pillow talk, but she might have smothered me in retaliation. I was less in danger of a slow, agonizing death at the bar of The Grill Room.

I freshened up at home, and spoke briefly to Colleen.

'I want to go back to my own place tomorrow,' she said. 'I appreciate your kindness in letting me stay here, but I feel like a specter inhabiting the wrong house.'

'Your mother raised again the possibility of staying with her for a while. I told her I'd put it to you.'

'I haven't changed my mind, and I won't.'

'You are aware that someone tried to set your home on fire?'

'I heard. Mom said you were going to take care of it.'

'I met with the people involved,' I said, 'or some of them.'

'What happened?'

'One of them ended up in the ER, but I didn't put him there. He might have demonstrated too much initiative. Not everyone likes a go-getter.'

'So it won't happen again?'

'I didn't say that. Firstly, the firebugs were operating at someone else's instigation. I haven't had a chance to confront him yet. I'll do that tomorrow, but I don't anticipate much more than a denial. The only positive is that the attack was aimed at Moxie and me rather than you, and the person responsible may have had his fun. Also, if he wants anything else thrown, he'll have to do it himself or go on a hiring spree. On the other hand, you remain a target for every other coward who secretly misses the days of lynch mobs. It's not going to be easy for you.'

'Nevertheless,' she said, 'I want to go back.'

'Then we'll continue with the protection detail: obvious at first, as now, but less so as time goes on. The Fulcis will need assistance, because I can't keep asking them to cover it all unaided.'

I thought of Mattia Reggio. Whatever my reservations about him, he could be relied upon for work of this type. He and the Fulcis could agree on a roster between them.

'But the costs are mounting, right?' said Colleen.

'We'll do our best to keep them down.'

'And all to prevent a prosecutor from turning me into a trophy on her wall.'

For the first time, I detected something resembling real rage. *Good*, I thought. She had a right, even a responsibility, to be angry. This was a fight, and she could either stand there and let her opponents brutalize her into submission or start counter-punching. I now realized that the first step was for her to stop hiding and return home.

'Which is why we can't let Erin Becker win,' I said.

As quickly as it had manifested itself, that brief demonstration of inner strength was gone, like a match flaring and dying.

'How is that going for us?' she asked.

Even though I remained convinced that it was better if she heard directly from Moxie about any progress on the case, I wanted to offer her something. Hope, however faint, remained hope.

'Mara Teller paid for her registration to the forum with a money order,' I said. 'I have a lead on the man who may have purchased it for her.'

'Why didn't she buy it herself?'

'Because she didn't want to be remembered, which means she may be known locally.'

'Just so she could attend a gas and oil conference, or sleep with my husband?' Colleen looked puzzled. 'It doesn't make sense.'

'I spoke with your therapist. She said you voiced a suspicion that your husband might have been unfaithful in the past, conceivably with the same woman. You never mentioned anything about that to me.'

'It was just a feeling I had when I first discovered the affair, but there was no proof. I was worried that I was jumping at shadows or creating false memories. I came to accept that I might have been mistaken. But even if I wasn't, would Mara Teller really have gone to all that trouble to renew some old acquaintance with my husband? It's an affair. It may be unsavory, but it's not a crime.'

'Abducting a child is, though,' I said. 'I keep leaning toward the possibility that she was less interested in your husband than in Henry.'

'So, what? Stephen shared the layout and security details of our house with her as foreplay?'

'She might have coaxed him into discussing his travel plans

with her. If she was targeting your son, it would be easier to take Henry when there was only one adult in the home.'

Colleen stared at her bare feet. The nail polish, I saw, was gone.

'An adult who was depressed, and drinking too much wine,' she said quietly. 'An adult who was capable of sleeping soundly through her son's abduction.'

That also bothered me. Had the opened bottle of wine been available for examination, we could have established whether it had been tampered with. But if that was the case, either Mara Teller had gained access to the bottle or someone close to Colleen had spiked it. From what Colleen told me, that could only have been her mother or husband. But it was idle speculation. The bottle was long gone.

'We're not going down that route again,' I said.

'You may not be,' said Colleen, 'but I am.'

I changed the subject.

'Did your husband ever mention an ex-girlfriend named Beth Witham?'

Colleen gave up on staring at her feet.

'Sure. He went out with her for a while, before we met.'

'A long while?'

'A couple of years. They broke up six months before Stephen and I became an item.'

'Do you know why they broke up?'

'He said she was a bitch. She wasn't always, but she turned into one – although that's what a lot of men say about their exes, isn't it? It may well be untrue. Is she involved in this?'

'Not beyond her past connection with your husband.' I tried to find a nice way to ask the next question, but there wasn't one. 'Colleen, did Stephen ever abuse you in the course of your relationship?'

'Did he hit me, you mean?'

'Hitting would be one form. There are others.'

'No,' she said. 'I mean, he's grabbed me once or twice, usually during arguments over money, or the amount of time he was spending away from home. His fingers left marks after, because I bruise easily. He was always apologetic, but I might have provoked him. I'd do that sometimes, just to get a reaction, and remind him I was in his life.'

The more I learned about the Clarks' marriage, the less appealing it came to seem. Obviously, I'd encountered worse, but it struck me as dysfunctional in a grindingly depressing way.

'Would you say your husband has a temper?'

'It may sound strange after what I've just told you, but no. Even during the worst of our fights, there was something half-hearted about his participation. Stephen doesn't really get angry, the same way he's never been what you might call excessively happy on any occasion I can recall, not even on our wedding day. The only thing that really engages him is work – and money, but the two go together for him. It wouldn't be enough for Stephen to win the lottery. He'd have to earn his wealth, so it could be an indicator of success in his professional life. His problem is that he's not good enough to reach the level he aspires to, not without outside help, but if you go looking for assistance in business, it can come across as a sign of weakness. It's compli-cated. Even when Stephen cultivated my father, I could see that it bothered him. He'd have preferred to be a self-made man, but that wasn't an option, and still isn't. It's made him bitter. I wonder what he'll be like when he's old. I don't think it'll be pleasant to witness.'

Some of which echoed the opinions expressed by Colleen's mother.

'And yet you stayed with him,' I said.

'I love him – for all his flaws, or because of them. I don't need him to be a corporate big shot. I just need him to be a good man, a good husband, and a good father. But I understand now that some or all of those things may be beyond him. They're not in his nature, or it could be that he ought to have found himself a different woman to marry. Beth Witham might have been the one, but I doubt it. Last I heard, she was working as a waitress, because Stephen mentioned that he'd seen her serving at a diner. That would never have been good enough for him, because he couldn't have introduced a waitress to his fancy friends. You still haven't told me why you're asking about her.'

'A source claims Stephen didn't break up with Beth,' I said, 'but that she dumped him after he beat her.'

Colleen shook her head.

'I don't believe that, not about Stephen.'

'Regardless, I'm going to speak with her tomorrow.'

'Why?'

'If your husband did hurt her, I want to know the circumstances.'

'No, it doesn't sound like Stephen.'

'You don't think he's capable of it?'

'It's not that,' said Colleen. 'I just can't see him caring enough to bother.'

She pushed herself from the kitchen counter.

'I'll be gone when you return,' she said. 'Don't take this the wrong way, but I really don't want to spend another night here. It's too quiet. I keep thinking I hear a child's footsteps at night, and they're not Henry's.'

I did not reply, except to say that I'd ask one of the Fulcis to come collect her. She didn't object. Then, quite unexpectedly, she walked over to me and kissed the corner of my mouth.

'Thank you,' she said. 'I think you're an extraordinary man. But you shouldn't be out here alone. If you are alone.'

Chapter LXVI

The restaurant area of The Grill Room was busy when I arrived, but the bar was quiet. I'd received a text message from Macy to say she was running late, but I had the *New York Times*, and the bartender served me an unpronounceable Italian red that made me feel sophisticated before leaving me to my reading. I was halfway through a review of a contemporary art exhibition – trying to learn a new and difficult language was supposed to stave off dementia – when a man in a dark suit, a dark tie, and a very white shirt entered and stood at a respectful distance. He smelled of new car.

'Mr Parker?'

'That's me.'

'Attorney General Nowak would like to speak with you.'

I didn't want to talk to Paul Nowak, not with Macy on her way and the promise of some quality time with her after, assuming she didn't pour my wine over my head for discussing Sabine Drew on a date night. Even without the Macy factor, I was aware that Nowak wasn't one of my cheerleaders, and my role in the Clark case wasn't going to alter that. Objectively, Nowak wasn't a bad guy, but he was a politician, which made him intrinsically untrustworthy. All politicians are ambitious, and ambition is a hunger that's never sated. It's a cousin to desire, even addiction. We're all prey to the former, whatever the variant, and whether it becomes a vice or virtue depends on one's principles. But politics, by its nature, requires compromise, and compromise and principles are like matter and antimatter. In the end, every politician fails someone, but the last person he wants to fail is himself.

'Are you his driver?'

'Yes, sir.'

'Is he in the car?'

'He's dining in the restaurant.'

'So let me get this straight,' I said. 'He called you to tell you to come in and inform me that he wanted a word, even though he's already inside?'

'That's correct.'

The driver kept a straight face, although whether through strength of character or because he'd swallowed too much of Nowak's Kool-Aid was open to conjecture. Moxie, I decided, would want to hear whatever Nowak had to say, if only out of inquisitiveness. Unfortunately, Moxie wasn't available.

'Tell him I'll be over in a minute,' I said.

'I'll wait to escort you.'

'I can find my own way. I've been here before, and I know what he looks like.'

'I'd still prefer to escort you.'

He might have been worried that I'd spring at Nowak's throat, or try to interest him in a hooker and cocaine before running to the newspapers with the story.

'I guess it's a job,' I said, 'but I'll still need that minute.'

I texted Macy to tell her to hold off on joining me and find somewhere else to cool her heels. *Nowak is here*, I added, by way of explanation. If she wanted to watch her career go up in flames, cozying up to me at the bar while Nowak choked on his meal would just about do it.

I put away my phone, picked up my wine, and followed the driver to Nowak's table. I wondered if it was just an unhappy coincidence that had led Nowak to dine at The Grill Room on the same night that a reservation had been made under my name.

Nowak was eating his main course alone at a table near the open kitchen. He had dark receding hair and a body built for short bursts of power. Nobody would have mistaken him for a male model, but women of my acquaintance, Macy among them, were prepared to grant him a certain appeal. He had the politician's gift of making you feel as though you were the only person in the room, while simultaneously looking over your shoulder for someone more interesting or important. I agreed with most of his views but would still have struggled to vote for him, even before he decided to use Colleen Clark as a vote-grabber, because I wasn't convinced his policies wouldn't change next week, depending on how the wind was blowing. I'd prefer to have taken my chances with the holistic veterinary woman, who was terminally politically disadvantaged by actually believing what she said.

The place setting opposite Nowak had been removed, but I saw stains on the table. The Grill Room didn't hold with stains. At some stage in the evening, Nowak had enjoyed, or tolerated, company.

'I always figured you for a grilled scallop guy,' I said, indicating what remained of the dish on his plate. 'They don't scream fancy.'

'What about the beurre blanc sauce they come with?'

'You probably hide that side of your character from the rubes. It's hard to present yourself as a man of the people with beurre blanc on your clothing.'

'That's why I always ask for it on the side.' He wiped his mouth with a napkin and gestured to the seat across from him. 'Sit, please – unless I'm intruding on a romantic evening?'

He cocked an eyebrow, and I wondered again what he knew or suspected.

'No, it's just me,' I said, taking a chair. 'All part of my ongoing love affair with myself. The gossip is that you'd like to see it broken up by depriving me of my license, followed closely by my liberty.'

Nowak set his knife and fork side by side on his plate, leaving half a scallop uneaten.

'I like to think I hold a more nuanced position on your activities, but I have to admit to an ongoing sense of puzzlement as to why no one has successfully managed to jail you or sue you. For example, you discharged a firearm on the streets of New York, which typically attracts a great deal of legal attention, as well as being a negligent thing to do.'

'I was young and foolish in those days.'

Which was entirely true, though only the first part was untrue now.

'Since then you've left more bodies and wreckage in your wake than the average hurricane, yet here you are.'

'Here I am,' I agreed.

This was the second time in twenty-four hours that someone had mentioned bodies and wakes to me, the other being Antoine Pinette. Maybe I needed to facilitate a meeting between him and Nowak. I had a feeling they might have more in common than an aversion to my existence.

'Someone – no, almost certainly more than one person – has been applying a finger to the scales on your behalf,' said Nowak. 'At the last meeting of the National Association of Attorneys General, your name even came up at the bar. For a man with very few friends at the state level across our great nation, you're remarkably resistant to prosecution. Even to raise the subject is to invite pressure: federal pressure. It's subtle but definite. I find that intriguing. It's led me to revise my opinion of you, if only slightly.'

'Why would that be?'

'Join the dots. You're no neophyte. I wouldn't be talking to you if I believed you were.'

'A man who wants to be governor of Maine almost certainly has larger political ambitions,' I said. 'He's not going to rock any boats until he knows who might fall overboard as a consequence, especially if it might be him.'

'That's very good. I may steal that for a stump speech.'

He spotted a passing server and tapped his wineglass for a refill.

'Can I get you something?' he asked.

'I'm still working on this one.'

'I was about to order dessert. I was thinking of tonight's special, which is their take on a Bête Noire, perhaps as a gesture toward your sometime employer, Mr Castin. I've always found him to be characterful from a distance, if less amusing at closer quarters. Erin Becker would concur on the latter, if not the former. He's giving her migraines over Colleen Clark.'

'You don't waste time, do you?'

'That's because I don't have time to waste.'

'Impatient both of delays and rivals, as someone once said.'

'Of me?' he said, with the eagerness of a man whose own name was his main Google alert.

'Of ambition in general. I was thinking about it earlier, even before I was summoned to your presence.'

'If it's not insensitive of me to say, given the tragedy in your past, you really need to find yourself a woman. If you already have one, you should consider spending more time with her, because sitting alone at bars is conducive to melancholy. So, Colleen Clark.'

'Moxie is her lawyer,' I said. 'If you want to drop the charges, he's the one to talk to. I can take a message, but you might have to spell some of the longer words. I'm not good with legalese.'

'We're not dropping any charges,' said Nowak. 'Clark is going to prison. It's just a question of sentencing.'

'That kind of confidence may play well on the fundraising circuit over a fried chicken dinner, but here it's only us. Colleen Clark's guilt hasn't been established, and is unlikely to be. Your evidence is thin, and Moxie is ready to shred what little of it there is.'

'I appreciate you're being paid to help prove her innocence, but when that bloodied blanket is shown to the jury, all bets will be off. This is theater, Mr Parker, and the prosecution gets to set the stage. Your client's role is already written, and we both know the ending.'

But the fact that we were having this conversation indicated Nowak had his doubts. What we had here was the prelude to a negotiation, one of which Erin Becker was either unaware or with which she was reluctant to be associated, even in a quiet corner of the Grill Room. Nowak was testing the waters, knowing that whatever was said here would be shared with Moxie.

'You'll need a unanimous verdict,' I said. 'If Moxie can't turn at least one juror in his sleep, he'll retire to grow lemons in Florida. And he doesn't even like lemons.'

The server arrived with a fresh glass of wine. As threatened, Nowak ordered death by chocolate, with some macerated berries to add spice to the autopsy.

'A conviction doesn't have to mean a long sentence,' said Nowak.

'Erin Becker has been making noises about upgrading to a murder charge. Twenty-five to life strikes me as plenty long.'

'The important word being "murder".'

'In this state "manslaughter" doesn't sound much better. That's still up to thirty years.' Maine didn't draw a distinction between voluntary and involuntary manslaughter. It was manslaughter, impure and rarely simple, with only the absence of malice to distinguish it. 'By the way, and for the second time, shouldn't you be having this conversation with Moxie?'

'What conversation?'

This was why I avoided lawyers, Moxie excepted, and only because he was also my lawyer.

'How does Becker feel about whatever it is that's currently not being discussed?' I asked.

'Erin wants to prove a point, but she'd also like the headaches to go away.'

'And redecorate the AG's office that you're working so hard to vacate? I hear she's big on chintz.'

'She's old-fashioned that way,' said Nowak. 'You tell Moxie from me that we require a conviction, but we don't need Clark to do hard time. I've read the literature on postnatal depression. I sympathize.'

He maneuvered his features into the required expression, barely avoiding having to use his hands to manipulate the muscles directly.

'We're not monsters in Augusta,' he continued, 'but there are two constituencies that need to be satisfied. The first wants to see Clark punished, while the second doesn't want to watch a woman being pilloried for a crime that may have resulted from psychological illness.'

'And both of them vote, right?'

His dessert arrived. Like most things to do with Paul Nowak, it was too rich for my blood.

'I've always believed,' said Nowak, 'that Janus should be acclaimed as the god of politics.' He ate a spoonful of chocolate. His eyes closed briefly in bliss. 'Do you want to try this? It's really very good.'

'We're not dating,' I said, 'and I think it may sit better on your stomach than mine.'

'You're not accustomed to the finer things in life.'

'Often by choice.'

'Your loss. Moxie Castin can line up enough expert testimony on the subject of childbirth, depression, and female psychosis to cause the spirit of Susan B. Anthony to descend on the courthouse and shed tears like rain, and we won't contest a word of it as long as we can work out a plea deal. Clark will have to do some time, but if she cops to manslaughter, we won't object to an EPRD of a year and a day from conviction, as long as it's done quietly.' An EPRD was an Earliest Possible Release Date. 'A year and a day: she won't even feel it passing.'

'I think she might, and it's not much consolation if she's innocent.'

'It may be all the consolation she's going to receive.'

'Plus you're forgetting something.'

'I am? I must be growing old.'

'Her child. If she were to take the plea deal, wouldn't she have to tell you what she did with her son's body?'

'Perhaps she blotted it out. With the proper care and treatment, it may come back to her. It doesn't have to be a condition of the plea.'

'So the boy's fate remains unknown?'

Nowak swirled the fruit into the chocolate and took another massive spoonful, revealing his tongue and teeth. He ate with the unselfconsciousness of the fundamentally arrogant.

'The boy's fate *is* known,' he said. 'Henry Clark is dead. The bloodstains say so. But, on reflection, you're right: we'll need her to tell us how she disposed of the child, if only to oil the wheels. If she does, we'll even let her attend the burial, as long as it's conducted in private and her husband doesn't object. By the way, did you attend the burials of your wife and child?'

Sometimes, when you take a punch, you have to make it seem as though it doesn't hurt. It can be hard, almost as hard as not throwing one in return.

'What do you think?' I replied.

'My wife and I don't have children. We're considering adopting. I asked because I can't conceive of what you went through.'

'That's not why you asked.'

'You're right.'

Any semblance of bonhomie departed as Nowak steepled his fingers against his lips, like a man in prayer.

'In my experience,' he said, 'which is wide, any crime against a cop's family causes the ranks to close tight. Police look after their own. It's a rule, but even rules need exceptions to prove them, and it turns out that you're one. Oh, they stepped up for you, your colleagues, because they couldn't do otherwise, but there was a marked slowness. You were not liked, even if none of them could have said why. It was as though you bore a mark only they could see, however faintly, or carried a contagion only they could detect, and they communicated the fact of it chemically to one another, like ants in a nest. What is that mark, Mr Parker? What is the contagion? I doubt you even know yourself.'

I set aside my wine and prepared to leave. I didn't want to drink any more, not in this company.

'I'll relay your message to Moxie,' I said.

'Be sure you do. It's the best deal he'll be offered in his career – the best that you'll be offered, too, because if we don't come up with a satisfactory conclusion to all this, there'll be fallout, and I'll be forced to examine why I don't like you. That conversation at the AG bar I mentioned earlier? Some of those present felt that it was time to fight the squeeze where you're concerned. Soon you'll overstep the mark again, and your rabbis, whoever they are, won't be able to save you. When that boat finally rocks, I won't be on board. I'll be watching from a deck chair on the shore, sipping a mint julep while you drown.'

It was obvious we were done. I stood. Nowak had soiled his side of the table with cherry juice and chocolate. The mess was making me nauseated.

'And there I was, thinking you were going to offer me a job on your security detail when you become governor.'

'If I'm ever in that much danger,' said Nowak, 'I'll kill myself.'

'I doubt that will be necessary,' I said, 'I'm sure you'll have no trouble finding someone to do it for you.'

Chapter LXVII

Passing on to Moxie the details of the conversation with Nowak could wait until morning; Moxie wasn't going to take the bait anyway. Had Colleen Clark been a no-hope client, he might have advocated accepting the plea deal, although even then he would have proceeded cautiously. Nowak might have been promising an EPRD, but Moxie wouldn't receive a signed agreement to that effect, and no one on the state's side would be under any obligation to keep their side of the bargain. In addition, it would involve Colleen pleading guilty to a crime that neither Moxie nor I believed she had committed, and promising to deliver a body she couldn't produce, which meant Nowak's offer was a nonstarter. Nonetheless, Moxie might feel obliged to share the substance of it with Colleen: cop a plea, claim traumatic loss of memory regarding the whereabouts of the body, engage with psychiatric support while in prison, and by the time she got out, someone else would be the focus of the mob's ire.

And Colleen might have considered accepting. Apart from the occasional moment of spiritedness, like the one displayed earlier in my kitchen, she was resigned to the machinery of the system mincing her up. It wasn't unusual. It wasn't even surprising. Her child was missing, she was estranged from her husband, and she was mired in a grief from which she could not even begin to free herself, however marginally, until Henry's fate was established. Because of all this, there was a real risk that, if presented with the prosecution's deal, she could be tempted to take it. She might even view the sentence as punishment for her perceived failure to protect her son. I'd seen stranger things happen in the course of criminal cases, and logic didn't enter into proceedings when someone was in Colleen's kind of pain. But should she show signs

314

of wavering, her son's fate remained the best card we could play. If she accepted the deal, any ongoing police investigation into Henry's whereabouts would end, and she might never discover what had befallen him.

I checked my messages. Macy was at the Bar of Chocolate, a dessert-and-wine place in the Old Port that had never, to my knowledge, been troubled by police custom. When I got there, she was seated at a table away from the small bar, an old-fashioned already in front of her, along with a slice of chocolate tart big and rich enough to make Nowak's Bête Noire look abstemious by contrast. I hadn't finished my glass of wine at the Grill – though I made sure it was added to Nowak's bill – so I didn't feel bad about ordering another. I joined Macy at the table, kissed her gently, thought about kissing her harder, felt her think about it too, and then put some distance between us before someone told us to get a room.

'So,' she said, once we'd recovered ourselves, 'what did Nowak want from you?'

'He wanted to talk about Colleen Clark.'

Macy drank some of her old-fashioned. As I said, we were trying to be careful about how we mixed the personal and the professional, but sometimes, as now, it was unavoidable.

'Did you want to talk about her – and do you?'

'Nowak didn't give me much choice, and I thought I should hear what he had to say. As for you: Yes, I want to talk about her. I may even need to.'

'Go on. Nowak first.'

'He was spreading chum on the water, but with no expectation of catching anything, because he's still sharpening the hook. He asked me to test Moxie for a plea deal, see if he's open to discussions.'

'What kind of deal?'

'Moxie produces a range of expert witnesses on postnatal depression, Colleen pleads guilty to manslaughter, and Nowak talks to the judge,' I said. 'Colleen serves a year plus, as long as she promises to act contrite after release. Whatever she might have done with her son's body gets kicked down the road as being too traumatic for her to face right now.'

'That's not a bad package.'

'Only if she harmed her child. That's what I tried to explain to Nowak, but he has one eye on a new color scheme for the governor's office.'

'He'll make a good governor,' said Macy.

'I'd dispute that, if he's willing to sacrifice my client for it.'

'I didn't say he wasn't ruthless.'

'Seriously?'

Macy took another sip of her old-fashioned.

'Damn it, I don't know,' she said. 'We really are talking about this, aren't we? And there I was, thinking we might have a proper romantic evening, like regular people.'

'Regular people don't have to seek out dark corners in case the cops, or potential future governors, catch them canoodling.'

'No, they don't. And is "canoodling" even still a word?'

'I'm older than you,' I said, 'so my vocabulary is richer.'

A young couple entered the Bar of Chocolate, bringing the clientele up to six. I didn't recognize the newcomers, but they looked like tourists, God bless them.

'Colleen Clark is innocent,' I said. 'She's been set up.'

'By whom?' said Macy, proving that all hope was not lost for the young, grammatically speaking.

'I'm still digging, but I think a woman named Mara Teller is at the heart of it, or that's the name she used to approach Stephen Clark. I'm getting closer to her. Portland PD had her first, but the investigators lost interest after that blanket showed up and Becker and Nowak began counting the column inches for a conviction.'

'All true,' said Macy. 'A blanket covered in a child's blood hidden in his mother's car will do that; and once Erin Becker became involved, the case got fast-tracked. You know how it works: there's only so much time, and no shortage of crime to fill it.'

'Plus, Furnish is a bum.'

'Furnish is a bum,' she agreed, 'but in this instance, he isn't completely to blame.'

'Is it okay if I blame him anyway?'

She patted my hand. 'Sure, honey, if it makes you happy. Meanwhile, your theory about the disappearance of Henry Clark requires taking something simple and making it very complicated. We're talking questions of access to the family home, a car, and a lot of planning.'

'I realize that.'

She watched me over the rim of her glass. I watched her back. It wasn't a chore.

'You're looking at the husband, aren't you?'

'I might be.'

'Evidence?'

'He's a louse.'

'We may need more than that before putting the cuffs on him.'

'All I have are broken threads,' I said, 'but they're starting to accumulate. By tomorrow, I hope to begin assembling them into a pattern.'

'You think Stephen Clark conspired with Mara Teller to abduct and kill his own child?'

She couldn't hide her skepticism.

'Well, when you put it like that.'

'Is there another way you'd prefer me to put it?'

'I can't think of one off the top of my head, but give me a minute.'

'I notice you're not rushing to dismiss it,' said Macy.

'No.'

'But why would he do that?'

'I don't know,' I said. 'Maybe Henry's death wasn't part of the deal. Stephen agrees to surrender his son to Mara Teller, for reasons yet to be established, but an accident occurs and the child is injured or killed. Now Stephen and Teller are yoked together: Teller has Henry's blood on her hands, and Stephen can't go to the police because he's complicit in the crime, one with which his wife has been charged. The best solution for all involved, Colleen apart, is that she should be tried and found guilty. Case closed.'

'When I hear it from you,' said Macy, 'it sounds almost plausible. But then, you do have that effect on me.'

'Before you go all dewy-eyed, I have one more complication to add.'

'Which is?'

Before continuing, I permitted her another mouthful of liquor. I thought she might need it.

'Sabine Drew,' I said.

IV

he left you, he left you,
and now you are ours.

Kathryn Nuernberger, 'You Are Afraid of the Dark'

Chapter LXVIII

To the northwest, Sabine Drew lay awake. Through the open drapes of her window, she could see the outline of branches against the starlit sky, like fractures in the cosmos, and hear the flitting of bats on the hunt for insects. She laid a hand against her breastbone and felt night sweat upon it. She made an effort to sit up, but her body would not respond, and when she tried to breathe, it was as though a hand had been placed over her nose and mouth. She began to panic, flailing against the bedclothes with her legs, even as her arms and torso remained rigid.

Suddenly she was no longer in her own bed, but lying in cold ground. There was dirt on her chest, dirt on her face, dirt in her eyes. The weight of it grew heavier and heavier, the light above slowly being obliterated until there was only darkness and the imminence of death. She was not alone. Henry Clark was nearby. She could hear him crying, could feel him straining toward a consciousness that was both hers and that of another, a man old but strong, still fighting even as the earth bound him to itself.

And a fourth was with them, a near-formless entity: hungry, alien, and yes, lonely. It still held Henry close, but it was also reaching for the man – a stranger, not the detective – reaching for *her*, because she was one with him in his final moments. She surrendered to its touch, intimate and searching, yet also uncertain. It tightened its grip, and curiosity turned to hostility.

Because it only likes children.

The pressure on her eased. She could move again.

The man was dead.

Chapter LXIX

Not unexpectedly, Macy wasn't pleased to hear Sabine Drew's name mentioned.

'That woman is a fraud,' she said. 'I don't even want to begin calculating the number of hours wasted on her wild-goose chase for a child who was already dead while we were searching woodland halfway across the state.'

'Is that what bothers you,' I said, 'the wasted hours?'

'You know damn well it isn't. Drew gave false hope to Edie Brook's parents, all for her own self-aggrandisement, but she wasn't the one who had to tell them that their daughter's remains had been found in the Scarborough marshes, half-eaten by crabs. We had to do that.'

'Drew told me she tried to speak with the parents, but they didn't want to see her.'

'Do you blame them?'

'Not in the slightest.'

Macy gave me the full force of her glare.

'I'm waiting for the "but",' she said.

'But I'm not sure I blame Sabine either. She was acting in good faith. I think she really believed she heard Edie calling to her.'

'I'm sorry, but her delusions don't excuse the harm she did. She was a sad spinster who discovered how to become the focus of favorable attention and liked it.'

'She admitted in my presence to overconfidence,' I said. 'She's also convinced that something deliberately misdirected her during the search for Edie.'

'Some*thing*?'

'Something that liked children and didn't want her interfering.'

'Did you eat or drink anything in her company?' asked Macy.

'Because I think she may have spiked you. Listen to what you're saying.'

I realized that I'd barely touched my wine. It tasted too sharp, but it was not the fault of the pour. Maybe I needed to be tested for COVID; that, or the poison of the Clark case was seeping into every aspect of my life.

'I know what I'm saying,' I replied. 'There are only three or four people in the world with whom I'd be willing to share this, because I'm aware of how it sounds. You're one of them, because you were on Sanctuary. You fought for your life on that island, and not just against Moloch and his people.'

At the turn of this century, an escaped criminal named Edward Moloch had led a band of mercenaries onto Dutch Island, at the eastern edge of Casco Bay, to hunt down his ex-wife and recover the money she had stolen from him. Dutch Island was better known as Sanctuary, because at one time a group of early settlers had retreated there to escape the depredations of the native population. The plan didn't work, leading to their slaughter. Three centuries later, Moloch's assault on the island represented an uncanny repetition of history, one that again ended in bloodshed. Macy had been a rookie patrol officer, assigned to Sanctuary to assist its resident policeman, Joe Dupree. She'd been blooded on the island, and also exposed to the peculiarity of the place. There had long been stories about Sanctuary and what might haunt it. In the end, Moloch and his killers were made privy to the truth of them. So, too, was Sharon Macy. Maine was old terrain with a long memory, a recollection that preceded even the arrival of men. Strangeness was endemic to it. It was why Stephen King couldn't have come from anywhere else.

'I should never have told you about that night,' she said.

'Some of it I already knew.'

'I'm not even sure about what happened on the island anymore. By now, I'm convinced I imagined more than I ever saw.'

'Have you ever returned?'

Macy actually shivered.

'Not since the last of the funerals.'

'Well, there you are.'

Her face softened.

'I've never discussed it with anyone who wasn't there, except for you, and you never once doubted me. I'd have known. I'd have seen it in your eyes, no matter what you might have said to the contrary.'

'No, I never had any doubts.'

'Because you've seen things, too.'

'And I wasn't lying about those either.'

'The only difference is you've never shared with me what it is that you've seen, or what you still see.'

Oh, Macy: I was either dating absolutely the wrong person, or absolutely the right one. I wasn't sure what I wanted. I think I wanted to walk away, but if I did, that would be the end for us. I cared for her. I was tired of being alone. And so, as with Sabine Drew at the Great Lost Bear, I found myself forced to reveal more of myself than I might have wished.

'I see my dead daughter.'

Seated by a lakeshore, seemingly somnolent, a dead child opened her eyes. Before her, the ranks of the dead immersed themselves in dark waters, to be lost from sight in the Great Sea. Jennifer Parker listened to her father's words. Her eyes went black.

'No,' she said.

Chapter LXX

I held Macy in my arms, soft and warm against me. I smelled the salt on her skin, and thought I could catch the glint of it in the moonlight: our scent and our sweat mingling with the essence of the marsh.

Colleen Clark was gone. A text had arrived from Paulie Fulci informing me that he had delivered her safely back to her own home. I was surprised he hadn't asked her mother to sign for her before handing her over. Nevertheless, Colleen was where she wished to be, although she would have no peace there, not while Henry remained lost.

'Why do you think Jennifer comes to you?' asked Macy.

The way the question was posed made her sound like a therapist engaging with a patient. After all, the likely explanation was that my pain had caused me to conjure up visions of my dead daughter, to glimpse her where she could not possibly be, because the alternative – the acceptance that she was no longer in the world – was too much to bear. I might even have been inclined to accept this were it not for the fact that I knew Sam, my living daughter, also saw and heard Jennifer. This, though, I had not shared with Macy, and would not.

'I'm not sure,' I said.

'She's never spoken to explain her presence?'

'If I told you that I hear her in my dreams, it would only be half true, but easier to dismiss. As in a dream, the contact and the discourse are not always willed, because I'm both the observer and the observed.'

'I'm not trying to dismiss it, just to understand.'

'I wish you luck,' I said, 'because I've struggled to understand from the beginning.'

I could have told her more. I could have explained how Jennifer had once returned to the house in which she had been killed in order to save my life. I could have described a conversation by a lakeside as I, wounded and dying, tried to decide whether to cease struggling and join her, or remain with the living. Even speaking aloud of Jennifer made her seem less real. The impossible shies away from scrutiny, and the numinous resists definition.

'Did you discuss Jennifer with Sabine Drew?'

We had not spoken more of Sabine since we'd left the Bar of Chocolate for Scarborough.

'She intuited that I could see someone. She said she hoped it was someone I loved.'

'That's an interesting word to use about her,' said Macy, '"intuited". I don't deny that she possesses a certain psychological acuity. She's not quite a con artist – I may reluctantly accept that her intentions are sometimes good – but she's not too far removed from one. Call it shared DNA.'

The smell from the marsh seemed to me to be growing oppressive, like low tide after a storm, underpinned by the remains of fish and birds rotting on the damp shore. I usually slept with one window slightly open, except in the worst months of winter, but now I got up to close it. Below, the marsh pools shone like mercury in the moonlight. I rested my head against the window frame, taking in the scudding of clouds across the moon and their reflection in an upside-down world.

'At the Bear, Sabine told me that she thought Henry Clark was in Gretton,' I said. 'Maynard Vaughn, the man who purchased the money order used by Mara Teller, lives in Dexter. The money order was bought in Dover-Foxcroft. Draw a line from Dexter to Dover-Foxcroft, and two more lines give you a triangle with Gretton as its apex. But Sabine couldn't have known about Vaughn, or Teller's link to the area.'

'Couldn't she?'

Macy joined me at the window, picking up a cotton blanket in which to wrap herself.

'Only if she was complicit,' I said, 'and I find that hard to accept.'

'Why? There are still people who are convinced she murdered Edie Brook.'

'Seriously?'

'It wouldn't be the first time a killer tried to misdirect an investigation, or keep tabs while claiming to be assisting.'

'And Verona Walters? Sabine certainly didn't kill her, but she did help locate the body.'

Macy didn't reply. She sat on the window seat to face the night. She really was beautiful, but I didn't know how long we could continue tiptoeing around in the hope of avoiding unwelcome scrutiny. Already, I felt sure, there were whispers. Nowak might even have heard some of them.

I knew what Macy was doing in expressing qualms about Sabine Drew. It was what any good investigator did: listen to what is being said, then ask *why* it's being said. Knowledge was power, and seldom shared except as part of a transaction. How was Sabine seeking to benefit from the information she was offering? For Macy, Sabine's testimony was tainted fruit, an effort at reintegrating into a community that had previously rejected her. But what if Sabine was telling the truth? In that case, what she wanted was peace: not only for herself but also for Henry Clark and his family.

'If you travel to Gretton,' said Macy eventually, 'are you going to bring Sabine with you, like a psychic bloodhound?'

'I might, if she's willing.'

'Why wouldn't she be?'

'She's frightened.'

'Of Gretton? It's a dump, but you're not planning to forcibly resettle her.'

'Of what's in there. Of whomever or whatever took Henry Clark.'

Macy tapped the glass.

'You see my reflection?' she said. 'This is me scowling derisively.'

'It's a good look for you.'

'I've had a lot of practice.'

'There's one more thing about Gretton,' I said, because I'd been doing my research.

'Which is?'

'Stephen Clark was born about five miles from town. He lived there until his late teens, only moving closer to Portland after his parents died.'

'That makes me doubt Sabine Drew even more,' said Macy. 'She could have read about his family history in the newspapers or researched his background to add plausibility to whatever line of bullshit she's trying to feed you.'

'True,' I said. 'But she couldn't have known about Mara Teller and the straw purchase of the money order.'

That silenced Macy, even if it didn't fully convince her. She took my hand.

'Let's get some sleep. We both have a long day ahead of us tomorrow. I'm worried I might have worn you out.'

I took one last look at the world beyond the window and felt a presence staring back at me. I now knew why the smell of the marsh was so profound. I could tell when Jennifer was close. I tried to find the shape of her, but she had hidden herself well.

'Hey,' said Macy. 'Bed.'

I turned away from the glass, and willed my dead child to keep her distance.

Chapter LXXI

The following morning Macy grabbed an apple from the kitchen, filled her massive to-go cup with coffee, and was off before I'd even managed to get my pants on.

Way to hurt a boy's feelings, I texted.

Aw, sweetums, came the reply, which about covered it.

I made a call to the Kopper Kettle to check whether Beth Witham was working. I was told she was busy with orders, and I said I'd try again later. I didn't add that next time it would be in person.

I contacted Tony Fulci, who had taken over watch duties from his brother at the Clark house. Everything was quiet the previous night, he said, although he did notice one change: Colleen had placed an electric candle in the front window of the house before going to bed. When she came outside to check on the effect, Tony had asked after its purpose.

'It's so Henry will be able to see it and find his way home,' she told him.

And I thought, *My God.*

'You still there?' Tony asked.

'I'm here.'

'I didn't know how to answer,' he continued, 'so I got back in my car and cried. I cried like a fucking baby. What does that say about me?'

'It says a lot, and all good.'

'You sure?'

'She couldn't ask for better men to watch over her than you and your brother.'

Tony digested this in silence, in the manner of a man forced to consume unfamiliar yet not unpleasant food. He and Paulie weren't

329

used to receiving compliments, so he wasn't sure of the appropriate response. In the end, he settled for 'Maybe.'

'What about Antoine Pinette?' he asked.

'We had a conversation. His idiot brother, Leo, was one of the firebugs, but Antoine wasn't with him, and didn't sign off on the attack. Bobby Ocean put Leo up to it, so Bobby's on today's visitation list.'

'I know where Bobby lives,' said Tony, 'if it helps.'

Admittedly, it was tempting to consider unleashing the Fulcis on Bobby Ocean's residence, like two wrecking balls in human form, but common sense prevailed.

'Don't think it's not appreciated,' I said, 'but let's keep that option in reserve.'

Tony acceded, if grudgingly. He told me the police were on the property again, if in smaller numbers than before, and he'd glimpsed Colleen's mother up and about in the house, in case I wanted to speak with her or her daughter. It couldn't hurt to talk to them, but before I hung up I warned Tony that the protection detail on Colleen would be ongoing until public interest in her began to fade. I mentioned bringing in Mattia Reggio. Tony didn't object. He might have been aware of my reservations about Reggio, but Tony and Paulie got on well with the older man because he had a wealth of stories about a generation of wise guys from the North Shore and Southie. For the Fulcis, it was like listening to a living George V. Higgins audiobook.

I phoned the Clark house. Evelyn Miller answered and said that her daughter claimed to have enjoyed a good night's sleep and was currently showering. They planned to take a trip to the outlet malls in Kittery, and browse the stores across the water in Portsmouth, before getting an early dinner. Colleen, they hoped, was less likely to be recognized among tourists and shoppers.

'I'll see if Mattia Reggio can drive you down,' I said. 'He's not as conspicuous as the Fulcis.'

It was hard to imagine anyone who might be more conspicuous than the Fulcis, so this was a low bar.

'I had hoped we could have some time to ourselves,' Evelyn said.

'Reggio won't intrude, and I'd prefer us not to take any chances.

If you get cornered by a reporter, or some fool with a vengeance complex, Reggio will be able to deal with it. If all goes well, you won't even know he's there.'

She consented to the shadow. I called Reggio, but his phone went to voice mail. I let five minutes go by before trying once more, again unsuccessfully. Part of Reggio's deal with Moxie was that he should be available from early morning to late at night. I tried the home number and Reggio's wife picked up. I'd met Amara once or twice. She came across as an interesting, strong-willed woman, even if she was never anything more than coldly polite with me.

'I was just about to call Mr Castin,' she said, 'in case he'd heard from Matty. He hasn't been in touch since late yesterday afternoon. That's not like him.'

'Did Mattia' – I wasn't about to start calling him Matty – 'say where he was going?'

'Somewhere up in Piscataquis, I think.'

I kept my voice neutral.

'Did he happen to mention why?'

The reply took time. I regretted that we weren't speaking face-to-face. I didn't want Amara to lie to me, if that was what she was planning to do. Lying was harder when it had to be done in person.

'He was trying to help with Colleen Clark,' she said. 'He'd been making calls about her, but he wouldn't share the details. Matty can be like that. He has his own office, and what happens in there stays there. Given his past, you can appreciate why.'

I could. A woman like Amara Reggio would have learned quickly not to ask questions about her husband's business. Even after he'd left that life behind, old habits would die hard.

'He wanted to prove something,' she continued.

'About the case?'

'And to you.'

'Why me?'

'He feels you don't like or trust him. You can deny it, but don't expect me to believe you. Matty respects you, for what it's worth. He wants to show you what he can do.'

Damn Mattia Reggio, I thought. Damn him and his hurt feelings. And damn me too.

'I need to know who he called,' I said.

'How do I find that out?'

'Did he use his cell phone or the landline?'

'His cell. He doesn't have an extension in his office.'

'Do you have online access to your cell phone account?'

'Of course.'

'I'd like you to go to it, take a screenshot of the recent calls, both incoming and outgoing, and email it to me. If they're not already logged by your provider, ask them for the numbers as a matter of urgency. If you can identify some of them, even to rule them out – calls to your children, say, or mutual friends – do that. Do you know the password for his computer?'

'I have it written down, but I've never used it. That's only for emergencies.'

'Use it now,' I said. 'Bring up the search history, if he hasn't cleared it. Look for notes he might have made, scraps of paper in the trash, anything that might indicate what he was planning to do. Take pictures and add them to whatever you send me. If you run into problems and want me to drop by, let me know.'

'I can manage,' she said.

She wouldn't want me nosing around in her husband's affairs. I had disrespected him, and now his wounded pride might have led him into harm's way.

'Amara—' I began, but she killed the connection before I could say anything more.

Chapter LXXII

I met Angel and Louis for breakfast at the Bayou Kitchen on Deering, which was one of their regular haunts since they'd bought their Portland apartment. They had already ordered by the time I arrived, because they knew I'd stick with toast and coffee.

'This joint is wasted on you,' said Louis. 'They ought to give you the bum's rush the moment you arrive.'

'They only let you in because you enhance its authenticity,' I said. 'It's always a good sign when the Black folk pick up on a southern place. Also, it keeps the racists away.'

Their orders came: Three Alarm Eggs for Louis, and a breakfast sandwich with all the fixins for Angel, which meant grits, home fries, *and* beans and rice on the side. Somewhere way back, Angel and Moxie Castin might have shared a common ancestry. I had to admit that my breakfast looked pathetic next to their offerings, as though I were suffering from some form of digestive ailment, but food wasn't my priority that morning. I was just glad for their company, but then rarely was I not.

We ate, and I told Angel and Louis of the previous evening's encounter with Attorney General Nowak, as well as my conversation that morning with Mattia Reggio's wife.

'Are you worried?' Angel asked.

'Not yet, but I'm getting there.'

'Reggio's no pushover. Wherever he went, you can bet he brought a gun with him.'

Angel was right, but there was a difference between busting heads and trying to get inside them. Also, back in his Office days, Reggio would have known what he was getting himself into and why. I was good at what I did, but right now even I couldn't find my feet in the Clark case because the ground kept shifting beneath them.

'If he does land in trouble,' said Louis, 'it'll be delayed retribution for his past failings.'

Louis harbored a marked dislike for career criminals of the Boston school, based on a point of principle: he took exception to most things that came out of Boston, including, but not limited to, the Red Sox, the Wahlbergs, and Aerosmith. Also, a man could die of hunger in Boston while trying to find a good diner, which was anathema to Louis.

'Regardless,' I said, 'we may have to go looking if Amara doesn't hear from him soon, so pack a toothbrush and a change of socks.'

'Like you, we've learned to keep a bag packed,' said Angel. 'What about Nowak?'

'I'll give Moxie an update when we're done here, but I know he'll politely tell Nowak to take a hike. The fact that Nowak even made the pitch indicates he's worried about Erin Becker squaring up to Moxie in a fair fight.'

'Do you think he knows about you and Macy?' asked Louis.

He and Angel had yet to spend any time in Macy's company. If they were uncomfortable with the idea of my dating police, they were keeping it to themselves.

'If he does,' I replied, 'he hasn't said anything to her. We're being circumspect, or as much as anyone can be in a town this size.'

'Can't last.'

'The subterfuge or the relationship?'

'The first certainly can't,' said Louis. 'As for the second, you're marked in a few states, but here is where the shadow is longest. As soon as the suits find out that it touches Macy, they may be tempted to turn the screws.'

He wasn't telling me anything I didn't already know, but the idea of Macy being forced to choose – and the choice she might make – bothered me. I liked being with her. I'd spent too long in solitude.

'We'll have to wait and see,' I said.

Angel called for the check, which was a rarity. Mind you, it didn't mean he was going to pay it. Angel routinely treated checks the way people with bad backs treated anything over ten pounds in weight: namely, as too risky to pick up.

'You ever see that interview Warren Zevon did with Letterman, shortly before he died?' asked Angel.

'Letterman's dead?' said Louis.

'Funny,' said Angel. 'Zevon's dead. Letterman's just old. He's got a beard like one of Noah's deckhands. Anyway, Letterman asks Zevon if facing death has taught him anything. Zevon thinks about it, and says "Enjoy every sandwich." The sandwich is a metaphor. Or I think that's what it is. It might also be an actual sandwich.'

'Please let there be a point to this,' I said.

'What I'm trying to say is, the Macy thing, just go with it. If it doesn't work out, you'll have had some good times. Doesn't mean it won't hurt, but it won't kill you either.'

The check arrived. Angel passed it to me.

'For the life tutelage,' he said. 'That kind of advice doesn't come cheap.'

I stepped outside to call Moxie. He was surprised to learn of Nowak's approach, but as anticipated, he took it to mean that the AG wasn't convinced Erin Becker could secure the required verdict at trial, and Nowak would accept a partial victory over a total defeat. Moxie also agreed that the fact Becker hadn't been present for the discussion meant she wasn't feeling the same degree of pessimism. It betokened a potential fracture in the prosecution's ranks, which might be helpful to our side.

'Where are you now?' asked Moxie.

'The Bayou Kitchen. We're on our way to talk to Bobby Ocean.'

'Who's "we"?'

'Use your imagination.'

'For the last time, are you sure this visit is absolutely necessary? You already put Antoine Pinette on notice.'

'Bobby overstepped the mark once. I want to be sure he doesn't try again.'

'And then?'

'I've done what I can here. We need to go hunting for Mara Teller.'

'All three of you?'

'Four. We'll be taking Sabine Drew with us.'

335

'I got some tea leaves here, if you think they'll help. I could also spring for a Ouija board.'

'She may have her own. One more thing: Reggio has gone dark, which Amara says is out of character. It could be nothing, except she believes he may have been working independently on the Clark case.'

'Give me strength,' said Moxie. 'Does she want to go to the police?'

'That would be a last resort. She's going to send me whatever she can find in his home office.'

'I can tell you he's not having an affair. She'd kill him if he did. I'll drop by to see her in an hour or two. If he doesn't surface by tomorrow, I'll take her down to talk to the cops myself. They'll be reluctant to designate him a missing person too quickly, but I may be able to have them spread the word. I know Reggio's not to your taste, but he's solid, and I like him.'

'I admit I may have judged him too harshly.'

'You?' said Moxie. 'Hush your mouth.'

Chapter LXXIII

The William Stonehurst Foundation for American Ideas occupied a dull, single-story nineties build off Clarks Pond Parkway in South Portland. The premises had formerly been occupied by a debt collection agency that went bankrupt, however that might have been accomplished, and the ghostly silhouettes of the company name remained visible on the exterior, along with the words RACISTS OUT and a swastika, both of which had been imperfectly painted over. Weeds grew through the cracks in the cement parking lot and a large animal, or possibly a regular-sized human being, had taken a dump in one of the spaces.

'So this is where the white folk are mustering to take their country back?' said Louis. 'I got to say, I'm trembling.'

'We're still working out the kinks,' I said. 'Sometimes you have to start small.'

Three vehicles sat in front of the building, one of them Bobby Ocean's black Hummer, which I'd seen around town. It was a recent purchase, acquired used, and among the last of the originals to roll off the line in 2010. Only blockheads drove Humvees, but Bobby still contrived to give them a bad image. I parked as far from it as possible, because the persistence of the William Stonehurst Foundation for American Ideas was proof that benightedness was contagious.

Lately, Bobby had been in the news for promoting assorted prepper, secessionist, and exit arguments, including the use of cryptocurrencies and decentralized autonomous organizations to found independent communities; and advocating that Maine, like Wyoming, should permit DAOs to incorporate as private companies as a step toward achieving that end. To be honest, I wasn't completely sure what a DAO was, even after Louis tried to explain it to me. I ended up with a vague notion of blockchains, tokens, digital interactions, and an absence of central leadership, which sounded like a good way to go about one's business without too much government interference. Whatever the reality, if Bobby Ocean was for it, I was against.

A faded NO MASKS sign was stuck to the inside of the glass double doors. Inside, a young woman typed furiously at a keyboard behind an overlarge security desk that probably dated from the previous tenants. The lobby appeared to have been given a fresh coat of paint, but it served only to make the furnishings look more worn, while the carpet could have done with being rolled up and burned. The wall behind the desk was dominated by a framed photograph of the titular William Stonehurst, aka Billy Ocean, beside a Betsy Ross flag.

'You know,' I said to Louis, 'your presence here might be regarded as unnecessarily provocative.'

'Inflammatory, even,' said Louis.

'Especially since you once set his late son's truck on fire.'

'It was an act of public service. You want me to hang back?'

'Hell, no,' I said. 'It was just an observation. This isn't a social call.'

The doors weren't locked, so the secretary couldn't do much to prevent us from entering. It was possible that she wasn't a true believer and was happy to have a job, even one as lousy as this one, but she knew enough about the operation to recognize that the foundation rarely entertained visitors from the Black community, not unless they were dropping off a UPS package. She didn't look any more enthused by the sight of Angel, who was proudly racially indeterminate, thus enabling him to cause anxiety to a broader range of ethnic groups.

'Can I help you?' asked the secretary.

'You know that replacement theory shit your boss peddles?' replied Louis. 'Meet the replacement.'

'We're here to speak to Bobby,' I said, wondering if it might not have been a better idea to leave Louis outside after all.

'Do you have an appointment with *Mr* Stonehurst?'

'No, but we're old acquaintances. He'll be happy to see us.'

She wasn't convinced, and I couldn't blame her. It was hard to conceive of anyone who might be happy to see the three of us together, or even individually.

'I'm afraid he's in a meeting.'

'Well, tell him to take off his hood and douse the cross with water,' I said. 'Company's here.'

Her hand slipped under the edge of the desk. Ten seconds ticked by before an inner door opened and a man stepped through. He was dressed in light blue pants, a matching shirt, and heavy black boots. The uniform was too tight, and he walked like the boots might be too tight as well, but then there was a lot of flesh to fill the available spaces.

'Shit,' he said. 'At least the day can't get any fucking worse.'

'How you doing, Whit?' I said. 'You a storm trooper now?'

Whitten Vickery had probably barely emerged from the womb before the obstetrician offered him twenty bucks to watch the door. He was a well-known presence around the bars of the Old Port on weekends, or on game nights when spirits might be set to run high. He also picked up a few hours at strip joints, on loading bays, and at Halloween hayrides, where he dressed up as a chainsaw-wielding maniac, helped by the fact that he had his own chain saw and didn't require a lot in the way of makeup. That said, he wasn't a bad fellow. He just didn't have a great deal going on in the conscience or intelligence departments, although he was smart enough to grasp that whatever Bobby Ocean was paying him to prevent any further graffiti incidents or hold off the Antifa hordes that might be preparing to besiege the building, it wasn't enough to compensate for facing me down, and it certainly wasn't enough to justify facing down me *and* the two men at my side.

'Work is hard to come by,' said Whit. 'You know how it is.'

'Tell me about it,' I said. 'I'm standing in the lobby of this dump, so I may have to dip my shoes in Lysol when I'm done. When did you start?'

'This morning. I got a call.'

It wasn't hard to piece together the sequence of events. After last night's incident at the Murder Capital, Antoine Pinette had informed Bobby Ocean that he was overdue a visit from me, and Antoine and his people would be sitting this one out as payback for the activation of Leo's arsonist tendencies. I was only surprised that Bobby hadn't located a rock under which to hide, but instead decided to brazen it out, albeit with hired muscle to protect him.

'They want to see Mr Stonehurst,' said the secretary to Whit. 'I told them he was in a meeting.'

Vickery sighed. He looked like a man who'd discovered half a worm in his apple and just figured out where the other half might be.

'I don't suppose,' he said, 'that you'd consider leaving without causing a ruckus?'

'If we did, we'd have to come back another time,' I said, 'so it would only be postponing the inevitable. I'd also have to disinfect a second pair of shoes.'

'Damn,' said Vickery. 'This was cash in hand, too.'

'You allergic to seafood?'

'No. Why?'

'I hear the Alfieros over at the Harbor Fish Market are looking for someone who isn't afraid of heavy lifting. They're good people, as straight as they come. You do right by them, and they'll do right by you.'

'Can I tell them you sent me?'

'Sure.'

'I'll get my coat. Then you can go straight in.'

He disappeared through the inner door.

'Wait a minute—' said the secretary.

'You ought to quit as well,' I said. 'You stay here long enough, and you'll end up giving evidence at a trial. You can do better.'

'Unless you're a racist,' said Louis.

'There is that,' I said. 'If you're a racist, this is your dream job, and who are we to deprive a woman of her dream?'

Whit Vickery reappeared carrying a navy peacoat and a Tupperware containing a sandwich, an apple, and a hard-boiled egg.

'Where's his office?' I asked.

He jerked a thumb behind him.

'Through there, first door on the right.'

'Is there another way out?'

'From the office? Only a window. Otherwise, there's the way you came in and a fire door at the back. You'll see it at the end of the hallway.'

The secretary moved to pick up the phone, but Angel was ahead of her and lifted it beyond reach.

'This isn't right,' she told Vickery. 'You're not supposed to walk away at the first sign of trouble. What kind of security guard are you anyway?'

'The kind who knows when he's beat,' said Whit. 'It's your call, honey, but if I were you, I wouldn't be hanging around to see what happens next. If it helps, I don't think they're going to hurt him.'

He waited in vain for confirmation.

'Much,' he added.

'I don't believe this,' said the secretary. She stood to grab her coat and bag. 'And I *am* allergic to seafood, so there's no point in my trying the fucking fish market.'

She came from behind the desk to join Vickery.

'Go for a walk,' I told her. 'Think about your future. When you return, we'll be gone.'

She found a pack of cigarettes in her bag and fumbled one into her mouth.

'I didn't like it here anyway. He keeps patting my ass and asking me to have dinner with him.'

'Bobby does love a buffet,' I said, 'but someone may have to cut off his hands to curb his other appetites. If you like, I'll offer him your immediate notice, and he'll pony up what you're owed in cash so you don't have to come back and beg. We can drop it off later.'

She lit her cigarette.

'Yeah, good luck with that.'

'Oh, we can be very convincing,' said Louis.

She regarded him for a moment before returning to her bag.

'Let me write down my address.'

Chapter LXXIV

Bobby Ocean had both aged and shrunk since the death of his son. His clothing hung baggily on his frame and his hair had gone from gray to pure white. I might have felt some sympathy had he not been such a poisonous individual, or had his physical diminution been accompanied by a corresponding dilution of his venom. Instead, the latter had become more concentrated: his recruitment of Antoine Pinette, along with his verbal and financial support for hate groups, was testament to that. I hoped that the difference of opinion with Pinette over the attack on the Clark house could lead to a falling-out between them, but I doubted it. They were both getting something they wanted from the relationship, although Pinette's current absence from the premises was a reminder to Bobby of the wisdom of leaving the rough stuff to the experts.

Bobby's office was nicer than the rest of the building, which wasn't saying a lot. The carpet was new, the chairs were unstained, and the walls were decorated with vintage photographs, maps, and paintings of Portland and its environs, as well as a trio of collotypes signed by Andrew Wyeth, perhaps to communicate to visitors that Bobby's soul wasn't completely blackened.

Bobby looked up as I entered. In his eyes I saw fading embers of resignation, tinged red at the edges by pure hatred.

'Don't you even have the fucking manners to knock?'

'I wanted it to be a surprise.'

'It isn't. I was told you might be making an appearance.'

'Antoine?' I asked. 'Pretty cold of him not to lend you moral support.'

'I'm not his keeper.'

'Just his enabler,' I said, taking a chair. 'You ought to pay him better. Maybe then he might show up when you need him.'

'Antoine does okay – and I was hoping he might have been mistaken about my having the displeasure of your company.'

'You should have stayed home if you wanted to avoid it.'

'I'm not going to hide from you. You're not worth the effort.' He sat back in his chair. 'Did you beat up on that useless slab of flab I hired as security?'

'He left under his own steam. I hate to tell you, but I think your secretary may have quit too.'

'Everyone flees before you,' he said. 'What did you do, wave your sword of self-righteousness in their faces?'

'I convinced them there were better employment opportunities available, but even welfare has more dignity. By the way, I told the secretary you were good for whatever you owe her. Don't make me into a liar. In case you're tempted to try out of spite, you'll be giving us the money before we leave, and we'll make sure she gets it.'

'You're a piece of work, I'll give you that.'

He got up to prepare a coffee for himself from the Nespresso machine behind his desk. I took the opportunity to glance at the material on the walls, where one of the newer, unframed maps caught my attention. I filed it to memory and was already looking elsewhere when Bobby resumed his seat.

'I could have offered you a coffee,' said Bobby, 'but I didn't want to. You still fraternizing with niggers and queers?'

'Gentlemen,' I said, 'I believe that's your cue.'

Angel and Louis ghosted into position from the hallway. To his credit, Bobby Ocean didn't drop his cup in fright or take to his knees to beg forgiveness. He stepped out from behind his desk, walked past me, and stood before Louis.

'You're the one who burned my son's truck,' said Bobby. His voice trembled slightly.

'That's right,' said Louis, whose voice didn't tremble at all.

'Your actions precipitated his death.'

'No, poor parenting did that.'

Bobby stared at Louis for a while longer, as though to take in every facet of his features in preparation for some retribution to come, before returning to his desk to glare at me.

343

'Tell me what you want,' he said. 'I have a foundation to manage.'

'This isn't a foundation, it's a dumpster fire. And you know why I'm here: you've been agitating firebugs.'

'That idiot Leo? Antoine told me about what he did. I'm not responsible for the actions of impetuous young men, however justified they might be. A child-killer can't expect to be treated with deference by the community.'

'A jury will decide what she is,' I said, 'if it gets to that stage.'

'Are you trying to tell me she's innocent?' He laughed. 'Of course, if you're on their side, they have to be innocent, right? You never make a mistake. Like God, you see deep into the hearts of men.'

'It was a dumb move to set Leo loose. It's only brought trouble to your door.'

'You mean you and them?' said Bobby, gesturing at Angel and Louis with utter disdain. 'You're not trouble, none of you. You think you're a step above everyone else, but you're just dinosaurs struggling in a tar pit. The world has altered around you, but you were too slow to notice, and now you're fighting a tide that's destined to overwhelm you. If my money and effort can speed the arrival of that happy day, I'll expend both until I'm broke and exhausted. But let me tell you, I intend to live long enough to see the expression on your faces when you realize how wrong you've been, and that all your efforts have counted for nothing. After that, I'll die laughing.'

He spread his arms, inviting us forward.

'So come on, what are you waiting for? Are you going to break up my office, bust a couple of ribs? Go ahead. I won't even bother to call the cops, because no pain or damage you cause can even begin to measure up to what I've already suffered because of you. Do what you have to or get out. You're making the place stink of piety.'

'I feel hurt,' said Angel to Louis. 'Do you feel hurt?'

'Cut to the bone,' said Louis.

I prepared to leave. What more was there to be said?

'Is that it?' asked Bobby. 'Jesus, it was hardly worth your while making the trip.'

344

'I arrived mad,' I said, 'but you cured me of it. It's hard to feel anger and pity at the same time.'

'Fuck your pity. You can take it to the grave with you.'

'Man still owes the lady money,' said Louis.

'Yeah, Bobby, I almost forgot. Cash only. I wouldn't want to be caught carrying one of your checks in the event of an accident.'

Bobby Ocean took a cashbox from a drawer, produced a fold of bills, and separated a small bundle of twenties.

'You sure that's right?' I said.

'She only works mornings.'

'Worked,' I corrected. I folded the bills and put them in my pocket. 'Next time you have a message to send, deliver it in person.'

'I'll remember that,' he said. 'Because there will be a next time.'

Chapter LXXV

The wind had turned cold and was now whipping trash across the lot of the Stonehurst Foundation. Only Bobby's Humvee and my car remained parked outside, Vickery and the secretary both having departed, presumably never to return.

'We could have inconvenienced him a great deal more than we did,' said Angel.

'He was ahead of us on that front,' I replied. 'What were we going to do: push him around, or burn the place down around his ears? It wasn't about making ourselves feel better, but ensuring he and his people were clear about the importance of distancing themselves from the Clark case.'

I unlocked the car. I wanted to get away from there before someone decided to link me with fascism and earmarked my car for the graffiti treatment.

'But he remains a long-term problem,' said Angel. 'For you, not to mention humanity in general.'

I took a last look at the miserable property, with its faded lettering and grim facade. It was a suitable outpost for the malignancy that Bobby Ocean represented, but he was the voice of the minority, whatever he might have believed to the contrary. The world was filled with better people than that. He and his kind would never utterly disappear, with an influence disproportionate to their numbers – because such was the way with loud, prejudiced men – but they would always be outnumbered by the rest, and fundamental decency had a habit of prevailing. Ultimately Bobby, like all his species, was a frightened creature: fearful of change; fearful of anyone whose color, creed, or language was different from his own; and most of all, fearful of those who refused to follow his path. Bobby Ocean was destined to die scared. But then, so were most of us.

'Time will take care of him,' I said. 'It has a habit of it.'

Louis, I noticed, looked doubtful.

'Anyway,' I added, 'the visit wasn't a total washout.'

'Why is that?' asked Angel.

'I got to take a look at the maps on Bobby's wall.'

'And that helps us how, exactly?'

I started the car.

'Because Gretton was marked on one of them.'

Chapter LXXVI

Not far from Gretton, Antoine Pinette stood amid tall trees, concealed by their shadows, the sound of the creek carrying to him on the breeze. Lars Ungar was beside him, a hunting rifle on his shoulder. The front of the house built from Kit No. 174 was visible through the pines, because they had ventured onto Michaud land.

'Tell me again what you saw,' said Pinette.

'A car went up to the Michaud place late yesterday afternoon, driven by an older man,' said Ungar. 'When it left again, it was being driven by Michaud's sister, with Michaud following in that old truck he keeps out back. The two of them returned in the truck an hour later, but with no car. Then after dark, Pris picked up on lights down by that house.'

Priscilla Gorman was one of the more mature women at the compound. She was also the original connection, via her brother, for the weapons and military equipment that had served to swell a number of bank balances in recent years, Pinette's among them. Back in 2013, Pris's brother had remarked to her about soldiers disposing of surplus materiel through Facebook and Craigslist. Mostly it was inconsequential kit – knives, helmets, scopes, gun sights – sold to bring in extra cash: the US military might have been renowned for many things, but paying its people generously wasn't one of them. Younger enlisted men were consistently broke, and that was before some of them got into narcotics, which had a habit of sending users deep into the red.

Pris's brother, a lieutenant based at Fort Dix in New Jersey, had problems of his own arising from a gambling jones, so when Pris suggested she might be in a position to find an outlet for stock, his ears pricked up. Pris introduced him to Pinette, who had years of experience in buying and selling illegal items, weapons included. By then, Pinette had done his research and concluded there was a significant market, both domestic and overseas, for spare machine gun and rifle parts, body armor, even military generators and gently used medical devices. Admittedly, the sale of weapon parts to other countries was in violation of the Arms Export Control Act, but if Pinette was troubled by the niceties of US law, he'd have found himself a proper job.

Pinette's crew started small, acquiring one or two containers at a few hundred dollars a time from trucks coming out of Fort Dix, before selling them for many multiples of the same. As the wars in Afghanistan and Iraq began to wind down, the military had commenced shipping huge quantities of used and unused equipment back to the homeland, so Pinette had no difficulty meeting the demand. Soon, he was dealing in entire truckloads of supplies, bought for as little as $1,000 or $2,000 apiece, and sending shopping lists by email to contacts in Afghanistan detailing components to be stolen to order and included in homebound consignments.

Aided by Pris's brother, Pinette gradually established a network of providers at five military bases in the eastern and southern United States, but they moved cautiously, turning down business rather than taking unnecessary risks. More custom meant bigger shipments, which required expanding the network, which increased the likelihood of getting caught. Pinette had learned from mistakes made by a group of soldiers and civilians down in Tennessee, who were successfully supplementing their income by selling military equipment stolen from Fort Campbell, Kentucky, until a combination of greed and arrogance led to their arrest. One of the non-coms in the chain had even invited prospective buyers onto the base to choose their own weapons at $500 a time, like Fort Campbell was a fucking outlet store. The surprise wasn't that they were caught, but that it took the Army Criminal Investigation Division three years to do it, which raised questions about the quality of personnel being recruited for ACID. It made Pinette glad he didn't pay taxes, if that was how the army chose to spend them.

Pinette's crew were soon clearing north of a million a year, and had so much cash that they started using some of the empty containers for storage, or burying wrapped bundles of bills in their own yards and those of selectively blind relatives who were paid to make sure their eyesight didn't suddenly improve – and that was before Pinette graduated from gun parts to the assembled weapons themselves.

This was a more delicate affair, but one necessitated by a contraction in the availability of general equipment as the Afghan and Iraqi gravy trains ground to a halt. Pinette's operation recalibrated accordingly, focusing initially on weapons marked for disposal, progressing to those being sent for repair, and finally arriving at unfired M4 carbines, M24 and M107 sniper rifles, and M249 squad automatics. These were harder to ship abroad, but there was a ready internal market, including criminals and elements of the far right, the latter stockpiling for the day when the Chinese invaded, or the UN, or maybe just the French.

There were the Mexican cartels, too, of course, who were always in the market for guns, but by then Antoine Pinette had been politicized, even radicalized, and he didn't favor dealing with nonwhites, whatever their hue. Two of his cousins had been ripped off by a Mexican dealer in New Springville, Staten Island, and when they went looking for the guy, his buddies killed them and dumped their bodies in Brookfield Park. Pinette didn't have any compassion for junkies, family or otherwise, but he had even less for immigrant drug dealers who killed and dumped white junkies when there were more than enough junkies of other races for them to kill and dump instead. In Pinette's view, it was time for Caucasians to take a stand before there were too few of them left to put up any kind of fight at all. This had drawn him into the orbit of Bobby Ocean, who embraced the idea of arming patriots, and had half-formed dreams of establishing a community of like-minded individuals in his home state. Bobby, in turn, had guided Pinette toward Den Hickman, who barely tolerated most white folk, never mind the coloreds. Hickman was not unwilling to ignore illegal activity on his land, so long as some of that money found its way into his pocket and he received the odd pity fuck from one of Pinette's women. Also, Hickman figured that men like Antoine Pinette and Bobby Ocean would be more than a match for Ellar Michaud, their proximity to his property serving to cast a further pall over his existence.

All of which explained how Antoine Pinette and Lars Ungar currently came to be regarding Kit No. 174 and speculating on what might have become of the original driver of the car glimpsed by Ungar. Pinette was sure it wasn't anything good. The Michauds were a strange trio, a reclusive brother and two sisters, all unmarried, tending an old house in the woods. Kit No. 174 gave Pinette the creeps. He wasn't a superstitious man, but he had learned not to ignore his instincts. They told him that Kit No. 174 was every kind of wrong.

'Have you taken a closer look?' he asked Ungar.

'I've been tempted, but trespassing didn't seem worth the hazard.'

'Hazard?'

'I guarantee the Michauds have sensors fixed up to let them know if anyone comes snooping,' said Ungar. 'When we first got here, I sent Sonny down to scope it, and he barely got within sniffing distance before Ellar came running. We stayed low on this side of the creek, but we could see Michaud scanning the area, like he knew we were out there.'

'Could be he's hiding something,' said Pinette.

'If he is, it's nothing worth knowing about. He and his bitch sisters live like throwbacks. They probably take turns with one another when the sun goes down.'

'If it's nothing, why bother securing the house?'

'Might be the family mausoleum,' said Ungar, and Pinette felt that shiver again. 'But I got to admit, I have ridden Michaud about it, because I can tell how much he hates us being here.'

'As long as he keeps his hate to his side of the creek.'

'Which he disputes.'

'Let him. The Michauds and the Hickmans will still be arguing over dirt and roots when this world finally burns.'

Pinette tried to tear his gaze away from the house, but found he could not. While it might have looked abandoned, he was not

351

convinced it was quite empty. Certain structures, even as they appeared to be uninhabited, retained about them a sense of occupation, as though a latent presence had infused the very boards. As he and Ungar observed the house, Pinette could not help but feel that the house was observing them in turn: not someone in the house, but the house itself.

'Antoine,' said Ungar, 'you still with us?'

Pinette started retreating up the slope.

'I need coffee,' he said. 'By the way, Sonny's not coming back. I had to cut him loose.'

Ungar didn't need to ask why. He'd heard about the beating delivered to Sonny at the Capital. It was unfortunate. Sonny had been their Internet specialist, trawling the dark web and chat sites for gamers to seek out potential recruits.

'Damn,' said Ungar, following his leader. 'I liked him.'

'So did I, but he fell into bad company.'

They crossed the creek to head back to their camp.

And Ellar Michaud watched them go.

Chapter LXXVII

The Kopper Kettle had been a fixture in Topsham since the 1980s. I knew a man who used to drive up there from Portland every Friday just to have the black pastrami eggs Benedict followed by a raspberry muffin. The rest of the week he ate like a rabbit that was off its feed, but Fridays were guilt-free.

I parked by the blue entrance awning shortly after 1pm, the Stars and Stripes flapping in the breeze. I could hear a bird singing nearby and picked out a little vireo standing by one of the diner's window boxes, which made me feel better about the world. I left Angel and Louis to get some air and intimidate passersby while I went to find Beth Witham. All three of us entering the Kopper Kettle together might have resembled a team of kidnappers.

Witham wasn't hard to spot, being the sole server on the floor and the only person under sixty working that day. She was built like a long-distance runner, so she probably wasn't secretly bingeing on those raspberry muffins in the back room. Her red T-shirt displayed tight, hard muscles on her arms, and she wore her dark hair tucked under a cap. She was a few years older than Colleen Clark, with the harried look of someone who was holding down more than one job. I knew that look. I saw it a lot in Maine. She wore no rings, but a tiny bluebird was tattooed on the skin between the thumb and forefinger of her right hand.

'The bluebird of happiness?' I said, when she arrived to take my order.

'I couldn't get the real one to visit,' she said, 'so I acquired a counterfeit. What would you like?'

'Just coffee, please.'

I placed a business card on the table, but she didn't pick it up. Judging by the hardening of her expression, that bluebird was ready to take flight.

'I thought someone might find their way to me,' she said. 'Which side are you on?'

'Justice, as distinct from the law. I considered having a special suit made, with an optional cloak, but I didn't want to come off as showy.'

'Save the charm,' she said. 'This isn't a seller's market.'

'I work for Moxie Castin. He's representing Colleen Clark.'

'Did she do it?'

'No.'

'But you would say that, wouldn't you?'

Had I been more musical, I could have set that exchange to a tune and claimed royalties.

'Not if it wasn't true. That pitch is for lawyers alone.'

She took the card and tucked it into the pocket of her apron.

'We close at two. I usually stay around to help clean up, but I'll see if I can take a pass today. I have to be at the Target at Topsham Fair Mall by three to start my second job, and I'll need to take a twenty-minute nap in the car before then or else I'll drop during my shift.'

'I'll try not to take up too much of your time.'

'You won't have to try, because I won't let you. There's a Panera close by, if you want to wait. It should be quiet soon enough.'

'I'll see you there. And thank you.'

'You haven't heard what I have to say yet.'

'You could have told me to take a hike,' I said, 'and then I wouldn't have heard anything but birdsong.'

She lifted her right hand and moved her thumb and forefinger, lending the illusion of movement to the tattoo.

'Tweet-tweet,' she said. 'I'll get you that coffee to go.'

The Topsham Fair Mall had a Renys, so I set Angel and Louis loose in it while I headed to Panera. Angel and Louis found Renys fascinating because it resembled a store from the middle of the last century, somewhere that would clothe you, feed you, and even equip you for the wilderness before sending you on your way with a smile and a lobster fridge magnet that you didn't need but cost only ninety-nine cents, so what the hell.

Beth Witham entered Panera at about two fifteen. She'd changed her T-shirt and dropped a fleece jacket over it, but the cap remained in place. I'd taken a seat by the window where we wouldn't be overheard, and substituted the cup of Kopper Kettle coffee with an iced tea that I didn't want. I offered to get Beth something, but she said she was good. She removed her jacket and placed it on the chair beside her.

'Do you run?' I asked.

'I have an old treadmill and some gym equipment in the garage at home, but I'm so tired lately that I don't have the energy to do more than a couple of hours a week.'

'That's more than a lot of others do.'

'But less than I used to. I got the virus right at the start of that whole mess and haven't felt the same since. I'm weary, and my stomach hurts. My doctor looked at me blankly when I told him, so I don't waste my money on him anymore. I'm not sure he even graduated med school, not unless he paid a bribe. But you're not a doctor, so what can you do about it, right?'

'I can sympathize.'

'That'll have to do, won't it? We may as well get started, for what it's worth. Ask your questions.'

'I'm interested in your ex-boyfriend, Stephen Clark.'

'Who told you that he and I used to be together?'

'A friend of a friend. Six degrees of separation falls to three in this state.'

'Can't deny what's true,' she said 'much as I'd like to when it comes to Stephen. What did you hear? Unless you're interviewing all his ex-girlfriends, in which case I might feel less special.'

'Does he have a lot of exes?'

'A few. He was a good-looking guy. Still is, judging by what I've seen of him lately on TV. He also wanted to better himself, which made him stand out from the rest of the boys I went to school with. Their ambitions didn't amount to more than a new

355

truck every third year, and manual labor that paid double on weekends.'

She took in the mall parking lot. She, too, had been ambitious, certainly for more than she currently had. Now, like so many people, she was holding down two jobs and worrying about getting sick.

'On the other hand—' she resumed.

'There's always another hand.'

'Yeah,' she said, 'sometimes one that packs a punch.'

'Was he violent toward you?'

'Is that what you were told?'

'Isn't that what you were implying?'

'How many questions do you think you've asked in your life?'

'More than I've heard answered, but that's true for all of us.'

'A philosopher too,' she said. 'My, my.'

I waited. It bore repeating: I was good at waiting.

'Have you met Stephen?' she asked finally.

'I have.'

'Did he put up a good front?'

'I'm still trying to decide.'

'That's all he is, pure front, but it took me too long to recognize it. He had aspirations, but none of the character or substance required to back them up. I watched his rage grow because of it.'

'How long were you together?'

'Two years. Not long, I suppose, but long enough.'

'For what?'

'For Stephen to reveal himself. You asked if he was violent toward me. The answer is yes, but only once. I didn't wait around to see whether it might happen again. I'd watched that story unfold between my parents when I was growing up, and I wasn't about to replicate it in my personal life. It was my mother, incidentally, not my father, just to counter any assumptions you might have. She drank and he didn't, but she had other problems as well. She was mentally ill, but people didn't talk about that the way they do now. Alcohol made it worse, although it was a function of her illness. She ground my father down, physically and emotionally, but he never once raised a hand to her in retaliation, and it

356

was never spoken of either inside or outside the home. He was ashamed, I think. He was a man being beaten by his wife – and he wasn't small either: not in stature, not in any way. He'd just stand there and let her hit and scratch until she wore herself out, then put her to bed. The thought of leaving her never arose. He loved her, you see. That was his tragedy. It would have been easier for him had he not.'

She scowled, but more at herself than me, annoyed at how much she had suddenly revealed. I thought she might be very lonely.

'What happened to them?' I asked.

'My mom died and my dad started living. He's with another woman now. She's good to him. They live up in Macwahoc. They visit when they can. It's easier for them to travel than for me.' She shook her head. 'Jesus, listen to me: Chatty Cathy, unburdening herself to a stranger. Look, the point is that I know violence and I won't stand for it. When Stephen hurt me – and he hurt me bad – we were done.'

'What led to the incident?'

'That's a very diplomatic way of phrasing the question,' she said. 'Another ex of mine once asked me what I'd done to Stephen to get him all riled up. Because I must have done something, right? I sent that one on his way, the asshole. You want to know what I did to enrage Stephen, Mr Parker?'

She leaned forward.

'I got myself pregnant, that's what I did. I ran out of birth control pills, was short on cash, and thought I had the dates all figured out so we could fuck without risk, but I was wrong. I could have asked Stephen to wear a rubber. He would have, because he wasn't difficult in that way, not like some I've met, but I thought it would be okay to ride bareback. I did the test twice, because I didn't want to believe the result the first time, even though I knew it was right. I could *feel* it was right. I didn't tell Stephen until I was sure. I was afraid to. I thought I had a good idea of how he'd react, but I was wrong about the degree.'

'Why were you afraid?'

'Because Stephen had told me over and over that he never wanted children,' she said. 'At first, I put it down to how immature some

357

young men can be. They're convinced they're going to be hand-some forever, and don't want anything that might tie them down. They're like bucking broncos, but life tames them. Gradually, I came to understand that Stephen was different. He *really* didn't want kids. He had this visceral antipathy to fatherhood. He didn't even like being around other people's children. What's more, he claimed to find pregnant women repulsive. He said that if I ever became pregnant, he'd dump me without a second thought. But that wasn't what he did.'

'What did he do?' I asked.

She took a long, deep breath.

'He punched me repeatedly in the stomach. He only stopped when I vomited. Then he dumped me.'

'Did you consider going to the police?'

'Sure, but I elected not to,' she said. 'I know it goes back to my father and how he remained silent all those years about being abused by his little wife. I felt ashamed. I was disgusted with myself for sleeping with – for *loving* – a man who could do that to me. I didn't want folks pointing at me on the street or talking about me behind their hands, because what happened would get out if I pressed charges. It was around that time I took up running and learned how to box. I wasn't going to be any man's punching bag again.'

'And the baby?'

'I miscarried not long after. I was only surprised it didn't happen sooner. Given what Stephen had done to me, I was sure I'd lose the baby that night, but I didn't. I was worried he might have damaged my insides, but I'm fine. I'd still like to have a child someday, or more than one, but it hasn't happened yet. Do you have children?'

'I have a daughter,' I said.

'What's her name?'

'Samantha. Sam. She lives with her mother in Vermont.'

'Do you get along with her?'

'I try to. She's an unusual child.'

'I like the name Samantha,' said Beth. 'I have a list of names for my baby, and they're all girls' names. Funny, but I've never countenanced having a boy. I hope I don't. Girls are more trouble for a couple of years, but they're smarter – and kinder too. This world isn't overflowing with kindness. We could do with more of it.'

She checked her watch.

'I'm sorry,' she said, 'but I really do need to take that nap.'

'I have a few more questions, then we're done.'

'Shoot.'

'You and Stephen grew up together, right?'

'We went to the same school, but he was a couple years ahead. We didn't start going out until after we'd both graduated.'

'Did you ever have cause to visit Gretton?'

'Gretton? What a shithole that was, and last time I drove through, it hadn't improved any. It did have a bar, though: the Junction, known as the Junco, that some of the boys liked, because age was just a number there. I'm surprised they didn't have high chairs and plastic sippy cups for half the customers.'

'Was Stephen Clark one of the boys who went to the Junco?'

'Sure. I remember he fucked a girl from Gretton in the parking lot. That was before we started seeing each other. The pack he ran with ribbed him about it for months after, so everyone knew. She wasn't even pretty, they said, just a local Gretton freak. It's a weird town anyway, but this girl had it in her bones.'

'Do you recall her name?'

'Lord, no. I doubt even Stephen could bring it to mind, once he'd sobered up after the act.'

'Does the name Mara Teller mean anything to you?'

'No, that's not someone I know.'

'It may not be important, but do you think you could find out who that girl was?'

'Seriously, after all this time?'

'Seriously,' I said, 'after all this time.'

'I can try. And let me guess: I shouldn't tell anyone why I'm asking.'

'It would be better if you didn't.'

'I can't promise I'll learn anything. I don't stay in touch with but a handful of people from my childhood.'

'I'd appreciate the effort.'

She was gathering up her things, preparing to go. I didn't have long left with her.

'How did you feel when you read about the abduction of Stephen's child?' I asked.

She didn't answer immediately. I'd noticed her taking her time throughout our conversation. Beth Witham was a woman who stepped cautiously.

'I thought it was a misprint,' she said, 'because I couldn't believe he had a kid of his own. I thought at first that it might have been his wife's from a previous relationship, but then I said to myself that Stephen would never have married a woman who'd had a child. He always told me he couldn't imagine fucking a woman who'd given birth, let alone marrying her and helping raise another man's son.'

'People change.'

'Some do: they get worse. The beating I took from Stephen was a hard lesson to learn, but I've always been grateful that I didn't end up married to him. There's something dead in him, rotting away deep inside. I bet it poisons him more and more with every year that goes by. Now ask me if I think he could have killed his son. Forget about alibis. Just ask me.'

'Do you think he could have killed his son?'

'No,' she replied. 'It's going to sound odd, especially after what he did to me, but Stephen doesn't possess the psychological strength to take a life and live with the consequences. He cried after he beat me. I think he was genuinely shocked by his loss of control. He's a weak man trying to find a shortcut to becoming a strong one. That never ends well.'

She put on her jacket.

'But if you asked me if I thought he'd let someone get rid of the child for him,' she continued, 'I'd say that was possible. What I still don't understand is how he ended up with a baby to begin with.'

'Accidents happen,' I said. 'You can attest to that.'

'Was it an accident?'

Now it was Beth Witham who waited for a reply. It turned out she was good at waiting too.

'His wife told me he wanted the baby,' I said. 'They had the child at his instigation.'

'So it wasn't an accident?'

'No.'

'Well, there's your final question,' she said. 'Why would a man who dislikes children, and finds pregnant women repulsive, elect to have a child? You run down the answer to that and you'll be closer to the truth about what happened to Henry Clark.'

Beth Witham, I concluded, was wasted at Target.

I walked her out. Angel and Louis were waiting by the car, each of them holding a Renys bag. They just couldn't resist temptation.

'Are they with you?' Beth asked.

'They're my associates.'

'They don't look like private detectives. Don't take this the wrong way, but they look like criminals. If they came into the store, I'd lie down on the floor with my hands behind my head.'

'Sometimes,' I said, 'that's precisely the effect we seek.'

'What do you figure they bought at Renys?'

'I shudder to think.'

She faced me so she could look me in the eye as she spoke.

'You have an idea where that boy might be, don't you?' she said. 'That's why you're not traveling alone. You're going to look for Henry Clark, and you know that whoever took him won't like it.'

I nodded.

'Do you think they might be in Gretton?'

'It's a place to start.'

'I'll get that name for you,' she said, 'but she was just a girl, one of many those boys fucked and forgot. I doubt she bore a grudge. Stephen did worse to me, and even I wouldn't have wanted to see his life collapse the way it has. No one would.'

'Yet someone did.'

'Or so it seems.'

It struck me, not for the first time, that in my line of work, I met more clever women than men. Perhaps it reflected a greater societal imbalance.

'When you find them, hurt them,' said Beth Witham. 'Then ask them about Stephen Clark.'

Chapter LXXVIII

Ellar Michaud and his two sisters sat in the kitchen of their home, the slow descent of the afternoon sun visible through the window behind them. Ellar had broken out a bottle of the gin distilled by Eliza from a brand of cheap vodka that otherwise threatened to induce blindness in the frail or unwary, enhanced with almond, juniper, and coriander. Aline didn't generally hold with drinking, and certainly not while it was still daylight, but these were exceptional circumstances.

There was no question but that the interlopers currently residing on Hickman land would attempt to investigate more closely Kit No. 174. Even had Ellar not been tracking the two men and guessed the direction of their thoughts, Lars Ungar had already revealed that his people were curious about the old house. If they succeeded in entering, they might well be curious about the dirt floor of the basement, even though Ellar had raked and smoothed it after the interment of Mattia Reggio. The house smelled of death, and not just recent death either. Generations of Michauds had been putting bodies in that ground since long before Kit No. 174 was raised. Decay, by osmosis, now infused its walls and boards; or that, Ellar thought, was one explanation, even as he suspected there was more to it, just as the permanent cold inside could be attributed neither to climate nor to the disposition of the dwelling itself. The wendigo made it that way.

Of course, the women disliked hearing that name used for it. Words like *wendigo*, *chenoo*, and *giwakwa* were not for civilized white people like themselves. Anyway, whatever inhabited Kit No. 174 was not beholden to the superstitions of the Mi'kmaq or the Abenaki. The tribes might have been aware of its existence, but they had not called it into being, and it was no god of theirs.

Instead, it had long ago allied itself to the Michauds, blessing their existences and those to whom they elected to extend the boon of its presence. The first Michauds had heard it calling and heeded the summons, the spirit having chosen them. In return for good fortune, it demanded only small offerings: a body upon waking, preferably a child, so that it might have company in the dark.

And it was true that the Michauds had always been fortunate. They traditionally enjoyed long lives and good health. Prosperity came their way – not so much as to draw suspicion, but sufficient for them to be able to dwell in comfort. Yes, there were occasional setbacks, though they seemed to coincide with moments of doubt in the Michaud clan: a questioning of their duty to the spirit, even its actuality. So it was better, it had been decided, not to interrogate, only accept.

Yet still Ellar vacillated, if silently, for he had learned to guard his speech around his sisters. Was it not in the nature of men to attribute patterns to coincidence, and in this way bring gods into being? Once they became trapped in that mode of reasoning, any departure was rendered fraught, and thus action, or inaction, reinforced belief. Might not the Michauds have created the entity, or the idea of it, because logic dictated that men originated gods rather than the opposite? If so, could they not also bring it to an end by withholding that same belief?

But it was easier for Ellar to indulge such speculations in private, or far from home. When he was on the land, or in the house itself, with his sisters by his side, he had less difficulty in believing. But credence did not denote outright acquiescence, and Ellar was worried. Enemies were gathering. For the first time in years, he felt vulnerable.

Ellar had read about the town of Prosperous, Maine, and the old chapel shipped there from the north of England centuries earlier. He had listened to the whispers about the Prosperous community, and learned that something was said to have dwelt beneath their ancient chapel, something transported with it from the old country; even some distant cousin of the wendigo, for who knew what manner of spirits preexisted men. That chapel now lay in ruins, destroyed by an explosion, leaving Prosperous in a state of terminal decline. A person could make of that what they wished, but one fact was indisputable: Prosperous had attracted the attention of the private detective Parker and suffered for it. Now Parker was involved in the search for Henry Clark, which had, in turn, led the man named Reggio to their door. Inevitably, others would follow.

At the kitchen table, Ellar spoke.

'We ought to have gotten rid of the house a long time ago,' he said. 'I wish it had never been raised to begin with. We might as well have lit a beacon.'

The idea behind its construction had been to install some part of the Michaud clan where the entity could be monitored, so they might more easily know when it woke, and move to appease it. It was also intended to serve the same purpose as a private temple or chapel: a signifier of familial belief. Finally, Ellar's great-aunt had wanted a place of her own in which to live, having grown tired of the company of her clan. It said much about the Michauds, Ellar thought, that she would have preferred to share her living space with a predatory wraith than with her own flesh and blood. Ultimately, she had died before she could take up occupancy, leaving whatever dwelt in the soil to possess and corrupt the house, or find in its flawed aspect a reflection of its own nature.

'It likes that place,' said Aline. 'The house has become its nest.'

'Did it tell you that?' said Ellar. 'It speaks to you now?'

But Aline wouldn't be drawn into an argument. Ellar guessed the gin might be having some effect on her, but Aline also had a different, more cryptic attachment to Kit No. 174 than he and Eliza. In summer, she would sleep there for a night or two, returning to them stinking of defilement.

'It doesn't have to speak to me,' she said. 'I know when it's at peace.'

'It won't be at peace for much longer if Hickman's settlers keep nosing around,' said Eliza, 'and we don't have time to go moving bones. Even if we did, their eyes are on us now. Any activity will only add to their suspicions.'

'I say we demolish the house,' said Ellar. 'We can plant trees, let the roots shatter whatever remains are left in there and drive them deeper down.'

'I told you,' said Aline. 'It doesn't want that, and neither do I. Who knows, we might even harm it. It could turn against us.'

Not for the first time in his life, Ellar fought the urge to grab Aline by the scruff of the neck to shake some sense into her – for all the good it might have done, Aline having long since developed a resistance to reason. If he did try to act without her consent, he could see her grabbing a rifle and taking up position on the porch of the house, daring him to take one step closer. He wouldn't have put it past her to kill him. Objectively, he realized, the three of them were crazy, but Aline was the craziest of them all.

'What options do we have?' Eliza asked her brother.

Ellar swirled the gin, conjuring from it a strong scent of almonds. If Aline ever decided to poison him, cyanide in the gin would be the way to do it. But he had an answer to Eliza's question. He'd been working on it ever since it became apparent that the outsiders weren't going to be leaving voluntarily anytime soon.

'We could move against Pinette and the rest,' he said.

'They outnumber us, and they're well-armed,' said Eliza.

'I wasn't advocating a gunfight. They're not the only ones who can cross creeks. I've taken a look at their camp. They're using hundred-pound propane cylinders to supply their needs. They've rigged hot-water showers, refrigerators, and heaters to a series of DuroMax generators, and haven't made a bad job of it, but that's a lot of propane. A leak, a naked flame, and the whole campsite could go up.'

Ellar could see Eliza picturing flowers of fire blooming in the night.

'What about the smell?' she asked. 'Won't that alert them?'

'You ever smell propane? It stinks like a skunk's spray. Hard to distinguish between them, unless you're born to the land. That would be the way to hide it.'

'There'll be an investigation,' said Aline.

'What of it? I can put together a firebox that'll burn to ash, leaving no trace.'

Ellar knew he was talking himself into an act that common

sense – those words again, so alien to his family – should have led him to reject, but he accepted that Aline might be right about retaining Kit No. 174, if for the wrong reasons. Destroying the house wouldn't cure them of the headache of the Hickman camp, because he and his sisters would never be free of surveillance as long as it was there. The camp was rapidly developing into a permanent settlement, as Ungar had hinted, which would escalate the existing dispute over boundaries and trespass; and it wasn't as though the Michauds could seek recourse through the law, as that would involve more strangers coming to survey the land.

But there was also the question of what Ungar or one of the others might already have seen, which included the arrival and subsequent departure of Mattia Reggio's vehicle. Witnesses, even ones as unreliable as a bunch of armed degenerates, would lead to a search, and a search could uncover bodies. Poulin, the town constable, knew better than to go peering under rocks unless it was unavoidable – he was a creature of Gretton, whether he realized it or not – but state or federal law enforcement would not be so inclined to a willed lack of interest.

'How soon can it be done?' asked Eliza.

Ellar had a couple of bottles of Rickard's Skunk Essence that he used for deer hunting off Michaud land. He'd also noticed a dead skunk by the side of the road outside Gretton earlier that day, and he couldn't see any reason why it wouldn't still be there.

'Best to act quickly,' he said. 'Then we can put an end to the whole sorry business.'

'Tonight?'

It was the time of the new moon, the darkest phase of the lunar cycle. Ellar saw a chasm gape before him and marveled that he had, with the aid of his sisters, contrived to create it.

'Yes,' he said, 'tonight.'

Chapter LXXIX

I called Amara Reggio as Beth Witham drove away, Angel and Louis beside me. I felt sadness and anger on Witham's behalf, not only because of her treatment at the hands of Stephen Clark but also for the fact that this bright, attractive woman was being sold short by life. Louis, had I mentioned it, would have dismissed this as my savior complex manifesting itself once more. What could I have said in reply? Nothing, except perhaps to point out that while not everyone could be saved, one had to behave as though they might be.

Amara had found nothing on her husband's computer, but she wasn't surprised by this, since Mattia used DuckDuckGo as his default browser. She had also gained access to their cell phone account and noted that Mattia, amid other calls, had contacted the same number three times on the night in question. It wasn't one she recognized, and she'd been tempted to try it before deciding it might be better to share it with me first. I asked her to read it out, and I added it to the dashboard notepad.

'I'll chase it down,' I said. 'You discovered nothing else?'

'No, but that's Matty all the way. When he dies, the paperwork won't pay for a lawyer's lunch.' She realized what she'd said, and followed it with '*Dio mi perdòni*'.

'He knows how to look after himself, Amara.'

'Not like he used to. I spoke to Mr Castin. He said you were the best there is at what you do. I wish I didn't have to rely on you because of how you've looked down on my husband, but I think Matty's in trouble. His silence tells me so.'

I didn't bother contesting what she'd said, or offer an apology. Neither would have been sincere.

368

'I'll be in touch as soon as I know anything,' I said.

I hung up, but didn't immediately call the number she'd given me. I didn't like taking unforced steps into the unknown. First, I wanted to establish who I might be calling. Sometimes, the simplest way to check for a user's name was to look for the number on Facebook. It was surprising how many people linked their phones to their profile, but I was certain that Mattia Reggio didn't move in those circles. My solution was to call David Southwood, who was the best reverse-lookup guy around. Most of the services that claimed to be able to trace cell phone users by their number were unreliable at best and scams at worst. Southwood was expensive, while much of what he did was illegal and therefore inadmissible in court, but his information was gold-standard. He answered on the first ring.

'What?'

Southwood wasn't big on idle chitchat. I'd never met him, and neither had anyone I knew. I imagined him living in a basement surrounded by screens, although judging by the prices he charged, it was probably a basement in the Bahamas.

'It's Parker,' I said.

'I can see that.'

I let the ensuing hiatus last for just slightly longer than a normal person might have found comfortable, but awkwardness was an alien concept to Southwood. In the background, I could hear fingers tapping at a keyboard, no doubt as intimate personal data passed before Southwood's eyes.

'I'd like a number traced.'

'Give it to me.'

I read out the digits.

'Just the name and address,' said Southwood, 'or do you want more? IRS, bank accounts, credit card records, vehicle registration?'

'It's urgent, so I'll settle for speed over depth.'

'It's always urgent. If it wasn't, nobody would ever call.'

I was shocked at what counted as unnecessary conversation. Compared to Southwood's usual level of interaction, it was the equivalent of a Hamlet soliloquy.

'How long?' I asked.

'There's a waiting list. Could be a few hours.'

'Move me to the top of the line.'

'There'll be a premium.'

'It's the nature of capitalism.'

Moxie would be good for the fee. He might complain, since it wasn't as though the IRS was sympathetic to deductions for illegal activity, but if the intelligence brought us closer to Reggio, he'd suck it up.

'Five minutes,' said Southwood.

He killed the connection. To my right, Louis cocked an eyebrow.

'So what are we doing?' he asked. 'Because right now it sounds as though we're looking for four different people – Reggio, Maynard Vaughn, Mara Teller, and Henry Clark – which counts as a lot of looking.'

I started the car. There was no point in sitting in a mall parking lot while it was still daylight and we had roads to travel. It was about ninety miles from Topsham to Dexter, most of it along I-95. I could cover it in an hour-fifteen, less if I really put my foot down.

'Dexter isn't a big place,' I said, 'so Vaughn shouldn't be hard to find. Let's just hope that whatever Southwood comes up with doesn't lead us back the way we came.'

Southwood was as good as his word. He called precisely five minutes after he'd ended our last conversation.

'It's a landline, registered to an Adio Pirato,' he said. 'I have an address in Roxbury, New Hampshire. It's on its way to your new private email.'

'You don't have my new private email.'

'Actually, I do.'

Of course he did. He probably knew more about me than I knew about myself.

'Because you opted for the gold plan,' he continued, 'I've also given you his car registration, contacts for his immediate family, and his rap sheet plus ancillaries. If you want financial records, that's platinum level.'

'If I need them, I'll get back to you.'

But Southwood had already hung up.

'Adio Pirato,' said Angel. 'I thought we might renew acquaintance with that fucking crook before too long.'

Pirato was the Northeast point man for the Office, responsible for the smooth running of the syndicate's operations beyond its main base in Providence, Rhode Island. When I'd needed to make contact with the Office during a previous investigation, Mattia Reggio had acted as the intermediary, and Pirato was among those with whom I'd been forced to negotiate.

I opened up Southwood's anonymized email on my phone. The 'ancillaries' included a confidential report from the Organized Crime and Gang Unit of the US Attorney's Office of the District of Massachusetts, outlining Pirato's suspected involvement in racketeering – specifically loan sharking, extortion, grand theft auto, and insurance fraud – as recently as 2020. No mention of anything dirtier, like murder, but only because Pirato was too wily a fox to leave a trail. It was a long time since he'd pulled a trigger, but that didn't mean he hadn't induced others to do so on his behalf.

I showed the email to Louis, who read it before passing it on to Angel.

'I could have told you all that,' said Louis. 'You should haggle on Southwood's fee.'

'Old-school rap sheet, too,' said Angel, 'though not any school you'd like to have attended.'

I dialed Pirato's number and got an answering machine. I left a message before contacting Amara Reggio, putting her on speaker so Angel and Louis could listen.

'That number you gave me, the one Mattia called the other night, is Adio Pirato's,' I said.

'Let's assume I know who that is.' Old habits died hard, meaning she wasn't about to discuss Pirato's character or professional interests over a phone line.

'I've left a message for him,' I said, 'but it might be useful if you left another. I'm not someone he'll be eager to hear from, so he may not be in a hurry to return my call.'

She assured me that she'd find a way to speed things up. I didn't doubt it.

We drove on.

Chapter LXXX

Dexter lay in a valley by Lake Wassookeag, where my grand-father and his buddies used to fish for trout. It was a vibrant small town by any standards, with a nineteenth-century library, a municipal golf course, and a small airport on its outskirts. The Dexter Police Department, which numbered perhaps six full-time personnel and assorted reservists, was housed in a whitewashed building on Main Street. I'd rarely had cause to deal with the Dexter PD directly, but it had a good reputation, which wasn't always the case with small-town law enforcement. It even had a K-9 division, and who doesn't like a dog?

We arrived at the station house just as a uniformed officer was locking up. The department was open for official business only from 9:00 a.m. to 3:00 p.m., so either he was running late or had forgotten his hat. Outside those hours, officers were available by calling the dispatcher, so we'd struck it lucky. I saw the brass on his collar as I got out of the car. Here was the chief of police himself, Lyle Drummond. He was built for blocking doorways, but looked friendly enough, even after I'd identified myself, meaning he didn't immediately try to run me out of town.

'Well, well,' he said, as he handed back my I.D., 'Portland's own Sherlock Holmes. Should I be getting ready to lose sleep?'

'I wanted to speak with one of your local residents, Maynard Vaughn,' I said.

'Huh.'

'Is that a problem?'

'Ordinarily, it wouldn't be,' said Drummond, 'except that Maynard has gone AWOL. He hasn't been seen since yesterday and he's a man of routines, except when he's off his meds, and that hasn't happened for a few years. We run a Good Morning

Neighbor program here, which means volunteers run daily checks on seniors and vulnerable adults, Maynard among them. He's always up and waiting for the visit because he enjoys the company, but there was no reply from his apartment today, and the other residents of his condo building say it doesn't look like he came home last night.'

'Did anyone take a look inside?'

'He leaves a key with the guy in the apartment next door, but the volunteer called us before doing anything, so one of my people was with her when she went in. There was no sign of any disturbance. The apartment isn't big, and Maynard keeps it tidy. It's a hangover from his time in the military.'

'Are you actively searching for him?'

'We haven't started combing the woods yet, but now that you're here, I may have to upgrade my level of anxiety. What did you want to talk to him about?'

I told him I was working on behalf of Colleen Clark and shared, as succinctly as I could, the relevant details of the investigation, including the purchase of a money order on behalf of Mara Teller by a man believed to be Maynard Vaughn.

'I don't know any Mara Teller,' said Drummond.

'I think it's a false name, but she might have been recognizable enough around here to enlist Vaughn's help.'

Drummond glanced past me. I turned to see Angel and Louis getting out of the car to stretch their legs.

'Who are they,' asked Drummond, 'Watson and Watson?'

Which I had to admit was kind of amusing.

'They take care of some of the heavy lifting,' I said. 'I have a bad back.'

'I might have heard stories about some shadows of yours,' said Drummond. 'But then if I was in your shoes, I'd also travel with reinforcements. Do you have a description of this Teller woman?'

'I can show you a photo, but it's not great.'

I pulled up the picture from the file supplied by Delaney Duhamel. Even cleaned up and enlarged, Mara Teller's features remained indistinct.

'You weren't kidding about the quality,' said Drummond, taking a pair of glasses from his shirt pocket to examine the image more closely. 'That could be my wife.'

'Great,' I said. 'Does she sleep around at conventions? If so, my work here is done.'

'Do you want to spend a night in a cell?'

'Not so much.'

'Then knock it off about my wife. She's a churchgoer.' He continued to look at the photo. 'You know, there's something familiar about this woman. I might have seen her around, but she's not local. If she was, I'd be able to identify her straight off, even with the blurring.'

'I'll email you a copy and you can let it percolate.'

Drummond gave me his card, and I returned the favor.

'By the way, who's the man with her in that picture?' Drummond asked.

'Colleen Clark's husband.'

I let him cogitate on that.

'You're thinking an affair?'

'He's admitted it,' I said, 'but only as a step above a one-night stand.'

'I haven't been keeping up with the small print. No more than that?'

'He says not.'

'You believe Teller, whoever she really is, might know what happened to the Clark boy?'

'If she does, she may also have harmed Maynard Vaughn.'

Drummond tapped my card against his gun.

'I'll circulate that picture,' he said. 'Someone else might have a better memory for faces. Spending the night in town?'

'No, we're moving on.'

'Can't say I'm not relieved. Mind if I ask where you're headed?'

'Gretton.'

I decided not to mention the detour we'd first be making.

'You ever been there before?'

'No.'

'Well, you won't be hurrying back for a second look,' said Drummond. 'It makes Dexter look like Vegas. So what's in Gretton?'

I finished emailing Drummond the image from my phone.

'If I'm right,' I said, 'Mara Teller.'

Chapter LXXXI

Ellar Michaud crossed the creek as the light was fading. He wasn't worried about being spotted by Antoine Pinette's crew, or even old Den Hickman himself. He'd been trespassing on Hickman land since boyhood, and these woods were as familiar to him as his own, so even without the camo gear he'd have been confident of passing unnoticed by a bunch of city folk. As for Hickman, his arthritis meant that he could barely walk unaided, and his approach was usually heralded by the noise and fumes of his piece-of-shit Chevy Avalanche. Hickman's wife was senile and their two kids had largely abandoned them both, although they surely still expected to be left the property when their parents passed away. It was no surprise, then, that Hickman had welcomed Pinette and his people onto his territory. They'd serve as entertainment, if nothing else.

Hickman had attempted to add a codicil to his will stipulating that it could not be sold to the Michauds in perpetuity, but his lawyer – who drank at the Junco and talked too much, hence Ellar's inside knowledge of the matter – had pointed out to Hickman that this condition would be difficult to enforce. Nothing prevented a future buyer from disposing of the property to the Michauds, in part or in whole, Hickman himself unlikely to be in a position to object from six feet under. Hickman, Ellar imagined, had likely been chewing on that particular quandary ever since. With luck, the indigestion would kill him.

Ellar didn't know how deep Antoine Pinette's pockets might be – certainly not deep enough to satisfy Den Hickman, even as the old fucker heard the Reaper sharpening his scythe – but the Michauds had been doing homework of their own on Pinette, aided by reports in the *Bangor Daily News* and the *Portland Press*

Herald. Months before Mattia Reggio fell into their hands, they were aware that Pinette's people had ties to Robert Stonehurst down in Portland. While Bobby Ocean, as the papers called him, wasn't Rockefeller rich, he was wicked wealthy by Maine standards, enough to be able to buy up the Hickman acres without batting an eye. If Ellar regarded Stonehurst as a potential buyer for the tract, five would get you ten that Hickman might be thinking along the same lines. This made eliminating the threat posed by Pinette, Ungar, and the rest all the more urgent. If Ellar was right, they were preparing for an outright purchase.

And then, ladies and gentlemen, Ellar Michaud and his kin would be royally fucked. They'd be forced to raze the old house for fear of drawing further attention to its nature and purpose, and according to Aline, the inhabitant wouldn't like that one bit. In revenge, it might decide to dispense with the Michauds. It had been part of this land long before their arrival and would persist long after they were gone, insinuating itself into the hearts and minds of those who succeeded Ellar and his sisters. In the meantime, the Michauds would succumb to whatever ailment it decided to visit upon them, because it was in them and of them. It was in the fruit they ate from the trees, the produce they grew in the garden, and the air they breathed. It had already infected generations of their family, permitting the contamination to remain largely dormant and rendering them asymptomatic, but that could easily change: a lump on Aline's breast, a telltale tumor in Eliza's mouth, dark blood in Ellar's stool. It was all well and good to speculate on the reality of its existence in daylight, but by night, in the woods that had birthed it, its actuality was harder for Ellar to deny.

He pushed these thoughts away. He and his sisters had settled on a course of action, even if a massive propane explosion was anything but subtle. Ellar was certain that the subsequent investigation, while revealing no trace of his involvement in the destruction, would uncover evidence of criminality on the part of Pinette's people. Ellar, during one of his previous recces of the camp, had seen military cases on the site, and before he died, Mattia Reggio had confirmed that Pinette was involved in the illegal sale of weapons. That would be sure to diminish any sympathy for the victims, as well as lead to awkward questions for Den Hickman and Bobby Ocean. Ellar wished old Den the best of luck selling land with a crater in the middle and the odd body part still lodged in the upper branches of trees.

Ellar came within sight of the camp. Already lamps were lit and fires burning. He could hear music playing, nothing to which he'd have opted to listen by choice. He wore night-vision goggles, but didn't think he'd need them; he was used to negotiating the darkness.

Ellar found a declivity, set aside his duffel bag, and waited for night to fall.

Chapter LXXXII

We'd arranged to meet up with Sabine Drew at Lagrange, where she would leave her car and travel on to Gretton with us. She arrived twenty minutes late to the rendezvous point.

'Sorry,' she said as I greeted her, 'I was just feeding my fish before I left.'

'You keep fish?'

'Ever since I was a little girl. I'm quite the expert by now, but I also find watching them restful. It's a private hobby.'

I made the introductions as she got in the back beside Angel.

'Have you been ill?' she asked him.

'Did he tell you that, or is it more psychic stuff?'

'Neither. I can see it in your face. Suffering leaves its mark, doesn't it?'

'Inside and out,' said Angel.

'Well, I'm sorry for it.'

'Thank you. By the way, are you a psychic or a medium? I wouldn't want to cause any offense by using the wrong word.'

'Both, I guess,' said Sabine, 'because the second feeds from the first. But really, I'd prefer not to be either one. What I can do has ruined my life.'

After that we proceeded in silence, apart from some Sarah Vaughan on Spotify. But as we drew closer to Gretton, I saw Sabine grow visibly more tense.

'I ought to tell you, Mr Parker, that I think Henry Clark has been joined by someone else.'

'Another child?'

'No, an adult male. He suffocated. I shared his panic as he died.'

'When was this?'

'Last night.'

'Who was he?'

'I don't know. I only felt his final moments because of Henry. I think he boosted the signal.'

We passed the town sign.

'You can let me out anywhere,' said Sabine. 'I'd like to walk around for a while. I'll be happier doing it with you three nearby, so if you could keep me in sight, I'd be grateful.'

I pulled up in front of a coffee shop and she got out. She paused to look left and right, as though to get her bearings, before walking south. The street was virtually empty of vehicles, with only a few people on the sidewalks, so she was easy to spot. If she started growing distant, I could just move the car.

'This,' said Louis with feeling, 'is all fucked up.'

Chapter LXXXIII

Antoine Pinette was driving along Gretton's main street when a woman in a multicolored jacket, her head in the clouds, stepped from the sidewalk and almost ended up under Antoine's front wheels. Had he not been abiding by the speed limit, he might well have killed her. He gave her a blast of the horn. She barely reacted, only peering at him with mild curiosity before yielding the road to him.

'These fucking rubes,' said his brother Leo, who was in the passenger seat. 'I swear, evolution sidestepped this place.'

Antoine took in the jaywalker, but her attention was elsewhere. He felt the strangest urge to stop and make sure she was okay. She reminded him of someone: not his mother, because Antoine would have run that bitch over without blinking, but a woman who might, in another life, have been worthy of his care.

'There's no way that woman is psychic,' said Louis, as we watched Sabine Drew step safely onto the sidewalk. 'It's a miracle she's survived as long as she has.'

But I was barely listening to him. Instead, I was squinting at the vehicle that had almost run her over.

'You know,' I said, 'that looks a lot like Antoine Pinette's car.'

Leo was still grumbling. He hated Gretton. Antoine didn't blame him, but this was work. Antoine avoided involving Leo in serious business affairs, but he'd decided to keep him close since the incident with the firebomb. The confrontation at the Capital still rankled Leo. Nobody wished to be humiliated in public, but Leo took indignity harder than most because he had so little dignity to spare.

Antoine had made it plain to Bobby Ocean that he didn't like any of his people being manipulated by him, but Leo most of all. He believed the message had gotten through, but couldn't be sure. Bobby hadn't been the same since his son was murdered, and whatever once passed for his impulse control was now seriously impaired. Currently on Bobby's shit list – apart from the usual lineup of negroes, Latinos, Jews, immigrants, feminists, queers, and socialists – was Den Hickman, who had begun to reconsider the wisdom of allowing strangers to situate themselves on his land. A couple of Antoine's associates had inadvertently frightened Hickman's wife by passing too close to the main house and now some aspect of her dementia had caused her to begin fixating on their presence, making life even harder for her husband. Worse, Hickman had become aware that his guests were storing more than the occasional misplaced pistol or semiautomatic in their camp, and had communicated his disapproval to Antoine, Den Hickman not wanting to spend his last days in a federal peniten-tiary. Also, none of the women were willing to give him pity fucks anymore, which had turned him ornery.

Recently, therefore, Antoine had gone from enjoying a secure operating base in Gretton – with the possibility of something more lasting on the horizon, funded by Bobby Ocean – to trying to keep an old cripple and his crazy wife calm, because the chances of killing the Hickmans and getting away with it in a community as small as Gretton were low, shading to none, even with a half-assed constable counting as the local law. Bobby was more ambivalent, but Antoine wasn't about to put anyone in the ground solely on Bobby's say-so, while the dream of establishing a new Eden in Piscataquis County had always been mostly Bobby's to begin with. For Antoine, it was just more convenient than working out of a lockup or junkyard.

More to the point, the final shipment of guns had arrived the day before, ready for distribution. It was about time to go to ground while exploring new income streams for the future. Antoine had so far eschewed the sale of narcotics, a hangover from the straight edge scene he'd embraced in his youth, but perhaps it was time to yield to pragmatism, since the defense of the white race wasn't going to pay for itself, and it wasn't as though he'd have to hand back all of his Minor Threat and Fugazi LPs. He had solid sources to whom he could turn for meth, even coke. There was a ready market for both, but coke dealing involved meeting a better class of individual, with all their own teeth. Consequently, the market was less volatile.

For now, the priority was to ensure everything went off smoothly with the transfer of the remaining weapons and equipment from the encampment. He and Leo would make one more attempt to convince Den Hickman to see reason before returning to the camp for the night. If they failed, Hickman would be Bobby Ocean's weight to bear. It was Antoine's guess that once Bobby calmed down, he'd see the wisdom in looking elsewhere, or even shelving those settlement plans. The difficulty with establishing a colony based on fear, hate, and anger was obvious: it would attract only frightened, hateful, angry people, all of them armed and with short tempers. Coop them up in some woods in Piscataquis with nothing to occupy them during the winter, and they'd quickly turn on one another. Jesus, already half these people couldn't agree on who they were supposed to hate more, while the other half were too contentious by nature to agree on anything at all. If you left them alone for long enough, they'd start punching themselves.

But Antoine wasn't about to cut himself loose from Bobby, not yet. He and Bobby shared a certain set of beliefs, even if they didn't always agree on methods, and Bobby's pockets remained deep. Only a fool turned his back on a ready source of funds, and Antoine Pinette was nobody's fool.

Chapter LXXXIV

The car that had come close to striking Sabine Drew was already vanishing into the dimness at the edge of town. There was no need to follow it. I knew where it was going.

'If Pinette is up here,' I said, 'it's to do with Bobby Ocean and that map on his office wall.'

'But not Henry Clark?' asked Angel.

'I've never imagined Pinette as a child abductor.'

Yet something Sabine had said at the Great Lost Bear came back to me:

Evil finds its own. It forms clusters.

As the words returned, so did Sabine herself, walking quickly back to the car. Angel opened the rear door for her.

'The boy was brought through this town,' she said. 'He left ripples behind.'

In Dexter, Chief Lyle Drummond was talking to a woman named Jen Blackmore. Like Maynard Vaughn, Blackmore lived on the margins, but her engagement with social services was more conditional and sporadic. Liquor was her demon and would kill her in the end. Regardless, she'd so far managed to survive beatings, exposure, and accidentally setting herself on fire, not to mention the damage alcohol consumption had inflicted on her body. Blackmore was in her forties, but looked sixty and smelled ripe. Still, when she was sober, or as near to it as she ever got, she was capable of clarity. She was also cleverer than she let on, noticed more than some people in Dexter and its environs might have liked, and forgot none of it. Right now, she was telling Drummond about Maynard Vaughn.

'He got into a car,' she said, 'down by the lake.'

'When was this?' said Drummond.

'Early yesterday afternoon. Can't say for sure, but the sun was still in the sky.'

'What kind of vehicle?'

'Light blue Chrysler. I've seen Maynard in that car before, or one like it. I took heed on account of how Maynard wasn't habituated to motor travel. That was way, way back, and there were two women in the car with him, one older, one younger. This time, I saw only the younger one.'

'And what happened?'

'The car pulled up, the driver said something to Maynard, he got in, and the car drove away.'

'Was Maynard under duress?'

'Not that I could tell.'

'I don't suppose,' said Drummond, 'that you happened to spot the license number?'

'I didn't have my glasses on,' said Blackmore. 'I mean, I could see it was Maynard, but those letters and numbers were beyond me.' She eyed Drummond slyly. 'Might there have been a reward, if I did get the plate number?'

'I'd have done right by you.'

Blackmore grinned at Maynard, revealing more gum than teeth. The remaining dentition didn't look like it would be occupying oral real estate for very much longer.

'How right?'

'Twenty bucks?'

'Huh,' said Blackmore. 'A twenty, just for a number.'

She whistled and produced a cheap cell phone from one of the pockets of her coat.

'That means a picture of the car has got to be worth at least fifty.'

Chapter LXXXV

Gretton had one motel, the Bide-A-While, with room rates so low we'd either traveled back in time or would be consumed alive by vermin in the night. Optimistically, if nothing else, the town also boasted two inns. Judging by the pictures on its website, the first promised prison mattresses and food to match, while the second screamed Gay Couple Heading for a Messy Divorce. We picked the latter.

'What now?' asked Angel, as we drove to the property.

'We find somewhere to eat,' I said, 'then start making inquiries. If Reggio came here, he might have talked to someone. A stranger, especially one with questions, would have enough novelty value to be remembered. We may also be able to find out what Antoine Pinette and Bobby Ocean are up to, because it can't be anything good.'

Which was when my cell phone received a call from a concealed number.

'Parker,' I said.

The voice that replied was old but firm, with the trace of an accent. Adio Pirato's parents might have emigrated from the old country before he was born, but it had left its stamp on their son.

'The last time we spoke,' he said, 'I hoped it would be the last time we spoke, if you know what I mean. You ought to make more friends, because I don't have any vacancies right now – or potentially ever, in your case.'

'I'll live with the loss.'

'It can't be worth your while making new friends anyway,' said Pirato. 'Your life choices mean you'll be dead before you get to know them well enough, or vice versa. Is this a cell phone?'

'Yes.'

'I don't like talking business on cell phones. Find a pay phone and call me back. You got a pen?'

I wrote down the number he gave me. We'd passed a gas station a block back, so I made a U-turn and pulled in. A pay phone – a rarity these days – stood beside piles of prepacked logs and a rack of propane tanks secured with a chain. The gas station attendant made change for me, and Louis filled up the tank while I called Pirato back. I could hear conversation and music behind him.

'How much trouble is Mattia in?' Pirato asked.

'Maybe none,' I said. 'Probably a lot.'

Pirato didn't bother stalling. Amara Reggio had vouched for me, which was good enough.

'Mattia asked me to check on a license number. I still know people.'

'Did you come up with anything?'

'I got it here.' He read out the license plate number. 'The vehicle is a blue 2016 Chrysler 200 sedan, registered to an Ellar Michaud, Private Road Seven, Gretton, Maine.'

'Is that all Reggio wanted?'

'We shot the breeze, but he was only interested in the car. Will there be recoil?'

'Not from me,' I said. 'If anyone asks, Amara found the imprint on a notepad in her husband's office.'

'That works. When you find out about Mattia, let me know. You can use that first number. The machine will pick up, but someone will hear.'

'I'll be in touch,' I said, 'for better or worse.'

I was already redialing David Southwood's number as I walked back to the car. Again, he picked up on the first ring.

'Yes?'

'I have a name and address for you,' I said. 'Ellar Michaud, Private Road 7, Gretton, Maine.'

'What do you want to know?'

'Find out if he has a sister.'

Chapter LXXXVI

We dumped our stuff at the inn. Contrary to expectations, it was run not by a pair of gay men but by a tiny retired woman named Bella whose tastes began and ended with exposed woodwork and ersatz Native Americana. Whatever happened over the next few hours, we wouldn't be leaving Gretton without causing a ruckus, and it made sense to have privacy to prepare for what was coming. We also needed somewhere for Sabine Drew to stay, because I didn't want her with us at the Michaud place. Our issues were with the living, not the dead.

David Southwood had gotten back to me with the information I'd requested and more. Ellar Michaud had not one but two sisters, both of whom lived with him on the family property. The older of the two was Aline, fifty-five. Ellar, at fifty-six, was the eldest child. The youngest by a distance, at thirty-eight, was Eliza. Both parents were dead, and the siblings were now the joint legal owners of a considerable acreage of land, one that had been in their family for generations.

Southwood emailed copies of three driver's licenses. Ellar Michaud was over six feet tall, and heavy with it. His sisters were smaller, but not by much, and neither was exactly pretty: in the right light, Eliza might have passed for inoffensively plain, and in the wrong one, Aline could have made a few extra bucks scaring crows. I compared the picture of Eliza Michaud with the blurred image of Mara Teller. The resemblance wouldn't have convinced a jury, but it was enough for me. I was looking at the same woman.

Three vehicles were registered to the address: a Buick truck, a white Nissan, and a blue Chrysler. None of the Michauds had a criminal record, though complaints of intimidation and trespass had been made against Ellar Michaud by his neighbor, Den

Hickman. The Michauds had filed no similar counterclaims, but it evinced a territorial spat that was always running hot without ever boiling over.

I was still looking through the license photos, familiarizing myself with the faces, when my phone rang again, this time from a number I didn't recognize. When I picked up, it was Beth Witham.

'I asked around about Stephen Clark and that girl from Gretton,' she said. 'A mutual friend said he couldn't be sure, because it was a long time ago, but he thought it might have been one of the Michauds.'

I gave nothing away. Beth Witham had come through, but I didn't know her well enough to confirm it for her.

'What can you tell me about them?'

'I never had anything to do with them. I know the family was old Gretton – I mean centuries – and kept themselves to themselves. The guy who gave me the name still lives up in Piscataquis, not far from town. He said people tried to stay out of the Michauds' way then, and still do, which was what made it so memorable that Stephen fucked one of them.'

'Are they bad news?'

'Not bad news so much as odd. You know, just not right. The guy said he heard locals used to approach Mother Michaud for help with work, or their love lives. Crossing her palm with silver, that kind of thing. She performed abortions, too, back before *Roe v. Wade*. I asked my dad about it, and he said it was true.'

I told her I was grateful for her help, then sat at the window of my room, moving between pictures of Eliza Michaud on my cell phone: one with Stephen Clark, her face slightly turned away from the camera, the other from her driver's license, staring straight at me. I was now convinced that Eliza Michaud had been responsible for the abduction of Henry Clark, but she had not been unaided.

Angel, Louis and I walked from the B and B to my car. Each of us wore a gun beneath our jackets, while I had a pistol-grip Mossberg 12-gauge shotgun stored in the trunk. It was a gift from Moxie, but so far I hadn't had any call to use it. I kept it in the trunk because I wasn't sure what else to do with it. I showed

Angel and Louis the email from Southwood and pointed to Eliza Michaud's picture.

'In the absence of a better candidate,' I said, 'that's Mara Teller.'

'They're all the right height for modeling work,' said Louis, running through the licenses and faces, 'but otherwise that's one grim family.'

Angel was still focused on Eliza Michaud.

'Why would anyone have an affair with her?' Angel asked.

'Who knows the ways of the human heart?' I said.

'Yeah, but what about the ways of human eyes? Though compared to her sister, she's a regular Aphrodite.'

'I don't think this was ever about an affair,' I said. 'It sounds like madness, but I'm starting to believe that Stephen Clark might have facilitated the abduction of his own child, and not in return for any sexual relationship with Eliza Michaud.'

Stephen Clark: a man who didn't want to be a father, and had beaten a previous girlfriend for becoming pregnant but later pressured his wife into having a child; a man with little interest in sex, but who seemingly had an affair with a woman he had once screwed years earlier in the parking lot of a bar.

'If not sex, then why?' asked Louis.

'I don't know. Take away sex and what's left? What could she give him that would justify handing over his son to her? What could she offer him that he didn't already have?'

'Money?' suggested Louis.

'Money doesn't feel right to me. That isn't what drives him.'

'So what does?'

'How about ambition?' said Angel.

And I thought, *Yes, that might be it*. Professional success and recognition were what Clark desired more than anything else, yet his own limitations prevented him from obtaining them. But how could Eliza Michaud have guaranteed his professional advancement? She lived in the woods with two older siblings, close to a remote, unloved town.

'I suppose we'll just have to ask the Michauds,' I said.

Lyle Drummond got in touch as we were passing Private Road 7 for the second time, trying to get some measure of the Michaud land. We couldn't see any buildings or lights, but we knew from Google Earth that the main house was in there, along with a second structure that might have been a ruin.

'Are you still in Gretton?' asked Drummond.

'You lied,' I said.

'I did?'

'It makes Dexter look like Vegas, not Reno.'

An animal ran from one side of Private Road 7 to the other: a weasel, from the length of its tail, embarking on a nocturnal hunt.

'To each his own,' said Drummond. 'You were asking about Maynard Vaughn. He was last seen getting into a blue Chrysler registered to an Ellar Michaud of Private Road Seven, Gretton, but the witness says it was a woman behind the wheel. The witness also says she saw Maynard in the same car at least once before, but that time with two women, including the same one who picked him up more recently.'

'How reliable is the witness?'

'She's a drunk who once managed to set herself on fire with denatured alcohol. That aside, she's more reliable than you might think, with an enviable memory that goes back years, decades. But even combined with what you told me, it's not halfway enough to get a warrant, not for a property outside my jurisdiction. But I was considering taking a trip up there tomorrow, once I've made the requisite courtesy calls to local law enforcement, and assuming Maynard doesn't show up in the meantime, which he may well do.'

'Who's the law in Gretton?'

'A constable, Poulin. He has full investigatory and enforcement powers, murder excepted.'

'Have you had dealings with him?'

'A few, but nothing consequential. My opinion, not for circulation, is that he's spent too long up there. I don't think he colludes in permitting lawbreaking so much as fails to see much of anything at all. If I'm arriving in his jurisdiction, I'll be obliged to inform him, but I might test the ground with the sheriff's office and the state police first.'

I decided to be open with Drummond. If things went south, he'd find out soon enough.

'We're out by the Michaud property,' I said. 'The man we're looking for came to Gretton in search of that same blue Chrysler.'

'Shit,' said Drummond. 'Look, I need to send this up the chain before we act, and that's not going to happen before tomorrow morning.'

'Last time I checked, we hadn't been deputized. I'm not sure the chain applies to us.'

'Don't be obtuse. It's already dark. You step onto that land now and you could legitimately be shot as trespassers. Jesus, if you three arrived uninvited in my yard at any hour, I'd shoot you on principle. Is it going to hurt to wait till there's light in the sky?'

I muffled the phone with my hand.

'No point in being shot at if we don't have to be,' said Louis. 'I've been shot before and didn't enjoy the experience.'

'You're getting old,' I said.

'It comes with not getting killed. As for you, if someone decides to shoot you, they'll have trouble finding a spot that doesn't already have a hole in it.'

'Angel?'

'I'm going to die somewhere,' he replied, 'but I'd just as soon it wasn't out here in the dark.'

'What about Reggio?'

'If he did go onto that property,' said Louis, 'and asked the wrong questions of the wrong people, he's already dead. If they didn't kill him, he's either alive there or alive someplace else, and that situation is hardly in danger of imminent change. In other words, us stumbling around at night isn't going to improve matters. But if you're intent, I got nothing better to do.'

'The moment Drummond starts reaching out to local and state law enforcement,' I said, 'word will spread. I've never met the constable around here, and have no idea of his loyalties, but we can't rely on his discretion when it comes to the Michauds. If we wait, we do so only until predawn, then we go in.'

'I can live with that,' said Louis, and Angel concurred.

I returned to the call.

'That took a while,' said Drummond.

'The perils of living in a democracy. We'll wait.' It was the truth, but also kind of a lie. We would wait, but not for Drummond.

'You make it sound as though you're doing me a solid,' he said. 'And there I was thinking it was the other way round.'

'Don't get all mushy. You can thank me later.'

'I'll add it to my list of things I look forward to doing, right below donating a kidney.'

'That's the spirit,' I said. 'Be a giver.'

Chapter LXXXVII

From his hiding place on the Hickman holding, Ellar Michaud watched Pinette's vehicle arrive at the camp. The lights strung from the trailers revealed the patched paintwork, and now here was Pinette himself stepping out from behind the wheel, accompanied by a younger man whom Ellar had seen around town with Pinette and Lars Ungar. There was some resemblance between Pinette and his companion, Ellar thought, even if the boy looked softer around the edges.

An older man with an unkempt beard emerged from one of the trailers and hugged Pinette before leading him to a panel van parked by a trash heap. Five or six of the men and women from the camp followed, leaving only a young couple seated before the fire, passing a bottle back and forth between them. Ellar looked for Ungar but couldn't see him. He might have been in one of the trailers, but if so, why hadn't he come out when Pinette arrived? More likely, he was away from the camp. This bothered Ellar. He really didn't like Lars Ungar. He'd hoped to watch him burn.

Ellar removed a sack from his duffel. It contained a dead skunk in a sealed Ziploc, along with two small bottles of Rickard's Skunk Essence. Ellar had located the three large propane tanks being used to supply the camp's main needs, as well as a couple of smaller tanks by two of the trailers, but he'd need time to cut the lines and prime the incendiaries. The dead skunk and bottles of essence would do the trick, but the distraction provided by Pinette's arrival was an added bonus.

Ellar secured the pack before setting it aside carefully. What it contained was delicate and he didn't want any breakages. Soundlessly, he prayed to a god that had no name, and in which he would have preferred not to believe.

Chapter LXXXVIII

Lars Ungar crossed the creek, that disputed border between the Hickman and Michaud lands. He was armed with a suppressed M4 carbine, which he had temporarily liberated from the latest, and final, shipment of weapons at the camp. An army surplus helmet, complete with netting, protected his head, and a night-vision monocular, permanently claimed for his own use, was fixed over his right eye, because Ungar didn't want to go stumbling into holes.

The main Michaud residence was some way distant, but Ellar Michaud and his weird sisters seemed to have a highly developed sensitivity to intrusion, which was one of the reasons for another piece of kit attached to Ungar's chest: a small video screen, linked to a camera mounted on his helmet. Ungar didn't ascribe the Michauds' extraordinary perception to any kind of sixth sense, no matter how odd the sisters might be, but instead continued to believe that there might be a more quotidian explanation.

Minutes after leaving the creek behind, Ungar came in sight of the old kit house. He sheltered behind a tree, lifted the night-vision lens, and gave his right eye time to accustom itself once again to natural light. When he was able to pick out branches against the sky, he activated the video screen. Instantly, the infrared beams of the security system were made visible as parallel bars of light set two and four feet above the ground. They surrounded the building, so that anything taller than a small deer would break both beams if it approached the property, probably activating an alarm at the Michaud residence. But a bird or bat flying through the higher of the two beams, or a fox passing through the lower one, wouldn't set any warning bells ringing.

Ungar ran an eye over the exterior of the building. If he were in the Michauds' position, he would have placed at least two cameras on the house itself, at or near the front and back entrances. That way, if the beams were broken, someone would quickly be able to establish the cause without having to hightail it over just because a doe decided to take the scenic route home.

But the presence of the beams raised an interesting question, namely what the system was designed to protect. Den Hickman had told Antoine Pinette that locals knew better than to go wandering on Michaud or Hickman land without permission – knew better than to go wandering on anyone's property without permission, because good fences made good neighbors. Gretton wasn't any kind of hunter's or snowmobiler's paradise, which meant landowners weren't much troubled by strangers either. This sense of isolation was one of the reasons that Pinette and Bobby Ocean had decided on Gretton as a base.

Yet even had the Michaud land been open to visitors, a complicated infrared security system looked like overkill for a dilapidated dwelling in the woods. Ungar supposed that there was always the risk of a fire spreading should kids have found a way inside to smoke weed and drink a few Coors Lights, although that possibility had already efficiently been dealt with by boarding up the windows on the first floor. The old wooden doors had also been replaced, or reinforced, with heavy steel plates, leaving the windows on the upper floor as the only weak points. There the glass remained unobscured, almost as though someone living inside didn't wish to be left utterly in darkness.

If someone *were* living in the old house, thought Ungar, it would explain a lot, including why it had been permitted to remain standing. The doors were clearly secured from the outside, which meant that whoever was inside would be closer to a prisoner than a resident. The more Ungar considered this, the more improbable it appeared that the house might be occupied. Nevertheless, he found that he, like Pinette, could not quite shake off a sense of habitation, and he had to remind himself not to jump at shadows.

Ungar made a single circuit of the house, staying low and keeping to the tree line. Even with the aid of the monocular, he struggled to find any obvious cameras at the doors, but that didn't mean they weren't there. Whoever was responsible for installing that infrared system obviously had enough technical aptitude to be able to hide cameras where they wouldn't be spotted. Ungar wondered where the juice was coming from. He thought solar power would be the most efficient way of powering a photoelectric beam setup, though he was no electrician. He left that to the camp expert, one of Pinette's cousins, who already had their entire circle hooked up for free to every premium cable channel known to man.

Ungar had come this far, and wasn't about to return to the camp without finding out what the Michauds were hiding. There was a certain amount of calculated risk involved, but the odds remained roughly in his favor. The Michauds weren't going to operate round-the-clock shifts to stare at a monitor relaying images of the house from hidden cameras, so the beams were the main alarm system. If they were broken, the Michauds would check the feed, but otherwise it might only be glanced at in passing. As long as Ungar didn't mess up, he believed he could make it to the house without being noticed. The doors were padlocked, but he had a crowbar in his pack as well as backup in the form of a sixty/forty solution of nitric acid and water stored in a small corrosion-resistant container, even as he hoped it wouldn't come down to using the latter. Depending on the thickness of the steel, he might have to wait a couple of hours for the solution to dissolve the lock. He didn't want to hang around for that long, just in case he suddenly found truckloads of previously unsuspected Michauds descending on his hiding place to teach him a lesson about respecting privacy.

Ungar took a deep breath and stepped gingerly over the lower of the nearest beams, keeping his head down so as not to break the upper one. He approached the house from the east, where the wall was windowless, and worked his way to the back door. This time, as he peered around the corner, he saw a camera. It was set above the narrow lintel, where a section of the wood siding had been removed so the unit was flush with the rest of the boards. Even in daylight, it would have been as good as invisible from a distance.

From his pack, Ungar removed a twelve-ounce can of Rust-Oleum black spray paint and gave the lens a good spritz. If the Michauds noticed the camera was no longer transmitting, they might, with luck, attribute it to a malfunction or a battery that needed recharging, and leave any further investigation until the morning. Should they not, Ungar had his M4 and was wearing a ski mask. If he had to shoot his way out, he would, but he was sure the sight of the M4 would be enough to give even big Ellar second thoughts, and unless he was storing secrets for the government in the old house, he wouldn't go making a complaint to the police about trespassing. If he did take it into his head to enter the camp and kick up a fuss, well, trespassing went two ways, and the camp would be obliged to protect itself against an armed intruder.

Ungar inserted the crowbar into the padlock and yanked. The lock was strong, but it gave the first time because Ungar was practiced at breaking locks: locks, arms, even heads. He slipped the bolt and pulled open the steel door. Behind it was the original wood version, the glass panes dusty, home to spiders and their prey. Ungar saw no alarm sensors on the steel; had he done so, he'd have hightailed it back to camp, since it would have meant the Michauds were already on their way. He tried the front door, which opened easily. This, too, was free of sensors, although he wasn't surprised: there wouldn't be much point in putting them on the inner door and not the outer one.

Now that he was inside, he dispensed with the night-vision monocular in favor of a high-powered Maglite. He progressed slowly, careful to test the boards before he leaned his full weight on them. The last thing he wanted was to put a foot through the floor and bust an ankle. Worse, he might fall straight down to the basement, which would leave him to lie in agony until some of his own people came looking for him, or the Michauds finally got around to checking on that camera he'd disabled.

The first floor was empty of furniture apart from two plastic chairs in what might once have been the living room. The wallpaper reminded Ungar of childhood visits to his grandmother's home in Rumford, with its tattered red drapes and smell of standing water. He felt as though he'd stepped back in time, but not to any era he might have elected to visit. It was obvious that the building was in some kind of regular use. The dust in the hallway was disturbed and Ungar spotted recent traces of mud. He glanced at the stairs leading to the second floor and saw that they had partially collapsed, leaving a hole like a toothed mouth. He decided not to bother with a search of the upper story. Whatever this house contained, it wasn't up there.

Which left the basement, accessed via a door under the stairs. It was the only inner door that was locked, which Ungar thought odd, but again his crowbar took care of it. When the door cracked open, Ungar was hit by a wave of warm air, when by rights the basement should have been cooler than the rest of the house. It smelled so rank that it was like being breathed on by someone whose innards were in a state of dissolution. For a moment, Ungar was even convinced that he might actually have heard an exhalation, though he put it down to the night breeze finding its way between cracks in the walls below.

Shielding himself as best he could, he shone his flashlight on the steps. They were newer than the rest of the house, and the beam picked up more mud on them.

'Hello?' he said. 'Anybody down there?'

He didn't feel foolish for asking. That primitive instinct was kicking in once more: he was not alone here. Why bother to lock a door in a house that was already secured from the outside, unless you were trying to keep someone contained? You locked them in to prevent them from roaming, from testing the steel doors and the boarded-up windows or trying to make their way past the hole in the main staircase to peer through the glass of the upper floors; perhaps even break them and cry out for help, or attempt an escape by jumping down to the porch roof.

But Lars Ungar received no reply from the basement dark.

He fixed the flashlight to his carbine, held the muzzle of the M4 on the stairs, and descended.

Chapter LXXXIX

Sabine Drew was dozing in her room. She wasn't hungry. Being in Gretton had relieved her of any appetite. The town was rife with badness. Whatever dwelt there had contaminated the land, air, and water, pumping its pollutants into the environment. She doubted if most of its residents were even aware of the contagion, they'd lived with it so long – they and the generations that had preceded them, because whatever was responsible had been in these parts for centuries, and its presence was as much a part of their existences as death and taxes. They probably attributed its effects to some combination of the weather, the economy, and the disposition of the streets and buildings. It was the curse of living in Gretton.

Sabine, drifting . . .

Of course, if you had half an ounce of sense, and a little grit and ambition, you left a town like this. If you didn't have options, were tied by family history to the land, or were just too damn lethargic to move, you stayed. You told yourself that there were worse places to live. You only had to turn on the TV to see that. Like the man said, better the devil you know. But in winter, when the cold had the town in its grip, or even in summer, when the sun never seemed to shine quite as warmly or as long as it did on other towns, you wondered at the aptness of that old saw, because whatever afflicted Gretton possessed neither face nor form. It was beyond reason. It simply *was*.

Sabine, going deeper, her eyelids flickering . . .

The Michauds, had they seen fit to contribute to the debate, might have offered a different interpretation. They were closer to it, and it to them. They had tried to give this presence a physical aspect, because to attribute a shape, a countenance, to the ineffable was the first step toward understanding the object of belief and one's relationship to it. For the Michauds, what dwelt on their land was not completely abstruse or transcendental. Line upon line of them had stared into the shadows, and as their eyes had grown accustomed to the murk, they had begun to perceive the lineaments of what gazed back at them. They had painted it, carved it. This she felt. This she knew.

Sabine, trembling, shaking on the mattress, the bedsprings singing a near-coital song . . .

Then the Michauds had done what comes naturally to those who try to map the numinous.

In the darkness between worlds, what was left of Henry Clark stirred at the sound of footsteps in the dirt.

Sabine opened her eyes.

'Get out!' she screamed. 'Get out!'

The Michauds had built a shrine.

Chapter XC

The beam of Lars Ungar's flashlight was fixed on the far wall of the basement. What he was looking at was so extraordinary that it served to distract him momentarily from the stench. Ungar had smelled dead animals and knew the fetor of putrefaction, but this was many degrees worse. Beneath the dirt floor, he guessed, was a body, or more than one.

Ungar did not move to investigate further, not yet, but stayed perfectly still as the beam illuminated the creation on the wall, a vision formed of paint, soot, and blood. It was vast, covering the available space, and resembled the interior of a volcano, a whirlpool formed of fire glimpsed through a fracture in the air-cooled black lava. But this was not a depiction of rock: the striations were too organic. It was closer to the carapace of a great insect, and what Ungar had at first taken for columns of smoke, or even charred branches, started to resemble an irregular multitude of limbs surrounding a slit that was almost vaginal. Taken as a whole, Ungar thought he might also be looking at a face, the features arrayed into some blighted approximation of humanity, as though the creator of the mural had set out to combine the most unsettling aspects of creatures that crawled through mud and lightless places with those that walked above them.

Ungar let the flashlight drift down with the muzzle of his gun to catch objects carved from wood, stone, and bone, some barely the size of his little finger, others as long as his arm, but each an attempt to replicate, either in whole or in part, the drawing on the wall. Some bore the yellow patina of age, while others were more recent, the material still fresh and white.

He moved the light away from the wall and allowed it to play over the floor. The dirt had been raked, the tool used for the task

402

still standing upright by the stairs, with a spade beside it. Ungar squatted low to examine the earth and thought it looked higher in the far corner. He expanded the beam and laid the M4 on the ground, so he would have illumination by which to work. He took the crowbar and probed at the dirt, pushing deeper until he met resistance. Whatever was down there felt soft; it yielded to the pressure.

Ungar set the crowbar aside, grabbed the spade, and began to dig until he uncovered cloth: an unbuttoned check shirt, and beneath it an exposed, distended male belly. Ungar progressed upward, from the navel to the head. He did not recognize the face, but the man's mouth was taped shut and his nostrils were filled with compacted dirt. He'd breathed it in because he'd been buried alive. Beside the first body was a second, but smaller: a child, male.

Ungar sat back on his heels and stared around him. He was in a charnel house, and now that he knew what the Michauds had been hiding, it was time to leave. The police would have to be called, but not before Pinette had moved the guns and materiel off Hickman's land. In the meantime, Ungar would assign someone to watch this place. He didn't want the Michauds to discover the incursion and try to move the bodies.

He reached for the M4 and was deafened by a blast that came from everywhere and nowhere at once, while simultaneously he felt a tug at his lower right arm. An instant later came the pain, and an absence where his right hand used to be, the wrist now ending in bone and torn flesh. He cried out, cradling the ruined limb, and turned to see the silhouette of a woman holding an over-under shotgun. The woman stepped onto the dirt floor, gradually moving into the ambit of the flashlight.

'You stupid, nosy fuck,' said Eliza Michaud.

She raised the shotgun and squinted down the barrel.

'No,' said Ungar, 'I got a—'

'I don't care.'

Eliza pulled the trigger, and Lars Ungar's head was gone.

Chapter XCI

Sabine Drew was waiting up for us in the living room when we got back. The innkeeper had retired to her quarters in a converted coach house at the back of the property, leaving the coffeepot, a decanter of sherry, and a classical music station playing low on the stereo. Sabine stood as we walked in.

'Something's happening at the Michaud property,' she said.

'Like what?' I asked.

'I don't know for sure. I think someone was out there who shouldn't have been. I heard – no, Henry heard – a noise, like gunshots.'

She saw the expression on Louis's face. It might have been described as neutral, but only if one were inclined to be charitable. Then again, it could be hard to tell what Louis was thinking. Rocks gave more away.

'I can tell that you don't believe me,' she said to him, 'but I'm not the only one who led you here. It was Mattia Reggio as much as I who brought you to this town.'

Louis continued to say nothing, leaving me to speak.

'I got a call while we were out,' I said. 'Reggio's car was found parked at a motel down in Pittsfield.'

Moxie Castin, a generous donor to the Maine State Troopers Foundation and an advertiser in the twice-yearly *Maine State Trooper* magazine, had received a boon in return from the state police. While it would have been premature to declare Reggio a missing person, the make and license of his car had been circulated, with a request for notification should it be spotted. Reggio's vehicle had been discovered less than an hour earlier in the parking lot of a motel on Somerset Avenue. The motel shared the lot with a strip mall and a couple of restaurants, although technically the motel's spaces were reserved, with signs on the wall requesting that mall and restaurant patrons park elsewhere. People often failed to notice them, or chose not to, and it wasn't worth the hassle of towing an errant car unless the motel was unusually busy, which it rarely was. It hadn't even registered with them until late in the day that Reggio's car didn't belong to a guest, and the police had spotted it before the manager had gotten around to deciding what to do about it. All of this I explained to Sabine.

'Do you really think he went down there after leaving Gretton?' she asked.

'If he did,' I said, 'he'd have contacted his wife before checking into that motel, but he didn't do either of those things. I don't think he ever left here, unless we choose to believe that he dumped the car and walked all the way to someplace else, and Reggio didn't even like walking to the curb.'

I leaned against the door. I ached, but some part of me always ached these days.

'We also found out more about the Michauds.'

Another good turn drawn from Moxie's list of creditors, this time a local lawyer, Curtis Cobbold, who was working for the Hickmans, or had been until Antoine Pinette showed up, at which point Cobbold decided that discretion was the better part of not going to jail.

'They're hardly the lifeblood of the community,' I continued, 'and you won't find them selling jam at the county fair. There are apparently two houses out on their property, but one is all boarded up, or was the last time anyone but the Michauds saw it. They don't bother people, and people don't bother them, except for their neighbor, Hickman, with whom the Michauds are in dispute over a boundary line. That dispute has escalated with the arrival on the Hickman land of some outsiders, a bunch of far-right extremists, except these aren't the usual sad incels and conspiracy freaks. They're led by a man named Antoine Pinette. I know Pinette. We had a run-in with him after his brother threw a firebomb at the Clark house. Pinette is up here as well. He might even be the one who nearly ran you over earlier.'

Sabine looked confused. 'How do they fit into all this? Could they be involved in the abduction of Henry Clark?'

'I don't see how, or why. Their presence may be a coincidence, or bad luck. It might even bear out something you told me down in Portland when we first met at the Bear.'

'Evil finds its own,' said Sabine.

'Pinette's objectionable, not evil,' I said, 'but the principle still holds.'

'So when are you going to confront the Michauds?'

'Not until we have a better idea of what's going on in there. We're going to wait until the dead hours, when they're sleeping, before we start sniffing around.'

'But we're also considering paying a visit to Pinette afterward,' said Louis, speaking at last.

'Why?'

'Because Antoine is smart,' I answered. 'If he's chosen to establish himself with Hickman, you can be sure that he's taken an interest in his neighbors. Right now, he may know more about the Michauds than anyone else in Gretton. But we'll take a look at the Michaud house along the way. No point in approaching Antoine from a position of total ignorance.'

'Will he help us?'

'Only one way to find out,' I said. 'We just came back to make sure you were okay, and to let you know the lay of the land.'

'That's very thoughtful, but I'll be coming with you.'

'Ms Drew,' said Louis, 'none of this qualifies as a Sunday social.'

'You know,' said Sabine, 'you can be quite patronizing when you choose.'

'He can be quite patronizing even when he doesn't choose,' said Angel.

'I want to be there at the close,' said Sabine. 'If Henry Clark is on the Michaud property, I don't want it to be cadaver dogs that find him. If you try to go without me, I'll find a way to follow.'

I gave up arguing.

'Then get some rest,' I said. 'We'll be leaving before dawn.'

She pulled up a footstool, settled into her chair, and wrapped a blanket around herself.

'I'll sleep here, in case you were thinking of forgetting to wake me.'

'Huh,' said Louis, 'you know us so well, it's like you're psychic.'

He was almost smiling, although it might also have been a grimace.

'I know enough to be frightened,' she said.

'That's not being psychic,' said Louis. 'That's just being smart.'

Chapter XCII

Ellar Michaud had learned the value of patience and stillness very early in life. His father, Normand, was a mean son of a bitch who never failed to return from a walk in the woods without a couple of fresh birch sticks with which to whip his children for any infractions, real or imagined, so it was better not to draw his attention. Their mother, Ivie, had limited herself to applying ointment to the marks after the beatings and reminding her offspring – as if any reminder was necessary – of the importance of not crossing their father. Both were now buried in the family plot to the north, but Ellar hadn't visited the grave since his mother's interment four years after her husband's. He didn't hate them, they and their attitudes not counting as unusual for that time or place, but neither did he spare much thought for where their souls might be residing. Aline missed them, though, especially her mother. It was Aline who continued to maintain Ivie's herb garden, filled with plants that had once doubled as abortifacients: wild carrot, wormwood, rue, centaury, pennyroyal, and more.

Ellar had monitored the comings and goings at the encampment, hoping that everyone would settle down and go to their beds, leaving him to work without the danger of being spotted, but activity was continuing well into the night. It looked to Ellar like the interlopers were getting a big shipment ready, their vehicle pool now swollen by a couple of old sedan deliveries. Occasionally, one of the group would head off to grab a nap or cup of coffee, but the work never stopped. If Ellar waited any longer, dawn would come and he'd have missed his chance.

With that in mind, Ellar had made his way to the far side of the encampment. He was armed with a Hi-Point C9 pistol and a scoped Armalite AR-10 tactical rifle, along with the Bushmaster knife he always carried. Pinette and the main group were currently about sixty feet to his right. They had set up a couple of portable lights, under which they were separating guns and equipment into piles, checking and double-checking the parts and mechanisms before storing them in tarps or smaller crates as required. The wind was blowing in their direction, so Ellar would have to work fast. As soon as he began spreading the skunk essence, it would carry to them and they'd begin searching for the source. He'd need to be good and gone before they found it.

Ellar set the two bottles of essence beside him before opening the Ziploc with the dead skunk. Although he'd been anticipating the stink, it made his gorge rise, but he doused it with plenty of Rickard's nonetheless. He left only the tail untouched, so he could pick up the skunk without tainting his gloves. When the job was done, he pulled the animal from the bag and tossed it into the trees behind him. It landed with barely a sound.

Ellar then sprayed the skunk essence on the surrounding grass. Rickard's was usually applied with a pipette, but Ellar didn't have time for that. He needed a lot of skunk and he needed it fast, but he stopped dousing as soon as the smell hit him full in the face. Even with a scarf over his mouth, he was struggling not to puke. He resealed the plastic bottles and put them in the bag he'd used for the skunk, just to avoid any chance of their being found later and the ruse being discovered. He was already scurrying back the way he'd come when he heard a shout of disgust from the group by the lights.

'Skunk,' someone said.

'Maybe more than one,' said another voice. 'Goddammit, that's bad.'

Ellar didn't bother looking to see if Pinette had sent anyone to investigate. It was enough that they'd registered the smell, until Pinette spoke up.

'You sure that's skunk and not a leak from one of the tanks?'

Ellar paused. He couldn't do his work if one of Pinette's people was dispatched to check the propane. He wouldn't even be able to move in the direction of the tanks for fear of being seen. Ellar saw a man walking toward the spot with the skunk and heard the first voice speak again.

'No, it's a skunk for sure. It's stronger over here. Jesus.'

Ellar knew that their olfactory functions would soon be so screwed up from the essence that they'd be unlikely to pick up any additional odor from the propane. He reached the main tanks without incident, squatted behind the largest, and removed the two incendiaries, constructed from sealed cardboard tubes filled with a mixture of potassium chlorate and sugar. Using the tip of his Bushmaster, Ellar made a hole in the end of each tube to add the detonator: a tiny vial of sulfuric acid. The vials were sealed with 316L stainless steel screw caps of his own construction, because the acid would eat through anything else.

He removed the steel lid from the first vial and replaced it with the thicker of two cork stoppers. He inserted the vial into the holes he'd made before turning the device upside down so the acid immediately began to dissolve the cork. When it reached the potassium chlorate-sugar mixture, it would ignite a powerful and very hot fire. Ellar had timed the dissolution rate on the cork and knew he had about eight minutes. Finally, he located the valve on the nearest tank and used the Bushmaster to cut an incision in the length of connecting hose. Instantly, he smelled gas.

Ellar slipped back into the trees and worked his way toward the two smaller tanks next to a trio of camper vans. There he repeated the procedure, this time using a cork timed for two minutes. He checked his watch. Four minutes had elapsed since he'd primed the first incendiary, which meant a gap of roughly a minute between the first and second explosions. He didn't know how much damage the initial blast would cause, as he couldn't boast a wealth of experience at turning propane tanks into bombs. He guessed it would be enough to destroy at least one of the camper vans and kill anyone unfortunate enough to be sleeping inside, as well as start a good fire; but it would also drive the rest of Pinette's crew back while they tried to figure out what was happening. With luck, that would put them well within range of the second, larger explosion. It wasn't a perfect killing box, but it would suffice.

Ellar grabbed his duffel and ran for the cover of the woods. He wanted to find somewhere safe from which to watch the conflagration. He didn't want to miss the show after going to the trouble of setting it up. He was almost at the trees when his right foot was yanked from beneath him, causing him to land awkwardly in a pile of branches that cracked loudly beneath his weight.

Unfortunately, so did his left arm.

Chapter XCIII

We pulled up at the entrance to Private Road 7 with dawn still an hour off. The road was now gated, although the gate wasn't locked.

'We could just head straight to Pinette,' said Louis.

'If we're wrong about him, and he's found common ground with the Michauds, we'll have played our hand and lost,' I said. 'We may also get ourselves killed. No, I want to see what's in there first. With luck, it'll include Reggio.'

'Are you just going to walk in and ask where your friend is?' enquired Sabine.

'He's not a friend,' I said, 'but other than that, yes. Besides' – I checked my gun to ensure the safety was off before restoring it to its holster – 'this is just a scouting mission, and there are many ways of asking.'

Angel got out of the car, checked the gate using the flashlight on his cell phone, and came back.

'It's got a little dual-beam alert to prevent it from being opened without activating an alarm,' he said. 'I could try disabling it, but it doesn't seem worth the trouble when we can just climb over or cut through the trees. That thing is only for people too dumb or careless to know better.'

I looked at Louis, who shrugged.

'These are last season's pants,' he said.

'Thank God for that.'

'What about me?' asked Sabine.

'You stay here. I understand your wish to help Henry Clark, but if we bring you with us you'll be a distraction, and that could get someone shot.' I eased the car forward, to where the verge was wide enough to allow me to park off the road. 'If you remain low, you won't attract any attention from passing vehicles.'

'What should I do if someone does come along, like the police?' Louis opened the door and prepared to join Angel.

'Lie,' said Louis. 'You're a white lady. They'll believe you.'

Sabine watched him go.

'Is he always like that?'

'Pretty much,' I replied.

'Doesn't it get wearing?'

'Only if you listen.'

We skirted the gate to enter the Michaud land, staying parallel to the road without using it. The gravel was pale, so anyone walking on it risked standing out, day or night. Something flitted through the shadows above my head. It sounded small and fast: a bat, hunting the last of the night bugs.

Gradually, the house came into view. Lamps burned behind two windows, but the thin drapes were drawn. The illumination flickered, and I could faintly hear the laughter of a TV audience: someone was up early, or late. I could see a security light positioned just above the front door, and guessed there would be another at the rear. If we stepped onto the grass or got too close to the edge of the trees, the light would bathe the yard, alerting whoever was inside.

I wasn't being truthful with Sabine when I told her we only wanted to scout the Michaud property. I now had no doubt that Reggio had visited and never left, despite the discovery of his vehicle elsewhere. But there remained a chance that he might still be alive, which meant one of us would have to gain access to find out. Ideally, it would first be useful to get close enough to be able to see through the windows, but the perfect was the enemy of the possible.

We moved to the back of the house. As anticipated, there was another security light above the door, but on this side the rooms were dark.

'Return to the front,' I told Angel, 'and set off the other light.'

It would attract the attention of anyone in the house, leaving the rear vulnerable.

'You want noise, too?' Angel asked.

'Noise would be good, but keep it low-key. I want to draw them out, but I don't want them shooting.'

Angel moved off, leaving Louis and me alone.

'Are you going in,' he asked, 'or am I?'

'Do you want to go in?'

'Not really.'

'Well, that answers the question, doesn't it?'

'What if Reggio isn't in there? Going to be kind of embarrassing for you.'

'Only if I'm seen, and then embarrassment will be the least of our worries. But these are the people we're looking for. Depending on what Reggio told them or whatever they figured out for themselves, they'll be on edge. Reggio's arrival will have tipped them off that the net's closing.'

The trees at the front of the house glowed brightly as the security light came on. It was followed by a clatter from the direction of the garage: Angel had gone to work. I waited until I heard the front door open before starting my run across the yard.

Which was when a woman carrying a shotgun emerged from the woods, her face and hands streaked with dirt. Her hair was longer and darker now, and the collar of her jacket was raised high against the chill of the night, but even so, I knew I was looking at Eliza Michaud, the woman who had called herself Mara Teller. She, in turn, recognized me. I could see it in her face. The time for dissembling was past. She already had the shotgun raised, and didn't halt her advance. She just kept coming as she fired.

Chapter XCIV

Antoine Pinette had covered his mouth and nose with a rag to protect him from the skunk odor, but it wasn't helping. His eyes were watering, it smelled so bad and beside him, Olin was gagging. From out in the woods, Leo waved a flashlight and shouted back at Antoine.

'I found it,' said Leo. 'It's dead.'

Antoine thought he sounded puzzled.

'Sure smells like it,' said someone else.

'No, I mean it's been dead awhile.'

Olin turned to Antoine.

'If it's been dead that long,' he said, 'how come we didn't smell it before now?'

Antoine heard a noise from behind him, like a big animal breaking through the undergrowth.

'The hell was that?' asked one of the women. Her name was Cass, and she carried a semiautomatic rifle on one shoulder. She was already antsy because her boyfriend, Lars, had yet to return from his scouting mission at the old property on the Michaud land, and Antoine was having a difficult time persuading her not to go after him. Now she unshouldered the rifle while Antoine removed the automatic pistol from his belt, both of them moving in the direction of the disturbance. Antoine tossed aside the rag, but the smell didn't strike him as any less strong, even though they were leaving the dead skunk behind. It was different, maybe, but—

'Clear the camp!' he shouted. 'We got a propane leak. Wake anyone who's sleeping and start—'

And the first of the incendiaries exploded.

Ellar Michaud's arm didn't hurt much as yet. He'd felt it break as soon as he landed and knew it was a bad one, but for the

415

present the shock was insulating him from the pain. He heard Antoine Pinette shouting about a propane leak, which confirmed what a smart son of a bitch he was. The noise of Ellar's fall had attracted attention, but if he tried to stand, he'd make himself a target; if he remained where he was, any flashlight beams would pass over him. Anyway, it wouldn't be long before Pinette and the others had more pressing problems to occupy them.

Although Ellar had been bracing himself for the explosion, it came sooner and louder than he'd expected. A wash of heat and flame rose from the camp, expanding as it went. Ellar felt it scorch his face and watched as the trees caught fire like great matches igniting. Moments later detritus descended on him as the wreckage from the camp, driven high into the air, came down on the forest. Ellar curled into a ball and put his right arm over his head to protect himself. A heavy object landed inches from his chest. When he opened his eyes, he saw a spiked shard of metal, about three feet in length and two inches in width, embedded in the dirt. Aline would have said that the entity was looking out for him because he was doing its work. At that moment Ellar might not have disagreed.

The rain of debris eased, but there was no longer any point in Ellar remaining where he was. A fire was blazing where the first device had gone off, illuminating the ground on which he lay, and soon he would be visible to anyone who glanced in his direction. But for the present, the occupants of the camp were still recovering from the shock of the first blast, and the second was imminent. A woman was screaming. Ellar knew that pitch. It was the sound of someone dying in pain.

Now the rest of the propane tanks exploded, this time closer to where Ellar was lying. The sudden light, noise, and heat were beyond anything he had ever experienced, and he was momentarily deafened. He was also convinced that, even at this distance, he was in danger of dying in the conflagration, so once more he made himself as small as he could while the woods grew bright as day. More metal and rubble came down, but Ellar only heard it land because his eyes were squeezed shut. Then the hard rain ceased, leaving only the crackle of burning. The woman, whoever she was, had stopped screaming, but other cries replaced hers. Ellar heard moaning, and a child weeping. He hadn't realized there might be children in the camp. It had only been adults out there until now. One of Pinette's women must have brought a kid with her – or more than one, because their kind were promiscuous. Ellar felt the mildest sense of regret, but no more. A child had no business being around a place like that, filled with guns and criminals. Some harm was bound to come to them, one way or another.

Ellar could make out people stumbling amid the smoke and flame of the ruined camp. He got to his feet, picked up his duffel with his good hand, and slung it over his shoulder. He checked the area around him to make sure he hadn't dropped anything that might alert investigators to the likelihood of the explosions being non-accidental, but the spot looked clear. True, the decoy skunk might cause problems, assuming Pinette or any of the others involved in that discussion remained alive to point to it, but an investigation would still struggle to lay the blame at the Michauds' doorstep, whatever accusations might be thrown around. Anyway, with luck the fire might reach the skunk and burn it, too.

And Ellar had an alibi: his sisters would swear he'd been at the house the whole time. As for his fractured arm, accidents happened. It wasn't the first break he'd suffered, and it probably wouldn't be the last. The injury would serve to strengthen his alibi, because his sisters would confirm that he'd fallen earlier that evening, but was too stubborn to get it attended to. A man with a broken arm wasn't going to be in any state to attack an armed camp.

Ellar cast one last glance at the conflagration before heading south toward the creek, and home.

Chapter XCV

The first explosion saved my life. Eliza Michaud jerked the barrel at the sound of the blast, sending the shot over my head to shatter the darkened window behind me. She pivoted to her left and fired the second round at Louis. It missed him and hit a tree, but I heard him swear as a shower of splinters erupted from the trunk. By then Eliza was retreating into the safety of the forest, beyond the reach of the light. She'd need time to reload, which would be our chance to take her.

Before I could move, another shotgun blast came from the ruined window over my head, nearly bursting my eardrums, but this time the firing was directed at the woods. Flattened as I was against the side of the house, I couldn't be seen by whoever was inside, but they were trying to prevent Louis from going after Eliza before she could reload. There came the distinctive sound of a shell being racked and the shotgun roared again. I couldn't see Louis, which meant he was lying low – always a good policy when someone turns a shotgun on you – but I couldn't stay where I was. It wouldn't be long before Eliza rejoined the fight, and my crouching against the white wall of a house while bathed in a halogen glow would not be conducive to a long and happy life.

A second explosion came from the north, this one bigger and louder than the first, and a ball of flame rose over the trees. Hoping that it might further distract the shooter, I duckwalked to the back door, found it unlocked, and eased it open. I was in a kitchen, which extended into a living area, the TV visible beside one of the front windows. There was no apparent connecting door from the kitchen to the room with the shooter, so I'd have to get to the living room and come in behind them.

A chunk of plaster erupted from the wall opposite, reducing a vase to fragments. Someone else inside the house had drawn the shooter's fire. It had to be Angel, coming in from the front. Despite the ringing in my ears, I picked up the sound of footsteps crunching over broken glass. The shooter was moving to tackle the new threat, and I moved with them. I reached the archway leading to the living room as a woman inched her way forward, the barrel of the pump-action roaming for a target. I let her take five more steps so she presented a clear target. Only then did I speak.

'Don't move,' I said. 'If you do, I'll kill you.'

Even with her back to me and her face concealed, I could tell she was weighing her options. They were only two: she could do as I said or she could die. I hoped she'd take the first. I never wanted to shoot another woman – or a man either, if it could be avoided.

Slowly, she lowered the shotgun.

'Set it down,' I said.

She did as she was told. Only when it was on the ground did I move in. I pushed her flat on the floor and searched her, but she had no other weapon. Angel arrived while I still had my knee in her back.

'You okay?' I asked.

He nodded.

'Check upstairs.'

I turned the woman onto her back. She possessed the hard features of a Dorothea Lange subject from the Great Depression. This was Aline Michaud.

'Mattia Reggio,' I said. 'Where is he?'

Her mouth moved, but only to form enough spittle to shoot into my face. I wiped it off. From where I knelt, I could see the underside of the kitchen table. A pink mound was lodged there. I thought I knew what it was: Mattia Reggio leaving his calling card, consciously or unconsciously. Perhaps he had known he might be about to die.

I returned my attention to Aline Michaud.

'I'll ask you again,' I said. 'Where is he?'

But 'My brother and sister will kill you for this' was all I got out of her.

Angel came back. 'Nobody else in the house, just her.'

'Reggio was here. I think he wadded his gum under the table.'

Angel went over and touched a finger to it.

'Soft.'

I leaned closer to Aline Michaud.

'If he's dead, his DNA will be all over that gum,' I told her. 'You've just been marked for a life sentence.'

'I don't know what you're talking about.'

'Find something to tie her up with,' I said to Angel.

'Where's Louis?' Angel asked, as he yanked the phone cable from the wall.

'Going after Eliza, I hope. Last I saw, he'd taken some splinters, but hopefully nothing worse.'

In retaliation, Angel pulled the phone cable tight enough around Aline's wrists to make her yelp.

'By the way,' he said, 'it sounds like someone's starting a war.'

'I think they came from the Hickman place,' I said, as I left the woman to his care. 'If it's war, it's been declared on Antoine Pinette and his crew.'

Chapter XCVI

Ellar Michaud had the creek in sight when he picked up signs of pursuit. His arm was now hurting like a bitch, not helped by a couple of tumbles he'd taken because the injury was screwing with his balance. At least it was the left arm, which meant he could still hold a weapon. He came to what had once been a healthy thicket of trees, now reduced to ruin by emerald ash borers. Den Hickman had already chopped the bulk of them, leaving only a couple to stand against the insects. The cut trunks lay piled by the creek, but Hickman hadn't done anything more with them, content to consign them to rot. Ellar got behind the pile, the creek to his back, and watched for movement. He thought it might be a lone chaser, but if so, they were making a lot of noise. Then again, they weren't carrying a flashlight, which was smart. The beam would have made them an easy target, but additional noise was the downside.

Ellar remained very still and tried to control his breathing. Sirens sounded, approaching from somewhere to the west. It wouldn't be long before Hickman's woods were crawling with police. Ellar needed to be home, with his clothes changed and his arm in a sling, before the law got anywhere near him. Nevertheless, whoever was out there would have to be dealt with first. Ellar didn't want them talking to the police, but neither could he leave the body to be found, because that would erase any doubts about the explosions at the camp being the result of an accident. He'd have to kill them, get the corpse onto Michaud territory, and hide it until he and his sisters had time to dispose of it. The police wouldn't be able to search the property without a warrant, and they wouldn't get a warrant without evidence of involvement. The incendiaries were designed to leave no trace, so the only major risk of apprehension lay in Ellar being seen crossing the creek – or worse, being waylaid before he could reach safety.

He felt a drop of moisture on his face, followed by another. It was starting to rain, which would help to erase any tracks he'd left. Within seconds, the droplets had become a downpour, and Ellar could barely see more than a few feet ahead of him.

A thrashing came from the rise above him and to the left, followed by the thud of a body landing hard, and a man grunting. The rain had caused his pursuer to lose his footing. Ellar squinted through the deluge and saw a silhouette pass between two trees, making its way down the slope toward the creek, clutching at branches so as not to slip again. Ellar could have taken him with the Armalite or the pistol, but he didn't want to make more noise than necessary for fear of drawing others to him. The man would pass directly in front of him. All Ellar had to do was stand by.

Another smaller misstep, another grunt. Closer now. Ellar eased the Bushmaster from its sheath. He'd have to discard it later. He hated ditching a good knife, but he'd take the $75 hit over a murder conviction. He inhaled, then held the breath as the man reached the stack of cut ash. The gradient eased as the hill neared the creek, and he paused to get his bearings, one hand resting on the nearest of the trunks, his back now slightly to Ellar as he faced the water. Ellar rose to jam the blade into the right side of his neck, where he could see exposed skin. He didn't want to risk a thrust to the body, only to hit a padded vest or holster. The man spasmed, causing the gun in his right hand to fall to the dirt. Ellar had the tree trunks for support, so it was easy for him to twist the blade in the wound. A spray of red joined the rain as he pulled the blade free and let the body drop. The dead man, familiar from the camp, was much older than Ellar, which might have explained why he'd struggled with the terrain. His hair was thin and straggly, and his beard nearly white. He resembled someone's grandfather and was therefore, in Ellar's view, old enough to have known better.

Ellar kicked the body down the slope to splash in the creek.

He went after it, grabbed it by the collar, and dragged it awkwardly through the water to the other side, where he concealed it as best he could in the undergrowth. Then, with the first light of dawn seeping into the sky, he commenced walking in the direction of Kit No. 174.

Chapter XCVII

I entered the woods behind the Michaud house with a sick feeling in the pit of my stomach as the rain came down. Among the trees was a woman armed with the ideal weapon for this kind of fight. At close range, say twelve feet or less, a 12-gauge loaded with No. 6 shell can cut straight through a four-inch telephone directory. It's a central, lethal blast, capable of carving a hole about six inches in diameter. The farther from the target the shooter is, the greater the diameter of the pellet spread. Up close, therefore, Eliza Michaud was sure to kill whoever she was aiming at, because few people hit with No. 6 buckshot at close range ever trouble a hospital. But I'd also come across one of her spent shells as I entered the woods, and its long brass base marked it as a magnum, which meant extra powder, so it could propel even more pellets. Louis and I had been lucky once. We weren't apt to be so fortunate again.

Well, relatively fortunate, because now I saw Louis. The left side of his face was perforated with splinters and his scalp was bleeding. The only positive thing that could be said was that none of the splinters had entered his eye.

'How does it look?'

'At least as bad as it probably feels,' I said.

'It feels like I tried to headbutt a porcupine.'

'I hate to tell you, but the porcupine won.'

The sun was coming up, which gave me some light by which to remove the largest of the splinters. The rest would have to wait for the emergency room.

'What happened in the house?' asked Louis, as I worked at his head.

'We took one woman uninjured: the older sister, Aline. Angel has rendered her harmless. No sign of the brother, Ellar, and we know where the second sister is at, give or take a few acres of woodland.'

'The fuck!'

'Sorry, that splinter wants to stay where it is.'

'Lodged in my brain, you mean.'

'By the law of averages, one of them had a chance of hitting the target, but it must have been a close-run thing.'

'You're funny like fucking Patch Adams. Did you get anything out of the sister?'

'Not much more than saliva and a threat, but Reggio had been there.'

'How do you know?'

'He left his gum stuck under the kitchen table.'

'Smart,' said Louis. 'Unhygienic, but smart.'

I tossed aside the last of the splinters I could get to.

'We could hold off until the cops arrive,' said Louis.

'But where would be the fun in that?'

'Says the man without splinters in his head.'

'Also, the police will be looking for the source of those explosions. By the time they get here, Eliza and her brother could be halfway to the next county.'

'Point taken. But you know, I seem to be getting hurt a lot lately.'

'You could always retire,' I said. 'Or learn to move quicker.'

'I'm too young to retire, and too old to accelerate.'

'Then you're screwed.'

'I guess so. Left or right?'

'Right.'

Louis sighed.

'You always pick the right,' he said. 'I don't know why I asked.'

'This time I had a reason.'

'Yeah, what?'

'If we trap her between us, you won't get injured on the same side of the head.'

'You're a good person,' said Louis, after a long, thoughtful pause that was almost certainly punctuated by visions of me dying painfully.

'Not just good,' I told him. 'The best.'

Chapter XCVIII

Eliza Michaud had panicked at the sight of the private investigator in the yard. Her blood had also been up after killing Lars Ungar and burying him in a shallow hole in the basement floor. Her spade had struck old bones as she worked, snapping a femur. A proper clear-out was long overdue, and as Eliza returned to the main house, she was contemplating how best to raise the subject with Aline. Her older sister preferred not to disturb the dirt too often.

These were the thoughts running through Eliza's head as the security light bathed the detective, Parker. Thankfully, she'd had the foresight to reload the shotgun along the way, even if her first shot had gone wild. The second, she believed, might have wounded the man with Parker, although not badly enough to put him out of commission, since he'd been able to return fire, driving her away from the yard and into the woods. So: two intruders, though there might be more. That was awkward. It was hard to strategize without all the necessary information.

The rain had soaked her right through, and she was very cold. She wished Ellar was with her. He must surely be returning from his successful attack on the camp across the creek. He might even have heard the gunfire, which would alert him to trouble. Eliza didn't want him to come across Parker unprepared. And she was worried about Aline: while Eliza's initial instinct had been to flee toward the creek in the hope of finding her brother, her concern for her sister had caused her to reconsider, which was why she was circling back toward the house. Parker might already have called the police, but even if he had, what of it? There was no evidence to link the Michauds to the commission of any crime. Armed prowlers had entered their property and they had defended themselves accordingly. True, Maine's castle doctrine permitted the use of deadly force only if the trespasser did not comply with an order to leave, which Eliza had not given, not unless two blasts from a shotgun counted. In an ideal world, if it came down to a legal argument, it would be her word against Parker's.

But last time Eliza had checked, nothing about this world was ideal. If Parker was in Gretton, he had a reason for it. It might be that Reggio had lied before dying, and had shared his plan to visit the Michauds; or Parker's inquiries had revealed some clue linking their family to the Clark woman and the disappearance of her child. But whatever had brought Parker to Gretton, it would be best if he never left. Killing him wouldn't solve everything, but it would solve a whole lot more than letting him live.

Eliza took a few moments to stop and listen. Like her siblings, she knew these woods intimately and had learned how to pass quietly through them. She doubted Parker had the same level of forest lore, so she'd hear him coming. Kit No. 174 was ahead, but looked undisturbed. She found cover behind a rise, put the stock of the shotgun to her shoulder, and calmed herself. When the muzzle found Parker, she would not miss again.

A familiar low double whistle came from close by. Eliza sagged with relief. She looked to her right and found Ellar. He put a finger to his lips and beckoned her to him. She scurried over, coming so close to whisper to him that their lips nearly touched.

'It's the private detective,' she said. 'Parker.'

'Alone?'

'I saw one other man. I think I wounded him.'

'And Aline?'

'I don't know. She was shooting at them from inside the house. I had to pull back.'

A sob caught in her throat.

'It's okay,' said Ellar. 'You did the right thing.'

He patted her awkwardly on the back, using the hand that held his gun. It was only then that she noticed he was protecting his left arm.

'Are you hurt?'

'I broke a bone,' he said. 'I was hoping to get home and have it tended to before the police came asking questions. There's also a body down by the creek that needs to be put in the dirt. We can't let it be found.'

'Then we have to kill them,' said Eliza, 'Parker and the other one, and we need to do it fast.'

'Or we could run,' said Ellar.

'What about Aline?'

'If they have her, she won't talk. If she's dead, she won't talk either.'

His gaze flicked past her as he searched the woods for any sign of their enemies. His callousness briefly shocked Eliza. This was their sister he was dismissing, but then Aline and Ellar had never enjoyed a good relationship. Eliza had always been the peacemaker between them.

'If we run, we admit our guilt,' she said.

'If they're here, sister, they already suspect us.'

'But who could they have told? If they'd talked to the police, the law would be hunting us. That's why we have to get rid of them. Let what they know die with them.' She stroked his face with the back of her hand. 'Or it may be that we'll be the ones to die.'

Ellar rubbed his cheek against her hand like an animal seeking comfort. It felt as though the Michauds' time was coming to an end. That might be as it should.

'Then we fight,' said Ellar. 'I don't know about whoever is with him, but Parker is good at what he does. You'll have to let him get close to have the best chance of killing him, but I don't think we ought to let him get that close. I can't handle a rifle with a busted arm, and you shoot almost as well as I do.'

'Better, even,' said Eliza.

'Let's see about that.'

'So what do you want to do?'

'We draw them to the old house and finish them there.'

Chapter XCIX

Louis and I heard the thrashing at the same time. We followed the sound until we came to the clearing, and there we found a second house. Its lower windows were boarded up, but both the outer security door and the old wood-and-glass front door were standing open.

If Eliza Michaud was in there, she would either have to wait until one of us was framed by the doorway before taking a shot, or position herself at an upper window in the hope that those magnum shells could do serious damage once we got near. But if she was still in the woods, she could shoot us in the back when we went to investigate.

Louis joined me behind a white pine that must have been at least a century old, so thick was its trunk.

'No reason for her to go in,' he said. 'If she did, she's trapped herself.'

'Or she's waiting for someone to head in after her.'

'Which is kind of the same thing.'

'Unless there's a back door.'

'I can find out.'

It was then that we caught a flash of Eliza Michaud's red coat among the trees on the eastern side of the house.

'So who's inside?' I asked.

'Maybe no one. It might have been open long before we got here.'

Still, we kept to the woods and out of shotgun range as we continued hunting Eliza, the doorway eventually gaping open to the left of us. The interior was entirely dark, yet I thought I saw something gleam for a second in the shadows.

I hit Louis hard in the back, driving him to the ground. The darkness of the house flared with light as the first of the rifle shots rang out, ripping through the leaves and branches above our heads. We scrambled for cover as the next bullets kicked up dirt around us. Then Louis was returning fire, emptying the remaining rounds of his magazine into the doorway from thirty yards while I opened fire on the red coat still visible through the bushes. Eliza Michaud, it seemed, had not been alone after all. Someone, probably her brother, had laid an ambush for us.

The rifle fire ceased. The red coat, meanwhile, remained where it was.

'Movement from inside,' said Louis.

Eliza Michaud stumbled onto the porch, her white sweater now bearing a series of red, spreading stains. An Armalite hung loosely from her right hand. She remained upright for a few seconds before dropping to the boards, but by then the life was gone from her.

'What about the coat?' I asked.

'Decoy,' said Louis. 'She must have hung it on a bush and let the wind take it.'

'Louis, there is no wind.'

A man's voice spoke from the undergrowth behind us.

'Dead men,' it said.

His next words were lost to gunfire.

Chapter C

I had tensed to receive the bullets, but none came. Instead, a corpse tumbled by and came to rest against a rock. I recognized Ellar Michaud from the picture on his driver's license, even with an exit wound that had removed his nose.

'Coming down,' said a voice I knew, and Antoine Pinette staggered to where Louis and I lay. The right side of his face was badly burned, that eye a ruin, and his right hand was a melted claw. The cotton of his jeans had fused with the flesh on his legs, and his blackened jacket had lost its sleeves. He smelled of smoke, fire, and roasted meat. He sat heavily on the dirt and pine needles, laying his gun beside him. He was dying, but why he was not already dead was revealed only when he spoke again.

'He killed so many of us,' he said, his scorched tongue distorting his words. 'But I got him, didn't I?'

'Yes,' I said, 'you got him.'

'Got him good,' said Antoine.

His chin fell to his chest. He breathed once, deeply – a final exhalation of satisfaction – and then was no more.

Chapter CI

There is no end of explaining to be done when bodies are involved, but I had experience of it, for better or worse. The first call I made was to Moxie, because we were going to need a lawyer. The second call, on Moxie's instructions, was to Curtis Cobbold, his legal contact in Gretton. Cobbold said he'd be with us as soon as he could get his pants on. The third call was to Angel's cell phone, alerting him to the imminent arrival of the police. The fourth was to Sabine Drew.

Finally, once everyone was on point, I called 911.

Aline Michaud spoke to police only when the Michaud family lawyer arrived at the house, and then to claim, not wholly incorrectly, that a trio of armed men had entered her property and she, out of fear for her life, had first ordered them to leave before opening fire when they did not. Upon being informed that her sister and brother were dead, she stopped talking.

Louis, Angel, and I gave our take on events, leaving out nothing. Sabine was also interviewed. While three of us were guilty of criminal trespass, we contested Aline's version and denied that any warning had been given before the shooting started. Had the situation remained that way – Aline claiming trespass, and her sister dead at our hands – we might have ended up behind bars, given Becker and Nowak's antipathy toward me. But once a Mincey warrant had been produced, the police were able to enter the house in which Eliza Michaud had been shot. There they uncovered the bodies of three males from beneath a thin layer of dirt, one recently deceased from gunshot wounds, the other two dead for at least a day or more. All had been stripped of identification, and the shooting victim was missing most of his head, but they were later identified as Lars Ungar, Maynard Vaughn, and Mattia Reggio. Survivors of the blasts at the Hickman camp testified that Antoine Pinette and another man, Barry Dresser, had witnessed someone they believed to be Ellar Michaud fleeing the scene of the explosions and had gone after him, despite Pinette being grievously wounded. Dresser's remains were subsequently found hidden under branches on the Michaud side of the creek with a hole in his neck.

All this unfolded over many hours. It was while I was sipping a cup of lukewarm coffee in an interview room at the Piscataquis County Sheriff's Office in Dover-Foxcroft, waiting for Moxie and Cobbold to get back from contesting threatened criminal charges and an imminent appearance before a judge, that Erin Becker arrived. By then I was tired, filthy, and had lost track of time, while Becker looked fresh and sharp in her business suit. She entered alone, taking one of the two chairs across the table from me.

'Should I get Moxie in here?' I asked.

'This isn't an official conversation,' said Becker. 'And it says a lot for your predicament that you're currently in need of not one but two lawyers.'

'Any conversation in a room with recording facilities is official, and a man can't have too much legal representation.'

'Would you be happier speaking in the parking lot?'

'I'd be happier speaking in the parking lot with at least one of my lawyers present.'

'I'm amenable. Give me a minute to make the arrangements.'

She left. When she returned, Moxie was with her, barely managing to hide his curiosity. My jacket was returned to me and Moxie and I followed Becker outside, where she lit a cigarette.

'You want one?'

We both declined. Her expression suggested this was a failure of character on our part, if one of many.

'We found a child's body with the others in the basement,' she said. 'We think it's Henry Clark, although that's not conclusive. Identifying the remains is going to take a while, but details have already been leaked to the press. We're preparing for a flood of references to a house of horrors.'

'What does Aline Michaud have to say about it?'

'She claims she had nothing to do with the old house,' said Becker, 'and her brother and sister were the only ones with access. Naturally, we're disinclined to believe her. I have no doubt we'll find her DNA in there if we look hard enough, and we'll be looking very hard. As of now, we haven't officially ruled out a link between the Michauds and Colleen Clark.'

Moxie opened his mouth to object, but Becker waved it closed with her cigarette.

'You did hear the word "officially", right? The charges against your client will be dropped as soon as we have a clearer picture of what's been happening in Gretton, but the attorney general has advised against any precipitous action.'

'Because he thinks that you and he can still come out of this ahead,' I said.

'The mystery of Henry Clark's abduction solved, at least three other murders closed, and who knows how many other disappearances explained?' said Becker. 'That represents a significant result, politically and legally.'

'You were prepared to burn Colleen at the stake for a similar reason,' I said.

Becker drew long on her cigarette and regarded the burning tip, like a pyre in microcosm.

'Now she's going to step down so Aline Michaud can take her place. The issue to be addressed is whether there's any advantage to be gained by immolating you and your friends as well. On that, opinions differ. The attorney general believes you should be prosecuted, and not only for criminal trespass. He feels he can make a charge of manslaughter stick for the death of Eliza Michaud, and is even optimistic about second-degree murder.'

'That man has his head up his ass,' said Moxie. 'I'd sooner vote for Satan.'

'Which is the point, isn't it?' I said to Becker. 'Nowak won't be attorney general for much longer. Everybody is about to move one rung up the ladder.'

'Precisely.'

'And you don't want to be the person responsible for prosecuting men who helped track down a family of killers.'

'I'd prefer not to be placed in that position. Magnanimity would be the smarter move.'

'And what would be the price of this magnanimity?' asked Moxie.

'Silence when the charges against your client are dropped, even if a "thank you" would be nice. In return, Mr Parker and his friends lose another of their collective nine lives, but no more than that. They'll still have their liberty, which would count as a legal miracle under the circumstances.'

'Do I have time to consult with my clients?'

'Sure,' said Becker, 'if it makes you feel better, but you know you'll take the deal.'

'And Colleen Clark?'

'No "I told you so" from your office, no statements to the press about the persecution of an innocent woman, and no civil suits against the Portland PD or the AG's office. You'll receive a quiet, low-key apology, and you'll accept it. Then she'll be left to mourn her child undisturbed.'

'I'm not sure that qualifies as a comfort.'

Becker tossed her cigarette butt under a car.

'No,' she said, 'I don't suppose it does.'

As Becker prepared to escort us back inside, I asked Moxie to give me a moment alone with her.

'If you're trying to get more than I've already offered, save your breath,' said Becker.

'I got more than I expected. I have no quarrel with you.'

'Then what is it?'

'Stephen Clark.'

'What about him?'

'He admitted to having an affair with a woman he identified as Mara Teller, but whom we now know to be Eliza Michaud. Stephen Clark was born not far from here. He grew up in this county, and I may have someone who can confirm that he and Eliza had a sexual encounter when they were younger. How could

Clark not have known who she was when their paths crossed again decades later?'

'You *may* have someone? What does that mean?'

'It's hearsay, admittedly, but I was told that Clark might have screwed one of the Michaud sisters in the parking lot of a bar in Gretton.'

'Presumably while intoxicated?'

'Nevertheless,' I persisted.

'Could you identify every woman you slept with when you were young, especially if you'd been drinking?'

'I know you'll find this hard to believe,' I said, 'but there weren't that many. Plus, I never claimed to be sleeping with any of them behind my wife's back, and my dead child didn't end up buried on their property.'

'Stephen Clark broke down when told that his son's body might have been found,' said Becker. 'He's under sedation. He says he made a terrible mistake with the Teller affair.'

'Which is the understatement of the year. What if it wasn't a mistake?'

'You're alleging collusion in the abduction and murder of his son. Why would he do that?'

'I don't know.'

And I didn't. I had only suspicions.

'We'll see what we can find,' said Becker.

But in the end, they would find nothing.

Angel, Louis, and I were released from custody within the hour. Sabine Drew had left a message to say that she was still at the Gretton lodgings. Although I wanted only to sleep, I knew I wouldn't be permitted to until we had spoken. Along the way, I contacted Adio Pirato, and told him about Mattia Reggio.

'He was always among the best of us,' said Pirato, 'though I know you wouldn't consider that to be a very high bar.'

'I may have done him an injustice,' I said, 'and contributed to his death.'

'Matty always went his own way, and he died doing the right thing. Don't take that away from him. Does Amara know?'

'The police have been to see her.'

'I'll head up there this evening. And I appreciate you taking the time to call.'

He wished me a good day and hung up.

At the inn, Sabine was waiting, looking distressed.

'I asked the police to let me enter the house,' she said, 'but they told me they couldn't do that.'

'Nobody outside the investigation will be allowed in until they've finished clearing it of bodies,' I said, 'and maybe not even then, not for a while. Ultimately, it will be torn down and the grass left to grow over it. If enough time goes by, the woods will reclaim the land and nobody will ever be able to locate the site again.'

'And the Michauds' property, what will happen to it?'

'They have some distant relations who might be able to lay claim, but it'll be sold one way or another. Hickman might try to buy it out of spite, though I doubt anyone will want to settle on it, or not until a lot of years have passed.'

'You know,' she said, 'it won't die just because the house is gone.'

'What won't die?'

'Whatever made its home in that place. Whatever poisoned the Michauds. I don't know that it can die, not like we do. Perhaps the best we can hope for is that it will be forgotten, and in being forgotten it will fade away.'

'Do you think the Michauds gave Henry Clark to it?' I asked. 'Is that why they took him, along with whatever other unfortunates might have ended up buried in there?'

'Yes, I do.'

'Why?'

'Who can tell?' said Sabine. 'Why did the ancients make sacrifices to their gods? To avoid angering them, and receive blessings and protection in return. What does the surviving sister say?'

'That she didn't know anything about it and it was all the work of her siblings, but that won't hold up under stress. Forensics will connect her to the house, which will put pressure on her to change

437

her story. Should she reconsider, and decide to open up, we may learn more about their motives.'

'She won't ever tell the full truth, whatever happens,' said Sabine. 'Why not?'

'I doubt she could even explain it to herself. She believed, and it was enough for her that she did.'

Sabine stared out of the window. I could feel her straining to reach the Michaud property.

'Why do you want to enter the house?'

'I want to comfort Henry,' she said. 'The best of him, the soul of him, is still in there.'

'And the thing you say is with him?'

'It's already retreating, going deeper. It doesn't like strangers moving through its spaces. It prefers being alone with its dead.'

'Soon they'll take Henry away from that place,' I said.

'Good. There'll have to be an autopsy, won't there?'

'Yes.'

'I hope he'll be gone before that happens.' She stared at her hands. 'Do you think his mother would like to say goodbye to him?'

I felt my eyes grow hot.

'Yes, I think she'd like that very much.'

Chapter CII

As Angel, Louis, and I drove from Gretton, Sabine with us, we passed the constable, Poulin. He was parked on the edge of town, just across from the sign welcoming visitors or bidding them farewell, depending on one's good fortune. I'd glimpsed him in the aftermath of the violence. He'd looked lost and ineffectual, which about covered it. Whatever happened from now on, his days in law enforcement were numbered.

I pulled up alongside his car. He peered in our direction, first casually, then with alarm.

'If it isn't Constable Poulin,' I said, 'the ever-vigilant.'

Behind me, Sabine wound down the window. She glared at him for so long that he was forced to look away. Finally, she spoke, but as though he were not present.

'He didn't know,' she said, 'but only because he chose not to. He was frightened of the Michauds. Many people around here were wary of them, and always have been, but he was truly scared.'

'Is that the case, Constable?' I asked. 'Were you too afraid of them to even examine the reasons for your fear?'

Poulin found his voice.

'You're blocking the road,' he said. 'If you don't move your vehicle, I'll issue you a citation.'

'I wouldn't want to put you to any trouble,' I replied, as I started to drive slowly away. 'We ought to respect the law.'

Poulin resigned the following day. Subsequently, a rumor circulated that he'd shot himself down in Louisiana, but it turned out to be untrue. He just kept on living, if you could call it that. But I doubt he slept well, and I hope he woke every morning to the taste of dirt in his mouth.

Chapter CIII

I met frequently with Colleen Clark over the days and weeks that followed. I was with her when confirmation came that it was Henry's body in the basement. I was with her when she went to claim the remains. I was with her when she buried her boy.

And I was with her one evening in the quiet of her kitchen as Sabine Drew held Colleen's hands in hers, the two women's eyes closed, the silence broken only by the ticking of the clock. The refrigerator and counters overflowed with food from neighbors who had come to apologize in person, a number of them in tears. Colleen had accepted without rancor their expressions of sympathy and atonement. I wondered then if what I had mistaken for her lassitude was more properly a kind of grace.

As Colleen and Sabine sat in unspoken communion, new scents entered the kitchen, traces of grass, pine, and fresh earth, and from somewhere both unbearably close and immeasurably far away I heard a child laugh.

'He's here,' said Sabine.

And Colleen called her son's name.

Chapter CIV

Stephen Clark attended Henry's funeral – of course he did – but he and his wife kept their distance from each other throughout the ceremony, and stood on opposite sides of the grave as their son was interred. Both wept, but Colleen's grief had a different essence to it, I think for many reasons. One of them, at least, I understood: she now knew she would see her child again, and that this was only a temporary parting.

Some intimates of the couple had, I knew, raised the possibility of a reconciliation. Stephen, they argued, had been wrong to believe his wife guilty, but in the face of such evidence, who might not have doubted their spouse? They could start again, have another child, and mourn their lost boy together. But others demurred, because who could forgive a man who would countenance such things about his wife? Somewhere between the two views, I supposed, was a pale version of what passed for truth.

And then there were those of us who could not bring ourselves to even look at him, but we were fewer.

This is what I think, though I have no hard evidence for it, and there are gaps I cannot fill: Eliza Michaud offered to help Stephen Clark achieve success in his professional life in return for his child. The pact might have been made before Henry was even conceived, or it may have been that Stephen did change, if only for a time, and thought he could play the role of a father, only to discover he could not, which made him vulnerable to Eliza's overtures. No, vulnerable is not the right word. Receptive. Stephen provided Eliza with details of the layout of his home, drugged his wife's wine so she would not wake when the Michauds came to take her son, and supplied them with the blanket in which to wrap him, a blanket to be returned to him when Henry was dead, and which Stephen would use to frame his wife.

How the DavMatt-Hunter accident might have been arranged also remained uncertain. According to witnesses, the truck driver could have done nothing to avoid the collision, and while the chauffeur had traces of oxymorphone in his system, he had used the medication in the past without impairing his performance behind the wheel. It might have been that, on this occasion, he had suffered some form of reaction to the opioid, causing him to become drowsy.

Perhaps it was only what it appeared to be: a misfortune that benefited Stephen Clark; a coincidence, and nothing more. Still, I was prepared to believe that the Michauds might have found a way to spike the chauffeur, but only because the explanation was more palatable to me than Sabine's: that the reach of whatever dwelt under Kit No. 174 exceeded the environs of Gretton.

Shortly after his son was buried, Stephen Clark moved into a new condo in Saco. One month later, his brother and sister-in-law called to check on him after he failed to turn up for dinner at their home, once they had established that he had also been out of contact with his office for two days. They discovered his body lying in the hallway and an open $400 bottle of Napa Valley Cabernet Sauvignon on the kitchen table, a half-full glass beside it.

According to a note found in the condo, the wine had been sent by a secretary at an oil conglomerate based in Taiwan, one with which Clark's firm had recently signed a lucrative and well-publicized contract, although the conglomerate subsequently denied all knowledge of the gift. The note indicated that one of the company's senior executives wished to speak privately with Clark to discuss a deal that might prove mutually beneficial, as they were impressed with his efforts on the contract and felt he was someone they could work with, perhaps on a discreet but lucrative consultancy basis. Clark was invited to participate in a scheduled online meeting, during which, it was suggested, it would be politic of him to display the opened bottle of wine. He was also advised not to commit anything to email. The secure link to the meeting, the note promised, would be sent thirty minutes before it was due to begin, at 8 p.m. EST. When his computer was examined, no such link was located.

Both the wine and Clark himself were discovered to contain large quantities of tetrodotoxin, otherwise known as TTX. The poison had been injected through the foil and cork of the bottle using a very fine needle. Clark would have begun to feel its effects within minutes of ingestion, starting with pain in the lips and tongue, quickly followed by sweating, nausea, and full paralysis. He had probably been trying to get to his cell phone as the poison took effect, but failed after dialing the first digit of 9-1-1. Death, given the size of the dose, would have occurred within four hours, during which time Clark would have been conscious and lucid, if in agony, and unable to move.

Colleen, when interviewed by police, seemed shocked at the news of her husband's murder, but admitted to not being especially saddened. The subsequent investigation revealed no evidence of her involvement in the delivery of the wine. It had been purchased using an over-the-counter preloaded credit card, paid for in cash by a bum in Concord, New Hampshire, who remembered only a woman in a surgical mask, the woman claiming to be medically vulnerable and never having regained her confidence following the COVID pandemic.

She had given him $20 for his trouble.

Chapter CV

The William Stonehurst Foundation didn't survive the bad publicity surrounding the activities of Antoine Pinette and his crew, not least their trade in stolen military equipment and weaponry. To save his skin, Bobby Ocean sold out everyone involved, so that even to have had passed Pinette on the street was, thanks to Bobby's evidence, enough to invite a federal warrant.

Bobby's lawyers were still cutting a deal to keep him from serving time when Leo Pinette, who had survived the conflagration in Gretton and was out on bail, shot Bobby to death in his office before taking a chair and calling the police to let them know what he'd done.

Chapter CVI

A few days after Stephen Clark's funeral, which his estranged wife did not attend, I received a midmorning phone call from Erin Becker.

'So someone decided to take justice into their own hands where Stephen Clark was concerned,' she said.

'In the absence of the law investigating him properly, perhaps.'

'He *was* investigated. He stuck to his story – he didn't remember Eliza Michaud from his youth, even if he did fuck her – and there was no proof that he was lying. I don't suppose there's any point in asking for your thoughts on the manner of his death?'

'None whatsoever. Are you leveling an accusation?'

'When someone dies oddly in this state, you immediately spring to mind. Do you know anything about TTX?'

'Only what I've read in the papers.'

'It's a natural toxin. It's found in certain fish.'

'And in some snails, worms, and newts,' I said, 'although I don't think I've ever seen a newt.'

Becker tried to figure out if I was being funny or not. I wasn't. I'd never seen a newt.

'Well,' she said, 'we're still trying to establish the origin of this particular dose, but it's a distinctive way to kill someone. Poison is usually a woman's weapon. So far, though, your former client is in the clear.'

'You don't give up, do you?'

'No, Mr Parker, I don't. You might bear that in mind when I become attorney general.'

She ended the call. I stirred the milk into my coffee and carried it to my office. I had bills to send and debts to pay. I sat at my desk, the window open to salt and sea. I thought of Sabine Drew, sitting alone in her home, listening for the dead.

'*You keep fish?*'

'*Ever since I was a little girl. I'm quite the expert . . .*'

I took my time over the coffee, then picked up my car keys and drove into Portland. There was somewhere I had to be.

Chapter CVII

The sign on the door of the Great Lost Bear said that it was closed for a private event. Inside, the Bear was buzzing, with food laid out on long tables and an open bar. Dave and Weslie Evans were seated at the front of four rows of chairs, guests of honor on the occasion of their retirement after more than forty years. As staff and patrons lined up to sing their praises, Dave and Weslie bore the distinctive expression of bewilderment that the naturally kind wear when confronted with public testaments to their decency, as though unable to recognize themselves in what they were hearing.

In one corner sat the Fulci Brothers, wearing T-shirts commemorating the event, theirs being the only ones made in 4XL. Beside them was Byrd Jackson, formerly the Bear's restaurant manager and now one of the new owners. She was speaking intently to them, and they were listening with equal concentration. When she was done, she kissed and hugged them both. They caught me looking in their direction, raised their glasses, and smiled. I saluted them back, as Byrd came over.

'Thanks for coming,' she said.

'I wouldn't have missed it.' Behind me, the door opened, and Angel and Louis entered. 'Neither would they,' I added.

There was a final speech, and a last round of applause, before a band began to play. I saw Macy working her way through the crowd to be with me.

'What were you saying to Tony and Paulie?' I asked Byrd.

'I was putting their minds at rest. They were worried they wouldn't have a place here, now that Dave and Weslie were leaving.'

'What did you tell them?'

447

'I told them that they'd always have a place at the Bear,' she said. Her eyes were shining. 'After all, where else would they go?' She kissed me on the cheek. 'Where else would any of us go?'

And the band played on.

ACKNOWLEDGEMENTS

This novel was begun in the fall of 2021, at the tail end of the COVID pandemic, before finally being delivered in the fall of 2023, and revised further in 2024. I note this only in response to those people, occasionally other writers, who like to remark that I 'knock' books out. If I do knock them out, it's sometimes very slowly.

My thanks, as always, go to my editors at both Hodder & Stoughton and Emily Bestler Books/Atria. Sue Fletcher at Hodder has edited me since my debut, while Emily Bestler has been my American editor since my second novel, *Dark Hollow*. Without their patience, expertise, and encouragement my books would be much poorer, if they were to be published at all.

My gratitude, too, goes to all those who work with Sue and Emily: at Hodder, they include Katie Espiner, Swati Gamble, Jo Dickinson, Rebecca Mundy, Oliver Martin, Alice Morley, Catherine Worsley, Helen Flood, Alastair Oliver, and Dominic Smith and his team; in Ireland, Jim Binchy, Breda Purdue, Elaine Egan, Siobhan Tierney, and Ruth Shern; at Atria, Lara Jones, Gena Lanzi, Hydia Scott-Riley, Dayna Johnson, David Brown, and many, many more. Dominick Montalto and Sarah Wright, meanwhile, persist in their efforts to catch my errors at copy edit and proof stage, while Jen Lechner was exceptionally generous with her time and knowledge when it came to advising on the legal procedures in the fictional Clark case. Whatever failings the novel may have are entirely mine. None of the above deserve any blame.

My agent, Darley Anderson, and his staff remain a source of comfort, assistance, and steadfast support, as does Clair Lamb, who acts as the right hand, if not of God, then of someone who occasionally has delusions of divine status. Clair, alongside Cliona O'Neill and Jennie Ridyard, also provided an extra pair of eyes at proof stage, while Cameron Ridyard gives me a window on the world, and vice versa, via my website, johnconnollybooks.com.

Finally, thanks to Cameron, Alistair, Megan, Alannah, and especially Jennie, for making all of this worthwhile.